The Apartment

on

Larkspur Lane

AUTUMN LAKE BOOK 2

BECKY DOUGHTY

BraveHearts
Press

The Apartment on Larkspur Lane: Autumn Lake Book 2
Copyright 2024 Becky Doughty

Published by BraveHearts Press

Cover Design: Mackey Designs

Author Info: BeckyDoughty.com

ISBN: 978-1953347022

1

Addison

~ ~ ~

ADDISON STOOD AS FAR away from the group gathered on the beach as she possibly could while still staying within hearing range. The sky overhead was just beginning to shift and sway, hints of iridescence coloring the edges of her vision. She narrowed her eyes in a futile attempt to bring into focus the muted kaleidoscope sky. It wouldn't help, she knew, nor would it hurry things up, either. The aurora borealis refused to dance across the sky on command, and if the film crew huddled around their tripods and insanely expensive equipment wanted to catch the light show on camera, they would have to wait until the capricious Northern lights were good and ready to make an appearance.

She hunched her shoulders a little higher around her ears, burrowing the lower half of her face deeper into the fur-lined hood of her parka. She breathed slowly, trying not to steam things up too much, which would only turn the fur into tiny slivers of ice that poked her in the face. Her teeth chattered and her voice shook as she let out a nasally, "Brrrrr." She rolled her eyes at the noise. "You sound like a cold sheep. If there even is such a thing." She often conversed with herself on these excursions.

Across the way, no one seemed to have noticed her withdrawal from the group, but that was exactly the way she wanted it. She only wished she could withdraw all the way off this bitterly cold island altogether. Preferably, without anyone noticing, and even more preferably—did that even make sense?—somewhere warm and cozy and... well, homey.

But of course, eventually, someone would need something that wasn't readily available to them, and all eyes would turn to search for her. *Addison, would you be a sport and grab me another memory card, please? Addie, darling, my macro lens is in my other bag. Can you hunt it down for me? Hey Addison. Since you're not doing anything right now...*

That was the real issue, wasn't it? Somehow, she was always the one with nothing better to do than to be at the beck and call of those who actually did have something to do.

"I believe there are many cold sheep during shearing season."

Startled, she spun around, both hands up in front of her in a straight-out-of-the-movies martial arts pose that had to look as ridiculous as it felt. She blurted out, "I'm karate!"

Addison squeezed her eyes shut for just a moment. *I'm karate? Really?* Then she thought better of it and snapped them open again. She'd learned early on that closing her eyes didn't make the bad things disappear.

The beam of her headlamp illuminated a bulky man-shape standing a few feet from her. He squeezed his eyes shut against the light, then turned his head slightly to avoid it. "Sorry, sorry. I didn't mean to startle you." He slowly brought both arms up at his sides in an I-come-in-peace posture.

The guy kinda looked familiar, but then, it could be just the beard. It seemed most of the men she'd met on this trip sported them. It probably had something to do with the wind chill factor and the potential for frostbitten chins. *If I had a beard, I wouldn't have to breathe shallowly into my fake fur.* The ridiculous thought had her shaking her head to clear it.

"I mean, I know karate. I can do karate," she amended, narrowing her eyes in what she hoped was a fierce expression. Although, of course, she'd already lost any credibility she might have otherwise had. *I'm karate.* Was it possible that she hadn't said that out loud?

Besides, even the karate she could remember from her childhood lessons was rendered completely ineffective by the copious layers she wore. There was absolutely no way she could do a roundhouse kick in her puffy, knee-length coat. Maybe if she just kept shining her light in his face, he'd be too blind to attack her.

But his expression confirmed her suspicions; she looked about as threatening as she actually was. Like a shivering fluffy pillow with a scowl.

Addison squared her shoulders. Lifting her chin a little, she said, "Sorry. I didn't mean to...." She made a few chopping motions with her hands, then grimaced, mortification creating a warm flush up her neck. "I'm—I'm going to go back. Over there." She pointed over her shoulder at the photographers on the beach. "I'm sure they're wondering where I've gone."

She was sure they weren't wondering any such thing, in fact, but this guy didn't need to know that.

Diamond Beach in winter.

Iceland in December.

At midnight.

What on earth was she doing there? Again.

Addison shoved her hands into her pockets and sent the guy a dismissive nod, barely able to meet his gaze. But before she could turn and flee, he lowered his hands to his sides and shrugged. "I know a place nearby that serves hot coffee."

That brought her up short. Hot coffee. She pressed her lips together and her gaze swung back and forth between the man and the group she'd come with. Oh, there was plenty to be had down the beach in the middle of that melee, but she was still trying to work up the courage to wade in again, now that she had finally broken free.

"It's good coffee, too. Not just hot." His slight Icelandic accent made the short sentences sound lyrical.

"Where?" Addison narrowed her eyes at him, her light once again forcing him to turn his head. "Sorry," she said, tipping the beam up a little. She could still see his face, but at least she was no longer blinding him. But she couldn't recall seeing any restaurants or cafes—any structures at all, in fact—within miles of where they were.

He shrugged again and pointed at the small contingence of vehicles parked close together some distance away. "In my van."

Addison rolled her eyes so hard that her head bobbed in a circle, too. "Nice try, buddy." How desperate did he think she was? She took one decisive step away from him.

"I also have *kleinur*. Both plain and dipped in chocolate," he added, wiggling his brows at her.

Like offering candy to a child, she thought, surprised to find that she was actually considering his offer. The classic Icelandic fried dough treat was one of the many delights to be experienced on the island. Not too sweet, crispy and flaky, perfect for dunking in hot coffee.... She eyed the van parked just behind the one she'd come in. Presumably, he was part of their group. "Dipped in chocolate?"

He smiled, his mustache curving up at the corners of his mouth. "Dipped in chocolate," he confirmed.

Addison turned back to study him again. The glint in his eyes told her he knew he was getting to her. What was she thinking? "I'm sorry," she said, shaking her head. "Who are you? I mean, did you come with us?" She gestured vaguely in the direction of the photographers.

"I am one of the drivers, yes. My name is Gunnar. I am Gunnar Ólafsson." He started to offer her his hand, then seemed to think better of it. He was attractive, she decided, in a winter wildernessy way. He had kind eyes, and as far as she could tell, under the facial hair and the bright red beanie pulled down over his ears, he was probably close to her age.

She was nothing, if not polite. "Hi, Gunnar. I'm Addison. Wedgewood," she added quickly, not missing the curious tilt of his head. Was it her name he didn't get? Maybe because in Iceland, a surname typically ended in *son* or *dottir*? She drew his attention to the group on the beach with a thrust of her chin. "Those are my parents. Carl and Vivian Wedgewood."

"I already know who you are," Gunnar said, his eyes crinkling in a smile that was starting to grow on her. "You obviously have not noticed me before now, but I noticed you already." He tipped his head toward the parked vehicles. "Hot coffee. *Kleina*. A warm car. How can you resist this?"

Addison was waffling, and she could tell that he could tell.

"I have music..." He drew the word out in a singsong lilt and shimmied his bulky shoulders a little. "How about Of Monsters and Men?"

It was so utterly and completely cliché, his suggestion of the popular Icelandic band. Addison couldn't bite back a smile. "Are you suggesting them because you listen to them or because you think I listen to them?" she asked.

Once again, Gunnar shrugged. "If you want to hear them; that is all that matters."

Addison hedged just a moment longer, the pull of the coffee and *kleina* making her mouth water. Finally, she capitulated. "I need to tell my mom where I'll be. In case she needs me for anything."

"She already knows," Gunnar said a little sheepishly. "She is the one who told me to find you."

Great. Just great. So the guy wasn't hitting on her at all. He'd been recruited by her mother to babysit. To feed and entertain her. Addison couldn't decide whether to be grateful—she was, indeed, cold and hungry, after all—or offended.

"Wasn't that nice of her," she said dryly.

"Yes," Gunnar agreed, seemingly oblivious to Addison's sarcasm. "A good mother always looks out for her children." He gestured again toward the van. "After you."

The biting wind had picked up a little in the time it took them to reach the van, and by the time Addison was settled into the passenger seat with a thick wool blanket draped over her lap, she was more than grateful to both her mother and Gunnar. The blanket had been his suggestion when he noticed that her teeth were chattering.

"From here, we can watch the lights just fine," Gunnar told her, nodding his head toward the view out the windshield. "I think it is more pleasant this way, don't you?"

"Absolutely," Addison agreed, watching with anticipation as he opened the large console between them and withdrew a thermos, two insulated mugs, and a brown paper bag.

"I'm sorry. I don't have cream or sugar. Just strong, black coffee."

"That's not a problem for me," Addison assured him. The smoky, robust aroma that wafted into the air when he unscrewed the lid of the thermos had her salivating. She peeled off her heavy wool gloves so she could hold the mugs for him to fill.

Several minutes later, fortified by the midnight snack, Addison settled a little deeper into the bucket seat and sighed contentedly, both hands wrapped around a second cup of coffee. She was starting to feel her toes again. "Thank you," she said, turning to look at the man in the driver's seat. "You might have just saved my life, you know."

"Really? So I am a hero now?" Gunnar winked at her from over his own cup.

For whatever reason, this guy made it easy for Addison just to be herself. Maybe it was the bizarre setting—although that was nothing new for her. Growing up as the only child of her famous photojournalist parents, Addison had borne witness to parts of both the world and humanity that most people never even knew existed. Winter in Iceland was no commonplace thing, but it wasn't even close to the wildest place she'd ever been.

Gunnar's smile was warm and friendly, and Addison nodded. "My hero." If she didn't know any better, she would have mistaken her behavior for flirting with the man.

"So tell me," Gunnar said when the silence between them started to get too loud. "Are you a photographer, too?"

Addison snorted softly and shook her head. "I'm the kind of camera operator who takes pictures from a moving car. They're always blurry and so nondescript that even I can't remember what the picture was supposed to be of."

He laughed out loud at that. "No. Surely not. The daughter of the world-famous Wedgewoods?"

"You've heard of them, then? Before this trip?" Addison asked. Not that she was exactly surprised. Her parents had been in the business for over three decades, and their names were credited with innumerable images and articles in countless forms of media around the world.

"Of course," Gunnar said matter-of-factly. "It would be difficult to find a home in Reykjavik that doesn't have at least one copy of *Edge of the World* on a shelf." The book was an awe-inspiring collection of photos captured during multiple visits to Iceland over the course of several years. Images of food, culture, the convergence of ancient and modern lifestyles, and the ever-changing landscape that made up the southwestern part of the island.

"Of course," Addison echoed, but not without a measure of pride in her tone. "I've always secretly wondered if I was adopted. I mean, I don't have a single artistic streak in my body." She tugged on a strand of her straight, dark brown hair that she kept trimmed just past her shoulders. "I look nothing like either of them. They're both blonde and beautiful and otherworldly, you know?"

"Otherworldly?" Gunnar said it like he didn't know what the word meant.

"Like creatures from another realm." Addison gestured out the window at the star-spattered sky that was beginning to vibrate with swirling shafts of blues and greens. "They belong in places like this. They thrive on the hunt, the pursuit of the next fantastic beauty on 'this round of green, this orb of flame,' as Lord Alfred Tennyson would say." She took a sip of coffee and looked away, feeling suddenly dull and lacking in substance in the long shadows cast by her glorious parents.

"And you are not otherworldly?"

"Oh, Gunnar." Addison sighed and shook her head. "No. I'm not otherworldly at all. I am *this* worldly. I'm a homebody. A put-down-roots girl. I am not a pursuer, a chaser of anything. I don't want to sleep in a new bed every night. I don't want to wake up wondering what side of the planet I'm on. I don't want to eat things I can't pronounce or go places where important things are lost in translation." She broke off, realizing she was beginning to rant. She pointed at the mug she held and shot him a suspicious look. "I'm talking way too much. Is there truth serum in this coffee?"

Gunnar chuckled. "Just Arabica beans; I promise you." He studied her for a few moments, then said, "So tell me something else, then." His expression had lost some of its joviality; was that concern she read there instead?

"What do you want to know?"

"If not this," he began, making a broad sweeping gesture with one arm. "Then what is it that you do want?"

Addison didn't even hesitate. "I want to wake up in my own bed and eat the same boring breakfast every morning. I want to feed my cat, water my plants, and do the crossword puzzle in the newspaper that gets delivered to my door every day. I want to check for mail in my own mailbox, and I want to drive to and from my nine-to-five job five days a week in my own car." She pressed her lips together to keep from listing even more things she wanted, lest she sound too pathetic, even though she knew it was unlikely she'd ever see this man again. *I want to be seen;* she didn't say aloud. *To be known. To belong. I don't want to be the new kid, the stranger, the alien, ever again. I don't want to fade into the background until I completely disappear.*

"What is your cat's name?" Gunnar asked after a few moments.

"My cat? I—I don't have one."

"But you said you wanted to feed your cat…" His words trailed off, and his brow furrowed in question.

"I know, I know." Addison waved a hand dismissively. "I meant that I wanted to do normal things that people do every day. Things that take place at the same time in the same place again and again and again. Dependable. Constant. Predictable." She sighed resignedly. "Boring."

"Do you—um…" He hesitated, then proceeded to ask the question anyway. "Do you have any plants?"

Addison shook her head. "I don't have any plants. Not a single one." She chuckled softly. "I'm pretty pathetic, aren't I?"

"No, no," Gunnar insisted. "It just seems to me that the things you want aren't so difficult to come by. Why don't you have a cat? Or a plant?"

Addison grimaced. "Promise you won't laugh?"

"I promise," he was quick to assure her.

"Well, I've never had either one. I don't know the first thing about taking care of some other living thing. I'm—I'm afraid I'd do it wrong. I mean, I suppose it's okay if a plant dies under my care, but a cat?" She shook her head. "It's probably better if I just keep it all in my imagination."

"Hm."

"What does that mean?" she challenged, feeling slightly chastised by the simple sound.

"If this is not what you want, then why did you come? I mean, it doesn't sound like a very pleasant way to spend your holidays. Your mother said you were staying in Reykjavik through Christmas."

Addison nodded slowly. "It's the only way I can see my parents. If I come to them."

"Ah. I see." His gaze shifted away from hers and she recognized immediately the look in his eyes. He was feeling sorry for her.

"What about you? Is this—" She gestured broadly the way he had earlier. "Is all of this what you want?"

Gunnar didn't hesitate, either. "I love it here. It's wild and vicious and intense and beautiful, and of course, the people here are all so attractive, yes? Like gods and goddesses."

"Well, of course," Addison agreed with a grin.

"But seriously, this is home to me," Gunnar continued. "Johann—the other driver. Have you met him?"

"Yes. I rode here in his van."

"Of course. He and I have been operating private excursions like this one for many years, and I wouldn't want to be doing anything else with my life right now."

"Wow." Addison sighed dreamily as she let his words sink in. The colorful northern lights continued to swirl and sweep across the sky, casting a surreal greenish tint over everything. "I wish I could be that certain about my own life."

Gunnar slid his stocking cap off and ran his fingers through his shaggy hair, drawing Addison's attention back to him. He really was an attractive man, she acknowledged. He had a broad forehead above a strong brow and clear blue eyes that made her think of the crystal blue chunks of iceberg that crowded the shores of Diamond Beach. His nose was long and straight, his mouth was quick to flash a smile, and the beard, although long, looked neatly trimmed, soft, and well cared for. She wondered what it would feel like to run her fingers through it.

"Does your beard keep your face warm?" she asked to derail the direction her thoughts were headed.

Gunnar grinned. "Why yes, it does." He reached up to scratch just under his jaw, then ran his fingers down the length of it in what seemed like a semi self-conscious manner. He caught her watching his movements and paused. "You want to touch it?"

She shook her head quickly. "No. Goodness, no," she insisted, far too adamantly than necessary. "That's all right."

Gunnar's soft chuckle had her burying her face in her cup again.

2
Addison

"Hey, girl," Natalie said over her shoulder as Addison moved around her to get to her own spot behind the ticket counter. "Did you ever hear anything from your yummy Viking?"

Addison shook her head as she scanned her badge and keyed in her password. "He's not my Viking. And no, I haven't heard from him, because I didn't give him my number."

"But he is yummy, right?" Natalie pressed, balling up a scrap of paper and tossing it at Addison.

She dodged the missile, then rolled her eyes. "I suppose, but it wasn't that kind of a... a thing."

A harried woman approached the ticket counter. Natalie turned to greet her. "Good afternoon," she said brightly. "How may I help you?"

Most passengers preferred to use the self check-in options. Those who came to the counter usually had questions needing answers or problems that needed to be solved. The raised voice of the woman Natalie was currently trying to assist was evidence of just that.

"The man at the security line said that this bag is too large to carry on, but I measured it at home according to what's posted on the airline website. I am not going to pay for my bag just because you people don't know what your own website says."

Out of the corner of her eye, Addison saw Natalie pick up a pen and nonchalantly add a slash mark to the unlabeled tally sheet on the counter next to her monitor. Whenever the two of them worked together, they kept a running tab of the number of times they heard the words "you people" in a given day.

Addison pulled up the check-in list for the flight that was scheduled to leave in a little more than an hour. "I can help the next person in line," she called out to a group of twenty-something women obviously traveling together. Five of them carried large tote bags that read "Vegas or Bust" and the sixth wore a sparkly tiara and a satin sash over one shoulder with the word "Bride" embroidered on it. Her tote read "What Happens in Vegas...." Addison knew the world was changing, but to her admittedly conservative way of thinking, the message on the bag read a little like a harbinger of trouble that was already brewing for the couple who hadn't yet shared their vows. But she smiled warmly, congratulated the blissfully beaming bride, and sent the ladies off with well wishes and a final "Take care of each other!"

When the line emptied again, Natalie wiggled her eyebrows at Addison, picking up the conversation where they'd left off. "So...." She drew the word out in a suggestive tone. "What kind of a thing was it, then?"

Addison snorted. "I was too busy holding other people's camera equipment, refilling thermoses, and trying not to freeze to death to have time for a thing." She eyed the sliding doors where an inconceivably young couple was attempting to herd their five children into the terminal ahead of them. They turned and headed toward another airline's counter.

Now it was Natalie's turn to roll her eyes. "Oh, you poor thing. Traveling the globe, seeing the wonders of the world, and all expenses paid, no less. You make it sound like torture."

Addison grimaced sheepishly. "Ugh. I do, don't I?"

"You know, if I didn't know you better, I might think your Viking—"

"Again, not my Viking."

Natalie dismissed her denial with a deadpan look. "I might think your Viking adventure was all a lie, that maybe you just stayed home on your time off. Read a book and played with your cat."

"I don't have a cat." The thought of doing just that, however, made Addison sigh longingly. A man hurried by, hauling a large suitcase behind him, the wheels of the thing refusing to work in tandem. He let out a frustrated growl when the thing wobbled wildly and almost tipped over, forcing him to slow down.

"I don't know why not," Natalie said. "You're about as cat lady as they come."

Addison laughed. "I'll take that as a compliment," she said before waving the next in line forward, a mom and her preteen daughter. She took the woman's driver's license, checked her suitcase, and printed out four boarding passes. The duo was heading to Los Angeles with a stopover in Dallas. "Here you go, Vanessa and Leah. Have a great trip."

"We're going to see family in Orange County," the woman said, touching her daughter's shoulder maternally.

The girl, Leah, rose up on tiptoe to try to see over the counter. "And we're going to Disneyland," she exclaimed in a voice hushed with anticipation.

"Wow." Addison gave her a bright smile. "You are going to have so much fun." She said each word with dramatic emphasis.

"Have you ever been out to California?" Vanessa asked, and Addison didn't miss the beat of nervousness in her question.

"I have," she said with a reassuring smile. "I've been on this exact route more than a few times. Are you familiar with the Dallas airport? You have a three hour stop there."

Vanessa was already shaking her head. "I've never flown before. This is a first for me," she said with a self-conscious smile.

"And for me," Leah interjected.

"Well, congratulations, you two!" Addison pulled open the small drawer under her counter and took out a couple of plastic airline stick pins. "You're earning your wings today." She leaned forward and said to young Leah, "You let your flight attendants know on both planes, too, okay? You might end up with a whole collection of these by the time you get home. And today is your lucky day, because I have it on good authority that you're flying with Sharon on this first leg of your trip, and she is just about the best flight attendant you could ever wish for." She'd text Sharon to let her know to watch out for the duo.

While the delighted Leah carefully pinned the little bauble to the front of her pink hoodie, Addison gave Vanessa a quick rundown of how to get around the enormous Dallas/Fort Worth airport using the tram system.

"And if you have any trouble, don't hesitate to ask an employee for help. That's what we're here for."

Vanessa gushed her appreciation, and Addison waved as the two headed toward the security check line. That kind of interaction was one reason she really liked her job. Her extensive travel experience gave her inside knowledge of different airports, destinations, cultures, and more, and she always got a hit of dopamine at being able to set nervous travelers' minds at ease.

At another break in customers, Addison bent over to pick up the crumpled ball of paper her friend had thrown at her.

"What you need, girlie, is a man," Natalie said, holding out the trash can toward her.

"I do not need a man," Addison contradicted, straightening up too quickly. She thumped her skull against the underside of the counter and dropped back to her haunches. "Ouch," she exclaimed through clenched teeth, reaching up to press a palm to her throbbing head.

"A real man," Natalie went on, undeterred. "Someone who exists in the real world. In *your* world."

"I do not need a man," Addison repeated, standing up more slowly.

"A man like that one," Natalie said in a loud whisper as she began typing furiously on her keyboard. She pulled her phone from her pocket and held it to her ear, doing a ridiculous job of trying to look busy.

Addison turned around, her hand still clutched to her sore head, to find a man approaching her counter. She froze.

Not just any man.

Noel Stewart.

She dropped her hand and prayed fervently that he hadn't heard Natalie's declaration only moments before. With a bright smile, she asked, "How may I help you?"

Tall, dark, and handsome... if there were an official photo to represent the ridiculous phrase, it would *not* be one of Noel Stewart.

No, Noel Stewart's photo would sit next to 'boy-next-door-you-clean-up-nicely.' He had stick-straight dark hair that kept wanting to fall forward onto his forehead. His eyes were coffee brown beneath a broad forehead, and the smudge of a shadow on his upper lip and jawline gave the guy a slightly rakish appeal. He wasn't tall—only a few inches taller than her own five-foot-six, Addison thought—and he had the lean physique of a guy who liked to play basketball with his buddies down at the park, rather than one who spent hours pumping iron in a gym.

She cleared her throat and tapped the screen on her monitor, not wanting him to think she was all but holding her breath as she waited for him.

Not that Noel noticed anything about her at all.

He greeted her with a distracted, "Hello," and set his ID on the counter in front of her. "I need to check in." After briefly meeting her gaze, he dug his cell phone out of the inside pocket of his navy blazer and started thumbing out a text.

Addison smiled brightly at the top of his bowed head and picked up his driver's license. "Hey, though," she said, then blushed furiously at her jumbled response. What on earth was she trying to say, anyway?

She ducked her head, glad he wasn't paying her any attention. She smiled down at his license a little too long—it was an awful picture, even she had to admit—then pulled up his information, checked him in, and printed out his boarding pass. How she wished she had the panache to say something clever or complimentary, something to encourage his attention. "Here you go, Mr. Stewart."

He looked up from the phone when she said his name, almost like he'd forgotten where he was standing.

With a sinking heart, she realized she could have said, "Hey, there, man of my dreams. Will you marry me?" and he wouldn't have noticed.

"Thank you," he said with a half-smile, then tucked the items into his breast pocket along with his phone. He paused like he was about to ask her something, and she leaned forward the tiniest bit. But he only patted the counter and said, "Have a great day, Addison."

"Uh, yeah." Heat flooded her senses when he said her name, making her forget how to respond. She stared after him as he made his way toward security. How did he know—? "Duh. My nametag," she muttered, reaching up to touch the plastic badge clipped to her uniform pocket.

Natalie was suddenly no longer busy. "That's him, isn't it?" she asked, sidling up to Addison. "Your lake man?"

"Not my lake man, Nat." Addison shook her head. She'd first seen Noel in Autumn Lake a few days before Thanksgiving coming out of Schnucks grocery store carrying a very full canvas bag and a bottle of San Pellegrino. It hadn't been a terribly cold afternoon, and he'd been dressed in what she'd come to think of as his signature look—a tailored sports coat over slim-cut pants. She'd sat in her car, staring at him as he hurried past her in the parking lot, his head down, his expression one of serious contemplation. He'd caught her attention because he'd seemed so out of place, like an actor who'd stepped into the wrong movie, and the look on his face told her he was very aware of how ill-fitted he was for the role he was suddenly playing. She'd felt an immediate empathy toward him, a response that had quickly turned to intrigue when he'd climbed into a big, black sedan with a Carpe Diem Resort logo in the lower right corner of the rear window. A guest or a staff member, she'd determined. So what was he doing slumming it over on the south shore, mixing it up with the locals at Schnucks Market? The folks on the ritzy north side of the lake had their own whole foods grocer, one that was much more conveniently located to the resort.

She'd crossed paths with him at a gas station the following week, too. Once again, she'd been sitting in her car, having just filled her tank, and he had pulled up on the other side of the pump in a dark gray sports car, presumably his own this time, and not a company car. He'd been talking rather animatedly as he got out, and it had taken Addison a few moments to realize he'd been using a Bluetooth device and not speaking to a passenger, or worse, himself, with so much enthusiasm.

Then a couple of weeks before Christmas, he'd shown up at the airport where she'd stepped in to help him at the finnicky self-serve kiosk. Up close and personal, his sophisticated urban image seemed to fall away, catching her by surprise, and Addison had gushed about it to Natalie for the rest of their shift.

Now she said, "I don't have Viking. I don't have a lake man. I don't have a man, period, and before you say it, I don't need a man, either."

"But that is him, right?" Natalie grabbed her by the arm and shook her, knocking her off balance. "That's the guy you were drooling over a few weeks ago, isn't it?"

Addison narrowed her eyes and pointed at her friend's mouth. "You've got lipstick on your teeth."

Natalie frowned. "Are you serious? Have I had lipstick on my teeth this whole time and you said nothing?" She rubbed frantically at the front of her perfectly pristine teeth. She stopped when she saw Addison's wry expression. Natalie made an impatient sound and rolled her eyes, but she was not to be deterred. "I *know* that's him."

Addison didn't confirm or deny it.

Natalie stepped up onto the baggage scale and leaned out past the counter to watch Noel walk away. "He knows your name, at least. That's something," she said, then let out a quiet whistle of appreciation. "Girl, you need to grab that—"

"Stop it," Addison chided. "I'm not the kind of person to 'grab' anything. Especially not something—or someone—that isn't mine already."

Natalie moved back behind the counter and shrugged. "Your loss." Then her expression brightened. "Hey. You want me to push him in front of an airplane for you? Steal his man purse?"

"What?" Bemused, Addison furrowed her brow at her friend. "What on earth are you talking about?"

"You know. Like in that *While You Were Sleeping* movie. You're totally Sandra Bullock here."

"Oh, please."

"Seriously," Natalie insisted. "I could knock him down and you could rescue him at the last minute, save his life, endear yourself to his family while he's in a coma, and then marry him. Or his way hotter brother."

"Wow. That would take a lot of effort, starting with the part where you'd have to lure him out onto the runway first."

"Hey, I know." Natalie tapped her temple and nodded slowly. "I could shove him right in front of Wendy's cart. Anyone who gets in her way is going down, down, down."

Addison snickered at the thought. Wendy was the airport's custodial day crew manager, and she took her role seriously. "If you did that, at least I wouldn't have to throw myself in front of a plane to save him. Wendy would just continue on her jolly way, and I could pick up the pieces and put them back together again."

"Maybe your Noel has a way hotter brother, too," Natalie suggested. "One who will travel the world with you."

"Again, he's not my Noel. And I don't need someone to travel the world with me."

Natalie ignored her. "One who might actually notice you."

"Gee, thanks."

"And the only way you're going to meet the hotter brother is if I put Noel in a coma."

"You are insane." Addison shook her head, then reached over and hugged her friend. "But I love that you'd be willing to go to prison to help me get my man."

"Or his hotter brother."

They were still laughing when the next customer showed up, but Addison's thoughts lingered on the lovely notion of having someone like Noel Stewart to come home to at the end of the day.

"It's never going to happen," she murmured softly to herself.

"Hush your mouth," Natalie reprimanded as she handed the man his boarding pass. Then she had to apologize to the guy when he flashed her a startled look.

When the customer had moved on and they'd stopped snickering, Addison tapped her badge. "The only reason he knows my name is because it's right here in big blue letters. I'm one of the invisibles, my friend. A nobody. We keep the world spinning so that the somebodies—like my parents or like Mister Noel Stewart and his even hotter brother—can focus on being somebody."

"Well, that's the saddest thing I ever did hear," Natalie chastised, planting both hands on her hips and glaring at Addison. "What's up with you talking so down on yourself, girlie?"

Addison sighed and managed a half-smile. "I don't know. Ever since I got back from Iceland, I've just felt out of sorts. Like I'm walking around in shoes that don't fit anymore. Or maybe they've never fit, and I'm just now realizing it."

Her friend cocked her head and gazed at her with narrowed eyes. Her expression wasn't unkind. More curious than anything.

"Why are you looking at me like that?" Addison hedged. "I'm fine. Really. I'm not going to run out in front of a plane or anything, other than to rescue Noel Stewart, of course. I'm just in a post-holiday slump, okay?"

"It's almost March. That's like me blaming these extra forty pounds on pregnancy weight, even though my baby is five years old."

"Hey," Addison admonished. Her friend wasn't as rail-thin as she'd been before her pregnancy, but she certainly didn't need to lose any weight. "Now look who's talking down on herself."

Natalie tsked. "You know what I mean. Maybe you need to take a vacation. And I don't mean a trip to some exotic place where you're going to be your parents' lackey. A vacation of your own," Natalie suggested. "Go somewhere *you* want to go and only do stuff that *you* want to do. Get away from all of this humdrum work stuff."

Addison was shaking her head before her friend finished speaking. "You forget, Nat. My passport is so full that it has a dozen foldout pages added to it. If I never travel again, it will be too soon."

"Then why are you so quick to jump on a plane when your mom calls?"

Addison shrugged one shoulder. "She's my mom. They're my parents. If I don't go to them, I don't see them."

"And you're their daughter, Addison," Natalie shot back adamantly. "Maybe they should come to you now and then. Spend a few holidays with you in your pretty little lake town. Do a photoshoot or something."

Addison snorted. "There's nothing here they'd want to photograph." She gestured out the window toward the parking lot. "Places like Autumn Lake aren't really my folks' cup of tea. They go where few have ever been before. They photograph strange and wondrous things."

"You're a strange and wondrous thing." Natalie chucked her under the chin. "And you're here."

"Ah. But they don't photograph me, remember?"

"Because you don't let them."

"They stopped taking my picture right about the time I hit my awkward, gangly, pimple-faced age," Addison muttered dryly. "When I became less wondrous and more strange."

"Hey now. That's my friend you're insulting." Natalie's words were drenched in censure.

Addison took a deep breath in, held it for the count of three, then let it out. "Sorry. Maudlin Mary over here."

Natalie's frown only deepened. "Don't you have any dreams for your future? Any plans for a career? Hobbies you love? I mean, this—" She extended an arm to encompass the surrounding terminal. "This can't be all there is for you, especially after the wild and wonderful childhood you had."

Natalie had all kinds of interests outside of work. Not only was she in a relationship with a man she planned to marry one day, but she was working on her business degree and had big plans for a career in financial management. She also had a five-year-old daughter, Avia, who was the cutest thing in the universe.

Addison sighed. "You're going to think I'm silly, but what I really want more than anything is a place to call my own. I mean, I love my little apartment, but it's not *mine*. I've been there for almost six years now, which is crazy to me. It's the longest I've lived anywhere in my entire life. But it still feels temporary because it's—" She broke off, trying to put her thoughts into words. "I want to put down roots in a place where I can grow old with someone I love, raise a whole brood of children who will love me so much that they want to live close to me and raise their kids so I can be an awesome grandma."

Natalie grinned affectionately at her. "So you're telling me that your life's dream is to be an awesome grandma?"

Addison chuckled and nodded. "Yep. Sounds about right."

3
Noel

THERE WAS SOMETHING IN the way she dipped her chin, in how she peered up at him from under lowered lashes. *Shy,* he thought. *Not coy.* Even the way she said his name, so proper and professional, made him pause and take notice. He'd almost asked her today if they knew each other from somewhere else, from some other time, but then he'd reconsidered. He knew how it would sound if they hadn't; a pickup line. He wasn't a pickup line kind of guy.

Even so, Noel found it difficult to ignore the surge of anticipation he felt every time he interacted with the woman behind the ticket counter. He'd noticed her the first time he'd flown out of the small Evansville airport, but he'd already been entering his information in the self-help kiosk when he glanced up and met her gaze. As luck would have it, the kiosk refused to process his boarding pass, and Addison had swept in to help.

As she'd tapped the screen to override the system, he'd subtly studied her profile, the hint of gloss on her lips, her long eyelashes that framed her big, green eyes. He'd have asked her out then and there if it weren't for how utterly impulsive that would have been.

Noel didn't do impulsive.

She'd had on a light floral scent, and when she got close, he'd had to force himself not to lean in and sniff her. There was something almost nostalgic about it, and it teased his senses long after he could no longer smell it. He couldn't decide what exactly it reminded him of; he just knew he really liked it.

It was probably for the best; he thought as he settled into a hard plastic seat in the waiting area at his gate. He had no business getting curious about a woman, not with all the things he was currently juggling. This was the third time he'd been in and out of this airport in as many months. "You just know her from here, you dolt," he muttered, chiding himself now for even considering engaging with her.

Noel's phone buzzed in his pocket yet again, but he ignored it. He would not respond to another text or call until he was on the ground at the other end of this flight. The morning had already been chaotic, his phone disrupting him with bid after bid for his attention, and Aunt Gigi's garbled texts were the icing on the cake. Why couldn't she proofread before she sent them?

He refused to feel guilty about not being accessible while he was in the air, or even in these few minutes before boarding his flight. Sometimes a man just needed to disconnect from it all, and here in the crowded waiting area, Noel relished the sense of detachment that came with ignoring his phone.

Besides, he had a book to read. He patted his messenger bag just to be certain the book he'd bought a couple of days ago was in there. He wouldn't start it until he was settled into his seat on the plane, but the thought of losing himself inside someone else's story had his anticipation building. He hoped *The World on Fire* lived up to his growing expectations.

Talk about impulse. Noel hadn't bought or even read a book in far too long. But the window display in the bookshop featuring the series with its fantastic artwork had caught his eye, and on impulse, he'd gone inside to check it out.

"Ah. Our own Mr. Archer," the proprietress had said when she'd come across him reading the back of the book. She'd pointed at the name on the cover. "He's homegrown. A local boy."

"Is it good?" It was a silly question. Of course, she'd say it was good. She was in the business of selling books, after all.

But the woman had surprised him; she'd studied him for several moments before responding. "I don't know that I'd call it good," she finally said. "It will transport you, though, and you'll come out the other end of it feeling both wrung out and hopeful at the same time." She grinned and waved a hand at the display. "I wouldn't have it in my front window if I didn't think it was brilliant."

Why Noel even dreamed he had the luxury of reading during this chaotic season in his life, he had no idea, but despite his reservations, the premise of the novel intrigued him enough to purchase the first in the series. He'd decided then and there that rather than going over his budget analysis for the monthly report on his upcoming flight, he'd break tradition and read on the plane instead.

Noel had worked in accounting for corporate Carpe Diem Resorts and Hotels for almost a decade, and last fall, he'd been offered a position as Financial Auditor at the company's high-end resort in the beautiful tourist town of Autumn Lake. The resort was only a half-hour drive from the thriving river city of Evansville, and centrally located between many major cities, including Nashville, Louisville, St. Louis, and Indianapolis. It was also less than a day's travel, whether by car or plane, to his only remaining family in West Virginia.

What had seemed like a dream job, however, had quickly become something of a nightmare. It had taken Noel about a week of reviewing and assessing the company's financial statements, control systems, and policies and procedures to realize that if things didn't change, and quickly, the resort was heading for some pretty rough waters.

From what he could determine, John Sheridan, the Operational Internal Auditor whose responsibilities had included the financial operations before Noel's position had been created, hadn't done anything as nefarious as embezzlement or tax evasion. But the resort's economic instability was evidence that the man wasn't equipped to cover the scope of the tasks expected of him alone. The purpose of separating the financial aspects from the rest of the operational processes had been to provide relief to the man.

Instead, John had taken personal offense at having some of his responsibilities taken from him, and he seemed determined to take it out on Noel.

Handling disgruntled or discouraged clients was something Noel was accustomed to. It came with the territory; money often did that to people. But he'd not expected it from John—or John's devoted assistant, Paula Swinton—especially since the three of them needed to work as a team to maintain the operational efficiency of the resort.

John, apparently, was not interested in being part of a team, and from what Noel could tell, John wasn't keen on letting Paula be a team player, either. The man somehow managed to keep her so busy—doing what, Noel wasn't sure—that Noel felt bad asking for her help with any of his own tasks.

At first, Noel had gone out of his way to refer to John for input, to seek him out with questions or concerns, but by the time he'd presented his first reports to the board of directors in mid-December, Noel had all but given up on winning John over. He began avoiding the guy unless interaction with him was absolutely necessary, keeping his head down and his mind busy, focusing solely on the duties of his own position.

In some ways, the tension between them eased up when he stopped trying so hard, but for Noel, the day-in-day-out stress of working with someone who seemed to resent his very existence ate away at him. It stirred up things inside of him that he'd thought he'd long ago laid to rest.

A man's voice boomed out over the speaker system, jerking Noel's attention back to the moment. "Good morning, travelers. Flight number 6125 is now ready to start boarding." He spoke quickly, his words running together, becoming almost indecipherable as he droned on, but folks seemed to know what to do, anyway. Noel was no exception, and he made his way to the ticket line, along with everyone else.

The plane wasn't large. It held about sixty passengers when at capacity, and with only one seat on one side of the aisle and two on the other, he didn't bother spending the extra money for business or first class. He'd been able to procure one of the single seats, and with a nod of greeting to the young couple across the aisle from him, he settled in and buckled up.

He pulled the book from his carryon, then shoved the messenger bag under the seat in front of him. Once they were in the air, the flight attendants would make their way through the cabin with drinks and snacks. But other than that, he had a few hours to disappear between the pages. And if he enjoyed the writing, he'd hunt down the other books in the series, and start making reading a priority in his life again.

Reading. Books. Fiction. Science Fiction and Fantasy had been his favorites. *The Narnia Series. The Lord of the Rings Trilogy. Dragonriders of Pern. Rats of Nimh. The Dune Saga.* Tales of wild adventures so far removed from the life he lived had been his escape when he was a boy.

He opened the front cover, pausing just a moment to appreciate the resistance of the binding, the way the pages of a new book hesitated to open up to him upon that initial cracking of the spine.

To his surprise, Noel found that he could, indeed, still squeeze through that imaginary portal and lose himself in the realm of other realities. The book swept him right out of his plane seat and into another world where the fate of the future rested on the shoulders of eight intrepid freedom fighters.

The fading beam of the headlamp cast a malignant glow over the mountain of refuse that blocked their way. Keeria squeezed her eyes shut, trying not to give in to the despair that nipped at her heels. She couldn't let the others see it, though. They were counting on her to get them out, to keep the flame of hope burning, no matter how improbable their survival seemed....

So caught up was he in the story that he was surprised when he felt the altitude change and realized they were already descending. He finished the chapter he was on—and of course; it ended on a precarious cliffhanger—and tucked the book away.

The moment Noel exited the plane and turned his phone on, reality came crashing back in the form of a slew of message alerts. Up until he slid into the driver's seat of the car he'd rented, Aunt Gigi kept insisting that she was ready to jump in her big old boat of a car and come get him. "You don't need to spend all your money on a rental, Noel," she'd hollered into the phone at him.

She hollered not because she was angry, but because she was hard of hearing, and she never turned her television off. Or down. He could just picture her sitting in her easy chair in front of the ancient TV, with her phone clamped between ear and shoulder, her hands working her knitting needles with lightning speed as she fashioned yet another comfortable cardigan made from recycled thrift store sweaters. She donated them to the nursing home where her husband had spent the last years of his life, and it always made her day to see yet another resident wearing one of her creations. "Cardigans are much easier to put on than pullover sweaters," she'd told him, maybe a hundred times. "Arthritis makes for uncooperative shoulder joints."

If it weren't for his aunt and her open-armed exuberance, Noel wouldn't be making this trip. Or any of the ones he'd made to Bald Knob over the last few years. He went back solely to visit her, to show his love and appreciation for the woman who'd been so instrumental in helping him find his way out of the darkness in which he'd been raised.

His father still lived in Bald Knob, too, but Noel hadn't seen the man in years.

Bruno Stewart was a hard, vicious human, and the fact that Bruno and Gigi were siblings boggled the mind. Noel's mother, Nita, had died fifteen years ago, the life simply leaching out of her far too prematurely. She'd been beaten down—beaten regularly, although she denied it every time anyone dared to ask about bruises, sprains, and even a broken bone or two—by the life of poverty, shame, and suffering Bruno had provided her with.

Noel had somehow managed to evade Bruno's drunken rampages that followed Nita's ragtag funeral. Gigi had insisted Bruno was "grieving something fierce, poor soul," but Noel thought it was much more likely that the man was angry about having to cook and clean for himself now that his wife was gone. He'd turned narrowed eyes in Noel's direction more than once in those days, a look that Noel knew all too well. A look that meant he'd better make himself scarce if he knew what was good for him.

Scarce, he'd made himself.

It was Aunt Gigi who had pressed a tight roll of bills into his hand during the wake when his father had been preoccupied with neighbors paying their respect. Her words had been an echo of his mother's, albeit a little less dramatic. "Finish school so you have that diploma, then git yerself on outta this holler, Noel. You got somethin' in you that needs to see the light of day. The mines ain't no place fer the likes of you."

The money she'd given him had gotten him all the way to Los Angeles before he'd run out, but he'd always been a hard worker, and labor jobs weren't difficult to find year-round in that part of the country. It had taken him almost a year, working his way up the coast, before he finally ended up in Washington State, where he worked even harder to complete his business degree. It was an accomplishment that felt to him like the final severing of ties that bound him to his old life, the ultimate spreading of his wings. His only regret was that his mother hadn't been there to witness it all. He hoped she knew that he'd gotten out, and that she was proud of the man he'd become.

Yet, here he was, driving too fast on the circuitous country road that would take him back to the place that used to be home. A place to which he no longer belonged.

4
Noel

In the early years after he'd left Bald Knob, Aunt Gigi hadn't been privy to his whereabouts, just in case his father got any notion in his head to wrangle it out of her. But Noel regularly sent her cash and short letters tucked into envelopes with no return addresses, even though he knew no dollar amount would be enough to repay her for what she'd done for him. On the rare occasions he called her, she thanked him profusely for what he sent and never asked for a penny more.

Until, during one of those calls, she'd told him about slipping on the icy sidewalk in front of her house, that she'd broken an ankle in the fall. "But not my hip or either of my arms, thank the good Lord above. I was able to scoot on my tush all the way up to my stoop where I could sit on the first step with a little dignity, I'll have you know. Then I just waited for someone to pass by, hoping they'd realize a little old lady settin' on her porch step in the middle of a January morning weren't no normal sight." She had chuckled at Noel's shocked exclamations and continued. "I was laid up in my easy chair long enough to knit up a whole mess of baby blankets. Pastor Schafer boxed them up and sent them off to an orphanage in Haiti. Can you believe it, Noel? My little ol' blankies got to travel the world. They've seen places this ol' girl can't even imagine in my wildest dreams."

After that conversation, Noel added another line to his cell phone plan and sent her a smart phone. "Go down to the high school and ask one of the kids to show you how to use it," he'd instructed. "Then keep that phone with you at all times. I won't have you sitting out on your porch step in the cold like that again. You could have gotten pneumonia."

She'd made a dismissive noise over the line. "Don't you know you can't catch a cold from bein' cold?"

Sending her that phone was a decision he'd come to regret at times, but one that had given him a certain peace of mind, knowing that she could reach him at a moment's notice.

Then three years ago, his father had suffered a massive stroke down in the mine, and Aunt Gigi had called Noel as soon as she'd gotten the news. Bruno had survived, but his paralysis was extensive, and from what the doctors could tell, he would no longer be capable of caring for himself.

In spite of his vow never to return to Bald Knob, Noel had made the trek back to the hollow, even though he knew his father wouldn't want or accept his help.

"You can keep your handouts," Bruno had railed in long, slurred syllables, saliva dribbling from the slack side of his mouth. In fact, when Bruno had made it clear that if he never laid eyes on his son again, he'd die a happy man, Noel had agreed wholeheartedly.

But for Aunt Gigi's sake, he saw to it that his father's transition from the hospital to the long-term nursing facility—the same one his uncle had been in—went as smoothly as possible, paying for everything Bruno's insurance didn't.

After his father's collapse, Noel traveled to Bald Knob when he could, even if only for a few days at a time. It wasn't to see his father, of course, but to make sure that his aunt continued to have everything she needed. It was his way of taking care of her because she was taking care of Bruno. In December, he'd spent the three-day Christmas weekend with his aunt, then had returned to Autumn Lake to put in some quiet, stress-free hours in the office before John returned from his long holiday vacation.

Noel had gone back to Bald Knob mid-January for two days to celebrate his aunt's birthday with her, and now here it was, not much more than a month later, and he was already heading back again. His aunt had asked him to come, something she never did, and although she insisted everything was fine, her request concerned him enough to make it happen. He'd put in several fifty- and sixty-hour weeks since the holidays; he figured he could take a couple of days away to set his mind at ease.

As he pulled into his aunt's driveway, he was pleased to see how nice her little yellow house looked these days. The lawn, although brown from the winter cold, looked well-tended. There were burlap bags tied around carefully trimmed rosebushes in the flowerbeds on either side of her newly painted front door, and the honeysuckle vine that rambled over the white picket fence still boasted a smattering of tenacious bedraggled leaves that had clung to the vines through the bitter cold of winter in the Appalachians.

By the time his feet hit the gravel drive, Aunt Gigi was standing out on her little stoop, waving both arms at him, her gravelly voice ringing out in welcome. "Noel Stewart! You made it! How was the drive? Are you hungry? How does breakfast for dinner sound?"

The barrage of questions was perfunctory, he knew, and he didn't bother answering any of them. "I like the green," Noel commented when she finally stopped to take a breath. He tapped the front door as he held it open for her. "When did you do that?"

"Oh, I had young Jeffrey Hahn paint it for me a few months ago. He was trying to earn some money to help pay for his mama's surgery—did I tell you about Emma's accident last year? She had a little fender bender coming out of the Piggly and busted up her nose something fierce. It didn't heal right, and she's had trouble breathing and gets these headaches that just knock her down for days at a time. There's a surgery she can have, but her insurance only covers part of it, so there's a chunk of change coming out of her pocket for it. Jeff—senior, I mean. You remember him, right? Didn't you two go to school together?" She didn't wait for a response. "Anyway, he is taking on any extra hours he can, but the boys are doing their share, too. I think they just want their mama back to normal. You know how it is when a mama isn't well."

She rambled on about the Hahn family's trying situation a little longer, then something she said reminded her of another family in her church who was going through some trouble of their own. "Shorty Cooper hasn't been able to go back to work yet, and times are hard for folks already, so I've been taking a meal or two over there a couple times a week, just to be sure they're getting some solid food in their bellies."

Noel sank into one of the chairs at the small table in the kitchen and listened to his aunt discuss her friends and neighbors without hardly taking a breath. Something was eating at her, he could tell, and he had no doubt it had to do with his father. He wouldn't press her; they'd get around to it eventually, he knew. For now, Aunt Gigi seemed content to talk about everything but Bruno.

She peeled off thick strips of bacon and laid them out in her iron skillet while she talked. In moments, the mouthwatering aroma of frying salted pork filled the room, and he was suddenly ravenous. "What can I do to help?" he asked, knowing already what her answer would be.

"Not a darn thing. You just sit there and look handsome," she said, jabbing a large metal spatula in his direction. "Would you like pancakes or waffles with your eggs and bacon?" It was a given that there'd be biscuits. Breakfast wasn't breakfast without biscuits, according to his aunt.

There was nothing healthy about Aunt Gigi's cooking. The pancakes were made from a mix, the biscuits from a generic brand pop-open can, the eggs were always fried to perfection in the hot bacon grease, and the white gravy would be riddled with sausage or bacon bits from the pan scrapings. But if home could be a taste rather than a place, it would be Aunt Gigi's breakfast for dinner.

If only he could package that taste up and carry it with him wherever he went. "Pancakes sound good to me. Can I set the table, then?"

"Nothin' like bacon dipped in maple syrup, right?" She thrust her chin toward the stack of plates on the counter beside her. "No need. I'll just load everything up on plates here and keep them warm in the oven. But if you insist on helping, the coffee is fresh. I'll let you pour your own cup. And crank open that window a little, will you? Don't want to set off that smoke alarm you insisted I have. I swannee, that thing is nothing but a nuisance, Noel."

The little kitchen had been painted recently too, Noel realized, and everything had a fresh, clean air about it, in spite of his aunt's penchant for fried foods and cigarettes. The window cranked open stiffly, and he made a mental note to squirt a little WD-40 on the mechanism while he was there. The chill air that drifted in felt good on his face, and he breathed in deeply, the comfortable sounds in the cozy kitchen soothing his spirit.

Noel poured his coffee and topped off his aunt's cup, too, then took a careful sip of the dark brew. It was much stronger than he liked it and tasted a little scalded, but he'd expected no less. His aunt's coffee pot stayed on all day long, and a fresh pot just meant that it wasn't the first one of the day.

Aunt Gigi set two heaping plates in front of him, one with fried eggs, several strips of bacon, and a couple of biscuits smothered in thick gravy, the other with a stack of pancakes. She scooted the croft of butter his way, then handed him the glass jug of real maple syrup she'd heated up in a pan of water on the stove. His aunt was a purist when it came to her syrup.

After setting her own piled-high dishes on the table, she dropped into the chair opposite him, then offered up a short prayer of thanks. For a few minutes, they ate in companionable silence, enjoying the first several bites of the homespun fare.

"How's Bruno?" Noel finally asked, forcing his shoulders not to tense up in anticipation of her response. He'd stopped calling him 'Dad' the day he left the hollow.

"He's fine, Noel. Just fine. Onery as a stub-tailed, toothless beaver, and just as helpless, too." She took a sip of her coffee. "There's a nurse at the home he's taken a shine to. Name's Debbie. Not in the romantic sense, mind you."

"In other words, he's not mean to her," Noel translated, his tone dry. "Give him time."

"No, no. It's more than that." Gigi shook her head slowly. "I think he's got a friend in her. She's not his type at all. She's bossy and pushy and won't let him tell her how it's going to be."

The opposite of his mother, Noel thought.

"From what I can see, she's been able to get him to do far more for himself than anyone else has in some time. She's new to the area, so I doubt you know her. Debbie Sholes is her name. Her husband teaches at the high school." She rose and went to the oven to pull out the warmed plate of extra pancakes and offered it to him.

Noel took two more, even though he was already full. She'd be offended if he didn't.

"Anyway, whenever I get over there to visit him these days, he's usually out of his bed, dressed, shaved, and hair combed and everything. I think he needed someone to believe in him. Someone who wasn't quite ready to give up on him."

Noel didn't meet her eyes. Was that just an observation or a leading statement? Was she accusing him of doing just that? Giving up on his father?

"Don't look so guilty, Noel," his aunt said with a rough chuckle. "I didn't mean that to come out like a reprimand. Most any other son would have shaken the dust off his boots and never looked back. You've done far more for that bitter old man than he deserves from you."

He still didn't look at her. He may have done everything he could in providing for his father, but he had, in fact, given up on him. Every time Noel showed his face at the nursing home, Bruno would snap and snarl and tell him he wasn't wanted there, so he'd stopped going, stopped subjecting either of them to each other's presence. And with that decision had come a great sense of relief. If he never saw Bruno's scowling face again, Noel had almost convinced himself that he would be just fine with that.

There was always a piece of his heart, though, that longed for the clasp of his father's hand on his shoulder, a pat on the back, the smile of a man who was proud to claim Noel as his son.

"I wasn't going to say anything until tomorrow morning, but I suppose there's no reason to wait." Aunt Gigi absentmindedly swirled her spoon in figure eights in her cup.

"What is it?" Noel prodded when she still hesitated.

She sat back in her chair and looked him in the eye. "He's asking to see you."

5
Addison

ADDISON STEPPED OUT OF the terminal into the blustery early evening. She tugged the collar of her coat a little tighter around her neck and peered out into the parking lot across the street, not looking forward to the trek out to the far lot where employees were expected to park. She shoved her hands into her pockets, clenched her teeth to keep them from chattering, and set off.

By the end of her shift, Addison was usually more than ready to get behind the wheel of her dependable, ultra-safe, fuel-efficient CR-V and head back to Autumn Lake. She really liked her job, but there were some days when it seemed that she spent her whole shift troubleshooting and problem-solving, and nothing lifted her spirit more than the thought of tucking herself into her little apartment in the lovely lakeside town she called home.

While she waited for the car to warm up, she plugged her phone into its car charger, pulled up her "Homeward Bound" playlist, and closed her eyes as the orchestral swell of 80s arena rock filled the interior of her vehicle. It pulsed through her, the beefy bass notes and pounding drums, the soaring vocals that rivaled any operatic number, in her opinion.

This was Addison's secret vice, her means to decompress after a long day of dealing with the rollercoaster of emotions that accompanied travelers. Not because of the cheesy lyrics or the heavy eyeliner and big hair. Not even because of the guys in spandex—which she could never bring herself to study too closely, anyway. That was all part and parcel to the genre. But there was nothing like the music itself to shut out all the noise of her wandering thoughts, her unexplored hopes and dreams, and her unmet needs.

"I need Noel Stewart," she murmured, and for a moment, she wasn't sure if she'd said it out loud or not, since she couldn't even hear her own voice over the throbbing melody. She glanced out her windows to make sure no one was nearby. She had no doubt that her music could be heard across the parking lot, even with her windows all rolled up, which was bad enough. She was too old to listen to her music this loudly, wasn't she? But to be seen sitting alone in her car talking to herself? She couldn't decide which was worse. Maybe they'd think she was singing along…

Except that there was no "they" around to witness her ridiculousness, no one to catch her in the act of being utterly and completely alone.

"Thank goodness Natalie didn't hear me admit to needing a man," she said with a dry chuckle. "Besides, I'm happy being alone," she insisted to the strip of her face she could see in the rearview mirror. She toyed with the necklace she wore, a gift her parents had sent her from their last trip to Java. From a herringbone chain hung a silver twisted wire tree sculpture strung with tiny jade beads as the leaves. It was larger than what she might have chosen for herself, but the craftsmanship was so fine, the wire lacing so delicate, and she'd been enchanted at first sight. It hung at the perfect length below the juncture of her collarbones, just visible in the open collar of her uniform, and she wore it to work almost every day.

"I'm alone, but I'm not lonely." Her thumb brushed over the texture of the jade leaves on the pendant. "I have crazy parents who love me. I have friends. I have a great job and I like the people I work with. I have an apartment that suits me just fine, and I really like my reliable car with its awesome sound system." She still couldn't hear herself, and for some reason, in some nonsensical way, that fact seemed to invalidate her words.

Addison sighed deeply and lowered the volume so that she could safely back out of her parking spot. She left the music low as she made her way toward the exit of the lot.

"Hey, Arnie," she said to the attendant manning the ticket booth.

"Hey, yourself, young lady." Arnie Bowman was a retired coal miner who had somehow survived his career with his hearing intact, his lungs in decent working condition, without any missing digits or limbs, and with a smile for everyone that passed through his lane. Addison loved knowing that she'd get one of those smiles from Arnie at the end of her workday.

"How's the book coming along?" she asked. There was no one in line behind her. She put her car in park so that she could chat without thinking about keeping her foot on the brake.

Arnie wasn't just a parking attendant these days. He was working on his third novel in a post-apocalyptic trilogy about a mining explosion that released a deadly toxin into the world, wiping out more than half the earth's population. Arnie had a way with words that drew her into the story, and she had been delighted to discover that she really wanted to know how everything was going to turn out. "Give me some good news."

"You are my biggest fan, I do believe," Arnie said with a wink. He tapped the computer monitor in front of him where he had a document pulled up; he worked on his manuscript between customers. "It's going along just fine, thank you very much. And no, I will not tell you how it ends." He leaned out the window of his ticket booth and cupped a hand near his mouth as if to prevent anyone else from hearing his next words. "I don't even know how it's all going to go down, so how can I tell you?"

Addison gripped her steering wheel and grimaced exaggeratedly. "Hurry up, Arnie. I need to know what happens next. I'm dying here."

"So is Panier Hellinthon, I'd wager." He tapped the side of his nose and nodded.

Addison's eyes grew wide. "No!" she exclaimed. "You can't kill off Panier. He's one of my favorites." She covered her ears. "Don't tell me anything else. I don't want to know, after all."

Arnie guffawed, then narrowed his eyes at her, although still smiling. "How you doing, my friend?"

Caught a little off guard by the question, Addison hesitated just long enough for Arnie's expression to grow serious. "I'm fine," she said, stumbling slightly over the word. She'd almost blurted out, "I'm happy," as though saying the words again would make them true.

"Rough day?" Arnie asked, seeing right through her bluff.

"Not bad, but I am ready to call it over," she admitted, wondering if she looked as out of sorts as she felt these days. Is that why he was asking? "I'm looking forward to curling up in my warm pajamas with a cup of hot tea and the last book in this really great trilogy by this author I know." Talk about his work and maybe he'd stop looking at her like he was trying to diagnose her. "If only he'd get cracking and release it to his adoring fans."

"Aha. I see what you did there." Arnie pointed at her, but apparently, he wasn't going to be distracted. He cocked his head to one side and said, "Forgive me if I overstep here, Miss Wedgewood, but you seem to me to be a little... oh, I don't know. Lost? At loose ends?"

It wasn't really a question. Nor could she take offense at his observation. It was exactly how she felt these days. Besides, Arnie would never say anything like that with the intent to be rude; he was a good man, and he'd become a good friend in the time she'd been working at the airport.

When she didn't immediately respond, Arnie nodded slowly. "I've overstepped."

"No, you haven't," Addison was quick to assure him. She scrunched her nose at him as she pondered her next words. "I don't think it's that I'm lost, exactly. I think it's more that I'm tired of... of—" She broke off, grimaced, then said, "I'm tired of wandering."

"Wandering, hm?" He considered that carefully, not hurrying to fill the silence between them.

"I've spent my whole life wandering. I have traveled the world, Arnie, wandering around in the footsteps of my parents. Literally. I just walk along behind them, going where they go, being wherever they are being." She made a dismissive sound at the back of her throat. "Whenever I can catch up with them, that is. So yeah. Not lost. Just wandering."

"As the great J.R.R. Tolkien once said, 'Not all who wander are lost.'"

"Exactly." She glanced in her review mirror, surprised to find that there were still no other cars behind her. "Maybe I'll go home and read the Lord of the Rings trilogy, since the trilogy I really want to read isn't finished yet."

Arnie waved away that attempt to distract him, too. "Do you know the rest of that stanza?"

"'All that is gold does not glitter; not all who wander are lost,'" Addison quoted. It was one she knew by heart. "I write those lines on the first page of my journal each new year," she explained. "I love the open-endedness of it. The idea that not only is there more than meets the eye, but also, that if we are only looking for what we expect to see, that we might miss out on what's really there."

"Hm," Arnie said with a slow nod. "Yes. That's about what it means to me, too. But the next line—do you know it, too?"

Addison shook her head. "I don't."

"'The old that is strong does not wither. Deep roots are not reached by the frost.'" He didn't expound, but just let the words linger in the air between them.

Did he know about her obsession with roots? Her brow furrowed as she considered the lines. "That almost sounds contradictory," she finally said, curious as to why Arnie had steered the conversation there.

"I wouldn't say contradictory, Ms. Wedgewood. No, I believe that although Tolkien appreciated the wanderer's soul, he was sending out a clear message that wandering—aimless wandering, in particular—could be dangerous. Wandering without purpose or direction could lead you into places you're not prepared for or expecting to end up. Go ahead and wander, yes, expand your horizons. But know where your old deep roots are and keep them tended so you don't lose your way. I believe that the verse in its entirety is about searching for, and *finding*," he emphasized, "our purpose on this road that we call life."

Addison nodded slowly, not quite sure how to respond. She shouldn't be surprised to hear Arnie unwrap so poetically one of the most iconic literary quotes known to man. He was, after all, a reader and a writer himself.

Arnie wasn't finished. "You know what I think?"

"What do you think?" Addison asked, not really sure she wanted to know, but humoring him all the same. Although, she added, "Before you answer that, do you think I can handle it?"

He chuckled and nodded his head. "You can handle it. Here's what I think. I think you are weary of wandering, not because you're lost, but because you have yet to be found." The crinkles around his eyes deepened as he studied her. "And everyone needs to be found."

"What do you mean?" Again, she wasn't sure she wanted to know, but there were still no cars behind her, and she couldn't just roll up her window and drive away, could she?

Arnie patted his chest over his heart. "In here. Your heart. It's waiting to be found. But if you keep wandering, how can anyone find it?"

"A man?" Addison shook her head, overwhelmingly disappointed in him. She had not expected him to play the 'you need a man' card. Natalie, sure. But Arnie? "You surprise me, my friend. I mean, I like men well enough, and there are times I even wish I had one in my life, but I—" She broke off, realizing she was starting to sound a little defensive. She took a stabilizing breath. "I'm not really interested in being rescued by a man right now, Arnie. I want to be rescued by me."

"Rescued?" Arnie shook his head. "Who said anything about being rescued?"

"You know what I mean. Found. Chosen. Rescued. Same thing." She heard the rumble of an approaching vehicle and sighed with relief as she watched a pickup wending its way through the parking lot toward the exit. "I'm not looking to be swept off my feet. I kinda like my feet planted firmly on the ground, in fact."

"You're putting words into my mouth," Arnie admonished gently. "I didn't say you needed a man. I said everyone needs to be found. To know where they belong. And yes, to whom they belong. Your people. Your place. Home." He patted his chest again. "Where your heart lies. That's what I think, Ms. Wedgewood. You'll find yourself, your way in life, your purpose, when you figure out where your deep roots are."

The truck pulled up behind her, his lights half-blinding her in her rearview mirror. Arnie was right. Cliché, yes. A little cheesy, definitely. But correct, nonetheless. She pressed the heel of her palm over her own heart in response to the dull ache that settled there. "I'm working on that, Arnie," she finally said, then reached over and patted the ledge of the ticket booth window. "And you need to keep working on that book. I'm desperate to know how it ends."

"Aren't we all?" he retorted with a ready grin. "You have a nice evening, now, you hear?"

"You, too, Arnie. See you tomorrow."

Half an hour later, Addison pulled into the narrow back alley that ran the length of the buildings along Larkspur Lane. Her apartment was perched above The Quill and Ink Shop, and behind the art supplies and stationery boutique were two parking spaces allotted for her use. She sat in her car after she took the keys from the ignition and stared at the second space, clearly demarcated by parallel white lines on the asphalt. It was rarely used, at least not with her knowledge, and tonight, it seemed glaringly empty.

"I should get a cat." She pushed open her car door and peered up at the little deck above her. She could just picture a fat tabby perched on the railing, waiting for her to get home so it could purr loudly and rub against her legs. "Here, kitty, kitty," she called out, letting her imagination play out. "Mommy's home."

The words echoed cheekily off the back of the tall brick building, and she smacked a palm to her forehead. "Wow, Adders. Just wow. You *are* a crazy cat lady and you don't even have a cat." She chortled self-consciously as she circled her car and headed up the narrow flight of steps, hoping that no one had witnessed her borderline madness.

6
Noel

"Bruno?" Of course, she meant Bruno. "Why does he want to see me?" Noel wiped his mouth with his napkin and leaned back in his chair. But it was a fair question; his father had made it abundantly clear that Noel was the last person he ever wanted to see again.

Aunt Gigi sighed, then said, "He's softened, Noel. That's the only word I can come up with to explain it. I probably wouldn't even go so far as to say that he's changed, but he's mellowed. In some ways," she added hastily.

Which meant that in most ways, Bruno was still Bruno. Noel frowned, stood, and started gathering the dirty dishes from the table. Gigi didn't stop him, which was telling. He stacked her plates on top of his, then carried the pile to the sink. "Do you think that's a good idea?" he asked, although he didn't need to hear her response to know what it would be. It was why she'd wanted him to return so soon after his last visit.

"I don't know that I'd call any idea of your father's 'good,'" she conceded. "But I do think his request comes from a genuine interest in knowing how you're doing."

"And that's not something you can tell him? Fill him in on how great my life has been without him in it?"

"Noel." It was a gentle reprimand, and he felt it in his gut.

"Sorry." He stood at the sink with his back to her, waiting for the tap water to turn hot enough to wash the dishes. Glancing over his shoulder at her, he asked, "Why didn't you just tell me this on the phone?"

Gigi pressed her lips together and gave a one-shoulder shrug. "I guess I was worried you'd find excuses to avoid coming if I did."

"You know me better than that, Aunt Gigi." It was his turn to gently reprimand her. "When have I ever not taken care of my responsibilities?"

"I know, I know," she said, practically over the top of him. "I also know your plate is full with that new job of yours. You work so hard, Noel. I just didn't want it hanging over your head like a black cloud."

A black cloud, indeed.

♥ · ♥ · ♥ · ♥ · ♥

NOEL TOSSED AND TURNED in his aunt's tiny guest room for most of the night, and when he crawled out of bed the next morning, he felt weighed down by trepidation and doubt. But he would go through with paying his father a visit, if only to make Aunt Gigi happy.

At sixteen, Bruno Stewart's first job down in the mines was to push the full tubs of coal gouged from the black seams over to the pit eye, where it would be hauled up the shaft to the earth's surface. Even as a young man, he was hard and hungry and more than a little mean. He was also determined to outwork everyone, and he quickly moved up the ranks. In his late twenties, Bruno had served his country for two terms in the military, and when he returned home, it was with a quiet, young—and pregnant—wife, Nita, a nurse he'd met at one of the field hospitals where he'd been stationed. He'd moved her into the home he'd grown up in, then picked up his tools and his safety gear pack and headed back into the mines.

The war didn't make the man any less mean. Nor did having a wife and baby at home.

In fact, the opposite was true. Bruno came out of the mines each day coiled like a rattler ready to strike, and his wife and son learned quickly just how volatile he was. Down in the pit, Bruno kept his rage in check—the crew members were brothers in arms to him, and he'd once told his wife, "Them boys are my real family, and don't you ever forget it."

Noel hadn't been much more than a toddler when he was old enough to witness his father lifting a hand to his mother. Old enough to remember the sound of that massive palm striking his mama's cheek, the way her head flung sideways at an impossible angle before she righted herself, her shoulders hunched, her chin down, and apologized for whatever it was that she'd done.

There were times when the gunshot of those slaps still ricocheted in Noel's memory.

When Noel was eleven, there'd been a methane explosion in the mine where his father worked. Bruno, the crew foreman at the time, had been delayed near the entrance, working out some details on a piece of equipment that needed repair, and had sent his crew on ahead of him right before it happened. The explosion had triggered a roof collapse, trapping eight miners in a chamber almost three hundred feet deep for four days.

Although he'd been knocked off his feet by the blast, in an act of superhuman resilience, Bruno had gathered himself immediately and began organizing a rescue strategy. Over the next four days, he'd proven himself to be a hero time and again, heading up one of the teams that went into the shaft to pull the men—or their bodies—out of the rubble.

Three of the miners had been killed outright in the explosion, two men sustained horrific crush injuries and didn't survive the four-day ordeal, and one more died in the hospital a few days later. The other two survivors had suffered injuries that caused long-term disability, and neither of them was able to work the mines again.

Bruno had never quite recovered, either. That explosion had taken his whole crew, his brotherhood, his family, from him and he'd been unable to save them. The dark cloud that he'd always dragged around with him roiled thick and murky with the impotent rage he felt over not being able to get his boys out of the collapsed shafts.

News crews and photographers had camped out in Bald Knob for weeks as the aftermath of the explosion and loss of life played out in their tiny community. Like a pack of prowling wolves, they'd pressed in, made rabid by the town's despair. Their empathetic expressions couldn't mask the twisted desperation that spurred them on to capture the most shocking moment, the most heartbreaking interview, the award-winning, iconic image that would represent to the world just how horrific life and death could be.

And how remarkable humans could be.

Bruno Stewart had been photographed hauling a broken miner out of the rubble, carrying him in a fireman's lift, the man's head and limbs dangling lifelessly in the macabre image. Tear tracks had streaked Bruno's coal blackened face, and the journalist had asked the right questions at the right time.

When the story came out, the whole town bought copies of the popular magazine, and Noel's teacher had given him his own issue.

Bruno had read only about half the article before he launched the magazine across the room in a fury that would burn for days. The journalist had quoted Bruno verbatim when he said, "I should have been in the mines with my crew, but since I wasn't, I should have saved them. I failed my brothers and their families, and I don't know if I can live with that."

Survivor's guilt, they'd called it.

Noel had hidden his own copy of the magazine under his mattress, taking it out only when he was certain his father wasn't in the house, or he was passed out in the other bedroom. The photos in the article were stunning, somehow capturing the relentless battle between suffering and hope during that terrible time, as the rescue operations worked day and night to free the men below. The community held a round-the-clock prayer vigil at a local church, and in one of the pictures, Noel and his mother huddled together in a pew, their heads bowed as they gathered with other believers to beg God for intercedence.

There was another photo in the magazine article, one that made Noel's gut churn. It was a different shot of Bruno, taken two days into the ordeal, looking like an avenging angel accepting a bottle of water from an adoring child.

The child had been Noel, and the water bottle had been his mother's idea. It had taken him over an hour to get his father's attention long enough to offer him the water... only to have it slapped from his hands in an angry outburst.

Bruno had grabbed him by the shoulders and shaken him until his teeth rattled. "You think my boys have pretty little plastic bottles of fresh water down there? You think they're okay sitting in that—that coffin, while I sit back and indulge in refreshments?" He'd spit the words out between clenched teeth, then shoved Noel away from him, making the boy stumble backwards. Noel had somehow managed to right himself and stay on his feet, but as he turned to flee, his father had roared, "Do you have rocks for brains, boy?" Then Bruno had slapped him in the back of the head so hard that he'd gone sprawling, face first, into the mud.

He had lain there, the pulse throbbing loudly in his ears, holding his breath, hoping against hope that his father was finished with him, that he wouldn't drag him up out of the mud and start in on him again.

When he'd finally convinced himself that he was alone, he'd pushed gingerly to his hands and knees and lifted his head slowly. Standing in the shadows between two of the news vans was a rail-thin girl dressed head-to-toe in black, her eyes huge in her pale face, her hands clutched tightly to her chest. She'd seen the whole thing; he could tell by the combination of fear and shock and concern on her face.

She took one hesitant step toward him, but Noel lurched to his feet and ran in the opposite direction.

The photo in the magazine had made the moment look like something good, something pure, hopeful. Everything that it had not been.

Noel hadn't even seen the photographer who'd snapped the shot. He'd been too busy focusing on keeping his neck from snapping under his father's rough handling. The fact that the wraith girl had witnessed it all had affected him even more than the abuse, and Noel had avoided the mine and the news crews like the plague after that, making sure he'd never have to lay eyes on her again.

It was after the mine disaster that Bruno had gone from being an angry, volatile man to a real-life monster. One of his favorite pastimes was breaking things. Dishes, mirrors, windows. Or punching things. Walls. Doors. His wife. Sometimes his son, too, if his wife wasn't available.

Everyone knew, but no one stepped in. Folks didn't do that back then, at least not in Bald Knob. And besides, Bruno Stewart was a hero, after all. Aunt Gigi would come to check on them, sometimes bringing food or first aid supplies when things got really ugly. Sometimes she'd bundle Noel and his mother up and take them home with her, the lines between her brows etched deep with misery. Sometimes she'd even courageously call Bruno out for being the cowardly monster that he was, raising his hands against the ones he was supposed to love and protect, but usually, only when the man was drunk enough not to care.

In fact, the only time Noel and his mother felt remotely safe was when they were holed up with Aunt Gigi and Uncle Thomas. It was a much-needed reprieve from the storm, even though they always feared there'd be retribution awaiting them on their return.

Today, Noel would lay eyes on the man that had far too many times laid rough hands on him, and his stomach churned just picturing his father's scowling face. "Let's get this over with," he muttered to himself, scrubbing his fingers through his spiky, sleep-mussed hair. Then he made his bed up and headed out to the kitchen, the smell of muddy coffee beckoning him.

Aunt Gigi took one look at him and clucked in sympathy. "Sit. I'll get you a cuppa Joe."

"Thank you," he said, pulling out a chair from the table in the middle of the small kitchen.

When she brought him the steaming mug, she leaned down and planted a kiss on top of his head. "It sure is nice to have a man sitting at my table again." She pulled a small, foil-wrapped chocolate heart, a leftover from Valentine's Day, he guessed, from the pocket of her apron and set it on the table in front of him. With a wink, she said, "Don't spoil your appetite now."

He picked up the chocolate and peeled back the fuchsia foil. He flattened the wrapper on the table and read the message printed on the inside of it.

"What does it say?" his aunt asked, glancing over her shoulder as she filled her own coffee mug.

"You are the sunshine in my day."

"Ain't that the truth," Gigi said with a firm nod. "You are my sunshine, Noel Stewart. And don't you ever forget that. Now, would you like some breakfast? I'll scramble the eggs so it's different from last night, and we'll have sausage gravy on our biscuits."

"Sounds great," he said as brightly as he could muster. His stomach was in knots, and the thought of a heavy meal right now wasn't exactly appealing.

"You don't have to go visit him, Noel." Aunt Gigi pulled a jug of milk and a box of sausage links from the fridge. "He doesn't know you're here. I can see it's weighing heavy on you."

"I know," Noel acknowledged. "If he really wants to see me, then I'll go, but honestly," he added, frowning down into his mug. The coffee was good and strong—and actually fresh—this morning. "I'm not completely convinced he really means it."

"Of course he does. Your father doesn't say anything he doesn't mean."

Noel studied her as she bustled around the little space. She pulled a can of prepackaged biscuits from the fridge door, walloped it much harder than necessary against the counter, and it popped open. "Woo-hoo," she chortled. "Don't you just love that sound?"

"Some things never change," he said, smiling at her antics. She was trying to brighten his spirits, he could tell, and he loved her for it. "You're just as crazy as ever, you know."

"Thank you very much," his aunt retorted, propping one hand on her hip. "May the day never come when I stop being this crazy."

"Amen to that," Noel chorused, but his thoughts went right back to his father. Was it possible that the man had, indeed, softened so much that he wanted to see Noel again? And why? Could it really be the first step in reconciliation?

Did Noel even want to reconcile after all this time?

Or was there something unsavory up the man's sleeve? Knowing Bruno, Noel couldn't help leaning toward the latter. The man wasn't known for his kindness, and Noel had never heard him apologize to anyone for anything in his entire life. Reconciliation was not a word that he could ever imagine associating with Bruno Stewart.

7

Addison

That evening, Addison found her own uncharacteristically morose company rather tiresome. So, she changed into fleece-lined leggings, a bulky sweater, and a pair of boots that would keep her feet warm and dry. Then she walked the block and a half to The Cracked Spine, the local bookshop owned by her friend, Claire Maitland.

She and Claire chatted for a few minutes, but it was a busy night in the shop. A group of teenage girls pushed through the door, setting off the chimes that signaled more customers, bringing their lively chatter in with them. "Hi, Claire!" one of them called out, the others chorusing along. "You look amazing!" And she did, Addison acknowledged silently. Part of Claire's charm was the cosplay outfits she wore to work, and this evening, she had dressed in the scarlet gown and simple white coif worn by Offred in Margaret Atwood's *The Handmaid's Tale*, her hair in a demure knot at the back of her neck. The red turned her pale skin to porcelain, her blue eyes to crystals.

Another girl added, "Hey, Addison." It stirred something warm and fuzzy in her chest to be recognized by them, to know that she was *known* by so many people. That she belonged. Arnie's words from earlier replayed in her mind. *Know where your deep roots are.*

"Peruse to your heart's content," Claire told Addison before heading off to assist them. The girls were obviously regulars in the shop and knew exactly where to find the books they wanted, but they met Claire with big smiles and the effusive hugs that teenagers seemed to dole out without hesitation. It didn't surprise Addison; Claire made friends with everyone. In fact, if it hadn't been for Claire, Addison might still feel like an outsider in the small town she now called home.

It had been the bravest thing Addison had ever done, applying for and accepting the airline attendant job. She'd known when she'd submitted her application that her life would change dramatically if anything came of it.

Her parents, much to her surprise, had congratulated her profusely when she'd been offered the job, and had encouraged her to take it. Years later, she could still remember everything as if it had been yesterday.

"We know you aren't really cut out to be road warriors like we are, Addie," her mother declared.

"You've been such a trooper all these years," her father agreed. "Gallivanting all over the globe with us. Attentive, helpful, always contributing wherever you can. That's just how you are."

"I was raised right," Addison replied, embarrassed by their sincere praise and doing her best to swallow the tears that threatened to spill. "But are you sure you'll be okay if I take the job immediately? I mean, I was supposed to go with you to Beijing next month."

"We will be fine, Addie," her mother said. "Beijing is our opportunity. Evansville, apparently, is yours."

"We'll be fine," her father repeated. "Do you remember Pete Mavis? He's been chomping at the bit to tag along on another trip with us."

"Oh, he'll jump at the chance to take your place," her mother added.

"Not that he could ever fill your shoes." Her father assured her. "No one could ever take your place. I'll wager you're going to be a tough act to follow, Addison Wedgewood."

"Thank you, Dad. Mom. I—I guess I'll tell them yes, then."

"Good girl. Don't second-guess yourself," her mother instructed. "You're strong. You're beautiful. You're brave. You've got what it takes. Now go make things happen."

Her father chuckled and nudged her mom with his elbow. They sat side by side at the table, squeezing together so they could both see the phone screen during the video chat with Addison. "My wild road warrior," he said to his wife, his smile one of complete adoration. Turning back to Addison on the phone, he winked. "My darling couch potato."

"Thanks, Dad. Although I'm not sure if that's a compliment."

Their engaging conversation was a bit out of character for her parents, and Addison couldn't help but wonder if maybe she should have abandoned ship long ago. She'd been so afraid to tell them, to disappoint them, and instead, they'd been thrilled for her.

Apparently, Addison did have a little of her mother's decisive alpha spirit in her, because within a week, she'd accepted the job, found the lovely apartment she now called home, and even bought the dependable little car she loved so much. She'd started her first day on the job only three weeks after accepting the offer.

And she'd never looked back.

"Did you find anything irresistible yet?" Claire made her way back to where Addison was perusing the post-Valentine's clearance table.

"Absolutely." Addison snatched up a box of chocolates and a bag of red and white saltwater taffy. Then she cocked her head at her friend. "Or did you mean books?" Then she pointed at the short stack of paperbacks she'd been setting aside to take home with her.

"You've got great taste," Claire said, quickly scanning the titles in Addison's pile. "And that chocolate is divine; only the best for The Cracked Spine."

"Of course," Addison said with a nod. "I would expect nothing less."

Claire straightened a stack of love poetry books and smoothed the corners of the raspberry velvet tablecloth, then slowly lifted her gaze to meet Addison's. "So…" she began, drawing the word out.

Addison set the box of chocolates down and turned her full attention on her friend. When Claire didn't continue, she prompted, "So?"

"I think I met someone."

Addison's mouth fell open in surprise. "You what? You… *think* you met someone?"

"Nothing's official or anything. It's just a guy who's been coming into the shop a lot recently, and you know how I am. No one is a stranger to me."

"No one." Addison fought back a delighted smile. She couldn't remember ever seeing her friend so… so *twitterpated*, as Bambi would say.

"Well, after the third time he'd been into the shop in less than a week, I asked if he wanted to get coffee and go somewhere so we could talk about the books he was buying. He picked up one of your friend's books, and you know how much I love talking about that series."

"And?" Addison asked when Claire paused a little too long. Surely there was more to the story than that.

"And..." Claire gave a little shoulder shimmy. "He said that he'd love to, but that it was too late in the afternoon for more coffee. So, we ended up walking to the lake and sitting on one of the benches on the shore for more than an hour. It wasn't busy here, and Tina had just gotten out of school and was happy to take over so I could slip away."

"It's still winter, girlie," Addison said, her brows lifting. "It's frigid down by the lake."

"It is, indeed," Claire said, a sparkle in her eye. "But we sat close, and when I started shivering, he put his arm around me to warm me up."

"And you let him?" This was a whole new side of her friend; one Addison hadn't seen before.

"Not only did I let him," Claire said, her cheeks coloring with pleasure. "I kinda snuggled up to his side, too."

"Who is it?" Addison asked, leaning forward in anticipation. "What's his name? Do I know him?"

Claire hedged a moment, then said, "Don't hate me. Promise?"

Addison's brows drew together. "Why would I hate you?"

"Because I can't tell you who it is." She grimaced sheepishly and reached out to take Addison's hand. "I want to; I really do. But I don't want to jinx it, you know. I get the feeling he's coming to Autumn Lake to get away from something. Or someone. I didn't press because I don't want to know. Because I really like him." She suddenly looked terribly vulnerable, something else that Addison hadn't seen in Claire before.

Addison tried not to frown. "Wow. That—I mean, of course you don't have to tell me his name. That's your choice."

"But?" Claire prodded, even though her expression told Addison she wasn't excited to hear her reservations.

"It's not really a but," Addison countered, squeezing her hand. "I mean, I love the thought of you meeting someone; and what better place than here at your shop? It sounds like the perfect meet-cute."

"But?" Claire repeated, pulling her hand free so she could rearrange a tray of heart-shaped page-corner bookmarks.

"I don't know. I guess it just sounds like there's potential for trouble, you know, with the whole 'getting away from something' you mentioned. You're talking about your heart, Claire, and I care about that heart. If this guy is attached…"

"I don't think he's attached," she said, shaking her head. "I didn't get that vibe from him."

"But he's got secrets?" Addison was trying to keep a positive perspective on things, but her concern was growing as Claire talked.

"I don't know that they're secrets," Claire countered. "I just feel like he's got a backstory that might be a big deal."

"Where is he from?"

"I—I don't know. But it must not be too far because he drives here."

Addison asked, "Do you know where he works? What he does for a living?"

Claire hedged again. "I'm not sure, but I know it has to do with helping people," she finally said. "I think that may be part of what he's dealing with. Like maybe there's a lot on his shoulders right now."

"Did he ask you for your number? Or give you his?" Addison reached over and covered Claire's hand with her own. "Or you can tell me it's none of my business, of course."

"It's okay," Claire said. "And no, he hasn't. But he has my number. It's on the shop bag and on his receipts."

Addison thought maybe she was being too much of a downer. Just because she couldn't find a nice man of her own didn't mean no one else should be able to. She smiled warmly. "I'm happy for you, Claire. I promise. You are kinda glowing, you know."

"I feel like I'm glowing," Claire agreed. "Like I'm floating about an inch off the ground." She lowered her gaze a moment, and when she met Addison's eyes again, she said, "I had to tell someone about him, or I would have gone crazy. But I don't want to worry about the 'what ifs' right now."

Addison thought she understood where her friend was coming from. That place of uncertain hope in something that seemed possible, but maybe not so probable. "He'll call, Claire," she said, reassuringly, even if she didn't fully believe it.

8
Noel

When they arrived at the nursing home, there were only a few cars in the lot, and most of those were in the employee parking section. Granted, it was the middle of a work week, but Noel had a feeling that it wasn't the kind of place where visitors lingered.

He offered Aunt Gigi an arm, and they headed inside the security door—a staff member named Sadie had to open it from the inside—then they filled out the visitor check-in form. Sadie recognized his aunt, but when she saw the name on Noel's form, she looked up at him with wide, surprised eyes.

Noel looked nothing like his father; he knew that. His mother's genes were strong in him, and even though he'd often wished he'd gotten at least some of Bruno's solid German bulk, it was not to be. Noel was of average height, naturally lean, his thick, straight hair without a hint of the curls his father had. He had his mother's features, too, and, according to her, he had her father's hands. Noel's hazel eyes, and perhaps something in the angle of his jaw, gave some evidence to Bruno's parentage, but every time he looked at his own reflection, he was relieved not to see any more of his father staring back at him.

"I'm Noel Stewart. Bruno's son," he said, smiling pleasantly at the young woman. It irked him to hear the mountain twang slipping back into his words, something he'd worked so hard to eradicate, but he figured maybe here, back in his hometown, it might work in his favor.

"You're his son?" Sadie questioned, frowning a little as she studied him. "I've never seen you here before."

Great. So now he was being judged for not visiting over the last three years. He hadn't even considered the likelihood of that kind of response.

He had a sinking feeling that no defense he could offer would redeem him in the aide's eyes, so he simply said, "I am."

"Our Noel here travels all over the country for work, Sadie. He comes when he can," Aunt Gigi interjected before Noel could come up with some polite defense. "Now, are you going to let us in? Or do we have to pass a private screening?"

Noel tried not to gawk at his aunt, unprepared for her brusque rebuke to the girl. But when he saw the warning look on her face, he stayed quiet.

"Sorry, Miss Gigi," Sadie mumbled, ducking her head to avoid the older woman's glare. "I'll let Debbie know you're here. Mr. Stewart had kind of a rough night. He's not... you know. Not feeling his best today." Sadie looked about ready to cry, but she squared her shoulders and added, "Debbie told me to check with her before anyone goes in his room."

"I'm sure she meant anyone but me," Gigi said, planting one hand on her hip. "So don't make me get feisty with you."

Noel blinked rapidly and dropped his gaze to his feet. He had to press his lips together to keep his grin locked down tight. His aunt was already far feistier than he'd seen her in a very long time. Poor Sadie.

"I'm sorry, Miss Gigi. I'm sure you know how he can be—"

Noel cleared his throat. This wasn't going well, and he had to intervene, quick, before his aunt said or did something she might regret. "It's fine, Aunt Gigi. If he's not up for a visit, maybe it's better that we try another time."

Gigi turned to Noel with a frown. "Another time? Honey, that man is clean out of time. He asked to see you. You're here. We're here." To Sadie, she said, "We're willing to brave Bruno's bad mood, you hear?"

One of Sadie's hands rested on the communication device clipped to her hip, her fingers toying nervously with the buttons. Noel could tell she desperately wanted to call for backup, but was too afraid to do so in the face of Aunt Gigi's... feistiness.

To his aunt, he said, "It might not be a bad idea to have Debbie give him a heads up, especially since I'm here."

Sadie, who apparently knew not to pull rank on Gigi, waited for the older woman to agree. Finally, his aunt let out an exasperated huff. "Well, I suppose. But our time is valuable, so please let Debbie know that we're well aware of what Bruno's ugly side looks like. And I'm not talking about his backside. I mean, his ugly inside."

Sadie turned away to avoid Gigi's steely gaze and paged Debbie.

It took three tries, but Debbie, sounding frazzled, finally responded. "Yes? I'm in the middle of something here."

"Miss Gigi and her—um, Mr. Stewart's son are here to see him."

Debbie didn't respond immediately, then asked, "Mr. Stewart's son?"

Noel heard a gruff voice, loud and insistent in the background, before the sound cut off. The devices apparently worked more like walkie-talkies than a cellphone.

Several long moments of empty static sounded over the radio before Debbie responded. "I'll be right there. Have them wait in the lounge, will you?"

After seeing the trepidation on the attendant's face and the disgruntled expression on his aunt's, Noel took the bull by the horns. "Let's go sit, Aunt Gigi. Sadie, is it possible to get a couple glasses of water?" He wasn't thirsty, but the girl seemed to be waiting to be excused.

"Sure. Yes. Absolutely." Relief softened the fear in the young woman's eyes, and Noel gestured for his aunt to go ahead of him into the somewhat dated but clean and cozy lounge. There was an enormous fireplace on one wall, and although it was no longer functional, presumably for safety reasons, the massive mantle was decorated with framed photos of the residents, and a large floral arrangement sat on the hearth in front of the grate.

Aunt Gigi dropped unceremoniously into one of the overstuffed armchairs and crossed her arms.

"Hey, Aunt Gigi, it's okay. He may not be up for a visit from me today, and I'm okay with that." Noel hoped to soothe her spirits with his gentle words, but truth be told, he wasn't going to be upset if today's visit didn't happen.

Aunt Gigi crossed her arms and made a noise in the back of her throat. "Well, you may be okay with it, but that doesn't mean I have to be." When she got emotional, especially when she was angry, her Appalachian twang got heavier. "Your daddy doesn't have much time left, and I think he's finally admitting that to himself. He was sincere when he told me he wanted to see you, and I'm holding him to it. There is nothing left to him in this world except for you, Noel Stewart."

"And you," Noel countered. "You've been good to him."

"Yep, and he don't deserve me, neither. But that's family, honey. And now here we are, and that little whippersnapper ain't going to tell us we can't see him. That's all there is to it."

"She was just doing what she'd been told," he said softly.

"Well, I told her to do something different." Gigi harrumphed and turned to glare out a window that looked out onto the parking lot.

Sadie, carrying a tray of drinks, entered the room and paused in the taut silence. "Um, I brought you coffee and water. I hope that's okay," she said, directing her words at Noel.

He rose, took the tray from her, and set it on the coffee table in front of his aunt. "That's perfect."

"Do you need anything else?"

"We need Debbie, that's what else," Aunt Gigi snapped, giving the young attendant a narrowed-eye glare.

"We're fine." Noel handed his aunt one of the large-handled ceramic mugs with its matching saucer. "Thank you for the drinks."

Sadie pivoted on her heel and practically fled the room.

"So, what is the beef between you two?" Noel asked, lowering back to the sofa with a glass of icy water. The one sip of coffee he'd dared to drink had made his jaw tighten reflexively at how bitter it was. Gigi could have his cup if she made it through hers and still wanted more.

"That Sadie girl put in Bruno's medical records that he was violent and aggressive, and they had to file an abuse report. He almost got kicked out of here because of her."

"You didn't tell me about this." Noel's brows furrowed in concern.

"I didn't tell you about it because it was a lie, and I was able to sort it all out on my own."

"She lied?" he asked dubiously. He knew his father, and 'violent and aggressive' seemed about right to him.

"An exaggeration, Noel." Gigi rolled her eyes. "I know your daddy is a mean ol' cuss, but he can barely lift his own head anymore. He needs help, and if girls like Sadie ain't equipped to provide the kind of help he needs, well, who can blame him for getting upset? But violent and aggressive? And supposedly unprovoked, she claimed."

Noel frowned and said, "That doesn't seem so out of character for Bruno. He's far more than just a mean ol' cuss, Aunt Gigi."

"I talked to him, Noel. I can understand him better than pretty much anyone here. He told me he needed help getting over to his bedside commode. But when he pushed his help button, that Sadie girl just went in there and reset it, telling him she'd be back to help him shortly. That happened four times in a row." She held up four gnarled fingers. "Four times. And every time, she just turned the call light off, promised she'd be back, and left him practically bursting at the seams. Which is exactly what he did."

Noel eyed her skeptically. "He burst at the seams?"

His aunt snorted with disgust. "He finally just soiled the bed right under him. Then he pushed that button again, and when she waltzed in all in a tizzy and started berating him for the mess he'd made, he grabbed her wrist and told her she'd better not leave him lying in his own filth if she knew what was good for her." Aunt Gigi grabbed her own wrist and shook it gently to demonstrate. "That's what she called violent and aggressive, Noel. His desperation for a little respect. Unprovoked, my great Aunt Tilly."

Her voice had grown tight, and Noel realized she was more than just angry.

"Old age, dementia, strokes like your daddy's, the way these bodies just break down and give up before we hit the finish line? It's a crime against humanity." Her words came out ragged and raw. "We are stripped of our dignity in ways we have no control over, and then some empty-headed young thing waltzes in and—and witnesses our utter frailty, then mocks it by not caring enough to try to understand? People like that Sadie girl just don't get it, Noel."

Noel sat forward in mute dismay. He held out his hand, palm up, relieved when she placed her own in his. He squeezed her fingers gently, at a loss for words that might comfort her.

"I know I'm next, Noel. I know it. But my daily prayer to the good Lord is that he takes me in the middle of the night while I'm asleep in my own bed, in my own house, all my faculties intact. I don't want to end up in a place like this with no one looking out for my dignity."

"I'll always look out for you," Noel insisted, stroking the back of her hand with his thumb. Her skin felt shockingly thin and fragile under his touch. When had that happened? "And if you don't want to end up here, then I'll hire someone to move in with you and take care of you at home, if that's what you want. Or you can come live with me." He meant it. He'd make a place for Gigi in his life, if that's what she needed. He owed her so much more than that.

Gigi pressed her lips together, her eyes glistening with emotion. Noel couldn't remember ever seeing his aunt cry, and this was probably as close to it as she'd get in public, if he knew her at all. Finally, she said, "You're a good boy, Noel. But you know as well as I do that I don't want to live or die anywhere but in this here holler. And live with you?" She tsked and shook her head, then pulled her hand free so she could pick up her mug of coffee. "No, thank you. Besides, you still have to figure out who you are without the shadow of..." She glanced down the hall that led to the residents' rooms. "Of all of this hanging over your head. I'm a part of your once was. I have no place in your what will be."

She said it so gently, so tenderly, that Noel couldn't even be offended by it. He didn't bother contradicting her, but as far as he was concerned, Aunt Gigi would always be a part of his life, even long after she was gone from this earth. "What happened with Sadie?" he asked, changing the subject. "She obviously didn't lose her job. Was there no disciplinary action taken?"

Gigi's shoulders squared, and her chest swelled with indignation. "What happened with her? Nothing, I tell you. They called me in and told me I needed to start looking for another place for your daddy, that they weren't equipped for that kind of behavior in their residents. Well, I refused to sign anything until I went down and spoke to Bruno. He told me what had happened, and I marched back down to the main office and told them I'd file a report of my own, *and* I'd start talking. They changed their tune pretty quick, let me tell you. Didn't want me doing that, as you can imagine. I have a big mouth in this town, don't you know it."

Noel nodded slowly, his heart full of pride and love for his truly feisty aunt.

"Eventually, I heard they had a little chat with that Sadie girl," she said, scowling again. She did so every time she referenced 'that Sadie girl.' "She got some kind of slap on the wrist and had to go through some dumb class on bedside manner or something or other, but they put her right back on the floor caring for patients." Aunt Gigi shook her head in frustration. "I don't want anyone to lose their job, mind you. It's tough to make ends meet in this life, I'm well aware. Besides, nursing homes like these are always understaffed. But I put my foot down about her not being allowed to work with Bruno. That was right about the time Debbie hired on, and it's been much better since then."

"Thank you, Aunt Gigi," Noel said, his voice rough with emotions. "I don't know what we Stewarts would do without you."

"I'm a Stewart, too, honey. I was a Stewart long before you came into this world."

"Family," he murmured.

"Family."

A tall nurse in bright pink scrubs, her blonde hair in a messy bun on top of her head, swept into the room on a cloud of antibacterial handwash as she rubbed her hands vigorously together. "Hi, Miss Gigi. How are you?" she asked, her movements brisk, economical. All business, this one, Noel decided. Without waiting for an answer from his aunt, the nurse turned to him. "You must be Bruno's son. Noel, right?"

He rose and shook her hand in greeting, then offered Gigi a hand up out of her chair.

"I'm Debbie. Your father's charge nurse. His cough kept him up last night, so he's in rough shape." The look she gave Noel made him tense; it wasn't going to be good news. "He's refusing to see anyone. I'm sorry. I know you've come a long way."

Noel wasn't surprised one bit. Nor was he disappointed. Not really. Why had he believed, even for a second, that the man who'd hated his very existence all his life would now be interested in reconnecting? Preposterous. Ridiculous. Absurd. *Fool.* The words danced and spun like mean-spirited imps in his head.

"Debbie," Aunt Gigi began, but the nurse held up a hand and shook her head.

"Miss Gigi, I've been in that room with him for the better part of an hour and he's in no condition to have visitors today. I think you know me well enough to trust that I wouldn't say so if it weren't true."

Noel looked back and forth between the two women, wondering if his aunt would get "all feisty" with Debbie, too. He, on the other hand, wasn't about to argue, and not just because Debbie clearly knew what she was doing and who she was dealing with.

If Bruno didn't want to see him, that was just fine with Noel.

9
Addison

The days were growing longer, but the weather stubbornly remained bleak. Outside the floor-to-ceiling plate-glass windows, the sky was gray and moody, the clouds heavy with rain that was probably waiting to fall until she got in her car to drive home. It was not quite winter, not quite spring, just cold and damp and muddy.

"Like my heart," Addison said with a sigh as she stood behind the counter at the entrance of the jetway, waiting for the first of the passengers to disembark from the plane. After working for the airline for so many years, she had experience in almost every position and filled in wherever she was needed. Folks getting off a plane rarely even acknowledged her as she smiled in welcome, but inevitably, if an attendant wasn't available to assist the passengers, someone would need something.

Affordable air fares meant fewer staff for many airlines, particularly at small regional airports like this one. And gate agents, especially, felt the crunch of that. They were responsible for a multitude of tasks that enabled flights to stay on schedule. They operated the jetways, maneuvering the bridge tunnels into position for passengers getting on and off the planes. They arranged for wheelchairs and unaccompanied minors, dealt with the fallout of inflight passenger emergencies, and directed travelers to connecting gates and baggage claim areas. They helped with cleaning the cabins between flights, cleared new crew members and standby passengers, and scanned boarding passes. They took care of gate-checked carry-on bags, dealt with irritable customers with last-minute travel issues, closed the gates, and pulled back the Jetways so the plane could leave. They answered endless questions, operated the system computers like skilled hackers, knew where the closest restroom/restaurant/electrical outlet/bar/lounge was from anywhere in the terminal. And they were required to do it all with a smile.

The job could be overwhelming on a good day, and, like so many of her days lately, today had not been a good day.

Addison was more than a little frazzled after dealing with a passenger who had made a horrible to-do after a turbulent flight from Dallas. The woman's complaint was not about the turbulence, though, but about the terrified little boy in the seat next to hers. "That... *child*," she ground out in a tone that let everyone know she wanted to call him something else. "Screeched like a stuck pig the entire flight." Her voice was loud and shrill enough to evoke a similar description of her own behavior. "He wouldn't shut up, and the mother just sat there the whole time and did nothing to stop his temper tantrum. It was bad enough that we all had to deal with your pilot's inability to do his job right—I have bruises on my ribcage from being thrown against the seat handles, you know. But to have to endure that, too? And no one would respond to my call button light, either. Talk about inept."

Addison had tried to explain that flight attendants couldn't get out of their seats during that kind of turbulence, except for in an emergency, but to no avail. The passenger made it clear that she considered her circumstances to be just such an emergency.

She'd demanded a refund for her ticket, and when that wasn't forthcoming, she threatened to file a lawsuit against the airlines, the woman and her child, and the flight crew for not stepping in. Addison had offered to take her name and information to pass on to management. "It's possible we can compensate you in some other way," she'd suggested, knowing that the company would likely issue her some air miles to use on a future flight.

The woman had adamantly refused. "You can't just dismiss me like this," she'd shouted, infusing her statement with profanity.

To Addison's relief, someone had notified security while she was dealing with the situation, and a few moments later, an officer had appeared and escorted the woman to the exit under the threat of arrest. She had shrieked obscenities the entire way out of the building.

It was only after she'd gone that Addison had noticed the young mother whose child had been so distraught on the plane. She'd stayed behind in the hopes of helping to set things right, and was now in tears herself. Addison had spent the last fifteen minutes trying to calm the woman, assuring her that she'd done nothing wrong, that her child, a delightful little boy who seemed to have recovered completely, was not to blame for his reaction to the traumatic experience. Addison took a measure of pride in the fact that she had somehow managed to do so without openly lambasting the vile woman who'd made such a fool of herself over the situation.

Now, all she wanted was for the next group of disembarking travelers—the last on her shift—to sweep past her and right on out of the building. Her smile in place, she stood at the ready at the boarding pass station near the open door of the Jetway.

When Noel Stewart exited the bridge, chatting affably with a woman on his other side and just out of Addison's line of sight, she shrank back a little further, hoping to blend in with the blue paint on the wall behind her. Of all the people in the world, she didn't need him noticing her. She knew without a doubt that she looked as frazzled as she felt. She glued her eyes to the monitor screen in front of her, intent on looking too busy to disturb, and pleaded under her breath, "Just walk on by, all you people. Walk on by."

It wasn't meant to be. "Hello, Addison, dear."

Addison plastered on a smile and looked up to see who had greeted her. "Barb!" she exclaimed in surprise, then scuttled around the counter to hug her friend. She stepped back and gave the attractive, motherly figure a quick once over. "You look stunning, as usual. Even after traveling all day. I'd forgotten you were coming back this week."

"Oh, goodness, Addison, but you do know how to make a person smile, don't you?" Barb Selway wasn't only a frequent flyer out of the little regional airport, but a friend, too. Addison had met the Selways during her first summer living in Autumn Lake. The town held an annual floating lantern festival, and Addison had braved going down to the lake on her own in a concerted effort to become a part of her new community. She'd struggled to get her lantern lit when it was time to set the beacons afloat and had been on the verge of giving up. Barb and Craig Selway, however, had been on a blanket nearby, along with their son, Rory, their daughter, Andrea, and Andrea's husband, Jeff. Barb had practically shoved Rory at Addison, insisting he help her with her lantern. "Scooch your chair on over close to us, dear," Barb had called out to her. "You don't want to get lost in this crowd."

They'd become fast friends that evening, and inevitably, Barb had all but asked Addison if she'd like to go on a date with Rory. The guy had good-naturedly gone along with his mother's machinations and asked Addison to join him and several of his friends for a fish fry the following evening.

To her surprise, Addison had enjoyed herself thoroughly. The group had been larger than she'd expected, at least thirty people around their age, and the fish had been fresh-caught right from the lake earlier that week. The deep-fried catfish and potato wedges and the flaky cheesy biscuits came from one of the seasonal diners on the boardwalk, and Addison thought it might have been the best meal she'd had since moving to the small lakeside town.

"You'll have to forgive my mother," Rory had said to her as they sat shoulder-to-shoulder on a log in front of the bonfire. "She wants me to get married and bring forth a whole new generation of Selways before she, in her words, 'is too old to roll around on the floor with them.'"

Addison had giggled at the imagery that conjured up. "What about your sister?" she'd asked him.

"Oh, Mom's pressuring them; believe me. But Andrea is married, so I've got some catching up to do, especially since I'm the older sibling and will hand off the Selway name." Rory had studied the dancing flames, the light flickering across the planes of his handsome face. He'd turned to smile amiably at her. "We don't really mind, Andy and me. Mom and Dad have a great marriage and loved being parents, and they want us to have the same 'overflowing joy' in our lives, too. Mom's words again, not mine."

"Does that mean you aren't interested in marriage and children?" Addison had asked him, a little relieved at the notion, truth be told. Rory was fun to hang out with, but she hadn't sensed any chemistry between them.

"Someday, sure. But right now, I'm busy. I work fifty-plus hours a week, and when I get off work, I want to be able to do this." He'd gestured around him at the group on the lake shore. "Come and go as I please, crash when I'm tired, stay up late if I'm not. I know I'm not ready for the responsibility of being a dedicated husband and father. It may sound selfish, but it's the truth."

"Actually," Addison had said with a shrug. "It sounds responsible to me. Like you know exactly where you are right now, what season of your life you're in."

Rory had bumped his shoulder against hers. "I think you and I are going to get along nicely, Miss Wedgewood."

And they did. Barb took every opportunity to mother her, especially once Andrea and Jeff moved away, and she and Rory treated each other with the casual ease of adult siblings.

Barb glanced back at the man who'd accompanied her to the counter. "Addison, you've probably met Noel Stewart by now. We were seatmates, and he tells me he's been flying in and out of this airport regularly over the last few months." She waved him closer. "Noel, if you need help with absolutely anything to do with flying, Addison is your girl."

"You're my girl," Addison quipped agreeably, attempting—and failing dismally—to play it cool. She flushed hotly. "I mean, I'm your girl. Well, not *your* girl. I'm not anyone's girl." Great. Could she make things any weirder? "And I'm not really a girl." Yep, she could. "I'm an adult. A woman," she finished lamely.

Barb's eyes widened as her gaze bounced back and forth between Addison and Noel. "Well, just in case you haven't, let me make the introductions official. Addison, this is Noel Stewart. Noel, this is my dear friend, Addison Wedgewood."

Noel stepped forward with his hand outstretched, his smile a little pained. "Nice to meet you, Addison. And on this side of the counter," he added. Thankfully, he said not a word about her mortifying rambling.

Probably trying to be polite while desperately wondering how to get away from Barb's freaky friend. She shook hands with Noel, but only nodded, too afraid of what might slip out if she attempted to use words.

"I'm surprised you two haven't run into each other 'on this side of the counter,' before now." Barb's smile was extra wide, a calculating gleam in her eyes. She looked a little scary, Addison thought. "Noel moved to Autumn Lake last November, Addison. He works at Carpe Diem. And Noel, this lovely young lady calls Autumn Lake home, too. Despite the fact that you've somehow not managed to run into each other out at the lake, you two just try telling me this isn't a small world."

Barb and her husband currently lived in Evansville, but they had a summer cottage on the south shore for most of their marriage and considered Autumn Lake their home away from home. In fact, Rory lived in the lake house year-round.

"Wow. Small world, indeed," Noel said, his smile growing warmer. "I haven't spent a lot of time on the south shore yet, but that's on my agenda, now that winter is starting to ease up a little."

"Oh, don't count on that," Barb said with a chuckle. "Lady Winter is known for being an unreliable narrator in these parts. Sunshine and daffodils one day, ice storms and seventy-mile-an-hour winds the next. Don't fall for her wily ways; she'll mess with us well into April or even early May."

Barb was right about that. In spite of forecasted warmer weather on the horizon, Addison knew by personal experience not to put away her winter wear until after May Day.

"So you two met through the resort, then?" she asked, frantically searching for a way to distract Barb from playing matchmaker. Because Addison had a feeling that was exactly what was going on behind that scary, calculating look on her friend's face.

Barb nodded. "We did." She put a hand up to the side of her mouth like she was divulging a juicy bit of gossip to Addison. In a mock whisper, she added, "The resort hired him to help them figure out why they aren't making money yet."

"Oh. I—I see." Addison wasn't quite sure how to respond to that.

Noel chuckled and shook his head. "That's not exactly why they hired me," he countered. "I'd say it's more that they want to know where the money they *are* making is going."

"I see," Addison said again, although, truth be told, she didn't see at all. The fancy resort across the lake was a bit like a world unto its own. It certainly didn't cater to the working-class folk who called Autumn Lake home. In fact, there were strong undercurrents of us-versus-them between the south shore locals and the north shore residents, a sentiment that had been perpetuated by the high-end North Shore housing development that had gone up on that side of the lake in the last couple of years. The mansions were essentially mini versions of the resort, and the people who bought those sprawling lots were the same people who vacationed at places like Carpe Diem. Inside the resort were several boutique stores, and last year, with the opening of a Fresh Thyme Market, a gas station, and a Country Club on that side of the lake, The North Shore community was practically self-sufficient. Other than for events like Autumn Lake's Fall Festival, the Christmas parade, or the Summer Lights Celebration, there weren't too many reasons for them to come to the south shore.

Autumn Lake had some wonderful shops in the downtown area, a few quaint restaurants that offered delicious fare, and during the tourist season, all kinds of lake activity rentals and services. But the resort had established themselves as a self-contained entity, and because they had their own version of everything—their own watercraft rentals, their own tour guides, their own restaurants, salons, clothing stores, and more—the money that should have flooded the community just circulated back into its own coffers.

In Addison's admittedly naïve opinion, that was part of the problem. The company came across as stingy and elitist, and the community that had originally welcomed them now saw them as intruders. *What comes around, goes around*, she thought, considering the possible financial instability that Noel and Barb were eluding to.

Of course, she didn't say so out loud, but the look on her face must have conveyed something of what she was thinking, because Barb said, "I think Addison could give you a little insight from her perspective, Noel." That gleam in her eyes made Addison take a step backward, subconsciously distancing herself from whatever plan the older woman was brewing. "She wasn't born and bred in Autumn Lake, but she's been there long enough to be a part of the inner circle. The locals love her and think of her as one of their own."

"Barb," Addison admonished in a voice made squeaky with embarrassment.

Barb reached over and patted Addison's arm. "Well, it's true, honey. You are a jewel of a girl, and everyone thinks so." To Noel, she said, "So why not now? Why don't we take advantage of this coincidental encounter? You're off in a few minutes, right, Addison?" She didn't wait for confirmation. "My husband won't be home until late this evening, and Noel, you were just telling me that you're light on companionship in town."

Addison saw his eyes widen at Barb's words. The poor guy obviously had no clue that he'd befriended the Midwest's most aggressive matchmaker in Barb Selway.

"We can go grab a bite to eat together, and you can get a local's perspective on what makes Autumn Lake so wonderful," Barb continued, charging ahead without giving them the option of refusing. "Have either of you been to Shoot the Moon? It's my favorite soup and sandwich place, and I don't know about you, but not having to cook tonight sounds like just the thing." Barb slid her hand down Addison's arm and grabbed her fingers in a quick squeeze. "I have pictures of the most beautiful grandchildren in the world to show you."

How was she supposed to say no to that? Addison shot an apologetic glance at Noel, who looked blindsided. She smiled helplessly, then to Barb said, "I guess that—that would be nice." Why, oh why, didn't she have a cat she had to get home to feed? She glanced down at her uniform. Under the button-down blue shirt, she wore a cranberry red turtleneck with tiny roses all over it. It would suffice, she supposed, although if she'd had any inkling that she'd be having supper with Noel Stewart, she'd have chosen something else, something a little less... matronly. She had some face powder and lipstick in her purse, though, and maybe even a tube of mascara, although how old it might be, she had no idea. She reached up and touched the clip at the back of her head; she could tell her hair had gone from sleek chignon to crooked messy bun over the course of the day. She'd just run a brush through it and leave it down. At least it was freshly washed.

Besides, beggars couldn't be choosers, right? Without Barb's well-meaning manipulation, supper with Noel Stewart would never even be on the table. "No pun intended," Addison said aloud.

"What was that, dear?" Barb cocked her head and smiled bemusedly.

Fortunately, at the exact same time, Noel said, "That works for me," and Barb's head swiveled toward him.

"Wonderful. Oh, I'm so glad I don't have to eat alone this evening. And it'll be my treat; I insist." She lifted a hand and waved off Noel and Addison's protests. "I'm missing those babies something fierce and having you two join me will help keep my mind occupied until Craig gets home." She checked her watch. "I've got baggage, so by the time I gather my things and call for a ride, you'll be off the clock, won't you?" she asked Addison.

"I should be, but I can give you a ride, Barb. Especially since you're buying my meal." She'd learned long ago not to argue with the woman about footing a bill. "I'll just meet you down at baggage claim."

"I didn't even think about that. Perfect. Thank you, honey." Barb turned to Noel. "What about you? How are you planning on getting back to the resort this evening? Maybe Addison could give you a ride home, too."

"Barb!" Her voice came out an octave higher than usual. The woman was too much.

Noel smiled graciously. "I appreciate the offer, but I have my car in long-term parking here."

"Oh, that's too bad," Barb said, pretending not to understand Addison's imploring 'stop-interfering-please-please-please' look. "Do you have something in your eye, honey?" she asked.

Had it not been for the young couple who approached at just that moment, asking for directions to their connecting flight, Addison might have said something she'd regret. As Rory had told her, his mother meant well, but man-oh-man. Once the woman got a notion in her noggin, she was like a dog with a bone. It's what made her a good businesswoman. It also made her a good friend, too, Addison had to admit. When Barb decided to adopt you, there was no trial period. It was a done deal.

"We'll meet you at baggage claim," Barb said, as she hoisted her pretty handbag a little higher up on her shoulder and started down the corridor.

"Are you okay with all of this?" Noel asked her as he made slow work of smoothing the strap of his messenger bag.

"You're fine," Addison insisted. "I mean, it's fine. Yes. I'm okay with it. Sorry."

Noel grinned. "You don't need to apologize to me. I'm looking forward to it." Then he lifted a hand in a quick wave and turned to catch up with Barb.

"Natalie is going to freak out," Addison whispered, imagining her friend's reaction when she told her in the morning. She still could hardly believe it herself. She stepped around behind the counter again to sign out of the station. The last of the travelers had trickled out of the Jetway, and she had several things to do before she could clock out.

As she slipped her arms into her coat fifteen minutes later, she said softly, "I'm going out to eat with Noel Stewart tonight." The very notion of it, especially when put into words, pulled her up short and made her breath hitch.

"And Barb Selway," she reminded herself, but that didn't make her pulse slow even the tiniest bit.

10
Noel

Noel still wasn't exactly sure how it had happened, but apparently, he was going out to eat with the lovely Addison Wedgewood. "And Barb Selway," he reminded his reflection as he washed his hands in the restroom near the baggage claim. He'd helped Barb haul her two enormous suitcases off the conveyer belt, and then loaded them into the back of Addison's compact SUV out at the curb.

"We'll see you at the café in fifteen minutes," Barb had said before climbing into the passenger seat.

Noel shook excess water from his hands, then carefully ran his damp fingers through his stick-straight hair, willing the styling clay he'd used that morning to wake up. He needed a haircut; keeping it short was the only way to avoid the irritated hedgehog look he sported when it started to grow out. That and the expensive hair products he'd discovered long after he'd left home.

So, Addison Wedgewood lived in Autumn Lake. That had to be the explanation of why she seemed so familiar to him. He must have crossed paths with her or seen her from afar somewhere out at the little lake town. Maybe one of the restaurants or a shop? "You'd think you'd remember," he chided his reflection, but he still drew a blank.

He pulled open the collar of his shirt and took a quick whiff. Satisfied that he was at least presentable, he took a fortifying breath and headed out to locate his car.

Shoot the Moon was much larger than he'd envisioned. Barb's description of it as a sandwich shop had been quite an understatement; the place was a full-service restaurant and bar. He was shown to a booth near the back where the two women were already seated next to each other. He slid in opposite them, accidentally bumping Addison's knee with his own as he did. "Sorry about that," he said, shooting her a warm smile.

"They're all right," she said, then grimaced, like that wasn't quite what she'd intended to say. She looked away and began toying nervously with the corner of her napkin.

He bit back a smile; he didn't want to do or say anything that would make her regret being there. But it did something to his insides to imagine she might be just as affected by him as he was by her. To Barb, he asked, "Am I late?"

"Not at all," Barb assured him. "But I'm glad you're here. I'm suddenly ravenous. And my treat," she reminded them both. "So order whatever you'd like."

Noel was accustomed to meeting with strangers, and so was Barb, for that matter. A fashion consultant, she had several private clients, but she also worked with upscale vendors, and one such shop was the Ash and Aster Fine Clothing Boutique at the resort. It was how he and Barb had first met. He'd paid visits to each of the in-house vendors at the resort, and she'd been at the boutique the day he'd checked out Ash and Aster.

It quickly became evident, however, that Addison was much more reserved than the gregarious Barb. She wasn't exactly shy, as he'd previously thought. She seemed more than content, however, to listen from the sidelines and let Barb and him keep the conversation going.

So, as Noel talked about his job at Carpe Diem, he did his best not to sound too boring. He was careful not to paint the resort in anything but the most glowing of terms. "No one likes the word 'audit,' right? So, I try to put a positive spin on it. My job as Financial Auditor is to pinpoint the company's financial strengths and help them find ways to take those strengths to the next level."

"I like that," Barb declared, dabbing at her mouth with her napkin. She winked at him, and then nudged Addison beside her. "It almost makes his job sound fun, right?"

Addison grinned over at him, her eyes bright with humor. "Almost."

Noel nodded agreeably, hoping his expression wouldn't give anything away. On the contrary, his job was not what he would call fun. Not by a long shot. John Sheridan made certain of that. Oh, he liked the work he did—he had always been a numbers man—but the current environment in which he did that work sucked all the pleasure out of it.

Addison didn't contribute often, but she seemed to enjoy listening to the small talk. At least she wasn't acting like she *wanted* to get away as soon as possible. Even so, her reserve had him second guessing himself. Maybe Barb was just being polite when she invited him to join them. Perhaps he should have excused himself the moment she'd veered toward Addison in the terminal, but he'd selfishly tagged along, happy for the chance to finally meet the woman who'd been on his mind so much over the last few months.

In the glow of the glass pendant lamp hanging over the table, Addison's dark hair shone golden. She'd taken out the clip she'd been wearing earlier, and a curtain of soft waves fell forward whenever she dipped her chin. She absentmindedly tucked it behind her ear, the sparkle of a small silver hoop earring catching his attention. Something about the motion mesmerized him, stirring that odd sense of familiarity inside him again.

He shook it off and took a drink of sweet tea to distract his senses. The last thing he wanted was to make things awkward. What could he say that would draw her out without making her feel put on the spot?

"So, Addison, how did you end up living in Autumn Lake?" he finally asked, curious about her answer despite how banal the question was.

To his surprise, Addison straightened in her seat and put down the sandwich she'd been working her way through. Her eyes twinkled when she said, "It was simply meant to be. I was in Nashville with my parents for an event and fell in love with the Midwest, so I started looking for jobs. I applied for a position at the Nashville airport, but when they called me about an interview, they asked if I'd consider Evansville Regional, instead. I was able to catch a flight from Nashville to Evansville for super cheap, had an interview with the gang here, and *voilà*," she said with a one-shouldered shrug. "They offered me the job, and I took it."

"Crazy girl," Barb interjected with a chuckle, but it was obvious to Noel that this wasn't the first time she'd heard the story.

"I had only three weeks to move and settle in, but I couldn't find a place to live that suited me here in town. At least not on such short notice. Too much money or not a great neighborhood, stuff like that. So, I expanded my search and stumbled on a listing in the town of Autumn Lake. It's an apartment in an old brick building right downtown, within walking distance of both the lake shore and all the local hangouts." She sighed dreamily. "It sounds idyllic, right?"

Noel nodded. "It does."

"Well, it *is* idyllic," she continued. "It's perfect. I knew I wanted to live in Autumn Lake the moment I pulled into town. And when I saw the apartment? Well, I was sold. My landlords, the Veringers, could have charged me double, and I'd have gladly paid it."

Noel settled back in his seat as she expounded on her home, thoroughly enjoying the way she spoke. She didn't seem to have a regional accent of any kind, at least not one that he could place, but there was a pleasant lilt in her voice that made him think of sunlit days in spring. He almost laughed at the thought; was he waxing poetic about this woman?

"But then, I'm not telling you anything you don't already know," Addison added, averting her gaze, but not before he saw the color in her cheeks. "You've been there. You know what it's like."

"You've been to Addison's apartment, Noel?" Barb asked, her eyes lighting up in surprise.

Addison made an odd sound in the back of her throat as she shook her head and exclaimed, "No, Barb. No. Sorry. That's not— No. I mean, no."

"Got it," Barb chuckled and patted Addison's forearm. "No, he hasn't been there."

"I—I meant the town," she said, meeting his gaze again. "You've been to Autumn Lake. You live in Autumn Lake, or at least you work there, so you already know how great it is."

"I do," he said, somehow maintaining his straight face. "It's a great little town. There's something almost out of time-ish about it, especially right now when there are so few tourists," he agreed.

"Like Brigadoon," Barb interjected, her gaze darting back and forth between Addison and him. "But then, you two are probably too young to understand that reference."

"Not at all," Addison insisted. "I love that musical. The possibility of stepping out of time and into some enchanted town? That would be something else." She shook her head, her brow furrowing a little. "But to me, winter in Autumn Lake feels a little like being backstage. The costumes and makeup are off, the fake accents and pretenses are set aside. Winter is when the town is at its most genuine, in my opinion."

Noel nodded slowly, appreciating her perspective. "I can see that. I suppose that's probably true with a lot of tourist towns." He cocked his head at her. "Do you consider yourself a local?"

"A Townie?" Addison asked after a moment's hesitation, a mischievous grin tugging at one corner of her mouth. "I think so. I've made real friends in Autumn Lake. People have taken me in as one of their own." She put an arm around Barb's shoulders and gave her a quick squeeze. "People like Barb and Craig and their family. It's home to me in a way no other place has ever been."

He waited, hoping she'd share a few more details about her past, but she seemed to realize that she'd been doing most of the talking and fell silent.

"How long have you lived in Autumn Lake?" he asked, desperate to keep her engaged.

"It'll be six years this summer," she said, then picked up her sandwich. But before she took another bite, she added, "And if I have things my way, I'll live there the rest of my life."

Something in the way she said it, the sincerity, the certainty of it, poked at a tender spot inside of Noel. A bubble of envy swelled inside his chest as he acknowledged that he wanted that sense of belonging Addison had.

He'd yearned for it his whole life. To belong somewhere. To know that he was good enough, that he wasn't just a burden, that he could pull his own weight. That he was an integral part of something bigger than himself. He'd been searching for that certainty for as long as he could remember.

He glanced over at Barb, and she smiled warmly when he caught her studying him. "You should spend some time on the south shore, Noel," she said. "I think you might get a better idea of what Autumn Lake is made of from that side of things. The resort is so lovely, but it's a vacation spot. Even the North Shore development is made up of homes built for folks who want to live in the shadow of Carpe Diem. If you want to get to know the heart of the town, then I suggest you get to know some of the locals, the people who call Autumn Lake home."

"You're absolutely right," Noel readily agreed.

"Well, you already know this local," Barb said, patting Addison's arm again.

Noel felt every muscle in his body tense. He'd seen the calculating looks the woman had been shooting back and forth between Addison and him the whole evening. He knew what she was about before she said another word.

"You should show Noel around, dear," she said. "Introduce him to folks. It's such a great connection for both of you, don't you think?" She winked at Addison, who almost choked on the last bite of her sandwich. "God usually has a reason for bringing people together, and it's up to us not to squander those opportunities."

Noel chuckled dryly, hoping Barb's lack of subtlety did not offend Addison. "Indeed, it is."

Barb sighed contentedly and pushed her plate away so she could set her purse on the table to rummage through it for her wallet. "Well, I don't know about you two, but I'm feeling the long traveling day. I'm ready to call it a night. Shall we?"

She paid the bill, and as they headed out into the chilly evening, she stepped between Noel and Addison and linked her arms in theirs. "I do hope you two will get together soon. Without me playing interfering third wheel, of course."

Noel grinned over Barb's head at Addison, but her gaze was fixed on her car across the parking lot. Even though he only saw her profile, her smile told him that she wasn't averse to the idea. The thought of seeing her again outside of work certainly sounded enticing to him.

"I'd like that," he said, taking a leap of faith.

Addison and Barb both turned to look at him, then Barb must have elbowed Addison, because she did a little sideways shuffle. "Right. Yes." Then she hurried to say, "Not that you asked or anything. I just meant that yes, I'd like that, too."

Barb released them both and swiped her hands together a few times. "Well. It seems my work here is done," she declared with great satisfaction. "Addison, dear, take me home. My day is catching up with me, and it's going to be all I can do not to fall asleep in the car."

Noel walked Barb around to the passenger side and held the door for her while she climbed in. Leaning into the window, he peered over at Addison in the driver's seat. "I don't have your number," he said, doing his best to ignore Barb's gleeful grin.

As soon as Addison gave it to him, he sent a text. A chime of crystal bells sounded from somewhere in the back seat. "Oh. My phone is in my purse," she said, reaching back to scrabble for the bag she'd tossed onto the floorboard behind her.

"It's okay." Noel chuckled and shook his head to stop her frantic search. "At least we know you didn't give me a phony number."

"Noel," Barb chided. "Our Addison wouldn't do something like that." He grinned at the collective 'our' she'd used.

"At least not in front of Barb," Addison quipped with a smile.

"I see how it is," Noel teased, relieved at her dry humor. "Text me—or call me—when you get home, okay? Let me know you made it there safely."

Barb beamed like a proud mama. "Oh, good. I was going to have you text me, honey, but I might be asleep by the time you get home. You call Noel instead, you hear? We need to know you're safe."

Addison nodded agreeably. "I will, I will." Then she said, "You two do know that I make this drive home multiple times a week without calling or texting anyone, and I've somehow managed to survive all this time."

"That's something that needs to change," Barb shot back, eyeing her with motherly concern.

Addison reached across the console and squeezed Barb's arm. "You worry too much. I've been on my own a long time, my friend."

"Well, maybe that's something that needs to change, too," Barb said, her voice gentle now, and suddenly, Noel felt like an outsider again.

He patted the frame of Barb's open window. "Ladies, thank you for the nice evening." He held up his phone as he stepped back. "I'll be watching for your text."

He heard Barb say, "Now that is a nice young—" before her words were cut off by her window rolling up.

It was bitterly cold, and he hadn't worn a heavy coat, having planned to go straight from the airport to the resort. He shoved his hands into his pockets, shoulders hunched against the brisk breeze that had kicked up while they were inside the restaurant, and he hurried to his car.

All the way home, he rewound the hour-plus he'd spent in Addison's company. In spite of how nice the evening had been, he realized that not once had she initiated any part of the conversation, nor had she offered anything personal about herself. The only thing she'd let loose about—she'd all but gushed about, in fact—was Autumn Lake and how wonderful a town it was.

A message that was very different from what he'd heard from resort staff and even some of the residents of the North Shore housing development.

In fact, the common sentiment he heard on the resort side of the lake was just the opposite: how odd and off-putting the locals were. Phrases like "backwoods mindset" and "hicks and hillbillies" and "those people over there." The term "quaint" when used had not been complimentary, and he'd even gotten a "Bless their hearts," a time or two.

It seemed that there was a carefully and not-so-subtly cultivated elitist mentality surrounding the resort. The North Shore Haves versus the South Shore Have-Nots. Even the geographical location of the resort, perched on top of a prominence above the shoreline of the lake, gave it an air of superiority, like it was looking down on the town.

Carpe Diem had brought a lot of money flowing into Autumn Lake, had created jobs, increased the number of small business opportunities, and had almost single-handedly turned the tiny lake town into a booming tourist destination. But the company and its constituents behaved like self-aggrandized benefactors, separate and rather aloof.

It made sense to him that the locals remained so disinclined to make the newer residents who were populating the North Shore development around the resort feel welcome. They weren't fools. The south shore locals knew exactly what the north shore folk thought of them.

A thought gave him pause. Was that how Addison thought of him? That would explain her reticence to open up to him this evening, and her eagerness to wax eloquent about the town. Although she'd seemed receptive to the idea of getting together with him in the future, he suddenly wondered if she might accidentally "forget" to text him when she made it home tonight.

11
Addison

It had been a long time since Addison had been out on a real date, and even though Noel hadn't officially called it one, she decided that she would behave as if it were. Oh, she'd play the tour guide if wanted her to, but she secretly hoped that wasn't on the agenda for the evening.

She'd texted Noel, as promised, when she'd gotten home the night after their meal with Barb. The conversation had been disappointingly brief, but the next day, Noel had sent her a message asking if he could call her after work that evening. *I've got meetings until late, so it won't be until around 8. Is that okay?*

The phone call had started out a little awkward, but Noel was a good conversationalist, and when they'd finally said goodnight, Addison was shocked to find that they'd been on the phone for more than an hour. She'd lain awake long after, replaying their interaction, hoping that the conversation was the start of something much bigger.

He'd also asked her out to dinner. "So that you can show me your town," he'd added when she didn't answer right away.

It wasn't that she'd been undecided. Her answer was a resounding 'Yes!' She'd just been savoring the moment. He'd taken it for hesitation on her part, she realized too late, and she'd made a concerted effort to be attentive the rest of the time on the phone. Hopefully, tonight her responses to him would convince him that she definitely wanted to spend time in his company.

Although the skies had cleared considerably over the last few days and the stars twinkled cheerfully against the velvet sky, it was still quite cold, especially at night. A pretty dress simply wasn't an option, so Addison pulled from her closet her favorite black trousers, high-waisted and wide-legged. They paired well with her wedge-heeled ankle boots, and the combination of the two made her feel tall and elegant. She wore a dark green wrap blouse with a ruffled neckline under a cropped blazer, and she blow-dried her hair out so that it hung soft and full around her face, the ends brushing her shoulders as she walked. She spent extra time and care on her makeup, too. She wanted to look different than she did at work, for Noel to see her as something other than just a gussied-up ticket agent.

"You'll do," she said to her reflection in the mirror, refusing to let herself wish for a smaller backside or thinner thighs.

Addison already liked Noel Stewart more than was reasonable, considering that until a few days ago, she'd only adored him from afar. But she could just tell that he was the kind of man romance novels were written about. Kind, patient, attentive, gentlemanly... she could list his glowing attributes for days, if given the chance.

As much as she'd like to believe the best about Noel, however, she'd seen enough of the world to know that a woman living alone couldn't be too careful. As soon as she got off the phone with Noel, she called Claire to fill her in on the details so that at least someone in the world would know where she was and who she was with on her date. "You should meet him at Juno's," Claire insisted. It wasn't really a suggestion. "So he'll know that the whole neighborhood knows he's taking you out."

"Good idea," Addison slowly acknowledged. She wasn't ecstatic about everyone knowing her business, but she understood the wisdom behind the suggestion.

"And you're going to call Juno and give her a heads up beforehand, too, right?" The Cracked Spine sat elbow-to-elbow around the corner from Juno's Coffee Bar. Both places were only a little more than a block away from Addison's apartment, so walking was almost always her preferred way to get there.

"You're going to bring him in here, right?" Juno asked the moment Addison told her about her plans with Noel.

"I'm way ahead of you. We're meeting there instead of at my apartment," Addison assured her friend. The coffee shop was, after all, a favorite stomping ground among the locals, and if Noel wanted to get to know Autumn Lake, Juno's was the perfect place to start.

Addison took one last look in the mirror, then scooped up her purse from the table. Just before pulling the door closed behind her, she paused and turned to survey her little apartment with a sense of satisfaction and pride. Over the years, her home had become a canvas on which she'd combined elements of her past, her present, and her hopes for the future. She had scoured every thrift store in a fifty-mile radius to find just the right furniture for the space. She'd found a burgundy velvet loveseat with deep, squishy cushions, a bentwood rocking chair and mismatched footstool, and a Tiffany style floor lamp with a stained-glass shade that she'd added a four-inch beaded fringe to. For a coffee table, she'd screwed together two rustic wooden crates back-to-back in which she shelved selections from her ever-growing To-Be-Read pile of books. She'd attached castors to the bottom of the contraption so it could be moved around easily, and topped it off with a large silver tray, on which were piled more books, a vase of dried, pale blue hydrangeas, and a scarlet and cobalt paperweight she'd purchased from a local glassblower during a trip to Cinque Terre in Italy. Goldenrod and sky-blue batik curtains she'd found in a street market in Ghana hung at the windows and she'd color-washed the walls of her kitchenette with a vibrant teal that reminded her of the water at Base-G Beach in Jayapura, Indonesia. The open shelves on either side of the window over the kitchen sink displayed her collection of mismatched ceramic dishes and cookware. The space echoed the bohemian spirit that lived inside of her.

The apartment had two bedrooms, but one was so small that Addison had to take apart the daybed she'd picked up at a garage sale and put it back together once she'd gotten all the pieces into the room. She'd added an old piano stool at the head of the bed that acted as a nightstand. On it was a touch-sensitive lamp and two Swedish Dala horse carvings, one in the traditional red, one in a vibrant, happy blue. It was her guest room, although it rarely got used as such. On the rare occasions when her parents came to visit, she gave them her room with the big bed, and she slept comfortably on the daybed.

Her own bedroom was a cacophony of color, too. Curtains made of patchwork strips of fabric hung at her windows, an antique wedding ring quilt covered her bed, and mismatched throw pillows were heaped in a jumble in front of her headboard. She tossed them to the floor every night, then took pleasure in arranging them back in place each morning after making her bed. Eclectic artwork—everything from driftwood and metal sculptures and macrame panels to flea market paintings and vintage mirror trays covered almost every square inch of her walls. She loved to fall asleep at night, studying the unique pieces, imagining the history behind each one.

Her room also housed a vintage mahogany bookcase that Addison was slowly and methodically filling with books that she'd fallen in love with.

She'd spent her whole life living minimally—a necessity with the Wedgewood's transient lifestyle—and the few books Addison had owned during her childhood were inevitable casualties with every move. Her mother had always reassured Addison that books were never lost or wasted if they were passed on to other readers, but saying goodbye to each one had been just as difficult as saying goodbye to any new friends she'd made.

Eternally grateful for digital books, Addison had a record of all her favorite reads over the years, and since moving to Autumn Lake, she'd been slowly reuniting with her "old friends" and filling those shelves one novel at a time. And of course, with a pal like Claire, who owned The Cracked Spine Bookshop, Addison was constantly adding "new friends" to her shelves.

With a sigh of pleasure and a satisfied smile on her face, Addison swept out into the crisp evening air, pulling her apartment door closed behind her, then double-checking to make sure it was locked. As idyllic as Autumn Lake was, the days of not having to lock one's doors was a thing of the past, something previous generations now boasted about in wistful tones.

It was still early, but Addison planned to stop by The Cracked Spine on her way to Juno's so that she could get Claire's stamp of approval on her appearance. Life was so different with friends, Addison thought as she made her way down the steps to the short alley behind the Quill and Ink. There was always someone familiar to talk to, to share life's ups and downs with. People who cared about the ins and outs of her world.

Juno and Claire, especially, were a huge part of why Autumn Lake was home to her. It had taken Addison very little time to settle into her job at the airport, but the constant engaging with people in need that her job required of her left her drained by the end of her day. For the first several months, she'd come home to her little apartment, eaten her dinner, and crawled into bed with a book.

On her days off, she'd wander around Autumn Lake, check out the shops, sit on the lake shore and people-watch, but it was such a relief to be at the beck and call of no one, that she'd not made any attempt to connect with the folks she called neighbors.

It was after she'd read the last of the small collection of books she'd moved with that she'd finally ventured into The Cracked Spine, several weeks after moving to town. Claire Maitland had approached her with a warm welcome and had immediately made her feel at ease as they discussed reading preferences and favorite books.

When Claire learned that Addison wasn't just a visitor, she'd left her shop in the trusted hands of Tina, her young assistant, linked arms with Addison and walked her around the corner to Juno's Coffee Bar where she'd introduced her to Juniper Thomas. Juno had demanded they sit at the bar—the assertive woman reminded Addison of her mother in so many ways—then plated them both up a meatball and roasted red pepper sandwich, on the house. The coffee was remarkable, the sandwich was robust and messy and better than any meatball sandwich Addison could remember having, and the conversation that followed had laid the foundation for some new and lasting friendships.

Addison had been introduced to Liz and Candy Needham a couple days later, and when summer rolled around and the small town nearly burst at the seams with tourists and summer lakers, she'd met the indomitable Penny Anderson, too. Penny, who'd come to live at Autumn Lake for good just this last fall.

Penny had brought her mother with her, and the two of them had moved into Hazel Poleman's guesthouse. Penny had big plans to turn the stately old home into a real bed and breakfast, and with her fiancé's help, they were working hard at doing just that.

The Garden Gate Guesthouse would be lovely when it opened up again this summer, and Addison got a little giddy knowing that she and her friends had a part in turning the old place around. Last year, when Hazel had admitted that she could no longer manage the place on her own, Penny had enlisted the help of her girlfriends to come up with a plan to keep Hazel from having to sell her family home. They'd taken to the gardens first, the enormous lot behind the house that had once been a nature's paradise with flower beds and moss-covered stone walls, espaliered fruit trees, herb patches, and a kitchen garden where Hazel had once grown almost everything she served to her guests. Over the years, it had become run down and out of control, and by the time they'd stepped in to help, Hazel had been just about to throw in the towel.

They'd called themselves The Garden Variety Lovers Club, just for the fun of having a name for their project, and they now met regularly out at the guesthouse, reveling in the reawakening splendor of the property.

Addison was still smiling when she stepped into her friend's bookstore. At The Cracked Spine, Claire was helping a young mother with two little girls find some books to give as birthday gifts. The girls, however, were clearly not pleased that they were going to have to give the books away and were begging for copies of their own. Addison sent her friend a little wave. Claire's eyes grew wide, then she mouthed, "Wow!" before turning back to her customers.

Addison had some time to kill, so she headed to the enormous table at the front window where Claire typically displayed books of interest. Sometimes they were new releases, sometimes they followed a certain theme because of a holiday or special occasion, and other times, she used the space to clear out inventory by putting out overstock on massive discount. It was inevitable that Addison would find at least one book she couldn't go home without.

The display still held what was left of the Valentine's Day overstock, plus a whole new selection of discounted books. The chocolates she'd purchased the week before were long gone—they'd been just as delicious as Claire had claimed. Addison eyed the last two heart-shaped boxes where they sat beside a stack of colorful pens and notepads, a few love-themed mugs, and a wide-mouthed jar of lapel pins shaped like the classic Sweethearts conversation heart candies.

For just a few moments, Addison let herself imagine that she might be buying a Valentine's Day card for Noel next year. Maybe a box of chocolates, too; one that they could share.

"Getting a little ahead of yourself, Adders," she whispered to herself as she picked up a book with a bouquet of roses on the cover.

"Hey, girl," Claire called out, rounding the end of the next aisle over and heading her way. She gave her a quick hug, and in a low voice, said, "I left that poor woman to the mercies of her girls. I knew if I stayed there much longer, I'd take sides with them. I mean, why on earth would you *not* buy your children books if they wanted them?"

Addison laughed and shook her head. "This is why your bookshop is still open and thriving while the big chain stores around the country are closing their doors."

"Because I believe books are as vital to our health as food and water and a good night's rest? Amen, sister." Claire reached out and took Addison by the shoulders, turning her this way and that. "My goodness, Miss Wedgewood, but you look amazing."

"It's not too much?" Addison asked. Her confidence was definitely bolstered by her friend's reaction, but she still felt vulnerable. This was a first date, after all, and she really wanted it to go well.

"Not even a little," Claire confirmed. "You are going to knock that man's socks off." When she saw the book in Addison's hand, she snatched it away. "Not that one." Instead, she skillfully plucked one from the middle of a stack of sherbet and pastel covered novels in the middle of the table. "Have you read this?" She held it out. "It's such a lovely book. It made me sad, then angry, then happy, and when I closed the book, I felt like I'd made a couple of new friends. I thought it was just the kind of book you'd enjoy reading."

A couple of new friends, thought Addison. The woman seemed to have a knack for knowing just the right book for the right person at the right time. "That does sound like something I'd enjoy," she echoed. "I'll take it."

"Good. Come. I'll ring you up." Claire started toward the front of the shop, then slowed as she passed a shelf of historical American fiction. "And what about one for your man?" she asked, perusing the titles on display.

"He's not my man." Addison said, wishing people would stop saying that. She was half afraid they'd jinx any possibility of it actually happening. "And I don't know if this is really a date or not. I'm not sure I should come bearing gifts just yet."

"A book isn't just a gift," Claire countered. "It's an introduction. You are telling him who you are by handing him something that's important to you, and you are learning a whole lot about him by his reaction to the book."

"But I don't know what he likes," Addison said, not nearly as certain about the notion as her friend was.

"Well, there's only one way to find out," Claire said, pulling a novel from the shelf. "This one. If it resonates with him, he's a keeper."

"What if he's read it?" Addison asked, still hesitant. The book Claire handed her was about an orphaned boy who'd been forced to become a man too soon in the time shortly after the Crash of 1929, and about the journey taken by him and three other young runaways on their quest for freedom from oppression. A New York Times Bestseller, the front cover claimed.

"Then you'll have a good excuse to come back here together and introduce him to me." Claire practically forced the book into her hands. "If he's read it, then he can tell you about it, since you haven't yet, right? And I guarantee that if he's read it, he'll want to talk about it."

"And if he hasn't read it, and he thinks books are for freaks?"

"Then you wouldn't want to be caught dead with a guy like that." The door chimes jingled prettily, and Claire glanced over at a group of teenage girls who poured into the shop, their boisterous chatter drowning out the soft music playing over the sound system. "It's been busy tonight," she told Addison. "Let's go ring you up and get you on your way."

12

Noel

Addison had said yes to the phone call that evening, which had given him something to look forward to during the meeting. But that night, while on the phone, she'd also said yes to going out to dinner with him.

Noel was surprised at how much he was looking forward to seeing her again. Especially in light of what he'd come back to at the office.

Apparently, while Noel had been in Bald Knob, John Sheridan had been stirring the proverbial pot back at Carpe Diem. Upon his return to work, Noel had opened his email to find a message from John informing him that there was a meeting the following afternoon, and that he was expected to attend. According to the succinctly worded missive, there were some accounting discrepancies that pointed at Noel letting things slip through the cracks, but no one had seen fit to attach the ledgers in question. Which meant that Noel would be going blind into the session with the CEO and a few others on the Board of Directors.

He'd meant to ask John what the problem was, even though it ate him up inside to do so. Since John was the one who'd brought the issue to the attention of those they reported to, he would have that information. Noel also thought that John was quite likely intentionally not giving anything away, just to keep Noel on his toes.

But what better way to thwart the man than to go ahead and ask him anyway? Surely, he wouldn't refuse to give him the information. Noel had gone over his files numerous times, but could find nothing out of order.

Unfortunately, when he arrived in the office the next day, he discovered that John had called in sick. Noel couldn't decide which was better; that he got a day without John's antagonistic rancor or that he had no idea why he was being called on the carpet.

The meeting, he soon found out, was not about any discrepancy in his accounting. It was, in fact, an emergency budget meeting because the resort's Hospitality Manager had to go on a medical leave for a high-risk pregnancy.

When Noel went back through his emails later that evening, he realized that it was only one email from John that was worded in such a way as to make it sound like Noel was under scrutiny. None of the others had alluded to anything but there being an emergency situation that needed to be sorted out, but Noel had read them through the lens of John's misleading missive.

Disheartened and discouraged by John's continued acrimony, Noel was at a loss as to how to move forward. This kind of undermining couldn't continue, but he didn't know how to put an end to it without getting their superiors involved. And getting the superiors involved was always a risky thing, partly because John had seniority on his side, but also because it would make Noel look less than competent to handle difficult situations. He was still new enough in this position to feel the need to prove his worth, which meant he needed to find a way to resolve the discord between them. Thank goodness the financial side of things was in impeccable order and above reproach.

So relieved had Noel been that he wasn't in any kind of trouble, that today, he'd brought the aloof department secretary one of the hazelnut lattes he'd noticed her drinking on several occasions. He also had a date with Addison Wedgewood tonight, and he refused to let anything John, who was still out with a flu bug, said or did get under his skin.

Although she'd agreed to a date, Addison had refused to let him pick her up from her place. He understood her caution, but he hoped she'd grow to trust him before too long. She'd told him the coffee shop was only a short distance from her apartment, but it didn't sit easily with him when she said she'd be walking. He'd moved to Autumn Lake from Carpe Diem headquarters in Chicago where a woman walking alone, day or night, was a potential target. He would insist on escorting her home; It would be well after dark by then, and he wouldn't be able to live with himself if he didn't.

Juno's Coffee Bar was lit up like a beacon on the otherwise nearly dark row of businesses along Camellia Court. The stringed outdoor lights on the patio shimmered in the cold air, the gentle breeze setting them to swaying just the tiniest bit. In spite of the cold, people sat outside at the little bistro tables, bundled up and sipping hot drinks and chatting amiably. A dog had its leash looped around a bicycle rack out on the sidewalk, presumably waiting for his human who must have gone inside. The pup sat on his haunches and accepted the affectionate greetings from patrons entering and exiting the shop.

Noel looked through the plate glass windows as he passed them, hoping for a glimpse of Addison. She'd told him she was friends with Juno, the proprietress, and that she'd most likely be sitting at the bar if she arrived before he did. But the place was surprisingly full for a Wednesday night, and he couldn't get a good view of the folks sitting on stools along the counter. He'd have to go in blind, just like he'd done at the meeting yesterday afternoon. "This time, though, I'm looking forward to what I'll find," he murmured as he reached the door of the shop and pulled it open.

Addison wasn't at the bar, but instead, she was sitting a table with three other women, engaged in an animated conversation. Their body language told him they were quite comfortable with each other, and when Addison tipped her head back and laughed, Noel's pulse ratcheted up. In that moment, he thought that she was quite possibly the most beautiful woman he'd ever seen.

Instead of interrupting her, he made his way to the counter, and to his surprise, he found an empty stool. He could hardly take his eyes off of the woman he'd come to spend the evening with, but he somehow managed to sit down without missing the seat. He could watch her all evening, he thought to himself.

"What can I get you tonight?" The woman behind the counter had long cornrows swept back from her face and tied in a knot between her shoulder blades. She had smooth mahogany skin and high cheekbones, and although her teeth weren't straight, her smile was wide and friendly and full of confidence. She studied him with dark eyes as she waited for his response.

"Hi," he finally said. "I'm Noel." He glanced back at Addison again, hoping she wouldn't think he was flirting with the arresting woman behind the counter. He wanted desperately to make a good impression.

"I'm Juno. Welcome to my coffee bar." So this was the proprietress of the place. Now he really wanted to make a good impression.

"Uh, this is my first time here," he said, then realized as soon as the words left his mouth that she was already well aware that he wasn't a regular customer. She probably knew all of her regulars by name.

"Noel," she said, her eyes lighting up. "Noel Stewart, by chance?" She wiped her hands on the towel tucked into her apron waistband.

"I am," he said. Obviously, the women had talked about him. Hopefully, in the best of lights, too. "I'm here to meet Addison."

Juno cocked her head toward the table where the four women still chatted.

"I know," Noel said, watching them. "I don't want to interrupt. I'm in no hurry."

"Well, I have no such reservations," Juno said, then let out a loud whistle. The whole café fell silent for one heart-stopping moment. All eyes turned toward Juno, who pointed with both hands at Noel. Not knowing what else to do, he stood, took a bow in acknowledgement, and then turned to smile at Addison.

She rose to her feet, her hand over her mouth, her cheeks turning pink. Was it embarrassment or pleasure that had her eyes sparkling like that, he wondered. Maybe a combination of both? He quickly crossed the room to her, and all around, the conversations started up again.

"I'm sorry," Noel said with a grin, reaching out both hands to take hers. "I was trying very hard to not be noticed, but your friend—"

"She is no longer my friend," Addison declared, shaking her head.

"We're your friends, though," interjected one of the women at the table. "Introduce us, girlfriend."

Candy, the one who'd spoken, and Liz Needham were sisters, he learned, and Penny Anderson was the third member of the group. Penny, Addison explained, lived in the big white house he could see from his apartment on the fifth floor of the resort. "It's one of the oldest buildings in Autumn Lake," Penny told him. "Still owned by the original Poleman family."

Juno made her way over to the table and slipped an arm around Addison's waist. "Don't hate me, sister. He was just sitting there mooning over you from afar, and I didn't want him scaring away any of my customers."

"Juno!" Addison gasped, pulling her hands free from Noel's.

Penny and Liz echoed her, but Candy held up a hand for Juno to high-five her.

Addison pointed at Candy. "*Et tu*, Brute?" Then to Noel, she said, "We should go. Get away from this riffraff."

"We're open until ten if you want to swing back by here for an after-dinner nightcap," Juno suggested. She leaned close and murmured something in Addison's ear that made her blush even more, if that were possible, then started back to the bar. "We have the best chocolate eclairs you'll ever eat," she called over her shoulder.

"She does," Penny confirmed with a nod. "You can't go wrong with pretty much anything Juno has in her pastry counter."

"Where are you two off to tonight?" Candy asked, her gaze darting back and forth between him and Addison. Of the two sisters, she was clearly the more talkative. Liz took a long sip of what appeared to be hot chocolate, if the mini marshmallows were any clue, but he wasn't fooled; she was sizing him up just as attentively as the rest of Addison's friends.

"Don't tell them," Addison said before he could respond. "They'll just ambush us there, too."

So, she hadn't expected them to all be here, he realized. That actually made him feel a little better; he'd begun to wonder if she'd gathered her friends for moral support. Surely, he wasn't that scary, was he?

"We won't follow you, we promise," Liz assured them. "I have to be up at the crack of dawn tomorrow."

"Liz is with the county water department," Candy explained. "She and her crew are working on your side of the lake right now, aren't you, sis?"

"In the North Shore development," Liz clarified.

"So? Tell us," Candy pressed. "Come on, Noel. We want to make sure you're doing right by our girl, here."

Noel looked at Addison and shrugged. These women were her friends. Maybe if he impressed them…. "We're going to Bella Tavola." To Addison, he said, "I hope you like Italian."

"We love Italian," Candy exclaimed, then amended her response with, "Addison in particular, I mean."

"I do like Italian," Addison assured him. The look on her face told him she was pleased with his choice.

"It's just north of Evansville, so it's not far down the road."

"That place is amazing," Liz said, and the three women turned and all but gaped at her. "What?" she asked. "I go to fancy places, too. I even own something other than jeans and t-shirts." She tugged on the lapels of her quilted flannel overshirt.

Candy squeezed Liz's hand affectionately. "Of course, you do, sissy."

"Well, if Liz says it's good, then you can count on it being good." Penny made a shooing motion with her hand. "You two go. Have a good time. It was really nice to meet you, Noel."

The other two women echoed the sentiment.

As they passed by the counter, Juno held a hand up to her ear. "I expect a phone call or at least a text telling me you're home safe," she said. "You take care of her, Mr. Stewart. She's precious to us."

"I will," he promised with a nod, oddly moved rather than offended by how protective Addison's friends were toward her.

Noel held the door for her, then followed her out into the chilly night air. It was cold, but not so much that they couldn't walk a little if she wanted to show him some of the night life in downtown Autumn Lake. He'd suggested it primarily because Barb had encouraged him to get to know the town through Addison's eyes. But honestly, tonight he was more interested in getting to know the lovely woman with him than the town.

"I've never been to Bella Tavola before," Addison said softly, glancing over at him. She seemed suddenly ill at ease now that she was alone with him.

"I haven't either," he admitted. "But it comes highly recommended. Are you hungry?" It probably wasn't the most gentlemanly question to ask, but that's what came out.

Addison let out her breath like she'd been holding it. "Yes," she exclaimed, practically on a sigh of relief. "I didn't take much of a lunch break today, and I was secretly hoping you weren't expecting me to pay for my supper with a town tour." Then she covered her mouth with her hand as if she'd said something offensive. "I mean, I'm happy to pay for my—"

Noel held out an arm for her to take. Sometimes walking beside someone new made it easier to converse comfortably. "I wouldn't dream of it. But I'm starving, too, so I say we head to the car. I'm parked just down the road there." He pointed at a sleek gray coupe spotlighted under a streetlamp. "That said, I'd love a town tour from you, if you'd like to give me one. Maybe we can plan that for our next date."

13

Addison

So, this was a date. Not only was he taking her to the gorgeous Italian restaurant she drove by every time she went to and from work, but he'd actually used the word itself. Addison was so glad she'd dressed up. She ran a hand over her purse and prayed she'd know if and when she should give him the book inside.

She thanked Noel as he held the car door open for her and waited until she was settled into her seat before closing it. By the time she was buckled in, he'd circled the car and was climbing in behind the wheel. "Nice car." It was a Nissan—she only knew that because she'd seen the hood ornament—and a sports car with only two seats. It smelled good inside, like leather and men's cologne, and she had to temper her desire to breathe in deeply of it.

"Thank you," Noel replied, then started up the engine. It wasn't as loud as she'd expected, which was a relief. They were a good fifteen minutes from the restaurant, and she didn't want to have to shout to have a conversation in the car. Or not to be able to talk at all.

"So those were your friends."

Addison looked over at Noel, glad when she saw him smiling, even though his eyes remained on the road. "They are. Juno was one of the first people I met in town, and although I'm super mad at her and plan to never speak to her again, I couldn't imagine my life in Autumn Lake without her in it."

"Could make things awkward if you never speak to her again."

Addison sighed dramatically. "I suppose you're right. Maybe I'll forgive her tonight when I text her to let her know that you got me home safely."

"Good plan." Noel nodded. "You know, I think I like your friends. I'm a little jealous, I have to admit."

Addison looked over at him, surprised by the admission. "You're jealous? Of my friends?"

Noel shrugged. "I'm kind of a loner by nature," he said. "Making friends doesn't come easy to me."

She frowned. "I find that hard to believe. You're so... nice." She cringed and turned away. Wasn't 'nice' one of the most friend-zone words ever used in the history of romance? How could she fix her faux pas without making things worse? "I don't mean you're nice. I mean—" Realizing what she'd just said, she broke off.

"I'm not nice?"

Addison heard the teasing in his voice. She had to save face. "Of course, you're nice, Noel. But not to me." What? What on earth was she saying? Why did things sound one way in her head, only to come out completely wrong when she opened her mouth? "I mean, you're very nice to me. You're more than just nice. I—I didn't mean to call you nice."

"Well, then," he said, drawing out the words a little. "What *did* you mean to call me?"

Addison sighed. Why did she always back herself into these corners? "I'm sorry. Sometimes I say things before I really think them through, and there's no delete or undo button."

"Isn't that the truth?" Noel agreed whole-heartedly.

Addison knew he referred to there being no delete button, but it sounded almost like he was agreeing that she spoke without thinking. She let out a rather unladylike snort, then slapped a hand over her mouth and nose, surprised and embarrassed at the sound.

Noel laughed out loud. He reached over and gently pulled her hand from her mouth. "Nope. There's no delete button, remember? Besides, I kinda like that you're comfortable enough to snort-laugh with me."

He didn't let go of her hand.

Addison didn't try to pull away.

Noel continued. "I'm really glad you agreed to go out with me tonight."

Somehow, even though he'd all but laughed at her, he'd done so in a way that put her at ease, that made her feel appreciated. "I'm really glad you asked me to go out with you tonight." To her great relief, every word that came out of her mouth sounded exactly the way she meant it.

Although the parking lot was full, within minutes, they were seated at a table set with a cream linen cloth and hand-painted dinnerware. Music played softly in the background; Addison was pretty sure it was Dean Martin, but she was too embarrassed to ask, just in case she was wrong. Shouldn't she know Dean Martin's voice? Shouldn't everyone in the world? Aromas of garlic and basil, butter, cheese, and red wine tickled the senses, and she couldn't resist sniffing the air.

"Smells amazing, doesn't it?" Noel asked from across the table. It was a booth for two, maybe four if people were comfortable with snuggling while eating. With the high backs on the seats, it felt quite intimate, and Addison suddenly wondered what on earth they'd talk about for however long it took to share a meal. Why, oh why hadn't she researched topics of conversations for first dates before now?

Just when Addison was starting to panic, a pretty young woman approached their table. She wore black pants, a white shirt, and a black apron emblazoned with Bella Tavola across one of the pockets. "Buonasera! My name is Michelle, and I'll be your server tonight." She set a basket of ciabatta rolls on the table between them, along with bottles of olive oil and balsamic vinegar, and extra plates. "Bubbly or flat?" she asked, holding up a bottle of sparkling water in one hand and a decanter of iced water in the other. She deftly filled their water glasses, then after a brief discussion of the menu and the evening's specials, she took their drink and appetizer order and left them to figure out what entrees they wanted.

"Do you know Italian?" Noel asked, peering over the top of his menu. The dishes were listed in Italian, but the descriptions were in English.

"Enough to say 'hello' and 'goodbye' and a few other niceties, but that's all," Addison admitted. "I'm embarrassed to say that's all I know about most languages. I only really speak English." She'd been all over the world, but had never been in one place long enough to take on anything more than a tourist's trappings of those places. As an adult, she felt almost guilty for having had such vast exposure, and yet to have been so unaffected by them. She loved the fabrics and trinkets and memorabilia that decorated her home—she remembered vividly the street markets and bazaars where she'd found her treasures—but she would be the first to admit that they represented her presence in their world, not the other way around.

"I'm the same way. I've met a lot of people working for Carpe Diem who are fluent in multiple languages, and it's pretty humbling. So, tell me. If you could learn one other language, which would it be?"

Addison pondered that for a moment, then said, "I know I should choose something more common, but I'd kinda like to learn Icelandic. Very few people in the world speak it, so it wouldn't come in very handy, but it sounds so epic to me. Or wait. Maybe Norwegian. Such a magical language." She swept a hand out in front of her. "It makes me think of snow queens and ice castles."

"Wow," Noel said, clearly surprised by her choice. "I would not have guessed either of those."

"Are you making assumptions about me, Mr. Stewart?" she teased.

"No, no," he said, shaking his head. "I'm just admitting that those aren't the first languages that come to my mind, that's all." He lifted his water glass toward her in a quick salute. "I love that you surprise me, Miss Wedgewood."

"Oh." She was saved from having to come up with a response by the appearance of Michelle, tray in hand, bringing their bruschetta and crab-stuffed mushrooms and the house's aranciata, a refreshing drink they made from fresh-squeezed blood oranges and carbonated water. They still hadn't decided on their main courses, but Michelle encouraged them to take their time.

"Each course of an Italian meal is meant to be savored. If you're focusing on figuring out what you want next, you'll miss out on what is in front of you."

When she'd gone, Noel rather philosophically said, "That's not a bad rule to live by."

Addison nodded slowly. "I was just thinking the same thing." Under the table, she accidentally nudged his foot with hers, reminding her of her embarrassing response when they'd bumped knees the first time they'd sat across the table from each other at Shoot the Moon. "Oh—sorry," she said, then took a sip of the tangy, sparkling drink.

"Are you playing footsy with me already?" Noel teased. They'd opted to share the appetizers, and he pushed the platter of mushrooms toward her. "Not that I'm complaining," he added. "Here. You start."

The food, all four courses of it, was as delicious as they'd hoped. The conversation, to Addison's surprise, was just as wonderful. Not because they talked about anything exotic or unusual—they covered many of the basics of getting to know each other—but because they seemed to find that sweet, comfortable spot that kindred spirits shared where words flowed freely around the few and far between moments of comfortable silence.

Granted, she let Noel do most of the talking. Addison was a listener by nature, and she wanted to know all about him. She already knew all there was to know about herself, after all. In some ways, the exciting years of Addison's life were in the past, and when she considered what she could contribute to the conversation that might make her sound more interesting, she came up blank. She was no longer that traveling vagabond child. She no longer went anywhere or did anything special, other than the few trips she'd gone on with her parents over the years since settling into Autumn Lake. Even her last excursion to Iceland; the most exciting thing about that had been sharing coffee and donuts with a handsome Viking while watching the Northern lights in the middle of the cold, winter night.

Okay. Even she had to admit when said like that, it did sound pretty exciting. But she didn't think the scenario was quite the thing to bring up on a first date with another man.

To her relief, Noel didn't seem to mind that she wasn't exactly verbose. He wasn't the kind of guy to brag about his accomplishments or to even talk too much; he just took it upon himself to keep the conversation going, and Addison appreciated that so much. Had she been responsible for such, the evening might have gone differently.

Noel's years of working for the auditing teams for corporate allowed him to travel all over the United States, and he regaled her with stories about the places he'd been, from Florida to California, New York, to New Orleans. "Indiana is one of the few states I hadn't been to. We have a hotel in Indianapolis, but they have their own internal auditing team."

"Is that what you are now? Part of an internal auditing team?"

His expression fell flat for just a moment, and a tiny spark of unease settled in her stomach. "Yes," he said. "Our team is small. Only me and one other person, plus our support staff."

"I see." She hesitated, then asked, "It sounds like a lot of work. Do you like it?"

"I like what I do, yes," he answered after a heartbeat, but his response felt evasive, although she couldn't put a finger on why she thought so.

"What about Autumn Lake?" she asked, wondering if she was pushing it too far. "Do you like living in our sleepy little town? It gets more exciting when the summer rolls around."

Once again, he paused before answering. "I live in a furnished apartment on the fifth floor of the resort. Inside the resort are two restaurants. One is casual and more family oriented. They serve amazing breakfasts. One of these mornings, I'll take you there. The other one, Lux Solaris, is fine dining. The chef is a magician. Both offer room service. There are clothing boutiques on the main level, a salon and a barber shop, a pastry and candy shop, and more. Even a pharmacy. Pretty much everything a person could need or want is ready at hand at Carpe Diem."

Addison wasn't sure where he was going with this, but she nodded encouragingly.

"To tell you the truth, I know very little about Autumn Lake. I feel a little like a prince in a tower over there."

"Oh." She hadn't expected that. She could suddenly picture Noel, five stories up, standing on a balcony looking down upon the quaint villagers across the water. It was not a pleasant visual. It brought to mind the division between the locals—the Townies—and the WOOTS, as they called the wealthy out of towners. The general consensus among the Townies was that the WOOTS believed themselves to be far superior because of their financial status and looked down on the locals as beneath them. Her friend, Alex, who worked for a local construction company, had once told her, "It's like they think of us as peasants to their nobility."

Addison hated the notion that Noel might be of that persuasion. And if he were, then what was he doing out with her?

"I'm embarrassed to say that I've been so busy just trying to sort out my job—among other things—that I haven't made the effort to discover my new home town." He sounded sincere, which made the unpleasant picture of him in her mind fade a little.

As gently as she could, she told him, "Well, you've been missing out. This is a special place full of special people."

Noel looked her in the eyes and said, "I'm finding that out, and I intend to rectify it."

Over decadent squares of tiramisu and tiny cordial glasses of chilled amaretto, Noel asked, "Do you have any pets? And please tell me you're not a snake person."

Addison shook her head. "I wish on both counts. I think having a snake would be cool, but I'm not cool. At least not cool enough to ever be a snake person, so don't worry."

Noel dramatically swiped at his forehead with the back of his hand. "Might have been a deal breaker, there," he said with a chuckle.

Addison smiled at his teasing, relishing in how much fun she was having. "I'd love a dog," she continued. "But with my work hours, I don't think it would be fair to the poor thing, stuck inside my little apartment all day. I'd spend the whole day at work worrying about the little dude."

Noel nodded understandingly. "Dogs do love their outside play, I hear."

"But a cat?" Addison went on, the secret thrill of the notion making her pulse kick up a notch. "Now that's something I can strive for. I think I'd make a pretty good cat lady, don't you? And cats are pretty independent; you don't have to walk them, right?"

"Not that I know of. I've only had dogs before, so I'm probably not the person to ask."

"Lucky," she murmured, imagining a young Noel romping around in a big back yard with a floppy-eared pup. "I've never had a pet in my life. Not even a pet rock."

"Never? Not even a fish?"

"Not even a fish. I haven't even owned a plant, and I love plants to the moon and back. I've got this little bay window with a wide sill in my apartment, and every time I look at it, I think to myself, 'That's where I'll put all my plants one day.' But I still don't have any because I'm just too afraid I won't be able to keep another living thing alive. Crazy, right?" she said with a dismissive shrug.

"I wouldn't call you crazy," Noel assuaged her, but then he winked at her. "But I'd venture to suggest that you haven't really lived until you've had a pet."

"Exactly." She pointed her fork at him, then took a sip of her water to wash down the last bite of tiramisu. "I agree whole-heartedly. But I still think I need to start with a plant or two. Then maybe a hamster." She wrinkled her nose at the thought. "Never mind. I don't think I'm a rodent person, either. A cat, I think. A very independent one."

"Sounds like a good plan to me."

By the time they left Bella Tavola, Autumn Lake was pretty much shut down for the night. The coffee shop was dark except for the warm glow of the light Juno always left burning in the window, and they were far too late to stop in and see Claire. Her friend was probably disappointed that she'd not met Noel, especially since the rest of the Garden Variety Lovers Club had done so at Juno's, but Addison would make it up to her on the weekend. Noel had asked her to spend Saturday afternoon with him, giving him a tour of her home town, and she planned to take him to The Cracked Spine as the first stop on their date.

Partly because it was so late, but mostly because he'd swept away almost all of her insecurities about letting a stranger know where she lived, Addison let Noel not only drive her home, but also escort her up the metal stairs to her little deck to make sure she made it inside her apartment safely.

"Would you like to come in?" she asked after unlocking her door. Did that sound too forward? They'd already had after-dinner coffee with their dessert at the restaurant. They'd spent the ride back to Autumn Lake in companionable silence, almost as if they were just as satiated by the evening's wonderful conversation as they were with the amazing meal. As much as she liked him, and she really did like him, she wasn't offering him more than the chance to say their goodbyes inside, out of the brisk breeze that was blowing in across the lake.

Addison still hadn't given him the book. She'd been waiting for just the right moment, and for whatever reason, they'd talked about everything, it seemed, except books.

Noel took her hand. His fingers were a little chilled, but it was late and the night had grown quite cold. "I'd love to, but I'm going to say goodnight here." Then, like something straight out of a Jane Austen book, he lifted her hand and placed a soft kiss on her knuckles. Before letting go, he said, "I'm really looking forward to spending Saturday with you."

For a moment, Addison stood there speechless at the gallant gesture. She opened her mouth to say something, then snapped it shut again. At that moment, she had the vivid inclination to drag the man inside her lair and demand that he kiss her—her hand, her mouth, her neck—again and again. Was he a master seducer, or was he truly that much of gentleman?

"Thank you for the wonderful evening, Addison," Noel said, his smile making her knees go wobbly. "It's in my top three since moving to Autumn Lake."

"Top three, huh?" she asked. "You'll have to tell me about your first and second favorites sometime." It was certainly top of the list for her. She couldn't recall another first date like it. In fact, as far as she was concerned, all other first dates she'd had might as well have never existed.

Noel cocked his head at her and shoved his hands in his coat pockets. "Who said this one wasn't in first place? I just said it was *in* the top three."

A bubble of joy swelled inside her chest and she pressed a palm to her sternum. "You are too much, Noel Stewart. I really had a good time tonight. Thank you."

Noel just nodded, then made for the stairs. He glanced back once, then started down.

Addison watched from her doorway as he disappeared out of sight. She heard his feet on the gravel parking area below.

Suddenly, she surged forward and leaned out over the rail. "Noel?"

He was standing at the bottom of the stairs, one foot on the lowest step, looking almost like he'd been about to come back up. "Yes?"

"I—I—um, do you like to read? We didn't talk about books."

Noel took one step up. "I do." He took another step. "Funny you should ask. I just finished the first book I've read in way too long. I hadn't realized how much I missed reading."

Addison still had her purse hitched over her shoulder. She moved to the top of the stairs. "What kind of books do you like?" Were they really having this conversation right now?

Noel shrugged one shoulder. "I read lots of business and mindset nonfiction, but that's for work."

"Do you like it?" Addison took one step down the stairs and stopped, her hand trembling a little on the cold steel rail. "Those genres, I mean."

Noel climbed two more steps. "I like to learn, so yeah. I guess I like it. But it's not my favorite."

"What's your favorite?" Another step down. Now there were only three steps between them and they were nearly eye-to-eye.

"I read fiction to step outside my own life," he began after a moment's consideration. He slid his hand up the rail to cover hers. "I like stories about other times, other places, other worlds. What about you?"

Addison wanted to turn her hand over and lace her fingers with his, but she wasn't quite that bold. "I—I'll show you on Saturday," she told him, hoping he wouldn't ask what that meant. She wanted the tour of her town, every stop, to be a discovery for him. Now that she knew he liked books, she couldn't wait to take him to Claire's bookshop.

Noel nodded, his eyes locked with hers. "I can hardly wait. The books a person reads says a lot about them, don't you think?"

"I do. Yes." She took a deep breath. "I hope you don't think this is too forward," she started, then frowned. Now that she'd put it into words, he'd immediately start thinking just that. She shifted her gaze to the rail where his hand still covered hers.

"What?" Noel asked when she didn't continue. "What is it, Addison?"

She bit her bottom lip, then decided to just be brave. Really, what was so scary about giving the guy a book? It wasn't an expensive gift—nothing like the cost of the meal that he'd just paid for. It wasn't a book on how to woo a woman or become a better man. It was just a book. One that would quite likely be a doorway through which he could step outside of his own life. "I have something for you."

"You do?" He looked positively delighted. That bolstered her significantly.

Addison pulled her hand free of his—reluctantly—and opened her bag to pull out the book. "This is for you," she said a little breathlessly, still nervous about the appropriateness of the gift. "I haven't read this one, but I've read other books by this author, and I've never been disappointed."

Noel took it from her, turned it over in his hands, and read the back cover quickly before holding the book against his chest. "Thank you. I didn't think this evening could get any better. I was wrong."

"Oh," she said, the sound coming out a little gushy. "I should have given it to you sooner. Sorry."

"Don't be sorry," Noel said, moving up one more step, then another, until he stood on the step below her. With her heels on, she still had a couple of inches on him, but who was measuring? He reached up and smoothed a hand down the length of her hair, toying with the ends, his fingers brushing her shoulder and making her shiver with pleasure. He murmured, "If you had given it to me earlier, we might not be standing here right now."

Addison's heart raced at his nearness, beating inside her chest as if it wanted out, wanted to throw itself at the man inches from her. "If you've already read it," she stammered, "I can exchange it for something else."

"I wouldn't care if I'd read it a hundred times, Addison." The way he said her name felt like a caress. "I wouldn't trade this book in for anything, because it's from you."

"Oh." Why did she keep saying that? It made her sound dumb as a rock.

"I like it when you say that," Noel whispered. Had he read her mind? "There's a world of meaning behind that tiny little word, isn't there?" Then he pressed his mouth to hers in a tender first kiss.

Addison didn't even hesitate. She kissed him back.

Noel pulled away and moved one step down, putting a little space between them. "I'm going to say goodnight now, Addison." And with that, he turned around and made his way back down the steps to the parking spaces below. He paused right before climbing into his front seat and held up the book. "Thank you for this. And I haven't read it yet."

A few moments later, his tail lights disappeared as he turned out of the alley onto the street and headed off into the night. Addison stood on the steps, her fingertips pressed to her lips, trying to hold onto the sensation of that oh, so sweet kiss.

14
Noel

HE COULDN'T STOP THINKING about her. About the silkiness of her hair under his touch. About her bottomless green eyes, the way she studied him while she listened to him drone on and on about his life. Had he bored her to tears?

Something about the way she smiled at him told him otherwise.

About that sweet fragrance she wore that made him ache for his mother. "That's not weird?" he muttered under his breath. "I shouldn't be thinking about my mother when I'm with a woman I'm—" He broke off, the direction of that line of thought catching him by surprise.

With a woman he was what?

He'd been about to say 'a woman he was falling for,' but... so quickly? Was it really that easy?

For the past decade, Noel had traveled all over the country to different Carpe Diem locations for his job. He'd been attracted to other women before, certainly, but because of his transient status, he'd kept them at arm's length. He'd dated, but always with the full disclosure that he was not in the position to make a long-term commitment, which often put an end to things before they really started.

He'd never really minded not being in a relationship, not having a family of his own, even friends, in the past. He'd seen little evidence that love was all it was cracked up to be in books and movies or even folklore and legend, and if he never let himself experience it, maybe he could save himself the pain he'd witnessed in so many lives.

Besides, there was always that secret fear lurking in the back of his mind that, although he didn't greatly resemble Bruno, maybe, just maybe, there were parts of his father still buried inside him. Parts that should never be poked at. Parts that were better kept locked up tight.

Now, for the first time in years, he found himself wondering what it might be like to be in a relationship with someone. With Addison Wedgewood, to be specific. And why not? He no longer had the excuse that he was in town only temporarily—unless John somehow managed to get him fired.

He eyed John and Paula through the glass walls of John's office just across the small reception area where Paula's desk sat. The two of them were bent toward each other, deep in conversation. The door was open, but they kept their voices low, making it obvious they didn't want Noel privy to whatever they were discussing, and every once in a while, one of them would glance his way. If they happened to make eye contact with him, Noel didn't look away to try to ease the awkwardness of the situation.

It was so childish, this game they were playing. Technically, Paula was Noel's administrative assistant, too, but he wasn't about to hand anything off to her. Which was why he'd been working such long hours; he was doing everything himself, something he hadn't had to do in many years. He'd never realized how much he'd depended on support staff in the past. He'd never take them for granted again.

That said, whatever was happening on the other side of the small Auditing Department, Noel had no intention of making himself vulnerable to their manipulative behavior. As far as he was concerned, John was nothing but a bully, and Paula, his sidekick. And Noel knew all about bullies. They didn't really need excuses for their behavior.

All he knew for certain was that the company had brought him in to take over some of the tasks that John hadn't been able to perform, and instead of acknowledging his limitations and being grateful for another team member, the man resented Noel, treating him like an enemy intruder, taking every opportunity he found to challenge Noel's contributions, to question his ability to do the job he'd been hired to perform.

Projecting to mask his own shortcomings. It was every bully's modus operandi, wasn't it?

Sometimes, when Noel looked at John from the corner of his eye, he imagined Bruno's face sneering back at him. He'd have to blink and look again to clear his vision, but the acid in his stomach took a lot longer to settle.

Noel snatched his phone off his desk and thumbed in a text. *Good morning, Addison. Feel like sharing one of Juno's famous chocolate eclairs with me tonight after work?* He sent the message before he could second guess it. Although they were seeing each other again in only a few days, Saturday seemed lightyears away. Getting through today would be much easier if he knew he had time with Addison to look forward to at the end of it.

It was almost half an hour before she responded. *I can't tonight. What about tomorrow?*

Disappointment coursed through him. He'd have to endure his own company for the night, something he was not looking forward to. Maybe he'd head into Evansville and catch a movie. Get out of the resort for the evening, even if it was by himself. *Tomorrow works for me.*

She responded right away. *Great! Meet you there at 7?*

He frowned at his screen. It would be nearly dark by seven. *Meet you at your place at 7? We can walk together.*

The three little dots that told him she was texting showed, disappeared, then popped back on screen again. He waited. And waited.

They disappeared again.

Should he take back the offer? Was he being sexist, not wanting her to walk the streets alone at night? This was a small town, after all, where everyone knew everyone else. At least on the south side of the lake.

Finally, her response came through. *Compromise. Meet at Juno's at 7, then you can walk me home.*

That sounded fair. And it didn't sound like she was offended by his offer. Maybe she wanted a few minutes to visit with her barista friend before he got there. He could be sensitive to that. *Works for me.* Then he added, *Started your book last night. Already got a hold of me.*

Her response came quickly. *That's a good thing, right?*

He grinned at her message. *That's a very good thing.*

"Hey, Stewart!" John called out to him from the open door of his own office, impatient and rude. It sounded like it might not have been the first time.

"What is it, John?" Noel kept his tone cool. He laid his phone face down on his desk, but barely glanced in the other man's direction.

"You're late getting me the new budget projections for next quarter."

Noel tried to slow his breathing, to quiet his heartrate, but to no avail. He sent John the full budget projections out of courtesy, because they were supposed to be team mates. He was only obligated to give the guy reports that directly affected him and his role in the company. He peered over the top of his monitor at John, but didn't speak right away, waiting for his calming techniques to work.

"Well? I asked you a question. You too busy playing on your phone to do your job?" The man was sneering at him, taunting him, his expression all but daring Noel to step into the proverbial ring.

He's hoping you'll do something to jeopardize your job, Noel reminded himself, but he didn't hold back the snide remark that slid off his tongue. "You got a crush on me, John? Seems like you're too busy watching me to do your job." He knew he was antagonizing him, that he was lowering himself to the guy's level, but sometimes, fools didn't speak any other language. "Check your email. I sent them to you several days ago."

"What did you say, boy?" John surged up from his desk, startling Paula, who scrambled backwards, nearly tipping over her chair. Fortunately, the thing had wheels, and she was able to right herself without mishap.

Noel froze, everything inside him going still, the room around him narrowing into a tunnel of darkness in which were only John and him, facing off. In a quiet, tightly-controlled voice, he said, "Don't call me boy."

But a fool, John certainly was. The man put his hand to his ear. "What was that, boy? Don't call you what?"

In his periphery, Noel saw Paula slowly get to her feet to sidle back to her desk. She left her chair behind in John's office.

Noel didn't move. This was not the right way to handle things. He knew it deep in his bones, but an all too familiar emotion had him in its grip and wouldn't let go. No one had stirred up this much moral outrage in him in a very long time.

No one had called him 'boy' in that contumelious tone since Bruno.

"Paula, would you give us a few minutes?" Noel asked, still in that carefully modulated way. He kept his gaze locked with John's.

The secretary made a frightened sound, scrambled for her purse from one of her desk drawers, then scuttled out of the office, pulling the door closed hard behind her.

Abandoned by his sidekick, John seemed to deflate noticeably. He stayed standing, but fumbled a little, pushing a few papers aside so he could brace his hands on his desk like he needed the support to remain upright. "You know she's calling security."

"I hope she does."

John scoffed. "Why? You scared of me, boy? You need someone to hide behind?" But he wasn't fooling anyone with his false bravado.

Noel stood to his full five-feet-ten-inches and shook his head slowly. "Nope. But I'm tired of the way you're treating me and I've decided I'm not going to sit here and take it any longer. I figure by the time Paula gets a hold of them and they get up here to the sixth floor, you'll be needing them to get me off of you." He rolled his shoulders, shook out his arms, and cocked his head from one side to the other like a boxer warming up before a match.

Oh, he wasn't going to fight anyone today—he wasn't stupid. In fact, he knew he should cut the act now before things got out of hand. But the look on John's face spurred him on. "You think you can bully me and get away with it? Let me tell you what happened to the last guy who tried."

"Bully you? What are we, in high school?" mocked John. But the way he shifted from one foot to the other belied his belligerence.

"He's lying in a hospital as we speak," Noel continued, making fists with his hands, then slowly, methodically, cracking his knuckles. "And he's not leaving that bed anytime soon." He shrugged. "Maybe in a casket, if there's anyone left in the world who will fork over the cash for one. I'd bet not, though. I'm thinking it's more likely he'll end up in one of those freebie plastic boxes you get from the crematory." He almost laughed at the irony of it all. He was telling this weasel the truth. Bruno wasn't leaving that room except in a body bag. And maybe, in some small way, Noel had, indeed, put him there. Maybe the burden of Bruno's guilt and shame over the loss of both his wife and his only son had become too much for the man to carry, and his body had malfunctioned on him.

"Are you threatening me?" John's voice shook, but to his credit, he stayed on his feet.

"Naw. Just sharing with you a few details about my life. Since you seem so interested," Noel added with a taunting smirk. "But if you'd like to come a little closer, I can give you a few more."

"Sounds like a threat to me," John shot back. Then he dropped hard into his seat and held up the cell phone that he'd been covering with one hand. "And it's all on record now." He tapped the screen, presumably to end the recording, and added, "You're going down, boy."

Noel had to hand it to the guy. John Sheridan was a much wilier opponent than he'd given him credit for. In his blind rage, he hadn't even seen the cellphone.

John hadn't grabbed the desk to steady his weak knees. He'd only pretended to fumble around, shuffling papers the way he had, to mask what he was doing. He'd either called someone or hit record somehow, and now everything Noel had just said was, according to John, on record.

I'm going down. Noel eased slowly into his chair. He should have known better than to stand up for himself. Hadn't he learned anything from his own past experience? Keep your head down and your mouth closed, because the bad guys always get the last word.

There was a knock on the office door.

"Come in," John called, his voice unsettlingly calm, his eyes locked with Noel's. The door opened, and Ace Jackson cautiously stepped into the room.

Noel had always thought the guy had the perfect name for a security job. Ace Jackson.

"Everything all right in here?" Ace asked, his gaze darting back and forth between the two men who sat behind their respective desks on opposite sides of the room. "Paula said you all might need security?" The expression on Ace's face said they weren't fooling him. It was obvious that he could tell something was amiss.

John shook his head slowly. "She must have been mistaken, Ace. Everything's good in here, right, Stewart?"

Noel met the security officer's eyes, ignoring John. Everything was *not* good in here. "I'm sorry she sent you up, Ace."

"So, she was mistaken?" Ace asked, his brows furrowing in suspicion.

Noel nodded. "A misunderstanding." The whole thing felt way too much like high school, like they'd been caught fighting in the hall between classes and were both pretending it hadn't happened. "Again, sorry to have bothered you."

Ace studied them for a few more moments, his gaze moving slowly back and forth between them. Finally, he nodded and said, "Gentlemen, please understand that we take calls like this seriously here at Carpe Diem." He knew there was still trouble brewing between them, and the statement was a thinly-veiled warning, a charge to behave, plain and simple.

Noel had a sinking feeling that Paula had done more than just ask Ace to check on them. He could only imagine what kind of scenario she'd painted for the man. And whatever she'd told him could now be backed up by the recording John held in his hands.

So why wasn't John acting on it?

Noel nodded. "Understood, Ace."

John held his arms out at his sides, palms up like he had no idea what the officer meant. "I'm just a man doing his job over here."

As Ace finally turned to leave, Noel clenched his teeth together, a wave of infuriation washing over him. He didn't look at John. He felt sick to his stomach.

15
Addison

Even with all the excitement of her date with Noel, Addison hadn't been able to get Claire and her mystery man off her mind. Not because she wanted to know the guy's name, but because she was so curious about what kind of man Claire would be attracted to. In all the years Addison had lived in Autumn Lake, her friend had never dated anyone; at least not that she was aware of. She often did things with male friends, but Addison had never seen Claire romantically attached to anyone.

She'd called Claire that morning before work to tell her all about her date with Noel, and they'd talked so long, they'd both been almost late to work. Addison wanted to know more about her friend's budding romance, so Claire suggested she come by the shop for supper.

"I'll bring chicken corn chowder and peasant bread," Addison offered, knowing her friend wouldn't say no to that. Claire did not excel in the kitchen, and she'd be the first to admit it. "And I'll stay to help you close for the night, too."

"I won't turn down free labor," Claire told her. "Jen was out sick this afternoon, so Tina and I have extra to do this evening."

When Noel texted about meeting for dessert at Juno's, she'd felt a little bereft at already having to put him off, but she wasn't going to drop all her plans so she could meet him for coffee. Besides, wasn't she supposed to play a little hard to get, at least at the beginning? Not be too available?

It was another busy night at The Cracked Spine, so Addison put the soup in the fridge in the employee room for Claire to take home with her, then headed back out to see what tasks needed her attention. She found her friend in a section of the shop dedicated to manga and anime, a corner that often got extra after-school abuse from groups of kids who were drawn to the racks of Japanese cartoons and artwork. The two of them worked on different shelves, reorganizing titles that had been perused and put back in the wrong places.

"Does anyone actually buy these?" Addison asked Claire. "Or do they just come in, read it all here, and leave you a mess to clean up after them?"

"They do buy sometimes." Claire smiled and shrugged. "Usually it's kids who are teaching themselves to draw and paint in the style, rather than readers, though." Today, she wore a schoolgirl outfit straight out of a Tim Burton movie. Her uniform-style black dress had a short, flared skirt and a white Peter Pan collar, and she wore black stockings and thick-soled black boots. Her long blonde hair was divided into two braids fastened with black satin ribbons and a matching ribbon tied around her neck. Even more dramatic than her outfit was the dark smudged eye makeup that made her sky blue eyes look enormous and otherworldly.

Claire had the face and figure that allowed her to get away with wearing anything, and that's exactly what she did. From one day to the next, one could never guess what she'd show up to work in. She drew inspiration from characters in the books in her shop, and whether she dressed as Alice in Wonderland, a Jane Austen character, or Tinkerbell—she even had a markedly female version of a Captain Hook outfit—she always looked amazing. It was clear to anyone who knew her that she loved every part of what she did, from the shop to the books to the readers, all the way down to the in-character clothes she wore.

"But I don't mind them coming here to spend their afternoons. It's better than having them sitting at home alone on their phones, don't you think? Here, they're reading, socializing, and getting their fill of an art style that doesn't get a fair shine in their schools."

"Sure," Addison acknowledged. "That's awfully good of you, though. Half of these books and magazines don't look new anymore. How do you sell them?"

Claire winked at her. "I have new copies in the stockroom. I just keep the roughed-up versions out here. If they're serious, they'll ask if I have them in stock."

"Well, aren't you a smart cookie," Addison teased.

"I am, thank you very much." Claire slid another magazine back into its rightful place. "Speaking of cookies and other delicious treats, how are things going with your resort man? Any updates? Has he called you today?"

Addison rolled her eyes. "Nice segue," she snarked.

Claire grinned capriciously. "You liked that, huh? But tell me. Are you going out again soon?" She sent Addison a hopeful smile.

Addison told her about the text exchange that afternoon and Claire grabbed her by the shoulders like she was going to shake her. "Wait. You are here working for free when you could be staring moony-eyed at each other over coffee and eclairs at Juno's? Why didn't you say anything? You know I would have made you go out with him."

"Exactly," Addison said with a wry chuckle. "Juno will still be serving eclairs tomorrow. I want to be here tonight."

Claire wiggled her eyebrows at her. "Playing hard to get, are we?" She turned back to the shelf she was straightening.

"No," Addison insisted, although that exact thought had crossed her mind earlier. Even so, playing hard to get was not her reason for being there with Claire instead of out with Noel. It was because, over the last few years, she had discovered just how important her friends were to her, and just how much she'd missed out on by not having girlfriends in her life before now. She wouldn't do anything to jeopardize those relationships; certainly not by prioritizing a new man in her life over them. "But maybe I'm making sure that I'm not too available," she said with a half shrug and a crooked smile. "I don't want to look as desperate as I really am. Hopefully, it won't backfire on me, though. Make him think I'm not interested." She shot a sideways glance at her friend, her insecurities billowing up inside of her. She felt so naïve when it came to the rituals of dating. "You don't think he'll find someone else to go out with tonight, do you?"

"Not a chance," Claire shot back. "First of all, we live in a teeny tiny town, girlie. Options are super limited based on sheer numbers alone. And I know you. No man in his right mind would pass you over for someone else."

Addison released a wry chuckle. "Ha. Not true. I've been passed over more times than you can count. I'm apparently something of a man repellent. Why do you think I'm still single?"

"You say that like it's a bad thing," Claire said, cocking her head to look at her. "Wouldn't you rather be single and happy than in a relationship with someone just for the sake of *not* being single?"

The way she said it gave Addison pause. It was obvious to those who knew Claire that the woman was quite content in her own single status. She'd once told them all during a Garden Variety Lovers Club meeting when the topic of marriage had come up, "My parents set the bar pretty high for what a relationship should look like, and I'm not willing to compromise my standards. I have high expectations for myself, too—I want to be the best and most whole Claire I can be, someone worthy of the man I'm holding out for."

It was a sentiment that had stuck with Addison, something she thought was a good rule to live by, and not just for whatever man came into her life. She wanted to be the best version of herself for her friends, and for herself, too. There were times, however, more and more often lately, that she ached for something—some*one*—to pour her love into. She'd experienced such loneliness during her younger years, and now that she had friends and a place where she really belonged, she'd discovered how rich a life she could lead by loving others.

She wanted to come home to someone besides just herself at the end of the day.

But maybe now was not the time to say so.

"Of course, I'd rather be single and happy," she said in response to Claire's question. And she meant it, too. She reached over and laid a hand on Claire's arm. "I may not need a man in my life, but I am so glad I have you and Juno and the rest of the gang. You're the best friends in the whole wide world."

Claire grinned, then opened her mouth to say something, when on the other side of the tall book rack, someone cleared his throat. They both froze, exchanging wide-eyed stares. How had they not known they had company?

Addison covered her mouth with one hand, mortified at the thought of someone overhearing their conversation.

Claire mouthed, "It's okay," and then slowly eased around the end of the shelf to see who it was, leaving Addison to hide among the comics. "Finding everything all right—oh!" Her tone changed noticeably, growing warm, dulcet. "Well, hello, again."

"Hi. Again. Forgive me. I didn't mean to eavesdrop."

That voice—could it be? No. No, no, no. Addison didn't dare peer around the end of the bookshelf to see for herself, but there was no doubt in her mind that it was none other than Noel Stewart in the next aisle over. What on earth was he doing at The Cracked Spine? He'd told her he hadn't spent any time on this side of the lake, but if the recognition in Claire's voice was any clue, this was not, by a long shot, the first time he'd been in the bookshop.

"The salesperson at the front was busy with another customer, but she told me I'd find you back here. I didn't want to interrupt..." His voice trailed off apologetically, and Addison cringed at the thought of what he might have overheard. What had they been saying? Had he heard the part about her being desperate? Playing hard to get? A man repellent?

"These tall shelves give people a false sense of privacy," came Claire's engaging reply. "And I, of all people, should know better than to have intimate conversations here." She finished the statement with a low laugh, a sound that sent a tiny tremor up Addison's spine. Her friend sounded awfully comfortable—almost intimate, to use Claire's choice of words—with the man.

Addison squeezed her eyes shut. She should just go home, now. But there was no way out of the manga corner without passing right by Claire and Noel; she'd have to lie low until he left.

"Don't apologize; you didn't interrupt. You—my customers—are the reason I exist in this world, and I'm just thrilled that you made it back to my little shop. I've been thinking about you and wondering what you thought of the book I recommended."

Addison sucked in a sharp breath; her worst fears confirmed. "She's flirting with him," she moaned behind her hand.

Claire Maitland was flirting—hard—with Noel Stewart. Was he—*her* Noel—Claire's mystery man?

"It was excellent," Noel responded with heartfelt enthusiasm. "Far better than I'd expected. I'm hoping you have the other books in the series."

Claire murmured something that Addison couldn't make out. It sounded like they were moving away.

She didn't want to risk being seen by them, but there was no way she could stay in the store, no way she could talk to Claire about him now. She scooped up the coat that she'd draped over the back of a chair close by and slipped into it, pulling the hood up to obscure her features. Then she crept stealthily to the end of the aisle, hoping to maneuver around the store in the opposite direction they were moving.

"The third book releases later this year, but I've got Book Two in stock," Claire was saying to him. "I'll take you to them. I've moved things around since you were last here."

"I don't want to pull you away from—" Noel hesitated, as though not sure how to label what he'd overheard, making Addison squirm in misery. "You can just tell me where to look. I'm sure I can find them on my own."

"Don't be silly. Like I said, you are my top priority. Come."

Addison took another step and peeked around the shelf. Her heart lurched to a painful, juddering stop. Claire's hand, indeed, rested in the curve of Noel's elbow, and from Addison's perspective, her friend looked like she was leaning into the guy. At least walking very close to him.

Addison had turned him down, and now he was here at The Cracked Spine—again, apparently—falling under her friend's beguiling spell.

And Claire Maitland wasn't just flirting with him. With her hand tucked into his arm that way, she was all but laying claim to him.

16
Noel

Of course, I'd rather be single and happy.

Addison's words played over and over in Noel's mind, and as much as he didn't want to believe what he'd heard, he couldn't ignore how sincere she'd sounded.

He'd recognized her voice as soon as he'd gotten close enough to hear it, and not wanting to interrupt, he'd pulled up short, waiting for an opportunity to break in. He had not meant to eavesdrop, just as he'd told Claire, but when Addison called herself a man repellent, he'd had to stop from launching himself around the corner to assure her that she was no such thing. At least not where he was concerned. Just the opposite, in fact. As cliché as it sounded, he'd been drawn to her like a bee to honey from the moment he'd seen her standing behind that airport ticket counter.

The rest of the afternoon in the office had been fraught with tension, especially after Paula returned. She'd been gone for over an hour before she tentatively stuck her head in the door, almost like she worried she was going to walk in on the two men duking it out. But both Noel and John were nose-to-the-grindstone at their computers, and although they both acknowledged her, not even John had much to say to her. She settled in behind her desk and got on her own computer, and for several hours, the only sounds in the office were the clicking of keyboards, papers being shuffled, and the noticeably efficient responses to the few phone calls that came into their department.

Noel had kept his head down, his gaze fixed on the charts dancing across his monitor, not even getting up to use the bathroom until it was time to call it a day. Once home, he'd recognized that he'd been in no mood to sit quietly in a theater after the imbroglio with John. But sitting around his apartment, stewing over the turmoil in his life wasn't doing him any good, either. After the childhood he'd endured, he also knew better than to head downstairs to the resort bar. The alcohol would only fuel the fire that was burning through his self-control.

He could feel Bruno's rage nipping at his heels, the terror of the boy he'd once been. The man he now was waged war against the memories. Why was his monster of a father haunting him, making him so susceptible to John's insults these days? A few months ago, he'd been able to let it all roll off his back. He knew he did his job well, and he knew part of the reason he'd been hired was because John couldn't manage it. Sure, the man's abrasive nature hadn't made things fun, but he'd been certain that over time, John would come to accept him as a team mate, even if they never became friends.

So why was Noel rising to the bait, trading insult for insult, jeopardizing this job that he'd worked hard to get, that he really wanted to keep? What had changed? Hadn't he learned how to handle small-minded, big-headed men like John?

The guy reminded him so much of Bruno; Noel didn't need a therapist to tell him as much. Unlike Bruno, John was lean and wiry and dressed in a suit and tie, but he was a bully and a manipulator through and through. Although Noel would likely never be victim to the guy's fists, he knew good and well that John had all but painted a bullseye on him.

He would not let his mind dwell on the image of punching John in the throat... it gave him too much sick pleasure.

How he wished he had someone to talk to. Not a therapist or a counselor; he'd done his time with them, and although they'd helped him find the tools that he needed to put the past behind him, to move forward into his own future without fear, what they hadn't been able to give him was friendship. It wasn't just romance he'd shelved over the last decade; his previous role performing audits for corporate had given him little opportunity to make and keep friends. Right now, he could really use one.

He finally opted to head around the lake to the bookstore to pick up the other books in *The World on Fire* series. Maybe he could get out of his own head and into someone else's for the evening.

Of course, I'd rather be single and happy.

Was it true? Is that really how Addison felt? And if so, then why had she agreed to go out with him again?

In hindsight, she *had* been slow to respond to his invitation. She'd been at work, of course, so he hadn't been expecting an immediate response. She'd also put him off for a day, which hadn't been a red flag, either, at the time. He had no doubt she had a full life before he showed up on the scene.

But now, having heard from her own mouth how she felt about being in a relationship, he couldn't help wondering. Had she just agreed to meet him again because she felt sorry for him?

Even worse, had she kissed him back the other night because he hadn't given her the option of *not* kissing him?

"Oh, stop!" he berated himself. "Talk about high school."

In the context of all that he'd managed to overhear before making his presence known, what she'd really said was that she'd rather be single and happy than in a relationship for the sake of a relationship. That was a good thing, a notion in which he wholeheartedly agreed. "Besides," he said as he closed the book he was struggling to focus on. "It's a little early in the game to be calling this a relationship, isn't it?"

Friends. He'd like to think they were at least friends. And he really needed a friend right now.

Not that he'd ever tell her about the monster in his closet. He'd never tell anyone about the father he'd left behind, a man who'd abused and humiliated his wife and son for the sick thrill of it. He'd never ask anyone to help him carry that burden; it was his and his alone to bear. If Noel had his way, Bruno would remain locked away in the dark recesses of his mind until the man did them all a favor and departed from this earth.

He's asking to see you.

"Wow. You, too?" What was with the women's voices in his head tonight? Now Aunt Gigi was talking to him, reminding him that Bruno had requested Noel's presence, only to refuse seeing him when he showed up. More cruel manipulation doled out by the one person who was supposed to put Noel's well-being above all others.

Maybe that was why he was feeling so vulnerable to John Sheridan's attacks lately. Maybe it had something to do with the fact that Bruno was once again pulling strings Noel had thought were long ago severed.

He couldn't lash out at his frail, dying father, could he? But John Sheridan? Noel felt an overwhelming desire to heap his thirty-plus years of repressed anger and resentment on the man with whom he shared an office.

Which only served to make him loathe himself. He was not a monster like his father.

Or maybe he was, and all it would take was the right person, the right trigger, to unleash that part of him that had been denied for so long.

"I hate you," he muttered through clenched teeth, his jaw tight, the muscles in his neck tense with impotence. "Why did you have to poke that stupid part of me that always hoped you'd finally, *finally* love me?"

To his dismay, hot tears formed in his eyes and began trickling down his cheeks. It had been a very long time since he'd wept for any reason, and even longer still since he'd cried over the loss of the father he'd never had.

17
Addison

ADDISON SAT IN HER car in the parking lot, phone in hand, trying to work up the courage to send the text she'd just typed into the message box. She had to do it. She had to send it now. If she waited the half an hour it took for her to get home, it would be too late.

She knew it wasn't fair to either of them to put it off any longer. If she texted him now, he'd still have time to make other plans for the evening.

"I should talk to Claire first," she said, her misery amplified in the close space of the inside of her car. If her friend confirmed her suspicion that Noel was the mystery man she had her eye on, then Addison would bow out. For one, she couldn't compete with Claire. She *wouldn't* compete with her, either. She'd loved seeing Claire gushing about the possibility of romance the way she'd done the other night, and if Noel made her that happy, then who was Addison to stand in the way?

The only plan she and Noel had was to tour the town on Saturday. It wasn't really a date, was it? Sure, he'd kissed her after their dinner out, but that was almost expected these days, wasn't it? Kissing—or even more—on the first date? And really, if she hadn't called him back up the stairs, he wouldn't have kissed her. So maybe he'd thought she was the one expecting it, that he'd only done so to oblige her.

"Ugh. An obligatory kiss." The thought made her stomach turn. Especially since it had been such a lovely, lovely kiss.

Why did dating have to be so confusing? What happened to the days when holding hands made a relationship official, when kissing was something reserved for serious dating? Addison often felt so out of touch, like she'd been born in the wrong era.

Noel, on the other hand, was a man of the world in his sleek navy suits and suede loafers, his soft leather messenger bag and precisely-trimmed hair. He smelled like high-rise conference rooms and business class lounges, and he spoke with the precise, practiced eloquence of a man who wanted to rid himself of his roots.

I get the feeling he's coming to Autumn Lake to get away from something. Or someone.

The echo of Claire's words swirled around in her mind.

Addison sent her text message, then she shoved the phone in her purse and put her car in reverse so she wouldn't be tempted to sit there and stare at her screen for a response. For the first time in years, she was grateful that it was Arnie's day off and he wouldn't be working the exit booth. She didn't want to have to try to explain the tears that she was trying desperately to blink away.

"Just why *are* you crying?" she berated herself angrily. She felt stupid for allowing herself to be so fully invested in someone she'd just begun to get to know. "You don't have the right to be hurt about this, you foolish, *foolish* creature. He doesn't belong to you."

But if Noel ended up with Claire? How would she bear it?

Her phone chimed in her purse, and she chastised herself for not turning off the sound. She couldn't even turn up her music to drown it out because her playlist required her to connect her phone. Her hand tingled with the need to root around for the device, to see his response to her cancellation of their plans. She clenched her jaw and kept her eyes fixed on the road.

At a loss for what else to do, Addison started singing loudly from the chorus of the first Bon Jovi song that came to mind. "I'm going down... in a blaze of glory!" Then she burst into tears.

She gave in and pulled over, partly because she was only torturing herself by not checking her phone, but also because it probably wasn't very safe to drive at twilight with tears blurring her vision.

I understand. I'm sorry. Maybe tomorrow night if you're feeling better?

She'd told him she wasn't feeling well and planned to make it an early night, all of which was true. She felt awful. Her stomach hurt, her head hurt, and she hadn't slept well the night before. She just wanted to go home, crawl under her covers, and put an end to this endless day.

How was she supposed to respond to that? She couldn't say she knew that she wasn't going to feel good tomorrow night, too. But now he'd seen that she'd read his message, not to respond at all would be even ruder than the way she'd just cancelled.

She thought of one of her favorite graphic t-shirts, a gift from Claire. Circling a stack of books and a cup of coffee were the words, *Sorry, I can't. I'm all booked up.* How she wished she could be that brassy in real life.

Finally, she texted, *Can I let you know tomorrow?*

He replied almost immediately. *Absolutely. I'm praying for you and the rest of your night.*

Addison's eyes blurred again as she read his response. Had any man, other than her father, ever said he was praying for her? It should have felt strange, awkward, even. She pictured him kneeling at his bedside, talking to God about her. It seemed almost too intimate to be appropriate.

Thank you, she texted back. The words were completely inadequate, but she was both overwhelmed and at a loss for what else to say. Instead, she plugged her phone into her speaker system and thumbed through her collection until she found the specific playlist she was looking for.

Songs to Sing and Cry Along With.

Then she sang—and cried—loudly all the way home.

Three hours later, Claire was practically yelling at her over the phone. She'd called as soon as she closed the bookstore for the night. "I called Juno first," she explained. "Hoping to get a feel for how she thought things were between you. I figured you wouldn't be home yet, or that you wouldn't want to be interrupted, wherever you were. But she said you two never even showed up."

Addison hadn't been asleep when she called, even though she'd made herself sleepy-time tea and had ignored the urgent need for chocolate. Instead, after tossing and turning for over an hour, she'd started scrolling through Petfinder and other online resources in search of a cat who might need her as much as she needed it. "I'm not feeling good," she said into the phone, trying not to sound defensive. Juno had called earlier, too, but Addison had let it go to voice mail. So that Juno wouldn't be worried, she'd thumbed out a quick message, telling her they'd had to reschedule last minute, but hadn't given her any more details.

"Really? What's wrong with you?" Claire's question came out more accusatory than concerned.

"There's nothing wrong with me," Addison said defensively. "I just didn't sleep well last night and I've had a bad sleep-deprivation headache all day. I didn't think I'd be good company."

"So, you're self-sabotaging," Claire shot back.

"Actually, no," Addison retorted. "I'm practicing self-care."

"By not spending time with a guy you've been mooning over for the last several months? A guy who wants to spend time with you, too?"

"And just how do you know he wants to spend time with me?" Addison threw off her covers and pushed to her feet. She couldn't sit still for this conversation.

"How do I know? Because he keeps asking you out, Addison Wedgewood. And not just for beer and pizza down at Patsy's, either. I'm talking a legitimate first date at a fancy Italian restaurant—a great first date, from what I gathered. Then a second all-day Saturday date during which he wants you to show him your town, and because the man is so besotted that he can't even wait that long to see you again, he asked to get together with you at Juno's for eclairs. Which is really quite bold, if you ask me, since he can't have missed the fact that your friends all hang out there. And he's reading the book you gave him, too," she exclaimed. "That's how I know."

Addison didn't know what to say without admitting what she knew. She turned the light on in the kitchen and filled her teapot with water. She might as well have a cup of something other than chamomile. She wouldn't be falling asleep anytime soon, not worked up the way she was now. Maybe a little caffeine would help her headache, at least.

"Addison," Claire began after a long moment of silence. She was no longer ranting. Now, she just sounded concerned. Worried, even. "Why on earth would you think he wouldn't want to spend time with you? You're right; I may not have met the guy, but from what the girls all say, he couldn't keep his eyes off of you the other night. So, what happened? Did he—did he say something stupid?"

"No. That's not it." Addison shook her head, even though Claire couldn't see it. She needed to calm down or she'd start crying again. She needed to just clear the air with her friend, period. She took a deep breath and let it out slowly. "I think he might be interested in someone else."

"Wait. What?" Claire was clearly offended on her behalf.

"Or someone else might be interested in him."

"What? Addison, who cares if anyone else is interested in him? He's interested in you."

"I care," Addison retorted. "And you have met him. In your shop."

Her announcement was met with silence. Finally, Claire said, "I'm so confused right now."

Addison set a ceramic pour-over cone onto a large red mug, then scooped some of her favorite Sumatran coffee into the filter. "The guy who came in last night while I was there. When we were straightening up the manga section."

"What?" Claire sighed loudly into the phone. "I feel like a broken record. What is going on? Start from the beginning."

So, Addison did. She ended with, "I'm not going to try to steal your mystery man, Claire."

There was no response from the other end of the line. Except... wait. Was her friend laughing?

"Are you laughing at me?"

"No, no," Claire insisted. "I'm not laughing at you. I'm not laughing at all. I'm... pondering."

When she didn't expound, Addison said, "I'll bite. What are you pondering?" The tea kettle whistled and she poured hot water over the coffee grounds, breathing in the earthy aroma that conjured up childhood memories of tropical rain forests and south pacific beaches.

"I'm pondering about how easily we humans can talk ourselves out of the good things in life."

"I'm not following you," Addison grumbled, although she thought she might have at least an idea of the direction Claire was heading.

"That man? Your Mr. Stewart?"

"He's not my Mr. Stewart," Addison interjected.

Claire's voice went soft. "Oh, honey. He's yours. I mean, I may have flirted with him a teeny tiny bit the first time he came in," she admitted, and Addison could picture her holding up her thumb and forefinger in an incremental measurement. "But let me set your mind at ease. He was and still is completely unresponsive to my oh, so considerable charm."

Addison could hardly believe that, but she said nothing, waiting to see where her friend was going.

"Why didn't you say something to me last night?" Now she sounded hurt. "Or come around and introduce us? Stake your claim on him."

"Stake my claim, Claire? Really? Because I'm the kind of person who does that." Sarcasm drenched her words, but the notion really was preposterous. "And I didn't say anything because I thought... well, I assumed he was your Mystery Man."

Claire snorted. "Good grief, woman. Don't you know that whole 'miscommunication-slash-misunderstanding' thing is the oldest and—in my humble opinion—the dumbest romance trope in the world? Besides, everyone knows what happens when you assume."

Addison pressed her lips together, still not ready to let her off the hook. "You could have said something, too, you know. I mean, you're the one who was flirting with him."

Claire made a dismissive sound, but she didn't contradict her. "Look. I'm not being facetious when I say this, but I'm sorry you misinterpreted my behavior the way you did. I wasn't trying to flirt with him. I thought he was being nosy and kinda rude standing there listening in on our conversation like that. It was none of his business, you know? So I tried to divert his attention away from you, get him to focus on something other than what he'd heard. He seemed reluctant to go, which made me even more determined, so I practically dragged him away." She sighed softly over the phone. "Now that I know who he was, I have a feeling he probably recognized your voice and was trying to decide whether or not to make his presence known to you."

Addison considered what she'd heard and seen through the lens of that explanation. The way Claire had almost flippantly dismissed Noel's claim that he hadn't meant to eavesdrop, how she'd linked arms with him, and yes, practically dragged him away. Her friend had essentially been acting on Addison's behalf, protecting her privacy.

It all rang loudly of truth. And the whole situation reeked of misguided assumptions due to a lack of communication.

"And just to set the record straight, Noel Stewart is not—nor has he ever been—my mystery man."

"He's—he's not?"

"He's not," Claire repeated. "And I forgive you for thinking I'm a shameless flirt, but only because you were willing to give up your man for our friendship."

"He's not my—"

"He is," Claire cut her off with a chuckle. "What's he's *not* is mine. At least we got that cleared up."

"So, who—"

"And no, I'm not telling you who mine is."

"I wasn't going to ask," Addison lied. She'd been about to do exactly that.

"So," Claire prodded, not even bothering to acknowledge Addison's denial. "How are you going to fix this?"

"Fix this?"

"Yes, girlie. You broke it, you fix it."

"But—how?"

"I'm going to get off the phone now so you can figure that out. We'll talk tomorrow after work, and I hope to hear good news by then. That gives you twenty-four hours, girlie."

"But—"

"I believe in you. You got this, Addison," Claire insisted. "Bye, now."

"Okay. Bye." But the call had already been disconnected.

Addison picked up her coffee mug and headed over to her sofa. She settled into the squishy cushions and pulled a chenille throw over her lap as she considered how best to untangle the mess she'd made of things. It was just after nine o'clock; was it too late to text?

She rolled her eyes so hard that she almost spilled her drink. "Are you eighty? No, it's not too late," she chided herself.

But she *was* in her pajamas. That made it *feel* later than it actually was. She glared at the phone she'd set on the couch arm rest.

"How do I fix this?"

18
Noel

Noel sat slouched in the armchair in his suite, watching a game he had no interest in. Maybe he should call it an early night. He needed his head on straight in order to deal with John again tomorrow. "One more day," he muttered under his breath, and then he'd have the weekend off and he'd be spending as much of it as he could with Addison Wedgewood.

"If she's feeling better," he reminded himself. Her cancellation of their plans that night had been a major disappointment, but he'd forced himself not to entertain any negative thoughts about why, just to take her reason at face value. She hadn't been feeling well, period.

He checked his phone again, but there was nothing from Addison. There was, however, the unanswered text he'd gotten from Aunt Gigi that had come in more than an hour ago. It had stirred up the embers of anger and resentment inside of Noel, and he'd found himself unable to come up with an appropriate response.

Bruno is asking for you again. I promised him I'd tell you. I understand if you don't want to come.

He stared at the words, recognizing them for what they were. She hadn't said "if you *can't* come." She knew he would be there if he wanted to be there. But she also knew without having to ask that he did *not* want to be there, and she didn't begrudge him his reasons.

Noel turned off the television and headed for the bathroom. He'd already finished the book Addison had given him, a moving tale of coming of age during the Great Depression, but he had Book 2 in *The World on Fire* series he could dig into. Had Addison read them yet, he wondered?

An hour later, his eyelids were growing heavy, but the story of the intrepid freedom fighters in *The World in Darkness* had him locked in.

The book took the reader deep into the belly of the earth, traversing the miles and miles of mine shafts that led from one underground community to another, small towns that had sprung up out of the dark as humanity found ways to survive below the scorched surface of the earth. Noel didn't even have to try to imagine what it was like down there. He'd been into the mines himself so many times, and reading the books gave him an odd sense of déjà vu. The descriptions and scenes were so profoundly accurate that it felt a little like traversing a parallel universe.

He jerked awake with a start, his heart pounding, his forehead damp with sweat, and his hands balled into fists. The book lay facedown on the blanket beside him where it had tumbled from his lap when he drifted off. Noel kicked off the covers and swung his feet over the side of the bed, pushing up to sitting, forcing himself to come out of the dream completely.

He'd been racing through the shafts, his headlamp growing dimmer at every turn, lost and terrified of what was coming after him. Sometimes, he'd caught glimpses of a raging, open-mouthed Bruno charging after him in the dark, other times, an army of undead creatures that had scrabbled their way out of hell itself. The tunnel he'd been in when he'd crashed out of the dream and back into his suite had taken a sudden, sharp descent into a black pit that echoed with the tortured calls for help from people stranded below, buried in rubble. It had felt like a chasm of hopelessness opening up at his feet, and behind him, John Sheridan stood with a phone in one hand, a short-handled miner's pick axe in the other. Noel had turned to face him, but John's headlamp had burned so bright and hot that it had blinded him. He'd raised his arms to cover his eyes, the movement knocking him off-balance, and he'd felt himself begin the terrible tumble backwards into the pit.

"Lord, please," he murmured, covering his face with his hands. "Help." He didn't know what else to ask.

The last few days in the office had been a study in walking on eggshells. All three of them were on their best behavior, chatting little and staying busy. But the tension was so thick that it was like trying to walk underwater.

John kept his phone out on his desk in a visibly prominent spot, almost like he was mocking Noel. Why didn't the guy turn the recording in? Or was that not the point? Was he just trying to keep Noel guessing?

Paula, he'd noticed, had found more than one excuse not to join John in his office to talk, and the few times they'd exchanged more than a few sentences, they'd either done so on the phone, or she'd stood in the doorway of his office, almost like a line had been drawn that she was suddenly afraid to cross. It was odd, Noel thought, but maybe the woman wasn't quite as blinded by the man's machinations as Noel had originally assumed.

Noel wasn't interested in playing games, so he didn't pretend that everything was just fine the way John seemed determined to do. He came in, picked up any messages or paperwork Paula had for him, then headed to his own desk where he plugged in. If John's goal was to stress Noel out by not addressing the elephant in the room... well, he was succeeding. But there was no way Noel was going to give the man the pleasure of knowing it.

Needless to say, his office had become the last place on earth Noel wanted to be. He was having difficulty finding satisfaction in completing his tasks, in balancing the books, in planning and preparing budgets. The thrill of ferreting out problem areas and creating solutions seemed to elude him these days. He was beginning to hate his job.

Noel stood up and stretched, rotating his head right and left, working the crick out of his neck from falling asleep reading. His stomach grumbled, not from hunger, but from stress, and he headed to the kitchen for a glass of water and an Alka-Seltzer. He wasn't sure if the stuff even worked, but it gave him something to focus on.

Something had to give. This couldn't go on. His sleep was disrupted on a regular basis, and Noel was not the kind of guy who could go night after night without a full seven or eight hours of shut-eye. He was meeting his deadlines at work, sure, but there was no sense of achievement there. Not like back when he worked audits for corporate. One of the things he'd loved about working for corporate was the ever-changing aspects of his job. He and his team would travel to different hotels or resorts, perform their external audits, create tasks and systems to be implemented, then move on. Each new assignment brought new challenges, new faces, new circumstances, and Noel had thrived on that. He'd known taking an internal auditing position would come with a little of the drudgery of monotony, but he hadn't expected it to feel like this.

"Maybe I'm just not cut out for permanency," he said aloud as he watched the activated seltzer tablet fizz crazily in the tumbler of water. "Maybe I made a mistake in taking this position."

Noel sighed and dropped into one of the chairs at the dining table. "I don't know how to fix this," he said, then took a big gulp of the soda water, his jaw tightening against the medicinal tang of it.

He should just confront John. Ask him what they could do to get to the other side of this.

Noel shook his head. He had a feeling it was too late for that. The gauntlet, so to speak, had been thrown down the other day, and there now seemed to be a chasm between the men, one with no way across.

Exactly how things felt between Noel and his father.

This was Bruno's fault.

It was always Bruno's fault.

His father's request had made him want to punch something. Worse, it had made him want to punch John, and that had been even more unnerving than the thought of Bruno asking to see him. His rage felt like it sat just below the surface these days, like it might only take a spark to ignite, and then it would burn like a wildfire out of control.

That could never happen.

He couldn't let it.

He wouldn't let it.

He would not become his father.

• ❤ • ❤ • ❤ • ❤ • ❤ •

GOOD MORNING, NOEL. JUST *wanted to let you know I'm feeling better. I'm at work today.*

Noel closed his eyes and sank back in his chair after reading Addison's text a second time. His relief was so great that it almost scared him.

Her cancellation of plans last night had been a major disappointment, but he'd forced himself not to entertain any negative thoughts about why, just to take her reason at face value. If she said she hadn't been feeling well, then he needed to believe her.

His phone pinged again. *Thank you for your prayers.*

He needed to respond. *I'm so glad to hear it. And thank you for letting me know. I was worried.* Was that too much? He didn't care. He sent the message.

A few moments later, her response came through. *I'm better. Please don't worry. Can we try again tonight? Or should we just plan on getting together tomorrow?*

"Yes!" Noel declared in a loud whisper as he sat forward in his chair and spun around so that John and Paula couldn't see him interacting with his phone. Not because he was doing anything wrong, but because it was none of their business. Somehow, he'd made it through the week without any more incidents with John, and he wanted to keep it that way.

He did not feel like waiting until the morning to see Addison again. In fact, he was going to have a hard time waiting through the rest of the day to see her this evening. *How about dinner at the Lux Solaris here? They make an amazing apple cobbler and serve it on very fancy plates.* He'd had the dessert with his meal several times; he couldn't get enough of it.

It took a few minutes, but Addison finally responded with, *I actually make a pretty mean apple cobbler, myself. I don't have any fancy plates, but would you like to come to my place for supper, instead?*

"Yes!" he exclaimed again. "Absolutely, yes." Of course, that wasn't what he sent her. He sounded much cooler in his text message. *That sounds great. What can I bring?*

The conversation ended when Addison texted that a line was forming at her counter. *I'll see you at 6:30.*

19
Addison

"So, I have another date tonight," Addison said to Natalie as they stood at their respective stations behind the ticket counter. Addison's shift was ending soon, but Natalie hadn't gotten in until noon, and they'd been running non-stop since. Right now, they had a short reprieve, and although Addison had given her friend a hint about things heading in a positive direction, she'd been holding in her good news all afternoon.

Natalie eyed her suspiciously. "With your Lake Man? Or someone else?"

"He isn't my Lake Man," Addison countered. "But I'm kinda hoping I won't be able to say that much longer," she said with a cheeky grin.

Natalie clapped her hands and turned from her monitor to give Addison her full attention. "I take it that means your dating your Lake Man tonight."

"I'm going on a date with Noel Stewart tonight, yes." She paused and reworded things. "Or rather, he's coming on a date with me. I'm cooking for him."

Natalie gasped and covered her mouth, her eyes wide. "Cooking for him? That is next level, you know. What exactly are you cooking?" She shook a finger at her. "You know this could either make or break the deal with a man, right?"

Addison giggled. "My thoughts exactly. I'm going tried and true home-cooking all the way around. My scrumptious hamburger soup—it's already in the crock pot."

"Yum," sighed Natalie, who'd reaped the benefits of being Addison's friend over the years as she'd learned to cook. Addison frequently made far more food than she could possibly eat on her own, and Natalie was the recipient of many of those leftovers. "I love your hamburger soup. Please tell me you made way too much."

"You know I did," Addison said, scribbling a heart on the corner of a used ticket stub and handing it to Natalie. "I also made bread last night, so even though it won't be hot out of the oven, it's fresh. Crusty, rustic, perfect for dipping in soup bread. Or maybe I'll make grilled cheese with it. That would go really well with the soup, don't you think?"

"Either way, you made two loaves, right?" Natalie held up two fingers.

"Of course." Addison shifted to lean her hip against the counter. "And he told me the restaurant at the resort makes a really good apple cobbler, so I promised him one of mine."

"Oh, my," Natalie sighed dramatically. "You know he's going to propose the moment he takes a bite of that. You're going to come to work tomorrow with a great big ring on your finger. I'd marry you for that pie if I were single." She grew serious. "So, what happened with him and Claire?"

Addison had shared her fears about Noel being Claire's mystery man. Natalie had encouraged her not to jump to conclusions, but she'd also agreed that it all looked and sounded a little suspicious to her. "It was a mistake," Addison said with a grimace before explaining what had happened. "You were right. I made assumptions that weren't accurate. Claire lectured me on communication. Essentially told me not to be such a trope."

Natalie chuckled. "I really like that girl. So, this is a kiss-and-make-up date, then?"

Addison rolled her eyes. "Hardly. He doesn't know I made an idiot of myself, so no. There will be no making up tonight."

"But there will be kissing?" Natalie teased.

Addison shrugged. "I guess we'll find out, won't we?" Her cheeks warmed at the thought, and she reached up to press her palms to them. Natalie leaned forward and hugged her tightly.

"I love seeing you like this, Addison Wedgewood. You're just all lit up inside. And you were so sad yesterday. I'm glad you sorted things out." She stepped back and glanced at the time on the monitor. "Fifteen more minutes to go, girl. I'm so excited for you!"

"Excuse me?" A woman with a cloud of silver and white hair approached the counter at a speed walk, her peach leather purse slipping off her shoulder in her haste. In her arms she held a cobalt glazed pot over the top of which spilled a plant with thick, paddle-shaped leaves, some of them tipped with burgundy.

"What a gorgeous plant," Addison exclaimed, switching into her professional mode and flashing the woman a bright smile. Taking live plants on planes wasn't prohibited, but the airline did have pretty clear guidelines on how they were to be handled in transit. Like any other carry-on item, it would have to fit in the overhead compartment or under the seat in front of the woman, and the whole thing needed to be wrapped in a plastic bag or in a closed container to prevent soil or moisture from spilling out of it.

"Oh, thank you." The woman hugged the pot, then ran a fingertip along the curve of a leaf. "This is a crassula ovata. A jade plant. She's a beauty, isn't she?"

"Where are you heading with her?" Addison asked, playing along. The plant did kind of look feminine with all its curves and blushing leaves. She smiled at the woman; this was how she pictured herself someday in her daydreams. A plant-hugging, cat-collecting cheery old lady.

"Right here, I believe," the woman said, a slight drawl pulling on her words. "I'm Hannah from The Daisy Chain. I'm looking for—" she broke off to flip over a tag hanging from the side of the pot. "Addison Wedgewood." Hannah looked up at them, her gaze moving back and forth between Addison and Natalie. "Would that be either one of you?"

Natalie was already pointing with both hands at Addison.

"I—I'm Addison," she said, her voice trembling a little. She was having trouble processing what the woman was saying. Who would be sending her a plant? Maybe one of her Garden Variety Lovers Club friends back in Autumn Lake? But why at work? It wasn't her birthday.

Hannah pressed her free hand to her sternum and let out a hefty sigh of relief. "Oh, thank goodness," she said, stepping forward to put the pot on the counter. "I was supposed to deliver this to you first thing this morning, but it somehow got put into a display case at the shop. We found it this afternoon while restocking, and I am just mortified. As soon as I realized our mistake, I hopped in my van and brought it directly to you. She's too precious, isn't she? Just look at her. Cute as a button." Hannah leaned in a little and said with a wink, "I won't lie, dear. I considered taking this beauty home with me."

"It's for—for me?" Addison stammered.

"Yes, silly," Natalie said, squeezing Addison's arm. "It's for you. And I bet I know who it's from, too. Read the card."

Hannah's eyes brightened with anticipation. "I love deliveries like this. Not the late part, mind you; the happy part." She pressed her hands together in a prayer-like fashion. Evidently, she wanted to know who the plant was from, too. "So often, I take bouquets and plants to sad events. I just get such a kick when a delivery is a happy surprise."

Addison's hands trembled slightly as she plucked the pretty envelope from the plastic holder stuck into the edge of the pot. She peeled open the flap and slipped the little card out, then read it silently.

"Out loud," Natalie demanded, looking like she might reach over and snatch it from her hands if she didn't comply.

"I'm glad you're feeling better. I'm looking forward to this evening." Addison looked up at her friend. "That's it."

Natalie let out a huff. "Aaaaand?" She drew the word out. "I'm going to assume this, but is it from the lovely Mr. Stewart?"

Addison could feel warmth creeping up her neck. She shrugged and nodded, then held out the card for Natalie to see. "'From Noel,' it says."

"Is that a heart?" Natalie jabbed a finger at the card.

"No," Addison declared, pressing the card to her chest. "It's a leaf in the design on the card."

"That is such a sweet message," Hannah interjected. "Is Noel your young man?"

"She's working on that," Natalie said with a capricious smile.

"Nat!"

"Well, whatever you're doing, honey, it looks like it's working." Hannah reached over and tapped the shop tag still hanging from the pot. "When you're ordering your wedding flowers, you remember The Daisy Chain. We do fabulous bridal bouquets. And I guarantee you, we won't come at the wrong time," she said with a self-deprecating chortle.

Addison opened and closed her mouth twice before she managed to squawk, "It's a little early for that."

Hannah shook her head, then reached over and patted Addison's hand. "There is no time frame on love, Addison Wedgewood. When Cupid lets that arrow fly, you might as well surrender. He's a perfect shot every time."

"Who said anything about love?" Addison shot back. "And I wouldn't say Cupid's such a great shot. I've seen a lot of hits and misses in the game of love, Miss Hannah."

"Oh, honey. He may not always choose his targets with their best interest at heart, but he never misses. Take it from me. The Daisy Chain is part of the business of love, and I know when Cupid's been up to his tricks." She leaned closer and patted Addison's hand again.

"Oh, Miss Hannah," Natalie said, stepping around the counter to give the woman a quick side hug. "I think I like you. A whole lot. And let me tell you; I'm going to be looking up The Daisy Chain myself one day soon."

"Well, isn't it my lucky day." Hannah pulled a silver business card holder from her purse and handed each of them a card with her name on it. "Ask for me personally—otherwise, you might get my daughter. She's a good florist, but even she'll admit that weddings are my forte."

To Addison, she said, "And you, my dear. Jades are one of the easiest house plants to care for. It's all on the tag there, but here are a few tips." She counted things off on her raised fingers. "If you're comfortable, she'll be comfortable. If you don't want her to get too big, just keep her in that pot. As far as watering, just stick your finger into the soil about an inch. If it comes out dry, she needs a drink. But generally, you can water her deeply about once a week." She brushed her hands together, and added, "And that's about it."

"Wow. That's it?" Addison asked. Could it really be that simple? "What about plant food? Or fertilizer or stuff like that?"

"Well, you can always give it a little scoop of used coffee grounds a couple of times a month. Succulents like coffee almost as much as we humans do." Hannah winked at her. "Used green or black tea leaves will also work if you're one of those weirdos who don't drink coffee."

Natalie clapped her hands. "You tell it like it is, Miss Hannah." To Addison, she said, "Girl, are you going to call that man right now to thank him?"

"I'm still on the clock," Addison hedged.

"At least text him to let him know you got this. He's probably sitting in his room, chewing his nails, wondering why you haven't called to thank him. He sent it this morning."

"And I'm so sorry about that again, honey," Hannah interjected. "I called him to let him know, and of course, I refunded his money. I just got his voicemail, though."

"Hey, Miss Hannah." Natalie nudged the older woman and gave her conspiratorial wink. "I find it intriguing that he sent our Addison here a living plant, don't you?" To Addison, she said, "Not cut flowers or something that will shrivel up and die. Oh no. He sent you a living, breathing plant for you to put in your home so that you will think of him every time you pass by it."

"Mmm-hmm," Hannah agreed coyly. "Very intriguing."

"You two are too much." Addison came around the counter and hugged Hannah, too, though. "Thank you. Especially thank you for making a special trip out here to bring this to me."

"I'm just so glad I caught you before you left for the day. He said you got off work at four." Hannah tapped her watch and blew out a relieved breath. "I just made it, didn't I?"

Natalie picked up Addison's phone from the counter and handed it to her. "At least text him right now and tell him you'll call him when you get home."

"I'll text him," Addison said, nodding.

Natalie and Hannah both stared at her, their expressions a perfect match.

"What?"

Natalie mimed pulling out her own phone and thumbing out a text, dramatically hitting the imaginary send button on her imaginary phone.

"Right now? With you two watching? No way," Addison declared. "I have to think about what to say. I don't want him to think I'm being too assertive."

"Oh. Because inviting him over for a home-cooked meal at your place isn't assertive at all."

"You did what?" Hannah asked, pressing a hand to her chest and ogling Addison. Then to Natalie she said, "She's already cooking for him?"

"She is, indeed. Meat and potatoes and apple cobbler, the little hussy."

Hannah let out a shocked gasp, and Addison wasn't quite sure if it was feigned or not.

"Wow, you two. Seriously? It's just food."

"There is no such thing as 'just food' when it comes to dating, my dear," Hannah countered, patting Addison's cheek. "Cooking for each other is a major step in the time-honored tradition of the mating dance."

"The mate—" Addison gasped, her words breaking off in a squeak. "I'm not—we're not—this isn't a m—mating dance."

"Tell her why you're cooking apple cobbler for him," Natalie demanded.

"What do you mean?" Addison said, frowning at her friend. "He said he liked it, so I'm making it."

"Ha," chortled Natalie. "It's a whole lot more than that, girl. He said he liked the one the fancy restaurant makes so you're showing him what a real cobbler tastes like."

"Very clever," Hannah said, wiggling her penciled-on eyebrows.

"It wasn't clever," Addison insisted. "I just make a good cobbler and thought he'd like it. I was trying to be thoughtful and cook things he likes. I was being nice," she added, wishing she didn't feel so compelled to defend herself. Although it was probably because what they were saying was pretty much spot on. She *did* want Noel to taste her cobbler, and she wanted him to never want another bite of the Lux Solaris cobbler again after tasting hers.

"*Very* nice, it sounds like," Hannah declared, her brows still dancing.

Natalie cackled gleefully at the older woman's sass.

"You know what?" Addison asked, shaking her head in surrender. She pulled out her phone, but instead of texting, she said, "It's close enough to four. I'm taking my plant and going home." Beyond Hannah, she could see Jennifer Tulley heading their way, straightening her name badge on her uniform in preparation for taking over for her behind the counter. "I'll text Noel when I get to my car."

"What? No!" Natalie exclaimed. "You can't deprive us like—"

Addison's phone beeped with a text message notification. All three of them froze. She slowly peered down at the screen. "It's him," she whispered.

"What did he say?" Natalie started bouncing up and down with anticipation.

"I can only read the first part, but I don't want to open it yet because I don't want him to see that I've read it so quickly." Her heart began to race.

"Why not?" Hannah asked, her brows furrowed. "That makes no sense to me. The man sent you a gift. Do him the honor of acknowledging it. Just because I messed up and left you hanging doesn't mean you should leave him hanging."

Addison felt almost reprimanded by the woman. "You don't think it'll make me seem... desperate?"

"No," scoffed Hannah. "It'll make you seem polite." Natalie nodded in agreement.

Addison slid open the message.

Hi Addison. Hope you're having a great day.

"He—he didn't mention the plant." Addison held the phone out so the other two women could read the text.

"He's waiting for you to mention it," Natalie told her.

"Well, what should I say?" she asked, but before they could respond, her phone pinged again.

I'm looking forward to spending this evening with you. I haven't stopped thinking about it—and you—all day.

"Thank him for the plant, you dork!" Natalie grabbed her arm and shook her. "As Miss Hannah said, don't leave the poor man hanging."

So, under the exuberant guidance of her unlikely coaching team, Addison thumbed out a response. *Hi Noel. My already great day got even better when Miss Hannah from The Daisy Chain got here. Thank you for the gorgeous jade! I'm looking forward to dinner, too.* The last line had been on Hannah and Natalie's insistence, and Addison hit 'Send' before she convinced them to let her delete it.

Noel's response came back in no more time than it must have taken him to tap out his message. *I'm glad you like it. I remember you said you were afraid you'd kill a plant, but jades are supposed to be super easy to take care of, so I thought it would be the perfect first plant for you. Besides, it reminded me of that necklace you always wear. The tree with the jade leaves.*

"Girrrrl," Natalie cooed.

"He sounds like a keeper to me," Hannah chirped.

Addison just smiled, at a loss for words to describe how she felt. She reached up to toy with the pendant hanging around her neck. Not only was he a good listener, but he noticed things like her necklace. She felt both seen and heard in a way she hadn't by a man in as long as she could remember.

Another text appeared. *I'm bringing a book to share with you; is that okay?*

"Oh, my heart," Natalie said, sighing on each word. "You'd better snap that up. The man wants to talk about books with you?"

Addison giggled. "Right? I mean, a week ago, the guy didn't even know I existed."

"Well, I wouldn't say that," Natalie countered, wiggling her eyebrows suggestively. "Our self-serve kiosks aren't *that* unreliable, and he always goes to your counter, not mine. He knew you existed, girlie. No doubt about it."

Hannah tapped Addison's phone. "You need to answer that boy. Right now. Don't leave him hanging."

20
Noel

The lights of downtown Autumn Lake sparkled against the night sky in the town's muted reflection shimmering off the lake. Even in winter, Noel thought, with the bare-branched trees and the quiet streets, it really was a charming scene. He could see why Addison liked coming home to this place at the end of the day.

He was more comfortable getting around the little town now that he was spending time over on the south shore. There simply weren't that many streets to get lost on, and the majority of the businesses that stayed open during the off-tourist season were fairly centrally located. "Everything is within walking distance," Addison had said on more than one occasion. "If I didn't have to drive for work, I might not even own a car."

Noel turned into the little alley and spotted Addison's upstairs deck festooned with twinkle lights. As he neared her parking spots, he realized she was standing at the top of the stairs, her shoulders draped in a fluffy, colorful shawl that fell around her almost to her knees. She wore her hair down and in one hand, she held a mug of something presumably warm in it. She waved as he pulled in and parked.

They exchanged helloes as he got out of his car and started up the steps. He'd taken note when she'd said she wasn't much of a drinker, and this evening, instead of wine, he'd brought a chilled bottle of fancy carbonated Rose Lemonade with him.

At the top of the stairs, Addison stood back to let him pass, but he paused in front of her. "You're a lovely sight for sore eyes," he said to her, and he meant it. He'd imagined this moment all day, sitting across the shared offices from John. Her smile was warm and open, and beneath the shawl, he was glad to see she had on comfortable, casual clothes. He'd dressed in jeans and a Henley, and had hoped it would be appropriate. He tried not to look too long at her pretty pink lips; he didn't want her to know how much he wanted to pull her close and kiss her again. "I hope this is okay?" he said, hoping his voice sounded steadier than he felt. He held out the bottle for her to see.

Addison took it from him. "It's perfect. I've never had this before. Thank you." She sounded as nervous as he felt.

He took a moment to look around the sparkly deck, appreciating her eclectic style. There was a small round table with a mosaic pattern on the top and two matching chairs. A lantern sat on the table, a jumble of tiny stringed lights inside it rather than a candle. An old fruit crate sat on end with a basket of magazines tucked inside, and hanging from the roof beam overhead was one of those nest chairs made of knotted rope with a colorful cushion in the seat. "Very cool," he said, nodding at the arrangement.

"Very cool," she echoed, wrapping an arm around herself, and shivering dramatically. "Freezing, in fact. Are you hungry?"

"I'm starving," he admitted with a self-conscious chuckle. His stomach loudly validated his words, making Addison grin.

"Then you've come to the right place. Come in, come in. It's cold out here." She lifted the mug in a gesture toward the open front door, and her shawl slid from one shoulder. Noel reached for the end of it before it dragged on the ground and gently arranged it back in place around her neck. He thought she shivered under his touch; he hoped that was a good thing.

He followed her inside the apartment, pausing just inside the door to let his eyes wander around the space, a combination kitchenette, dining, and living room. The deck had been only the top of the eclectic iceberg compared to the inside of her home. Bold colors and delicate patterns combined to make the room feel both cozy and creative. None of the artwork matched, the furniture was grouped together in surprising ways that somehow worked. Parts of the wood floor shone at the edges of a collection of vintage carpets, and in one corner of the room was a beanbag chair the size of a loveseat.

"That's my favorite place to read," Addison said, following his gaze. "On winter mornings, the sun comes in that window and warms the room up nicely. In summer, I'm usually out on my deck with my coffee." Her expression shone with pride over her little domain.

"This is amazing, all this color and style. It suits you."

"Thank you," she said, her voice coming out a little breathless. She slipped out of her shawl and draped it on a coatrack, then continued while he followed suit. "I do love this place. I've totally made it mine. I don't own it, of course, but it's mine while I'm here, and my landlord pretty much lets me have free reign."

"For good reason," Noel declared. Then he saw the plant on the kitchen counter next to the sink. "Is that—?" he asked, pointing at it.

"Isn't she the cutest?" Addison asked, her cheeks pinking prettily. She crossed over to it and rubbed a waxy leaf between her thumb and finger. Shyly, she said, "I've named her. Emerald, because of the color, but Emmy for short."

Noel nodded. "Emmy. I like that." He felt a little silly talking about the plant that way, but the smile on her face as she looked adoringly at the thing made it all worth it.

She asked him to pour their drinks while she dished up their food. "It's simple fare tonight," she said. "Nothing fancy. Just hamburger soup and grilled cheese."

"Sounds amazing to me," he replied. It smelled amazing to him, too, the aromas rich and heavy in the air around them. He saw the look of surprise on her face when he held her chair for her, but she thanked him softly and waited until he sat before she took a sip of the pink lemonade he'd brought.

"Oh, wow," she exclaimed, her eyes sparkling. "This is yummy. Zingy!"

Noel chuckled as he, too, tasted the bright, refreshing soda. "Good word. You should try their ginger beer. Talk about zingy."

Regardless of who he was with, Noel always bowed his head and offered up a quick, silent prayer of gratitude for the Lord's provision before his meals. He'd never truly gone hungry as a boy, and he knew that was more than some in his childhood community could say. His mother had made miracles happen in the kitchen with what little they had, often going without herself so that Bruno would have his fill. And Aunt Gigi had taken it upon herself to supplement Noel's nutrition with afterschool snacks that were essentially full meals. Sure, there had been a lot of processed filler foods, but both women had grown large kitchen gardens, and he'd learned to eat his vegetables early on. He'd also learned to thank the women who prepared his food, and to thank the good Lord for providing the food for them to prepare.

But he noticed Addison pause, too, after she set her glass down. Sure, she could be waiting to see if he had everything he needed, but something in his spirit recognized it for what it was. Or what he hoped it might be. He took a chance. "Would you like me to say a blessing?"

"I—I'd like that," she said, her stammer not one of nervousness, he decided, but of unexpected pleasure.

As Noel bowed his head, the savory aroma of his meal wafting around him, there was nothing ritualistic or trite about his prayer of gratitude. In a few heartfelt words, he thanked God for the delicious food, for Addison's skill in the kitchen, and asked the Lord to be a part of every minute of their evening together. The prayer was short and simple, just as it usually was, but his heart overflowed with the knowledge that he was not alone in this world.

As he lifted his head, he realized that his shoulders were relaxed, his hands loose in his lap. This place, this woman, being here with her was a balm to his soul today. He smiled over at her, wishing he could tell her as much.

Across from him, Addison studied him, her gaze soft, evidently waiting for him to start first. Noel picked up his spoon. "This smells incredible, Addison."

"Thank you," she murmured, then they dug in, almost simultaneously.

It was, indeed, as delicious as it smelled. With the first spoonful of the soup, Noel closed his eyes and reveled in the flavors that filled his mouth. The broth was rich and spicy, but with a slight tang to it that gave him a juvenile desire to lift the bowl and drink the stuff. The vegetables were well-cooked but not mushy, and the ground beef was extra tender.

"This is not 'just hamburger soup,' Addison. And I already know this isn't just grilled cheese." He held up the thick slice of toasted bread with melted cheese on top, a thin slice of tomato in the center of it. "Would it be sacrilege to dip this?"

Addison laughed self-consciously. "Not at all. Although I can't promise it won't leave crumbs in your soup."

Noel didn't care about that. The combination of the buttery, yeasty bread, the aromatic roasted cheese, and whatever spread she'd put on it with the savory tang of the soup made him close his eyes again in wonder. "Wow," he murmured when he'd swallowed the enormous bite he'd taken. "Just wow."

"It's not too spicy?" she asked, even though he thought it was obvious he didn't find anything wrong with it. "I use cayenne pepper and smoked paprika in the soup, and sometimes it can be a little much. But I add some brown sugar to offset it. That's Havarti cheese on the sandwich, one of my favorites, and instead of butter, I use homemade aioli. If you don't like the tomato on top, just pull it off. I promise I won't be offended. I hope it's good." She was, indeed, nervous, he realized. She had absolutely no reason to be.

"Perfect." He set the open-faced sandwich down and wiped his fingers on his napkin. "I think this might be the best meal I've ever had in my life," he told her. And he meant it.

When she brought out the apple cobbler topped with creamy dulce de leche ice cream, Noel thought he'd just about died and gone to heaven. "It's my grandmother's recipe," she told him. "On my mom's side. My mom isn't much of a cook, but she made sure I knew how to make Grandma's apple cobbler the right way. And she insists that it's best eaten with dulce de leche ice cream. It's her favorite ice cream in the world, though, so she'll eat it with anything. Or by itself."

It truly was like no other cobbler he'd ever had before, and the ice cream did, indeed, pair perfectly with it. The Lux Solaris cobbler he'd thought was so good didn't even hold a candle to Addison's, and he effused so much about it that she finally threatened never to make it for him again if he didn't stop.

They cleared the table and cleaned up the small kitchen, working effortlessly together like they'd been doing it for years. He was curious about her job, and she regaled him with crazy stories about some of the travelers she'd interacted with over the years at the regional airport.

Once they were settled on the sofa in Addison's cozy living room, Noel brought up the subject of *The World on Fire* series he was reading. "It's post-apocalypse stuff, and you may not like the genre, but have you heard of it?"

Addison's eyes were bright as she listened to him. "I haven't just heard of it; I've read it," she said with a nod. She set her coffee cup down on the coffee table in front of them and got up to circle the couch. From a bookshelf nearby, she pulled out two hardcover novels and hugged them to her chest. "You're right in guessing that I'm not a huge post-apocalypse or sci-fi reader." She plopped back into her corner of the sofa and set the books on the cushion between them. She leaned toward him, and put a hand to the side of her mouth as though divulging a secret. "But I happen to be tight with the author, so I took a chance on it. And wow. Am I glad I did." She flipped open the cover of *The World on Fire* and nudged the book toward him.

"Wait. You're saying that you know Arnold Archer personally?" Noel asked, staring wide-eyed down at the author's signature. "Claire, right? Is that her name? At the bookstore here in town?" Addison nodded and he continued. "She said he was a local boy, but I didn't realize just how local." Was this Archer guy competition? The look on Addison's face told him he might get a run for his money with the author.

Grinning broadly, Addison held up two fingers pressed together. "We're like this."

Hmm. He would not be jealous. He cleared his throat. "Is it a trilogy? Is there a third book yet?"

"A trilogy, yes. At least that's what he says. I have a feeling his fans are going to want more, though. The third one isn't out yet; Arnie says it's supposed to release this fall, though. I can hardly wait. I'll probably reread the first two books before then, just to be in the zone." She eyed the empty mug he'd set down on the coffee table beside hers. "Would you like some more coffee?" She started to get up, but he stopped her with a hand on her knee.

"Wait a minute," Noel said, staring down at the flyleaf again. "Tight with the author, you say? As in, how tight?" He pointed at the elegantly scrawled words on the page.

21
Addison

ADDISON GIGGLED AT THE half-serious expression on Noel's face. "It's not a proposal," she said, having forgotten until that moment that Arnie had scribbled the words, *Let's live on a prayer together,* above his signature.

"Looks pretty close to one to me," Noel quipped. It came out sounding almost like an accusation, and Addison shook her head as she settled more comfortably into her spot.

"I was listening to my music in my car and he heard it," she explained, feeling a little self-conscious about the admission. "I have a thing for 80's hair bands."

Noel furrowed his brow. "I'm so lost. This Arnold Archer guy just happened to be walking by—or driving by?—your car and overheard the music you were playing? I'm assuming it was Bon Jovi."

"It was, yes," she said, grinning at his attempt to reason it out.

"So he just happened to overhear it... and then what? He pulled out a book and signed it for you?"

Addison laughed and shook her head. "For your information, a lot of authors have day jobs. Arnie is one of those authors."

Noel picked the book up and waved it between them. "This guy has a day job? This is good stuff, Addison. I know mines—my father was a miner—and this guy knows mines, too. Maybe even better than I do."

"Well, he should. He's a retired miner, too, after all."

"So..." Noel dragged the word out, clearly having a hard time accepting her words at face value. "Are you telling me that he works with you at the airport?"

"Not exactly *with* me, but at the airport, yes." She was enjoying doling out the juicy bits a little at a time. "And I bet you two have crossed paths several times."

"Okay. Now you're just being cruel." Noel put down the book and crossed his arms.

Addison's mouth went momentarily dry as he cocked his head and gave her what she could only call 'sad puppy dog eyes.' He was so cute, so boy-next-door handsome, that she was finding it hard to take a deep breath. "Maybe I shouldn't tell you," she managed to say with a cheeky grin. "I mean, he does use a pen name. Maybe he wouldn't want me telling anyone."

Noel scooted a little closer to her and stuck out his bottom lip.

"Oh, my goodness," she snorted, covering her eyes with both hands. "That is the most pitiful expression I've ever seen. Stop it."

"I won't tell anyone," he cajoled. From between her hands, she saw him hold up three fingers. "Scout's honor."

"Are you even a scout?" she challenged.

"Depends on who's asking."

"I am, you dork." She dropped her hands and gave him a mock threatening glare. "Fine. I'll tell you. But if you betray my trust...."

"I would never," he vowed, crossing his heart.

"Arnold Archer is the pen name for Arnie Bowman."

"Ah. I see what he did there. Bowman. Archer. Nice." Then he lifted his gaze to the ceiling, clearly trying to sort things out. "I know that name. Both names, obviously. But I feel like I actually know who Arnie Bow—Arnie!" He spun back to her, his eyes going wide with surprise. "Arnie at the parking lot exit? Super friendly guy at the ticket booth, right? That's Arnold Archer?"

Addison was grinning again, nodding slowly, feeling remarkably proud of her friend. "He's brilliant, don't you think?"

"Yes. Brilliant, yes!" Noel exclaimed. "What is he doing sitting in that ticket booth?" he asked, stunned by the revelation.

"He's writing books; that's what he's doing," she declared. "And he's writing books *because* he's sitting in a ticket booth, according to Arnie. He took the job because once he retired, he found he was terribly bored, and he was starting to drive his wife crazy being at home all the time. He thought it would be a nice change for him to sit there in the sunshine all day greeting folks. You know, after working so hard underground all his life. But then he started to get bored in the booth, too. So now he brings his laptop and writes his books in between cars passing through his line."

Noel shook his head in disbelief. "I'm... flabbergasted."

"Next time you leave the airport, you be sure and tell him how much you like his books. He still can't believe people read them, even though Claire says they fly off the shelf."

A strange expression crossed Noel's face. "Speaking of Claire and the bookshop, I'm a little surprised we haven't run into each other here in town before. It sounds like you're in The Cracked Spine fairly often, and I've been going in there a lot lately."

"Oh, well, I'm sure we've just been in at different times," she said a little breathlessly. Had he seen her in there the other night? She'd been so sure he hadn't.

"Actually," Noel continued, moving the books to the coffee table and turning in his seat a little so that he could look more directly at her. "I think you were there the other night when I stopped in to pick up *The World in Darkness.* I could have sworn I heard you talking to Claire. I didn't want to interrupt, but I'm curious. That was you, wasn't it? Night before last?"

"Um, yes, I was there," she admitted reluctantly. And here, she'd thought she could get away with never having to admit she'd been such a fool that night. "That's why I couldn't join you for coffee. I'd promised Claire that I'd help her out; she was short a staff person, you know? And I'll use any excuse to putter around The Cracked Spine."

Noel nodded slowly, his expression growing serious. "I apologize up front, because this isn't going to make me look good, but I wasn't intentionally eavesdropping, okay?"

"Okay," Addison said slowly, dreading what was going to come out of his mouth next.

He hesitated, then took her hand. He studied her fingers, rather than meeting her eyes, but she thought that might be more for her benefit than his. "I overheard you say something. Do you mind if I ask for... well, for clarification? I know you weren't talking to me, that what you said wasn't meant for my ears, but I don't want to misunderstand or misread things between us."

Wow. So, this is the way she should have handled things. *It's called communication, Adders. It's what grownups do.* "It's okay. You can ask."

"I heard you say that you'd rather be single and happy."

Addison sighed and nodded. She had, indeed, said pretty much those exact words. "It's the truth," she explained. "But I said it in response to Claire asking if I'd rather be single and happy than in a relationship just to not be single."

"Right. I heard her ask you."

Then what was his question, she wondered, relishing the way her hand felt tucked into his. Her heart was pounding so hard that she could feel her blood throbbing in her veins.

"I guess I'm wondering how you feel about us," he finally said. Now he did look her in the eyes. "Let me be really forthright. I've been thinking about you all week, hoping that I've been on your mind, too. And Addison, I don't want to be an obligation to you."

"You're not an obligation," she whispered when she could find her words. "And I've been thinking about you all week, too."

"Thank goodness." Noel let out a great sigh of relief, closed his eyes, and leaned his head back on the cushion behind him. The sound he made sent a flurry of tingles skittering just under her skin. He cracked one eye open and turned to grin at her. "I was afraid you'd concocted a story about not feeling well just to get out of going out with me. But then you invited me here tonight, and I couldn't help hoping...." He let his words trail off.

She couldn't lie to him. She simply couldn't. She stared down at their intwined fingers and said, "Actually, I kinda did. I mean, I felt awful, so that part wasn't made up." She sighed, hating how silly she felt.

He squeezed her hand encouragingly. "What is it, Addison?"

"I thought you... and Claire. I thought the two of you might—" She broke off, unable to finish the sentence. Her cheeks were hot with embarrassment. "I jumped to conclusions."

"Ah. Claire of The Cracked Spine." Noel fell silent for so long that Addison finally chanced a look at him. He was studying her with a broad grin on his face. "You have nothing to worry about there, Addison. That woman scares me a little. She is *not* my type."

"Really?" Addison ducked her head again, hoping she wasn't getting all blotchy. "I mean, look at her. She seems like she'd be everyone's type."

"I'd much rather look at you."

"Oh." Addison picked up *The World on Fire* just for something to do with her free hand.

Noel took the book from her and set it on the armrest beside him. Then he tugged on her hand, gently drawing her toward him. "We can talk more about books tomorrow." The rumble of his voice made him sound a little dreamy. "Come here."

She let him pull her closer to him on the sofa. Shoulder to shoulder, hip to hip, thigh to thigh they sat, Addison barely breathing at the rapture of the moment. She'd imagined the possibility of this for months, and suddenly, here she was, snuggling—*snuggling!*—with the actual man of her actual dreams. How was it possible?

"This is nice," Noel said, resting his cheek against her head. "I'm glad you're here."

"You are, too," she managed to say, the butterflies doing a happy dance in her stomach. "I mean, I'm glad. That you're here, too. And that you're glad." *Ugh.*

Noel chuckled softly, then turned and pressed a kiss to her temple. "I like the way you talk when you're nervous."

Addison, mortified, covered her face with her free hand. "Don't make fun of me," she groaned. "You make me nervous. But in a good way, I mean. And then my tongue forgets how to work."

Noel turned slightly toward her, wrapped his fingers around her wrist and lowered her hand so that he could see her face. He didn't let go. "I wasn't making fun of you, Addison. It makes me inexplicably happy to know that I make you nervous in a good way." He waited until she gave him a side-eyed look. "You do the same thing to me."

"But your tongue seems to work just fine," she shot back, her gaze lowering to his mouth. *Such a nice mouth...* Her eyes widened in censure as she tried to rein in her wayward thoughts. "I mean, your mouth works." She wasn't making things better. "You talk just..."

Her words drifted off as Noel leaned closer and pressed the mouth in question against hers.

The kiss lasted only a few moments. His lips were warm and firm against hers, and to her embarrassment, she sighed out loud when he pulled away.

"You are lovely, Addison Wedgewood," Noel said, resting his forehead against hers. He let go of her hand so he could cup her cheek, his thumb tenderly stroking the corner of her mouth. Then he settled back into the sofa again, wrapping an arm around her shoulders and drawing her closer to him, until she was resting snuggly against his side. After a moment's hesitation, she leaned her head on his shoulder, and then it was his turn to let out a sigh of satisfaction.

After a long, comfortable silence, she heard him say her name. "Addison?" It sounded like he was talking underwater, though.

"Hmm?"

"Hey, Addison." His voice was low and soft, a gentle murmur near her ear.

Suddenly, she stiffened and tried to sit up. She'd fallen asleep. Oh, good grief, she'd fallen asleep on him! "I'm so sorry, Noel. I guess I—I just drifted off."

Noel didn't let her pull away. "Please don't apologize," he said. She could hear the grin in his voice. "I'm not complaining. You can fall asleep in my arms anytime you want."

"You're teasing me again." She stopped trying to move away from him, but squeezed her eyes shut.

"If teasing you makes you turn that pretty shade of pink, then I'm not so sure that's a bad thing." He planted a playful kiss against her temple, then lifted his arm from around her shoulders. "I think it's getting late, though."

Addison sat forward and scooped up her phone from the coffee table. She gasped when she saw the time. "Oh goodness. Noel. It's after one in the morning."

"It is?" he asked, then yawned as if on cue, making both of them laugh. "Guess we should call it a night." He got to his feet, then offered her his hand to help her up, too.

When she tried to step back, he didn't let go. The look on his face gave her a momentary jolt of concern. "Are you okay?" she asked. He was so close she could see the fine lines of black that striated his brown irises, and she almost couldn't bear it.

"May I kiss you goodnight?" he asked, his voice low and husky, his eyelids lowering as his gaze moved to her lips.

She nodded without hesitation.

The kiss was soft, tender at first, then grew more passionate, more intimate. She pressed one hand to his chest, the other, almost of its own accord, slipping up to curve around his jaw. She'd been right; there was absolutely nothing wrong with his mouth. It was working just fine, indeed.

They finally broke apart, both a little flushed, and she shifted her hands to his waist to steady herself.

"Wow," he murmured, dipping his head a little to look her in the eye.

"Yeah," she said quite breathlessly, but she didn't care. "Wow."

Noel took a deep breath and let it out slowly. "My heart is racing. So, it's not just me?"

Addison shook her head. "Mine, too," she whispered.

The room was quiet for a few moments, then he took her hand again and led her around the coffee table toward the door. He released her long enough to slip into his jacket, then took her in his arms again. "Thank you, Addison, for tonight. Everything about it was perfect. I'm so glad we didn't wait until tomorrow to get together."

"I am, too," she said, smiling up at him. "I'm glad you liked my cobbler." He'd declined taking any of it home, telling her he'd rather eat it with her than all alone in his suite at the resort.

"I'm forever changed after tonight, Addison. You've ruined me for all other cobblers."

22
Noel

THE WEATHER COOPERATED WITH bright sunshine in spite of the brisk, March chill that swept in off the lake, and Noel and Addison spent all of Saturday together. They toured the town, Addison showing him her favorite haunts. At the bookshop, Claire was hosting a children's reading hour, so they didn't visit long, but the pretty proprietress seemed thrilled to see them there together.

They ate lunch at Juno's Coffee Bar, and Noel agreed that he'd never tasted a roast beef sandwich quite like the one Juno was known for. While there, the other women from Addison's Garden Variety Lovers Club showed up, including the indomitable octogenarian, Hazel Poleman, whose family was part of the founding members of the town, and Judy Anderson, Penny's mother. Penny Anderson had bought into Hazel's guesthouse, and the two of them, along with the help of Penny's fiancé, Ward St. James, were converting the place into an upgraded bed and breakfast that would open to the public this summer.

Ward had also made an appearance to pick up an order of sandwiches to go. Noel had already met Ward since his family's boat repair business was contracted to service the fleet of water craft over at Carpe Diem. "Once the weather's better, we need to have a day on the lake," Ward suggested when he learned that Addison was giving Noel a tour of the south shore. "Give you an on-the-water perspective of our town."

They joined the regulars at Patsy's Pizza for supper, and Addison shocked Noel by annihilating him at the pool table. "Where did you learn to play like that?" He didn't miss the fact that everyone who'd witnessed the game didn't seem surprised at all by her victory.

"My mom taught me how to play, but my dad taught me how to win. He wasn't one of those parents who lets their kid win without earning it, either. If I wanted to beat him, I had to do it fair and square."

"How old were you when you won your first match?" Noel asked, enjoying the little bits and pieces of her life he was getting to know.

"It was on my sixteenth birthday, and no, he didn't let me win, not even as a birthday present. It's been a back-and-forth battle ever since. My mom just rolls her eyes and leaves the room when one of us racks up."

Sunday morning, he attended Addison's church with her where they sat with several of her friends. He felt like they were quickly becoming his friends, too, which surprised him. He was good with people, but like romantic relationships, he'd never really made platonic relationships a priority. He'd always just considered himself a loner by nature, but now that he was letting himself contemplate putting down roots, he found that he really liked the idea of being a part of a small community again, in a place where everyone knew who he was.

They had a wonderful Sunday dinner with Penny, June, and Hazel at the Garden Gate Guesthouse where Ward and his parents also joined them. There was a lovely little bay between the guesthouse's dock and the jut of land where the St. James's home sat, and during their after-dinner walk—so that they could burn off enough calories to make room for brownies and ice cream—Penny insisted Noel and Addison come out and use her little boat any time they wanted to. The water in the cove was surprisingly calm. "It's almost always like this," she assured them. "The perfect spot to spend a lazy afternoon adrift on the water."

"Good spot to drop a line in the water, too," Ward added.

It had been a long time since Noel had gone fishing, but he'd escaped the chaos of his childhood home countless times by heading down to his favorite fishing hole. He'd often brought back supper, too, which is likely the only reason Bruno hadn't restricted him from doing it.

Sunday had ended with shared leftovers in Addison's apartment, a place in which he was quickly growing to feel at home. They'd held hands while watching a movie, then he'd kissed her goodnight on the twinkle-lit deck, anticipating the plans they'd made for the following day.

As the days went by, Noel found his thoughts consumed by the delightful and charming Addison Wedgewood. Although he and John barely acknowledged each other these days, tension at work between them had grown so fraught that Noel dreaded going in each morning. The knowledge that he got to spend time with Addison after the day was over buoyed him up like nothing else had in as long as he could remember.

Much of their time together was with friends at the pizza place or the coffee shop, or browsing books in The Cracked Spine, but Noel always treasured most the time he got to spend alone with Addison in the apartment above the stationery store. The whole apartment could easily fit into his suite of rooms at the resort, but stepping through her front door was like entering a whole new world for him, one he wanted to explore to his heart's delight. He loved discovering new bits and bobs in her place, trinkets, art, books, and more, that gave him insight into what felt like 'the secret world of Addison Wedgewood.'

On the last Sunday of the month, Addison invited him to join her and her friends for a movie at Autumn Lake's drive-in, an outdoor theater that had closed a decade ago, but had reopened one night a week during the pandemic a few years earlier. The Monday Movie Night had garnered so much local support that the town had decided to keep it ongoing.

Monday nights at the drive-in, according to Addison, was something akin to family reunions during the off-season. "We still go when the summer lakers are here, but it's not the same. If you're going to be a local, though, you've got to experience it before May. You don't even have to worry about getting there early for a good spot. Every spot is a good spot when it's just us Townies."

A drive-in movie. The thought conjured up all sorts of romantic ideas for Noel, but if what she said about it being a family reunion was true, he wouldn't be spending much time alone in his car with the fair Addison Wedgewood. But he was fine with that. He was thoroughly enjoying getting to know her friends, and he hoped they felt the same way about him.

For the first time in his life, Noel wanted to belong somewhere. He wanted to be a part of something, not just temporarily, but long term. Maybe forever. He was falling for Addison, but he was also falling for her town, and her friends, and the community that she was so intricately woven into.

As he lay in bed waiting for sleep to overcome him, a voice that sounded eerily like Bruno's said, "You may want it, but why would they want you? You're nothing but a little parasite. You'll never amount to anything worthwhile. Stop kidding yourself; no one wants you around. Just ask your buddy, John Sheridan."

A counselor had once told Noel that he couldn't choose the things his father said or thought about him, but that he could choose whether or not to believe them.

He didn't want to believe the words Bruno had flung at him a hundred thousand times in his childhood, but it was a whole lot easier said than done.

Even so, Noel fell asleep with thoughts of Addison in his head and a smile on his face, and he slept better than he had in as long as he could remember. By the time he returned to work on Monday morning, he felt rejuvenated and back on track, ready to face down John's bullying with patience and self-control. He made it to his desk a half an hour earlier than usual, and had already emptied his email inbox by the time Paula arrived. She said a quiet, almost apologetic, "Good morning," and settled in behind her desk, too.

John, however, had other plans. He showed up half an hour late, but he didn't come in alone.

23

Addison

For a Monday, the airport was surprisingly busy. Natalie's shift didn't start until noon, and although the other full-time ticket agent, Marcus Pratt, was on the clock, the guy moved slower than molasses, which meant Addison spent the morning running around like a chicken with her head cut off. By the time Natalie showed up, she was more than ready to take her lunch break.

"You go eat, girl," Natalie told her, making a shooing gesture toward the break room. "You can fill me in on all your Noel news when you get back."

Addison wasn't terribly hungry, but she needed coffee, and she knew she'd better eat something along with the caffeine or she'd end up wiggy, or worse, with heartburn all afternoon. She sat down and unwrapped the tuna salad sandwich she'd brought from home and ate half of it while she waited for the fresh pot of coffee that she'd put on to brew. Natalie would appreciate a cup or two as well.

Her feet were a little sore after the busy morning, but that was partly due to that fact that she had taken Noel to several of her favorite flea markets and thrift stores the day before, and she hadn't thought to change out of her church boots into something better for lots of walking. With thoughts of Noel making her smile, she propped her feet up on a chair and picked up her phone, hoping to see a text from him. There was nothing there.

Maybe he was on his lunch break, too. She could text him, couldn't she? "It's okay to text him first, Adders," she prodded herself.

She squared her shoulders and tapped out her message. *Happy Monday, Noel. Hope your day is going well. I had a great time with you over the weekend. Looking forward to movie night with you.*

Was it too much? Too bland? She hit 'send' before she started second-guessing herself.

Twenty minutes later, the other half of her sandwich was gone, and she was halfway through a second cup of coffee, but she still hadn't gotten a response. "He's at work," she said aloud, trying to convince herself that there was nothing to worry about.

Back at her station and in between customers, she regaled Natalie about the wonderful weekend she'd spent with Noel. She didn't tell her that he hadn't responded to her text all afternoon.

"Are you doing something this evening?" Natalie asked.

"That's the plan," Addison said. "I invited him to join the gang for Monday Movie Night at the drive-in." Her friend had brought her little family to the event a few times over the years and needed no explanation. "I'm not sure about supper yet, but I'll probably cook something for us before we go."

Natalie shot her a questioning look. "You're not sure yet?"

"We just haven't confirmed the details," she said, hoping she sounded more confident than she felt.

They talked about menu options, but Addison got the feeling that Natalie was going along with the conversation with some reservations. A notion that was confirmed when her friend finally asked, "You should just text him. Ask him if he wants you to cook something. Maybe he doesn't know a meal is part of the package."

Addison sighed. "I did. At lunch time."

"And he still hasn't responded?" When Addison shook her head, Natalie asked, "Why don't you go take a break and call him, then?"

"He's at work," Addison hedged. "He might be in meetings or something."

"He also might *not* be in meetings," Natalie said, giving her a stern, but kind look. "We're not in high school, Addison. You're allowed to expect adult behavior from a guy, which includes common courtesy. It's been almost four hours since you texted. Most meetings don't last four hours."

"You make it sound so cut and dried."

"It is cut and dried. Just call him. If he can't pick up, he won't."

In the break room, Addison pulled out her phone, hoping to see a response from Noel. Still, there was nothing. His phone didn't show if he'd read her text or not, so she couldn't assume he'd seen it. With butterflies in her stomach, she dialed his number.

The call went to voicemail, and in a falsely chipper voice, Addison said, "Hey, Noel. I'm getting ready to head home in about an hour. I'm just calling to see if you'd like to come over for supper before the movie. I'm making chicken coconut curry. Call me back when you get a chance." That didn't sound pushy, did it?

Ten minutes later, she left the break room. The line in front of Natalie's station was long, and Addison quickly signed in and started helping travelers. She gave her friend a quick shake of the head in response to Natalie's questioning glance.

Noel still hadn't called or texted when Addison clocked out, nor had she heard from him an hour later when the timer went off for the Basmati rice she'd made to go with the curry.

Most of the food ended up in containers in the fridge, her appetite having also made a no-show. She almost bowed out of going to the movie altogether, but realized if she stayed home, she'd just go stir crazy, wondering why Noel was ghosting her.

She spent the evening with her friends, waving off their questions about Noel's absence. "Work stuff," she told them, because presumably, that's what it was. She didn't want to think that it might be because he was having second thoughts about spending time with her. "He couldn't make it tonight."

24
Noel

By the time the meeting with Human Resources wrapped up, Noel was exhausted. He hadn't even tried to deny John's accusations or to defend himself. It was all on record, and since Paula had fled the office that day at his request, there were no witnesses who might be willing to fill in the missing parts of that conversation.

John had painted Noel as a bully, as an instigator, stating that he'd come into his position with an agenda. "From the moment he walked into my office," he'd stated. "I felt threatened in every way. He did everything in his power to make me feel incompetent, unnecessary, and irrelevant. I was willing to let it go, hoping he'd eventually come around and recognize that I wasn't the enemy, but then he threatened me with physical violence, and I couldn't just let it roll off my back." When asked what John thought Noel's motives were, he said, "I honestly don't know. I suppose he was intimidated by my seniority and my extensive knowledge of the operations of this company."

Everything that Noel believed about John. He felt manipulated, gaslighted, and at a complete loss on how to counteract the complaints without sounding guilty as charged.

He did, however, know his rights. He had accepted the written complaint, listened to John's accusations, endured the incriminating replay of the audio recording of his verbal altercation with John, and had listened in silence to all the potential outcomes that might result from the situation. When they finally gave him the floor, Noel had stated calmly that he wasn't comfortable offering a rebuttal or signing anything until he'd spoken with a lawyer. He agreed to cooperate with HR's full investigation under the guidance of an attorney. They offered him the option of discussing his version of things with an HR representative instead, but he felt certain that the odds were stacked against him, and that his fate would be better handled by legal help from outside the company.

John had pushed for Noel's temporary suspension until the investigation was over. Noel refused to agree to it. They compromised by giving Noel the rest of the week off with pay, and the assurance that it would not go on his personal record as a suspension if the investigation found him innocent. Noel was sure his attorney would have something to say about all of that, but he honestly wasn't upset about having a few days off to process all of this.

He couldn't stay at the resort to process, though; that was for sure. Nor did he want to stay in Autumn Lake where he was certain to run into people who were involved in or knew about his current circumstances. It was a small town, after all, and Noel knew all about small towns and how quickly gossip spread in a place where everyone knew everything there was to know about everyone else. But where should he go? He couldn't go back to Bald Knob, even though he knew Aunt Gigi would be thrilled to have him there for any reason. But he couldn't face his past with his future up in the air. He certainly couldn't face Bruno right now, not with the situation with John front and center in his mind. The correlation between the two men was too real, and Noel knew that he was far from the being in the right frame of mind to deal with either one of them.

Fortunately, John had stayed away from the office while Noel collected his belongings, including his laptop and his phone. His heart sank when he saw the cheerful message from Addison that had come in right after he'd been escorted to human resources. What on earth was he supposed to say to her?

When his phone rang just as he was leaving the office and he saw that it was her, he let it go to voice mail. He resisted the powerful urge to call her back and tell her all about his terrible day. There was no way he could explain why he'd reacted to John the way he had without telling her about his past. He would never burden anyone in his life with those dark years living under the monster shadow of Bruno. His childhood could stay in the past where it belonged. It was not part of his future.

Back in his suite, he changed out of his office attire into a pair of gym shorts and a t-shirt, intending to head down to the gym where he could let off steam on a treadmill. But as he bent down to tie his trainers, a sense of panic hit him. He couldn't show his face anywhere right now, not if he knew what was good for him.

They all know you're incompetent, boy. John's just the first one to call you out on it. Bruno's sneering voice sent toxic tendrils of impending doom curling around his heart. His pulse began to race, his scalp prickled, and his hands started shaking so hard that he couldn't tie his shoe laces.

He recognized the signs for what they were. He was on his way to having a full-blown panic attack.

They didn't happen often, at least not anymore, but when one struck, it was truly an attack. And no matter how hard he tried to be prepared for them, he was inevitably caught off guard every time. Wave after wave of gripping anxiety forced him to his knees, his breaths coming in short, panting gulps of air. He lifted his arms over his head, hoping the motion would expand his chest cavity and give his lungs more room, but to no avail. Leaning forward until his forehead was pressed into the carpet, he covered his head with his hands and began to pray.

"Oh God, please help me. Please help me," he gasped out between breaths. "Please."

25
Addison

Tuesday morning dawned with still no word from Noel. She mustered the courage to send him one more message. *Good morning, Noel. I hope you're okay. Should I be worried?*

At work, she went about her tasks, grateful that she'd been at her job long enough that she could practically do things on autopilot. When Natalie arrived at noon, she didn't even ask. One look at Addison obviously told her everything.

By the end of the day, she just wanted to go home and cry. How had she read things so wrong? Nothing about Noel had painted him as the kind of guy who did stuff like this, who just disappeared after spending so much time with her over the last several weeks. She'd thought they really liked each other, especially when he held her hand and kissed her goodnight the way he did.

"Maybe I've just been reading too much into things," she admitted to Natalie as she logged out of her station. "I mean, I've definitely given him a tour of the town, which is all he originally asked for."

"Yeah," Natalie said with a sarcastic scowl. "But I've never heard of tour guides who were expected to provide home-cooked meals and kisses."

Addison shrugged. "Maybe we're just country bumpkins and don't know big city expectations," she said, trying to keep the sour note out of her voice. "I mean, it's possible he was just taking advantage of the extra services I provided." She made air quotes with her fingers around the words, 'extra services.'

Natalie narrowed her eyes at her. "Hopefully, they *only* included food and kissing."

"Nat. Really? You know me better than that." The memory of sharing a few hours in the company of a certain Icelandic tour guide flashed through her mind. He'd shared his *kleinur*, homemade or not, and a few kisses with her under the Northern Lights, hadn't he?

Maybe that was just the modern way of things, after all.

"And we're not country bumpkins, girlie," Natalie argued. "For Pete's sake, you've traveled the world."

Addison shook her head. "I just don't get it, then."

"Why don't you drive over to the resort and confront him? That's what I would do." Natalie would, too. She wasn't the kind of woman to let a man take advantage of her. She knew what she wanted and didn't accept any less.

Addison shook her head again. "I can't. I'm not like you, Nat. And we've only been seeing each other—if I can even call it that—for a few weeks. No one has said anything about making things official."

"I think spending every non-working waking moment together automatically makes it official," Natalie countered. "Just because he didn't pass you a note asking if you want to be his girlfriend."

"Right? That's what I thought, too. I just feel so naïve, you know? I mean, there were probably red flags that I missed, but because I don't know what to look for in a—a—"

"A player?" Natalie suggested, one eyebrow raised sardonically.

"Ugh. No. That makes him sound so awful. And maybe I'm the problem. Maybe I'm not girlfriend material. It's not like I've had a lot of experience in that area. Maybe I'm just not... *enough* for him."

"Now you stop that immediately, girlie. Don't let this guy make you change the way you feel about yourself. No one should have permission to do that, you hear?" She gave her a tight hug. "You, my friend, are not the problem here. He is."

Addison hugged her back, but said, "I still find it hard to believe that he's that kind of guy."

"Yet, after today, evidence seems to prove otherwise," Natalie countered.

Addison frowned and slung the strap of her purse over her shoulder. She sent her friend a concerned look. "What if he's been in an accident or something awful like that, and he can't respond? Wouldn't it be awful if I was sitting here thinking the worst of him, while he's lying in some hospital bed somewhere?"

"Don't even go there, you hear?" Natalie shook her finger at her. "You just pray that thought right out of your head."

"But if that were the case," Addison admitted a little sheepishly, "at least it wouldn't be because he didn't want to be with me."

"And you would feel absolutely terrible if that were, indeed, the case, wouldn't you?"

Addison let out a frustrated sigh and nodded. "I'd feel like the worst person in the world if something bad happened to him."

"Then go home, enjoy that delicious chicken curry you didn't get to eat last night, and indulge in some you time. Read a book. Or go to your friend's bookstore and find something new. Binge-watch a new show. Something to keep your mind off that man. You are not allowed to mope around, you hear?"

"Good food. Good book. Good show. No moping. Got it." Addison gave Natalie a brave smile. "Thanks for being my friend. I love you. I'll see you tomorrow."

Wednesday passed in long, restless hours of confusion and concern. She berated herself for being so affected by Noel's behavior. They'd only just begun to see each other, so it wasn't like she had a right to expect anything from him. At the same time, she couldn't help replaying every moment they'd spent together trying to sort out what had gone wrong.

Had she said something that had offended him? If so, why not just say so? Surely, she wasn't so intimidating that he couldn't tell her if she'd made some kind of a faux pas, was she?

Natalie had insisted that Addison had good reason to drive around to the resort and talk to him face to face.

"I don't even know his suite number," Addison had said, shaking her head.

"Then ask for him at the front desk. It's not like he's a guest there."

"I'm not going to do that," she told her friend. "I don't want to embarrass him."

Natalie was a take-the-bull-by-the-horns kind of girl. She would have gone to the resort Monday night and refused to leave until the man spoke to her. But she understood Addison well enough to know that wasn't her nature, and she didn't keep pushing her in that direction. "I hate that he's done this to you, Addison, but if this is the kind of guy he is, maybe it's best that it's happened so early in the relationship."

"If you could call it a relationship," she said dismally.

"You were relating, weren't you?" Natalie shot back.

"We were," Addison acknowledged. "And I thought we were relating quite romantically, too."

"So, stop beating yourself up. He's the loser in this scenario."

But Addison couldn't get the notion out of her head that there was more to it than him simply losing interest in her. Something must have happened to so abruptly change the direction they'd been going. They'd spent almost every evening after work and weekends together, reluctantly leaving each others' company at night's end, and now, complete silence?

"It's called ghosting for a reason," Natalie said, her voice gentle. "People do it all the time. It's their problem, their weakness, not yours."

"But when it's done to me, it becomes my problem."

"Only if you stick around for it."

Their conversation played out over and over in her mind as she got ready for bed that night. It was still early, but she had a good book that she'd started at Natalie's suggestion yesterday, and there was no reason not to spend the last part of her evening reading in bed.

But once she was in her super soft knit jammies, her mug of tea on her nightstand, she sat on the edge of her bed and stared down at her phone.

"I have to try one more time," she finally decided. "I can't give up yet."

Noel, please know that I'm thinking about you and praying for you. I do hope you're well, but I have big shoulders if you ever need them. Hugs.

She sent the message, then set her phone face down on the nightstand and slid her legs under her plush bed covers and picked up her book.

26
Noel

THE TEXT FROM ADDISON came in just as Noel had finished putting away his leftovers. He'd spent a good part of the last two days preparing for and meeting with an attorney about his situation, and now that the mess was somewhat out of his hands, he was able to breathe a little easier. His stomach had been in knots since Monday morning, and it was only this evening that he'd gotten a little of his appetite back. What he really craved was something homecooked from Addison's kitchen, but the food from the Lux Solaris downstairs was good, and he'd eaten more than half of his meal, which was definitely a step in the right direction. He washed and dried his hands and picked up the phone, his chest tightening at her kind words.

He couldn't continue to ignore her. He was a better man than that. But what could he say to her? What if his attorney, Joyce Patterson, couldn't fix this for him and he ended up having to leave town with his tail tucked between his legs? Or worse, in handcuffs?

Yes, but what if things *did* go his way? What if Joyce, who'd assured him he had nothing to worry about, was right, and this would all blow over instead of blowing up? He didn't want to lose whatever this was between them, and now that he had someone on his team, he needed to try to make amends with this woman who was quickly becoming important to him.

He began tapping in a reply. *Thank you. I've needed your prayers.* But then he erased it all and touched the call button instead. He owed her a phone call after two days of radio silence.

After the third ring, Noel was sure she was just going to let his call go to voicemail. But then, to his great relief, she answered in a breathless voice.

"Hello?"

Just the sound of that single word made his pulse race. "Hey, Addison. It's Noel."

"Hi, Noel." He could hear the questions, the hesitation in her voice, but she only said, "It's good to hear from you."

He took a deep breath and let it out slowly as he crossed the room to drop into the corner of the plush sofa. "About that," he began, squeezing his eyes shut and rubbing his brow with his free hand. "Forgive me for not calling earlier. I—I have my reasons, but I think they're probably going to sound like excuses, no matter how I spin them."

"Noel," she said, interrupting him when he paused to take a breath. "You don't have to explain anything to me. I'm just glad you're all right." She paused, then said, "You *are* all right, aren't you?"

Noel hesitated, biting back the automatic "I'm fine," response that was ready to fly out of his mouth. Instead, he opted for honesty, albeit minus any gory details. "Actually, I've been dealing with some serious trouble at work that has consumed my time and energy over the last two days. I feel like I'm just coming up for air for the first time, but it's only a reprieve. I think things are going to get worse before they get better."

If they get better.

But he didn't say that out loud. "Anyway, I'm glad you called," he added, hoping she wouldn't push for explanations.

"I'm glad *you* called," she corrected, her voice sounding lighter. He thought she might be smiling on the other end of the phone. "I texted. You called."

"Right. Yes." He chuckled, then took a deep, slow breath and let it out again. "Your voice is a balm to my soul right now," he said, and as the words left his lips, he realized just how true it was.

"Oh, good," she said on an exhale, almost like she'd been holding her breath. "But I'm sorry about the trouble at work. The way you talk about your job makes it seem like such a perfect fit for you."

He sighed and wondered how much to tell her. As though reading his mind, she continued.

"You don't have to tell me anything about it. I'm not probing for details. I just want you to know that I am aware how important this job is to you, and I can understand why trouble at work would feel overwhelming. I want you to know that you have someone on your team." She paused, then added, "I'm here for you. That's all."

"Thank you," he managed to get out around the lump that had risen in the back of his throat. How long had it been since he'd felt certain there was someone at his back besides Aunt Gigi? This was why people had friends, wasn't it? "That means a lot to me."

"And not just me," Addison said, a note of determination in her tone. "My friends have fallen in love with you, too, Noel. You've got a group of us rooting for you."

Too? He let that sink in and smiled. He wasn't so naïve to think that Addison had truly fallen in love with him in so short a time, but the idea of it made the pressure in his chest lift a little. The notion also echoed his own thoughts earlier; maybe they hadn't *already* fallen in love with each other, but it was definitely possible that they were in the process of falling *for* each other. Which made his smile broaden.

He hadn't smiled in two days, and it felt good. "Thank you, Addison," he said again. "It does my heart good to know that."

There was a pause on the other end of the line, then she said, "Would you like to come over for supper tomorrow night?"

For some reason, her invitation made him want to weep. It felt like she was offering him shelter in a storm, a safe place to land after flying too close to the sun. At Addison's apartment, he wouldn't have to worry about running into anyone who knew about John's charges against him. He wouldn't have to be constantly looking over his shoulder while sharing a meal with her in the sanctuary of her colorful little home.

He must have paused too long, because she let out a self-conscious little cough and said, "I mean, I understand if you're busy. I just thought it might be nice to –."

He cut her off with a decisive, "Yes. Yes, I'd love to see you tomorrow. I'd love to have supper with you. What can I bring?" He was desperate to get out of his apartment, but even more so to see her smiling face again. He'd missed her fiercely.

"Nothing," she told him, and he could hear the relief in the single word. "You know I cook almost every night, anyway. Um, would you rather have meatloaf or chicken tacos?"

"Wow, options?" He practically hummed with enthusiasm. It had to be moments like this for which the old adage, 'The way to a man's heart is through his stomach,' was coined, because a wave of deep appreciation and affection for Addison Wedgewood washed over him at the thought of her preparing a meal for him. It didn't matter what she cooked, he realized. Just the fact that she wanted to feed him made him warm all over.

They decided on meatloaf; Addison claimed she had a recipe her mother had clipped from a newspaper more than twenty years ago. "Do you remember the basketball player, Penny Hardaway?"

Noel wasn't much of an athlete himself, but he liked sports, especially basketball. "Absolutely. He's coaching now. A legend."

"Yeah, well, this meatloaf is his mother's recipe, if you can believe it. It's one of our family favorites."

"Penny's mom's meatloaf recipe. Wow. I can't wait to try it."

"And I can't wait to make it for you. You've never had meatloaf like this before." He could almost picture her rubbing her hands together in anticipation.

They talked for several more minutes, Addison sharing an anecdote from work that made him smile. An elderly gentleman had come to her for help in locating his lost wife. They'd found the grandmotherly woman in the airport's playroom helping out an overwhelmed mother traveling with three little ones. "By the time I left them, Mr. Chamness was doing silly magic tricks for a rapt audience, and the couple had all but become honorary grandparents to the rowdy bunch. The mom—her name was Nancy—went from crying tears of frustration to tears of joy, especially when they discovered they'd be sharing the same flight." Addison sighed dreamily when she finished telling the story. "I just love it when I can help people who really need it."

Noel marveled at how much pleasure this woman got out of what most folks would consider a mundane job. He knew it wasn't all sunshine and roses for her. He'd seen her face that day he and Barb had exited the plane together, her initial reaction when Barb had greeted her. He'd seen her pull herself together and put on a brave face so she could be engaging with them. In spite of the difficult days, she was the kind of person who seemed to find the good in situations, in people, that others typically overlooked.

When they said goodnight a short while later, Noel was surprised to discover how much better he felt. His shoulders had relaxed and the tightness in his chest had let up. He took a few long, slow breaths and reveled in the sensation of peace that washed over him. "Thank you, God," he murmured, letting his head rest against the back of the sofa and closing his eyes. The relief he felt just being able to talk to someone other than himself at the end of the day was palpable, but to have someone like Addison Wedgewood as that 'someone' made it so much more than just relief. She lit something up inside of him, something that made him feel valued, like he was more than just the man in the suit behind the numbers. He had a feeling she had that affect on just about everyone who came in contact with her.

Did he make her feel valued, treasured, in the same way?

He pondered the question as he got ready for bed. He, in fact, had done just the opposite, hadn't he? By not responding to her attempts to engage with him until now, he'd surely made her feel unimportant, or even expendable. Not valued. Not treasured. By not even acknowledging her with a quick text to let her know he'd received hers was unpardonable. How much more selfish could he get?

By the time he'd showered and slid between his sheets, he was determined to do everything he could to make sure she knew what an amazing person she was.

The next morning began with a phone conference with his attorney. "Do not leave town," she advised him when he suggested he might go back to Bald Knob for a few days. "The only reason I'm not pushing for you to return to the office is that they're essentially giving you paid leave. But I've requested a written statement from then that this time away from the office is not a disciplinary action. If they haven't sent it to me by the end of the day, you're going back to work tomorrow morning, understand?"

That made sense to him. Honestly, he'd rather be busy working than spending the long hours of his days pacing the confines of his suite.

"Depending on what that statement says, even if they assure me that it's not a disciplinary action, I may insist that they send Mr. Sheridan home and have you return to work. If he is the one requesting that he not have to interact with you, then he should be the one on leave, not you."

Noel had worked with Joyce on a few other cases in the past, but never had he hired her as his personal defense attorney. He'd never had a need to before now. She was part of a firm the resort contracted with, and although her services were quite expensive, he was confident in her ability to cut to the chase with his situation. It was why he'd refused to sign anything on Monday that Human Resources had given him. He wasn't going to do anything more to jeopardize his position, one that he wanted to keep more than anything, now that he'd talked to Addison. If Joyce told him to jump, he'd ask her how high. If she said to stay put, he'd stay put.

As soon as he got off that phone call, he tapped in a quick text to Addison. *Feel like meeting me for lunch today?* He'd take her anywhere she wanted to go, even if it meant eating from one of the vendor kiosks at the small airport. *I'm off today and can pick you up,* he added. He hadn't told her about his paid leave the night before, and he didn't want her to worry that she'd be inconveniencing him.

I'd love to, came her reply a moment later. *I take lunch from 1-2. Will that work for you?*

He'd already checked out a few restaurants close to the airport; he wanted them to have enough time to enjoy a meal without having to rush through it. He'd landed on a Cantonese restaurant, having recalled that, during a conversation out at the Garden Gate Guesthouse over the weekend, she'd said one of her favorite comfort food meals was pan fried noodles and pork dumplings.

He arrived at the airport well before one, armed with another potted plant, this time, a young peace lily that sported lush green leaves and white-tipped spears shooting straight up out of the middle of it. "It's just getting ready to bloom," the woman at the flower shop had explained when she'd recommended the plant to him. "Each of these flowers should last for months."

Noel had explained to her that the recipient was new to keeping plants, but the florist had assured him the species was easy to maintain. "And it's a lovely gift for a friend. Peace lilies are all about harmony and hope, and of course, peace. In some cultures, it's symbolic of restoring balance after difficult times, of finding beauty in life."

He'd dressed carefully, wishing the dark circles under his eyes weren't so prominent, and took more care than usual to get his hair under control. He really needed a haircut; maybe he'd get that done this afternoon since he was in Evansville already. He'd found a no-nonsense barber downtown near the River Walk who managed to cut his hair exactly the way he wanted it with very little direction.

When he stepped up to the sliding glass door of the terminal at 12:50 pm, Addison was standing at the check-in counter talking animatedly to her coworker. Natalie, he thought Addison had said was her name, was grinning and nodding in response to whatever Addison was saying.

They both turned and looked at him as the door swooshed open and he stepped inside, the blast of warm air in the terminal a relief from the brisk breeze that had picked up that morning. The weather channel was forecasting rain and possibly sleet tomorrow, but today was still clear, albeit crisp, with only a few cotton ball clouds dotting the sky.

One of Addison's hands went to her mouth at the site of him and his plant, making him smile. Beside her, Natalie pursed her lips and nodded, as if to say "Well done, sir. Well done."

In fact, when he approached the counter, she did say, "Well, look who knows when to show up bearing gifts," in a tone that made him realize that she likely knew he had some making up to do.

He carefully set the heavy ceramic pot on the counter. "I come bearing a white flag," he said. He was prepared to go all out to make things right. "I'm sorry about the last two days, Addison. This is a peace lily."

"Isn't that a funeral flower?" Natalie asked, one eyebrow raised suspiciously.

"Nat," Addison said with a quick sideways glance at her friend. But she reached out and ran a fingertip over the shiny surface of one of the leaves.

A slight flush crept up Noel's neck and he could feel his cheeks warm at Natalie's not-so-subtle challenge, but he recognized the mama bear in her for what it was. "I suppose it could be," he said agreeably. "They're symbolic of healing and hope." He turned and locked gazes with Addison. Without looking away from her, he touched one of the taller blooms that was almost completely unfurled. "It's called a Peace Lily because it looks like its waving white flags of peace." He smiled softly, hoping she perceived even a small measure of his sincerity.

"Nice," Natalie said, nodding again. She cleared her throat when Addison didn't speak.

"Wow. It's beautiful," Addison gushed self-consciously, her cheeks coloring prettily. She tucked a curl behind her ear and lifted her eyes to Noel's. "Is it—is it for me?"

Natalie chuckled softly and nudged her with a hip. "It's not for me, woman." Then she wrapped her arms around the pot and carried it over to her own station. "But I'll plant-sit for you while you're at lunch. Get out of here, you two."

On their way out of the airport parking lot, Addison had introduced Noel to Arnie Bowman, the author he knew as Arnold Archer. The man had been exceedingly gracious and humble, had promised he'd sign his books at Noel's request, then another car had pulled in behind them, forcing them to move along. They'd spent the rest of the short drive to the restaurant talking about Arnie, both of them waxing poetically about how remarkable the man and his stories were.

The food at The Cantonese Palace was just as delicious as the online reviews claimed it to be, but then his enjoyment of it might have had more to do with the company he was with. Addison sat across from him making pleasant sounds of appreciation with each bite of her food, making him grin with satisfaction as he watched her wholeheartedly enjoy her meal. She had removed her uniform shirt to reveal a square-necked lightweight sweater the color of deep water. He couldn't say for sure if it was more blue than green or the other way around, but it hugged her voluptuous curves in a pleasantly distracting way.

He wondered if she liked what she saw when she looked at him.

His conversation with Joyce that morning had heartened him considerably, and although he still didn't feel like dragging out his dirty laundry for Addison to see, he found it surprisingly easy to give her a few pertinent details. "My position was created to relieve some of the task load from my coworker. Understandably, he's felt challenged by my presence. Were I in his shoes, I, too, would wonder if my company thought I wasn't capable of performing my duties. I can see why he might worry about my presence."

"You sound very sympathetic," Addison responded, her brow furrowed like she was trying to understand.

"I've tried to be," Noel continued, shaking his head slowly, a coil of shame twisting in his gut. "But he hasn't exactly been receptive."

"Ah." She took another bite of sticky rice. She didn't say more.

"I think he's been looking for something to pin on me since I first got here, and last week, I gave him what he wanted." He shrugged and looked down at his nearly empty plate, then lifted his gaze back to meet hers. He didn't want to withhold the truth about his actions to her; she needed to know what she was getting into, if she was going to, as she put it, 'be on his team.' "I lashed back at him and he recorded it. There's really nothing I can do to deny what I said to him."

Addison put down her fork, her brows drawn together in concern. "That sounds awful, Noel. The whole situation, I mean. That you've been under this kind of pressure all this time? No wonder you let off some steam."

Noel grimaced. "That's a nice way of putting it. My coworker is calling it harassment and verbal assault and threats of violence and a hostile work environment. There were a few other choice phrases, too."

Addison reached across the table and touched the back of his hand. "Hostility and violence? That doesn't sound like you at all, Noel. I mean, I know we haven't known each other for long, but I just don't see any of that in you."

Noel turned his hand over and wrapped his fingers around hers. "Thank you, Addison. I wish you knew how much it means to me to hear you say that." He looked her in the eye, needing her to grasp the seriousness of the situation. He was tired of talking about it, of thinking about it, but it wasn't fair to her to let her think John's accusations were completely unfounded. "But I hope you know that everyone has a breaking point. I mean, I wasn't violent," he amended quickly. "And I didn't assault him, not even verbally. But I certainly wanted to."

Addison made a quiet scoffing sound. "We've all had visions of punching people in the throat."

Her response, made so matter-of-factly, caught him by surprise, and he laughed. "Surely not you, Miss Wedgewood."

"Oh, surely me, indeed," she declared, straightening in her seat and squaring her shoulders. But she didn't withdraw her hand from his. "Why, just the other day, this guy made plans to take me to the movies, then he ghosted me. And that was even after I offered to cook supper for him," she said in a dramatic tone, pressing her free hand to her sternum. "A jackanape. A ne'er-do-well. A blackguard," she declared. "Believe me, I entertained a few visions about what I'd do to him if he happened to show up at my ticket counter again."

"Clearly deserving of a throat punch," Noel uttered in mock horror. He knew what she was doing, moving the conversation away from the unsettling situation he was in, and he squeezed her fingers in silent appreciation. "I'm glad you've moved on from that guy. He sounds like a real... what did you call him? A ne'er-do-well? Jackanape?"

Addison giggled like she was going to continue the silly banter, but then pressed her lips together in a gentle smile. "All kidding aside, Noel, that's not who you are. A jackanape, I mean. Nor do I believe, for even one moment, that you are anything your coworker has accused you of. I'm sorry you're in this situation, and I can see that it's really gotten to you." She leaned forward and reached across the table for his other hand, then clutched both of his, hard. "If there is anything I can do to help out in any way, I'm here."

Noel nodded slowly, for a moment overwhelmed by her vehemence. Just then, a waiter approached their table, and Noel let go of Addison's hands. "Everything is delicious," he told the smiling young man who asked if they were enjoying the food.

They ordered another pot of jasmine tea and a plate of almond cookies to share, and for a few moments after their server cleared away their dirty dishes, they sat in silence, the fragrance of the hot tea swirling between them.

Finally, Noel said, "You're doing it, Addison. Being here with me, I mean. Yesterday at this time, I felt like the loneliest man in the world," he admitted. "I was ashamed to talk to anyone, and I didn't know what to say to you."

"Am I really so scary?" she asked softly. She picked up her small porcelain tea cup and blew over the surface of it before taking a sip.

Noel gave her an exaggerated rueful look. "Well, you just admitted that you wanted to punch me in the throat."

"I did not," she retorted, rolling her eyes. "I said I entertained visions of what I'd do to you the next time I saw you."

"And what, exactly, were those visions, if they weren't about committing bodily harm against me?" he asked, then took a sip of his own tea, his eyes fixed on her face over the rim of his cup. Was she blushing? Or was it just the temperature of the delicious drink?

Addison set her cup down and shrugged. "Honestly?"

"Honestly," he insisted.

"I was worried you'd been injured and were languishing in some hospital somewhere with no friends or family to visit you. Of course, I imagined your phone had been lost or destroyed in whatever tragic accident had befallen you—"

"Languishing? Befallen me?" Noel grinned at her. "I don't think I've ever heard anyone use phrases like that outside of a book before. Or jackanape, either, for that matter."

Addison gave him a narrow-eyed look. "Well, my dearest friends are books, or the characters in them. How else am I supposed to speak?"

"I like the way you speak, Miss Wedgewood. So refined." She really was blushing. "So elegant."

"Thank you," she quipped, a pleased smile spreading across her face. She bit her bottom lip, then said, "I'm glad no tragic accident has befallen you, by the way."

"I am, too. If it had, I wouldn't be here sharing this amazing meal with you." He held her gaze and added, "I can't think of anywhere I'd rather be right now."

"Nor I," she said, blinking, but not looking away.

27
Addison

For Addison, the rest of the week went by in a whirlwind rush of too-long work days and not-long-enough romantic evenings spent in her apartment. She and Noel cooked together, watched movies together, and discussed the books they were reading, until one or the other of them reluctantly did the mature thing and called it a night.

She knew Noel was worried about his job, but he had all day to contemplate the possible outcomes. So, she intentionally found other topics of conversation to distract him from the unsettling circumstances in which he found himself. Oh, she let him talk about it if he wanted to. She made sure to give him the space to unload if that's what he needed, but in general, she wanted her home and the time he spent with her to be a vacation from the mess of things. *Let me be your staycation,* she wanted to say to him, but she kept the silly thought to herself.

After receiving the requested paperwork from Carpe Diem, Noel's attorney gave him the go ahead to take the rest of the week off so she could sort through the situation. "Joyce says she's certain this can be handled out of court, which is good," Noel told her on Thursday night. "But she said I need to be prepared for the possibility that this incident could remain on my record, which really stinks."

"Ugh," Addison said consolingly. "I really wish someone would speak up about his behavior. Surely, someone has witnessed it."

"It's only Paula who sees it, and she's definitely his ally. He's the epitome of professionalism whenever anyone else is around."

Addison crossed her arms and huffed out a breath. "Then I'm praying that Ms. Paula has a change of heart and comes clean."

Noel gave her a dubious look. "That would take a miracle."

"Well, I believe in miracles, don't you? And I'm not going to stop praying for one."

By Saturday night, she had no doubt that she was falling head over heels for Noel. On top of their growing camaraderie, each evening when he arrived on her doorstep, he came with another potted plant in tow. Now her pretty bay window was arrayed in colorful pots overflowing with lush, vibrant leaves and trailing vines.

There was Emmy the Jade from the first delivery, and Portia the Peace lily. "Portia means 'offering,'" she told him as they admired the collection with the small-town lights outside the window as a backdrop. "Since you brought her as a peace offering, I figured it was apropos."

"Very," Noel said with a self-deprecating chuckle.

An English ivy that vined its way up a two-foot spiral willow branch frame was named Ivy. "Not very imaginative, I know," she acknowledged. "But she looks like an Ivy to me, so why fight it?"

He nodded solemnly at her logic. "Absolutely."

"This is Phil." She lifted a trailing vine covered in heart-shaped, glossy green leaves. "He's a Philodendron scandens, and again, not very creative, but since he's the only man in the house, I felt like he needed a good solid sturdy name. Look how he wraps his arms around his ladies." She had draped the vines of the philodendron in and among the other plants.

"You're the man, Phil." Noel played along, high-fiving one of the plant's leaves, then following suit and wrapping one arm around Addison's waist and drawing her closer.

"This is Peaches," Addison continued, brushing a fingertip over a downy kaleidoscope-colored coleus leaf. *This*, she thought to herself with an internal sigh of satisfaction. *This is what I've waited my whole life for.*

Noel glanced at her and then back at the neon chartreuse leaves laced copiously with deep red veins. "I've never seen a peach that color before."

"It's not the color," she explained. "It's the peach fuzz. Feel it."

"Ah." He complied, stroking one of the large serrated-edged leaves.

"And this," she said, gesturing with both hands at a tropical beauty on a short wooden stool on the floor in front of the window. "This is Tuesday."

Noel hadn't been able to spend that morning with Addison – he'd had phone calls to make – and had sent the three-foot tall Monstera deliciosa in his stead. The terracotta pot was too big to sit on the window ledge with the others, and when she asked the delivery man from Daisy Chain about the tall fibrous stick in the center of the plant, he'd explained that the Monstera was a vigorous climber and needed the moss stick's support as the plant would grow more than an inch a month for the next couple of years.

"She could grow tall enough to touch my ceiling if I take good care of her," Addison exclaimed, beaming first at the plant, then at Noel.

"Tuesday?" He gave her another questioning look.

"Yes, because she's Wednesday Addams' nicer, prettier sister," Addison reasoned with an impish grin. "She's a Monstera—a monster, see? But she's lovely and sweet, unlike that awful Wednesday." Tuesday was, indeed, quite stunning with her dinnerplate-sized, glossy, split leaves spearing off from a thick main stem that was anchored with twine to the moss stick.

"Tuesday. I think it's a perfect name for her." He smiled at Addison, a glow of satisfaction in his expression. "I'm glad you like them. They look like they're happy, too."

Addison turned toward him, slipped her arms around his waist, and hugged him fiercely. "Thank you, Noel. I think I feel kinda like a new mom." She giggled and leaned away to glance over at the collection in the window, then back up at him. "I have very colorful children, don't you think?"

"They take after their mother," he agreed, before bending his head and pressing his mouth to hers.

The kiss started out slow and sweet, Noel's arms enveloping her in a full embrace, his hands on her back, his palms moving up and down her spine. Then one of his hands slid up to cup the back of her head, his fingers tangling in her curls, and he angled his lips on hers to take her in more fully. Addison let out a soft moan as she melted into him, and she wondered momentarily oif her legs would give out beneath her. Then she stopped thinking altogether and lost herself in the nearness of him.

When they finally pulled apart, she rested her forehead against his shoulder as she tried to catch her breath. "You should stop buying plants for me," she managed to say.

Noel leaned back so he could look at her, his expression concerned. "Why? Especially if you love them so much."

"Because," she replied, her voice growing steadier. "I—I don't know. Just because. I mean, I know they're not cheap, especially this time of year. And what if I kill them?" The thought of doing just that made her feel aghast. "I've never been a plant mom before, remember?"

His expression softened into a gentle grin. "You won't kill them. I'll help you keep them alive."

Addison gave him a dubious look. "You're a plant person?"

Noel shook his head. "Nope. But there are two of us now. We're team mates, remember? We got this. You and me."

You and me. Addison reveled in the way that sounded. "We got this," she echoed softly, then tipped her head back so he could kiss her again.

He picked her up for church Sunday morning, then they had sandwiches out on her pretty little deck. The sun was out, the sky was clear, and although it wasn't exactly balmy, the air held that anticipatory current of the coming of spring. But Addison could tell Noel was feeling the weight of returning to work under the dark cloud of the unresolved circumstances around his job. She could only imagine the mental and emotional battle going on inside of him, and she asked God to help her be supportive without being overbearing.

"Do you want to head down to the boardwalk?" Addison asked when he'd gotten up a second time to wander over to the railing. "It's such a nice day, I'd hate to spend the rest of it inside." When she was stressed, she could curl up in a chair with a good book or a movie and lose herself in someone else's world, but she could see that Noel might go stir crazy if he didn't do some kind of activity. *How different we are,* she thought to herself. Did they have anything in common? Should she be worried?

An hour later, they sat on a bench down near the shore, pressed together against the chilly breeze that swept in off the water. The sun was sinking low on the horizon, casting liquid gold over the rippling surface of the lake. Noel seemed calmer, less agitated, and Addison was surprised to find that she, too, was much more relaxed. She hadn't realized how much she was affected by his stress level.

"You haven't talked about going back to work tomorrow," Addison said gently, her head resting on his shoulder. "I'm reluctant to bring it up, because I have had such a wonderful day with you, but I don't want us to tiptoe around it, either." She left it as a statement, an opening, rather than a question. She didn't want him to feel obligated to talk about it if he didn't want to.

Noel sighed and tightened his arm around her shoulders. "I'm not sure talking about it is going to help much." He paused, then added, "I'm just trying to stay present in this moment, Addison. It's moments like these—moments with you—that are going to get me through the next week or two."

Warmth flooded through her at his words. "I'm glad," she said simply.

He pressed a kiss to the top of her head. "Thank you for not letting me just... disappear."

"I would never—you could never just disappear." She patted her sternum, and with a burst of uncharacteristic boldness said, "You're front and center here, Noel Stewart."

He said nothing, just rested his head against hers and sighed with what she thought was contentment, which made her immeasurably happy.

Disappear. She pondered his choice of words. What exactly did he mean by that? She'd used the same word to describe herself, that she was the kind of person who could disappear into the background of her parents' larger-than-life lives. But Noel wasn't a wallflower like she was. Did he really think she was an "out of sight, out of mind" kind of person? Or was there some deeper meaning there?

She wanted to ask him to clarify, but just then, her phone rang, startling them both. "It's my dad," she said with a smile, recognizing the ringtone. "My parents." Should she take it? No. Like Noel had just said, she wanted to stay present in the moment with him. "I can call him back later."

"Don't do that on my account." Noel got to his feet. "I'll give you some privacy."

"Don't go." She grabbed his hand and didn't let him move away. "I can talk to them later." They were currently in California, so they were two hours behind her, which meant she could get back to them any time before midnight and they'd pick up. "Let me just text them to let them know."

When she'd tapped out her message and sent it off, Noel sat back down slowly. "Are you sure? They won't be upset?" There was real concern in his expression.

"Upset?" Addison shook her head. "No. We talk or text a few times a week, depending on where they are and what time zone they're in."

"You're close with them, then?" He studied her, the guarded look in his eyes making her sit up a little straighter.

"I am. I'm an only child; they have always been my best friends. Well, my dad is, at least." She chuckled and shook her head. The breeze blew a thick strand of hair across her face and she brushed it away, tucking it behind her ear. "And that's not a secret. My mom knows and approves. She's not really the nurturing type."

"You never really talk about them."

"I know," she acknowledged sheepishly. She rarely talked about her family with him, mainly because he usually skirted the topic of his. Deliberately, she was pretty sure, and that made her cautious about discussing how fortunate she was with her own. She knew her relationship with her parents had its issues, but other than her desire to put down roots in a community in which she belonged, her parents had gifted her with an exceptional childhood, and she well knew it. She might have been a third wheel on their trips, but they'd never once even considered the idea of sending her off to some stable relative to raise or even a boarding school, not even when she'd asked them to do so. She could hear her father's adamant voice in her head. *You're ours. Why on earth would we even consider letting anyone take you from us?* They may not have always known quite what to do with her, but she'd never doubted, not even during the loneliest moments of her life, that she wasn't deeply loved. She hunched one shoulder and glanced over at him. "It's a little weird, though, don't you think?"

"What is? That you don't talk about your parents?"

"No. That my dad, and by association, my mom, are my best friends." She turned to gaze out over the lake, trying not to worry about what his response might be.

"I don't think that's weird." He paused, then added, "I think it's rare, but not weird."

"Really?" She peered back at him over her shoulder, but his expression was unreadable. Still holding his hand, Addison shifted on the bench so that she was facing him. "I've told you we moved around a lot when I was growing up. And because of that, I didn't really have any long-term relationships, other than them. I mean, I had my book friends. But in real life, Mom and Dad were the only steady parts of my life. The constant parts."

Noel gazed down at their clasped hands. "I think that's… remarkable."

"What about you?" she asked, trying to keep the note of trepidation out of her voice. She sensed that she was walking on shaky ground, and the tightening of his hand around hers all but confirmed it. She pushed on, regardless. "You've told me your dad was a coal miner, but you've never mentioned your mother. In fact, I think I've only ever heard you talk about your aunt. Aunt Gigi, right?"

Noel nodded slowly, not meeting her gaze. "My mother died when I was a teenager," he said bluntly, his tone startlingly bitter.

"Oh, Noel," she murmured, squeezing his hand. How was it possible that they'd been dating for over a month already and she hadn't known such an important detail about him? Why hadn't she asked before now? "I'm so sorry. I can't imagine going through that."

Noel shook his head. "It was a long time ago." He spoke in a flat tone, obviously not wanting to talk about it. As usual, every word about his childhood seemed to have to be pried out of him. She'd stopped asking him weeks ago for any details, letting him dole out tidbits here and there on the rare occasions when he did. She knew he came from a coal-mining family from somewhere in West Virginia, that he'd had a dog named Clyde, and that he'd made friends with a stray cat down by the creek where he fished one summer.

But they were in the thick of things now, and she was desperate to know more about this man she was falling for. He hadn't yet changed the subject, so she pressed on.

"What about your dad?" she asked. "Are you two close?" Aching for the young man Noel had been when he'd lost his mother, she hoped with all her heart that his dad had been a bulwark for him. A strong father figure would explain why Noel seemed so steady, so sure of himself.

Noel scoffed, the sound ugly and full of derision. "My *dad*." He spat it out like it had been doused in vinegar. "He and I don't..." He broke off, then began again, his jaw muscles clenched tightly around the words. "We don't get along. We never have." He pressed his lips together, but she could hear the words, *and we never will,* as if he'd spoken them out loud.

"I'm sorry," she said again. She hesitated, not wanting to be nosy, but she couldn't bear the thought of a young Noel dealing with the loss of his mother without any support. "What about your Aunt Gigi, then? If you don't mind me asking."

"My aunt. Bruno's—my father's sister." For a moment, she thought he wouldn't say anything else. But then he turned toward her and his expression softened. He met her eyes and tried to smile. "Aunt Gigi... well, she saved my life. I'm here because of her."

"I'm glad," Addison whispered. "I'm so glad to know that, Noel."

"I think you'd like her. I *know* she'd like you. She's a little rough around the edges, but she's good people."

"She sounds like my kind of people," Addison told him, then leaned forward and planted a soft kiss on the furrow between his brows, wanting nothing more than to soothe whatever dark thoughts the conversation had conjured up. "I hope we get to meet each other one day."

Noel let out his breath in a long exhale. He shook out his shoulders and scooted forward on the bench. Turning to her, he smiled. "Ready to head back?" he asked, making a show of shivering. "It's going to get chilly out here once that sun sets."

It was getting chilly, she realized, and not just because of the topic of conversation. The wind was picking up, the lake had grown a little choppy, and her ears were cold. "Sure. Feel like splitting a pizza tonight since we'll be walking right by Patsy's Pizza?"

"Take out or dine in?"

She didn't even have to ask him which he preferred; she could see the truth all over her face. "Take out. We can watch more of Candy's show."

That was one thing they had in common, she realized. They both liked watching home improvement shows. Addison had pulled up Candy Needham's fixer-upper show and they'd both been equally entertained.

"Sounds good to me. No cooking, no dishes." Noel laced his fingers with hers as they headed up the boardwalk toward the pizza place. "I still can't get over the fact that your friend has her own television show. It's a little surreal, you know?"

"Had," Addison corrected him. "But yeah, she's fun to watch, isn't she?"

"But you said she's not going back to TV. What's she doing now?"

"Candy is starting her own restoration business. Probably here in Autumn Lake, although I'm not a hundred percent sure of that. She's living with her sister right now while she works out the details. There are some legal hoops she has to jump through; some non-compete stuff, I think. But I've seen photos of her work outside the television show, and let me tell you, Noel. She's tiny, but she's mighty. Mighty talented. Mighty creative. Mighty tough, too."

Back in her apartment with their extra-large marguerita pizza—something else they discovered they had in common—and a side salad—because according to Patsy, having salad with pizza cancelled out some of the carbs—they settled onto floor cushions in front of the coffee table and pulled up *Fix that Find* on the television.

Later that night, after Noel had left, Addison phoned her dad. He didn't answer, but called her right back via video chat.

"Sweetheart!" he exclaimed in greeting, the volume of his voice making her laugh. He always talked much louder than necessary when they were on speaker or video.

"You don't need to yell, Carl," her mother said in her naturally brusque tone. If Vivian was the force behind the Wedgewood's success, Carl was the heart of the team. It worked well for them, and Addison didn't doubt the deep abiding love between her parents.

Her dad didn't lower his volume at all, but she quickly realized it wasn't because he was ignoring his wife, but because he had exciting news to share. "How would you feel about putting up with a couple of visitors next week?"

Addison gasped. "Are you serious? This isn't an April Fool's joke or anything, is it?" When her dad laughed and shook his head, she went on before he could say anything. "When? And how long can you stay? I'm sure I can take some time off." She propped her phone on her nightstand

and plumped the pillows behind her back against the headboard of her bed. "You know I'd love to have you come any time at all, but what's the occasion?"

For photographers, her parents were comically awkward during video chats. The angle of the camera gave both of them very large foreheads, and there had to be a light above them, because her dad's hair looked markedly thinner than it actually was. It had been only a few months since she'd seen them, after all, and he'd still sported a full head of sliver-streaked hair in Iceland. Dad beamed as he leaned closer to the phone, distorting his features even more. "The occasion is that your mother decided we needed to take a week off and go visit our daughter."

"Now I know you're not serious," Addison said and rolled her eyes.

"No, darling," her mother interjected. "We are serious as a heart attack. We were just going through our collection of photos from Reykjavik and we realized there were none, Addie, *none* of us with you in them."

"Oh. Well, we didn't go there to take pictures of me." Addison was a little taken aback by the conversation.

"Maybe not to take photos of you," her mother said. "But we did ask you to join us so that we could spend some time with you since we knew we wouldn't be together for Christmas."

"I was with you the whole time," Addison insisted. "Practically every waking moment, in fact."

Her father jumped back in. "Exactly, Adders. *You* spent time with us. *You* took time away from your busy life—"

"It's not all *that* busy."

Her dad continued as though she hadn't said anything. "To come see us, and *we* didn't make the effort to stop working long enough to even acknowledge that with a picture of us."

"But you know I don't like being in your pictures. And that's how it works with us. I love going on your trips with you when I can. I had a great time in Reykjavik." A vision of Gunnar the Viking on Diamond Beach popped into her mind and she quickly kicked it back out. There was no room for him in her head anymore.

"Addison." It was her mother again, her no-nonsense tone resonating through the phone speaker. "In case you don't already know this, you, darling girl, are more important to us than any photo or trip we have ever taken. And if you know how much I value my work," she said with on arched brow. "You'll know that's saying a lot."

Addison chuckled softly. "Thanks, Ma."

"I'm serious, darling. Carl and I have been talking about how much we miss you, and we both realized—"

"Belatedly," her father declared. "Much too belatedly, in fact."

"Yes," her mother agreed, not even pausing to chastise him for interrupting her. "We both realized much too belatedly that as much as we miss your knowledge and experience and attention to detail on our trips with us, it's you and your precious heart that we miss the most. You are irreplaceable, Addie, even after all this time."

"Oh. Well, thank you," Addison said, feeling her cheeks grow warm at this unprecedented praise.

Her mother pointed at her through the screen. "It's true. But what we have missed most these last several years is you. Your light, your sparkle, your laugh."

"Mom," Addison murmured, embarrassed and equally thrilled at the things her mother was saying.

"We miss seeing the world through your eyes," Vivian went on. "We have gotten too caught up in seeing only through the lenses of our cameras."

On the phone screen, her parents reached for each other's hands. Her father leaned in close to the camera again and said, "What we're saying, sweetheart, is that we want to see more of you."

Addison couldn't blink away her tears fast enough and she leaned over to grab a tissue from the box by her lamp. "You guys," she said after dabbing at her eyes. "I would love to see more of you, absolutely. Come tomorrow. Come tonight! Anytime, and I mean that."

"Besides," her dad added in a far too casual tone. "We'd like to meet this young man you've been talking about."

28
Noel

To his surprise and great relief, Noel arrived at work on Monday morning to discover that both John Sheridan and Paula Swinton were out sick. Whether it was because he was back in the office or because they were both taken out by the same bug, he didn't care. He had work piled up and waiting for him, something he hated to let happen, and the knowledge that he wouldn't have to even see John's scowling mug or Paula's prim pursed lips for a whole day while he caught up had him pumping the air with his fists in exultation.

With a fresh cup of coffee and some binaural beats music playing through his ear pods, he started his day by sending Addison a text to wish her good morning. She made him promise not to send her any more plants, at least until she found another spot for them in her apartment, then she asked him how things were going.

I feel like I've been granted a miracle, he texted back. *I'm the only one here today, and I plan to make good use of having the office to myself.*

He ended the conversation with plans to meet her for supper at her apartment. *I'm bringing the meal, though. I want you to try the crabcakes from Lux Solaris.* He considered just taking her to dinner at the resort's fine dining restaurant, but he wasn't prepared to encounter anyone who might be embroiled in his and John's work debacle. Once things were settled, though, and *if* everything worked out the way he hoped, he'd bring Addison to the Lux Solaris, and they'd celebrate with a top shelf bottle of champagne.

That evening, Addison excitedly told him about her parents coming to town for an unprecedented visit. "I think they're going to make it a regular thing, too," she practically cooed. "Taking time off work to come see me, I mean."

Noel was thrilled for her. He loved seeing her so happy, and he couldn't help wondering how different his life would have been if he'd had the kind of relationship with his parents that Addison did. It was unfathomable, considering the people who'd raised him, and he shook his head to unravel that thought, lest it tangle him up in knots. Maybe not of her own volition, granted, but his mother had all but abandoned him to the monster who was his father, and his father hadn't seemed to care that Noel had all but disappeared from his life.

Until he'd had his stroke. Even then, Bruno had ranted and raved at Noel for helping him.

And now he wants to see me? He scoffed dismissively at the question that popped into his mind. Bruno didn't want to see him. He wanted to jerk Noel around; that's what he wanted. He wanted to get in a few more vicious jabs, even if they were only metaphorical, before he took his last miserable breath.

"They are excited to meet you," Addison said, snapping him out of his dark thoughts.

Noel narrowed his eyes at her, trying valiantly to dredge up his good spirits again. "Oh, great. What have you told them about me?" He was only teasing, but part of him actually did worry. Did they know about his trouble at work? About those days when he'd ignored their daughter? Did they already have a preconceived idea of who he was?

He'd never met the parents of any of the women he'd dated in the past. He'd never wanted to meet any parents before now.

She snickered at the look on his face and reached over to caress his cheek. "Don't worry. They're really nice, and they'll love you because I do."

Noel froze at her casual statement. She loved him? Her expression remained open and sincere, and it occurred to him that it was quite possible she didn't even realize what she'd just said. *They'll love you because I do.*

She'd just said she loved him. He hadn't misheard her. It had come out so naturally, so unfettered, and he was certain he knew Addison well enough to know there wasn't a disingenuine bone in her body. If she said it, she meant it, even though it was quickly becoming apparent that she hadn't intended to say so. He replayed her words in his mind, committing them to memory. *Because I do. Because I do. Because I do.*

"Then I'll love them, too; I have no doubt," he finally said, choosing to tuck her unintentional revelation into his heart for now. He wasn't quite ready to unwrap the gift her words offered; not until he knew better how things would turn out at work.

They sat together on the squishy sofa, Addison turned sideways, her legs crossed so that she was facing him. "I have something to show you," she said, leaning over and picking up a large coffee table book. She held it out to him.

"What's this?" he asked, peering down at the incredible image of the Northern Lights swirling over enormous ice blocks on a beach. The book was entitled *The Edge of the World.* "*Where* is this?" he amended.

"That's a rare sighting of active Aurora Borealis in the southern hemisphere on Diamond Beach in Iceland." Her smile was almost shy, but there was something else shining in her eyes. He thought she seemed proud of the book.

"It's stunning," he said as he ran his fingertips over the image. He looked over at her, waiting for her to explain.

"My mom took that photo a couple of years ago," Addison said quietly, then she pointed at the air just off the edge of the book cover. "I was standing over here. Behind that rocky outcrop."

Noel's eyes widened. "You were there? You saw this in person?" Well, that certainly explained the light in her eyes.

Addison nodded slowly, almost sheepishly. "Yeah. I mean, I was only there to help. And to hang out with my parents." She pointed at the names at the bottom of the cover. Carl and Vivian Wedgewood. "That's them. They're photojournalists. This is one of their books from a series they did on Iceland." She was talking fast, nervously, almost like she felt the need to convince him that what she was saying was true. "And we were just there again last December to do a follow-up magazine article on it."

"Wow. Addison, this is incredible. I mean, you were there. You witnessed this." They were exclamations, not questions. Why would she make something like that up? Besides, her name was on the cover of the book. Or her parents' names. Noel opened the cover and began turning pages, handling the glossy heavy paper carefully. He felt like he should ask for a pair of those gloves people used when handling precious artifacts.

He glanced up to find her watching him, her cheeks pink, her bottom lip between her teeth. She smiled hesitantly and asked, "Pretty cool, huh?"

"This is beyond pretty cool." He opened to a double-page spread of a wide angle shot taken inside an ice cave of such a crystal blue that it made him blink.

"Ice caves in Vatnajökull Glacier National Park," Addison said, pronouncing the Icelandic name as though she'd said it a hundred times. Maybe she had, he thought with a grin, turning another page. "And that's Silfra," she said, pointing at a lake with water so clear it looked like glass. "It's a fissure that formed between two tectonic plates and it's filled with natural spring water."

There were people in snorkeling and diving gear in the water. "You can swim in that? Isn't it freezing?"

Addison nodded. "You can! It's a diver's paradise. They come from all over the world to explore it. Wait until you get to pictures of the world renown Blue Lagoon. The water there is geothermically heated and supposedly has healing and anti-aging properties. It's this basin of milky blue water dropped into the middle of jet-black lava mountains."

There was photo after photo of scenery that looked right out of Middle Earth, food so colorful and unfamiliar to him that he had to ask repeatedly what things were, and names of towns he knew he'd never be able to pronounce.

Finally, he closed the book and gave her a long, hard look. "So tell me something."

"Okay. Sure," she said, bringing her knees up in front of her and wrapping her arms around them. Her feet were bare, her toenails painted a metallic emerald green.

"Your parents are photographers."

"Yes. They take pictures of amazing sights around the world."

"And that's what you meant when you said that you'd done a lot of traveling." It wasn't a question, and he already knew the answer.

"Yes. That was my childhood." She shrugged, then added sheepishly, "We've been to countries in all seven continents."

Noel set the book back on the coffee table and reached over to put both hands on her knees. He leaned toward her, his face less than a foot from hers. He tried to keep his expression serious. "And you let me try to impress you with all the places I've visited here in the United States?"

"Oh. Well, you *were* impressed," she began, then shook her head, her cheeks growing pink with embarrassment as she stumbled over her words. "I mean, I *was* impressed. I am impressed. You've seen parts of our country that I haven't, parts I may never see, since my parents prefer taking pictures in far-off lands and hard-to-get-to locations. I really loved listening to you talk about it all."

He rolled his eyes and straightened up. "Now you're just trying to placate me."

"I am not," she insisted, grabbing his hand tightly, her expression turning to one of real concern. She pressed a kiss to his knuckles. "I mean it, Noel."

Noel squeezed her hand back and grinned. "I believe you," he told her, but still shaking his head. "I'm just shocked that you didn't tell me about this before now. I mean, wow. Wow!"

She scrunched up her nose and looked over at him from under her lashes. "I always feel like I sound like I'm bragging when I talk about my past. Or at least, I feel like that's what other people think it sounds like. And ironically, all I've ever wanted is this." She made a sweeping gesture around the room, her smile soft with pleasure. "A place to call my own where I'd wake up in the same bed every morning. To have good friends—maybe even a few best friends, although I know that's kind of a contradiction in terms. But I think you can have more than one best friend. One friend who's best at making you laugh, one who's best at being there when things are tough. One who's best at helping you make those big decisions in life. Am I making any sense at all?"

Noel smiled and nodded. "Makes perfect sense to me." Everything about this woman made perfect sense to him.

"I listen to you talk about all the places you've been and those you still want to see, and I can only imagine how simple my little world here in Autumn Lake must seem to you." She cupped her hands like she was holding a small ball. "But in all my life, my heart has only ever wanted a place to call home, to belong, and to have people in my life whom I've known long enough to really, truly love." She drew her shoulders up just a little, and he thought maybe she hadn't meant to admit quite so much.

He slid over so that he could put his arm around her and pulled her against his side. She relaxed and draped her legs across his lap, resting her head against his shoulder. "A place with a window full of plants?" he asked, then pressed a kiss against her temple.

"And a cat or two." He could hear the smile in her voice.

They sat that way for several minutes, Noel marveling at the life Addison had lived. How was it that someone so well-traveled, so savvy about the great big world they lived in, could be so happy and content with such a simple life? He gazed around her apartment with new eyes, seeing different parts of the world reflected in the eclectic, colorful décor. It shouldn't work, all jumbled together the way it was, but somehow, it did. It all felt like it belonged there, pieces of her life surrounding her.

I want to belong here, too, he thought to himself. *I want to be an important enough piece of her life to have a place in her world.*

He had to sort things out at work first, he knew. With his job on the line, he wasn't willing to make any commitments or promises he couldn't keep. But he found himself praying for a miracle, just like Addison had told him to, because he kept finding reasons to want to stay and make a life for himself here in Autumn Lake.

Paula didn't return to work until Wednesday, but John remained a no-show. Noel greeted her perfunctorily, then went immediately back to his work. The secretary was dressed neatly in one of the prim skirt suits she seemed to favor, her hair carefully styled and sprayed into the immovable helmet she wore to work every day. She sat at her desk in her usual proper posture, shoulders back, ankles crossed, but she looked pale, the dark circles under her eyes alluding to more than one sleepless night.

At first, he tried to ignore her obvious misery. Eventually, though, in spite of his feelings of resentment toward her, he found that he couldn't just sit by and pretend nothing was out of order. He wasn't a monster, after all.

Noel picked up his cup and drained the last of his coffee, then he pushed to his feet. "Excuse me, Paula?"

Her head snapped around so fast, he worried she might have hurt herself. "Yes?"

He held up his empty mug. "I'm going to grab another cup of coffee. Can I bring you some?" He wasn't even sure she'd had any yet; he didn't see her flowery mug anywhere.

"Oh." She flushed, then glanced around her desk before folding her hands primly on her lap. "I guess I left my cup in my car."

"I have an extra one in my desk," he told her, reaching for the bottom drawer where he had a stash of 'just in case' odds and ends. "You're welcome to use it."

She swallowed audibly, then blinked rapidly and averted her gaze. Was she crying?

"It's clean, I promise," he said, trying to lighten the mood.

"Thank—thank you." Paula's voice came out a little above a whisper. "That's very nice of you. I—I'd love a cup of coffee."

"Sure thing," he said, extracting the black stoneware mug from the plastic bag in the drawer. He held it up. "How do you like it? Cream? Sugar?"

She made a valiant effort to smile at him. "Just black. I only doctor up my coffee on the weekends. Makes it feel special that way," she added, then ducked her head as though worried she'd admitted something too personal to him.

Noel smiled encouragingly at her. "Drinking it black is definitely more business-like."

Paula nodded and shot him another shy smile. "Right?"

Noel started for the back of the office where there was a small refreshment station consisting of a sink, a mini-fridge, and enough counter space for a coffee maker and little else. There wasn't even a microwave. But the coffee maker was a high-end single serve brewer, and all three of them made good use of the machine.

She thanked him again when he handed her a steaming cup a few minutes later, then held it close to her face and breathed in deeply of the rich aroma. Instead of returning to his desk, he paused a few feet away, putting enough space between them so as not to make her feel crowded. She looked up at him. "It smells wonderful."

Noel nodded, took a careful sip of his own hot drink, then in a quiet voice, asked, "Paula, I don't mean to overstep, but is everything okay? Are you feeling alright?"

Paula set the mug down and slowly straightened the small stack of envelopes she'd been addressing. When she lifted her gaze to his again, there were definitely tears in her eyes. "You've always been very... very kind to me," she began, then opened a drawer and pulled out a tissue from the box tucked inside. She didn't use it; just twisted it in and around her fingers while she spoke. "John has been—well, he's been my boss for many years, and I'm good at working with him."

That was an odd way of phrasing things, Noel thought, trying to keep his expression neutral. He nodded, hesitant to speak or ask for clarification. He wanted to know where this train of thought was leading, and he was afraid that if he interrupted, she'd withdraw. She was obviously feeling vulnerable, if the tears were any indication, and he wa beginning to feel a deep empathy for the position into which she'd been put. Paula was supposed to be support staff for both of them, but her loyalty would reasonably lie with John, if for no other reason than that they'd worked together long before Noel came along.

She pressed her lips together, presumably considering how best to say what she seemed compelled to get out. Then she sighed, but still didn't meet his eyes. "He's been... good to me. But then, I've never challenged him, even when I don't agree with him."

A trail of electricity sparked up Noel's spine and he straightened. What exactly was she saying?

"I don't know what happened between you two." The tissue was quickly becoming tattered in her hands. "And I don't think I want to know."

I don't know either, he wanted to tell her, but he kept his mouth closed, wanting her to keep talking. He took another small step back, not wanting her to feel intimidated in any way. He sipped his coffee quietly while she gathered her thoughts.

Finally, her voice tremulous, she said, "I really need this job. My son..." she began, then broke off. Paula had a large framed photo of her son, Tyler, and daughter-in-law, Janice, on her filing cabinet. When Noel had first moved to Autumn Lake, Paula had been friendly and welcoming, and she'd told him that Tyler was living with ALS. She hadn't given him much more information than that, but Noel had done enough research since then to know that time was a precious commodity, and that it cost money to make the most out of what little time Tyler had left.

Paula cleared her throat and tried again. "Insurance will only cover so much, and caring for Tyler is Janice's full-time job," she managed to get out. She finally met Noel's gaze. In her eyes, he saw fear, desperation, love for her child, and a steely determination to do whatever she must. "John has seniority, history, connections here."

"And I'm the new guy," Noel finished for her. He said the words gently, without judgement. He understood. He really did. John Sheridon was a bully, and like all bullies, he knew his sidekicks' weaknesses. Paula Swinton believed that she had her job because she was good at working with John, not because she was good at her job. And John let her believe that in order to keep her subservient, even when she, in her own words, didn't exactly agree with him.

"I'm sorry," she said so softly he almost couldn't make the words out. "I can't afford to lose this job."

Noel wanted to say that he couldn't afford to lose it, either, but that wasn't true, was it? He was a single man with few obligations. Sure, he helped provide for Bruno's care, but he knew well that his father was living on borrowed time. He had Aunt Gigi, but she didn't need his money. Her husband had seen to it that her needs would be met after he died, and although she lived very frugally, his aunt truly didn't want more than what she had. In fact, all she really wanted from him was his time and company. Other than that, Noel could go anywhere, work anywhere, do anything he wanted. He'd made sure of that.

"Excuse me," Paula said, getting to her feet. "I need to step out for a minute."

Noel realized he hadn't responded to her apology. "Of course," he said, moving quickly to the door of the office suite to hold it open for her. "And Paula, I understand your situation," he said as she started past him. "You do what you need to do to take care of your family."

Paula met his gaze again, opened her mouth as if to say something, then closed it, her lips forming a tight line. She nodded and hurried out.

John returned to work the next day wearing a surly grimace. He didn't look in much better condition than Paula, but Noel wasn't about to ask after his wellbeing. He didn't plan to engage with the man in any way, whatsoever. Joyce had instructed him to get up and leave the office if John started anything, and Noel planned to do just that, even if the man said so much as 'hello.' Someone like John could turn even the most banal salutation into an opportunity for attack. Noel had seen it happen a thousand times or more with his father, and he wasn't falling for it.

To his surprise, however, not once over the rest of the week did John and Paula sequester themselves in his cubicle like they'd done so many times before. In fact, the secretary appeared to be far busier than she usually was, her fingers flying over her computer keyboard, her eyes fixed on the screen of her monitor. Her inbox of paperwork was empty at the end of every day, and Noel had never seen her desk so tidy. If he had to guess, Paula was doing her best to avoid engaging with John, too.

"I'm not living under any false hope that she'll shift her allegiance," he told Addison one evening over chicken chowder and crusty buttered bread. "But I have a lot of sympathy for her. I wouldn't want to be in her shoes right now."

"I love that you have so much compassion for her, Noel. I'm still praying for miracles. For John's heart to change or something else that seems highly improbable right now. Nothing is impossible with God, right? I truly believe that."

Noel nodded, although he wasn't sure he agreed with her a hundred percent. His aunt claimed that he was living proof that God changed lives. "The fact that you choose to forgive your father and care for him in spite of everything he put you and your mother through is nothing short of a miracle in action." But she hadn't witnessed his debilitating panic attacks or seen inside his head when he felt overwhelmed and consumed by the same rage with which his father had scared him so much as a young boy. Aunt Gigi couldn't possibly imagine how hard Noel worked to not become a man—a monster—like Bruno. She didn't see the ever-present fear that hovered over Noel at all times: fear of losing control, fear of not being good enough, fear of being sucked back into the black hole out of which he'd crawled all those years ago.

Addison must have read something telling in his expression, because she leaned forward across her little table and covered his hand with hers. "I believe in you, Noel. I believe that things are going to turn out the right way, and that we will see God at work in this whole process. I'm not glad for any of this; don't get me wrong. I hate that you're going through this." She snorted softly and added, "I hate that I can't do anything to fix it, either, except to feed you and be here for you."

He met her gaze, lifted her hand to his lips, and kissed her knuckles. "You have no idea how much those very things mean to me, Addison. I love that you have so much compassion for me." He turned her hand over and pressed a soft kiss into her palm.

She didn't look away, even though he saw the color suffusing her cheeks. "I like taking care of the people I—" She broke off, swallowed, then said, "The people in my life. It's what I do best."

Noel was sure she'd started to say 'the people I love' and it stirred up a fire inside of him to think he belonged in that group. But he wouldn't press her to acknowledge it; not yet. Not because he didn't feel the same way about her. He *did* love her, he fully realized in that moment.

Which was why he wouldn't let himself tell her just that. Because he loved her, he only wanted the best for her. And if things completely unraveled at Carpe Diem, he would be leaving Autumn Lake under the shame of a shattered career, and it would be all his fault.

He couldn't saddle her with that kind of a future.

29

Addison

Carl and Vivian Wedgewood arrived on Thursday night the following week. Addison hadn't asked Noel to go with her to pick them up from the airport, partly because she selfishly wanted to be able to focus all her attention on her parents their first night in town. But there was also a part of her that worried that Noel might not feel comfortable meeting them for the first time at the airport and possibly feeling like a third wheel as he witnessed what she knew would be their very public display of affection. At least between her and her dad. Not with Noel's relationship—or lack thereof—with his own father being what it was.

Her parents had been to Autumn Lake before, but never for more than a couple of days, depending on what their assignment schedule allowed. Addison planned to use every last moment of their eight-day visit to help them fully grasp why she loved her Autumn Lake community so much. The weather was absolutely glorious and was supposed to stay that way for the next two weeks. In gardens everywhere, daffodils and tulips, peonies, and the early season irises were vying for attention. Folks with water craft were taking full advantage of the spring sunshine. Addison had even made plans with her Garden Variety Lovers friends to spend tomorrow, the first Saturday in May, out on the water in the bay at the Garden Gate Guesthouse. Between the whole gang, they had two john boats, three jet skis, and the St. James' family boat on which Ward promised to give them a tour around the lake.

She hoped that by the time her parents left for their next assignment, they'd already be looking forward to coming back for another visit.

Friday morning, she came out of the tiny guest room to find her parents already bustling around her kitchenette, Dad whipping up a batch of his famous smiley face pancakes, and Mom standing over the coffee maker with a slightly befuddled expression on her face. She hadn't bothered brushing her hair yet, and the bedhead knot she sported made Addison giggle.

"Good morning," she said, stepping up behind her mother and wrapping her arms around her waist in a quick hug. "Do you need any help with that?"

The aroma of freshly ground beans competed with the scent of maple syrup warming in a pan on the stove, but no matter how many buttons—and there were only three of them—her mother pushed, the coffee maker wouldn't turn on.

"Try plugging it in," Addison whispered, reaching over to do so.

Vivian sighed and rolled her eyes. "Oh, good grief. This is why your father always brings me my first cup of coffee in the morning. I can't do anything without a little caffeine in my blood stream." She bumped Addison with a hip in a good-natured gesture, then headed for the table and dropped into a chair. "I'll just sit over here and wait to be served."

"It's how we prefer it anyway, love," Carl said, turning from the cast iron skillet long enough to give Addison a quick hug. It was true; Vivian was absolutely useless in the kitchen, although Addison suspected that her mother didn't try very hard to amend her inadequacies. But then, why should she when her husband and daughter were perfectly content with the way things were?

"I love watching you two do your complicated domestic kitchen dance," Vivian said, smiling adoringly at the two of them as they worked in tandem to put together breakfast.

Addison poured her mother the first cup of coffee and brought it to her, along with a carton of extra creamy oat milk and a honey crock. "This is local honey," she told her mother. "A woman named Kimber Tate has this amazing little homestead down the road about a mile outside of town. We'll go by her produce stand while you're here. She has such great stuff there, and it's always changing, depending on what she pulls out of her larder or garden. She also sells some of her baked goods at Juno's Coffee Bar—you remember Juno, right?"

"Of course, I remember Juno," her mother said indulgently. "Now there's a face I'd love to photograph. Those eyes." Vivian shook her head, a knowing look on her face. "That woman has seen things, Addie."

Addison nodded. Juno, did indeed, have a story, but it wasn't one she freely shared with the world. In fact, Addison had been friends with her for more than three years before she heard how her friend had turned her life around like a phoenix rising up out of the ashes of her past.

"Oh, Mom," Addison gushed. "If you could get a good picture or two of Juno, I'd be tickled pink. I only have a few with her in them and none are great. She's always the one who offers to take the picture, and even when we force her to be in on them, she always seems to be ducking behind someone or looking the wrong way."

"Then I'm putting that on my bucket list for while we're here."

"You have a bucket list?" Addison asked, grinning back and forth between her parents. "Pray tell, what is on this Autumn Lake bucket list?"

Still at the stove, her father said, "Well, we want to spend time with you, get to know this boyfriend of yours, and hang out with your very cool friends." Carl then made a valiant attempt to flip a pancake high into the air. It flipped just fine, but landed on the edge of the counter and toppled off onto the floor, uncooked side down. "Oops."

Vivian pushed up from the table and came immediately to his aide. "I've got this," she said, patting him on the backside before grabbing a paper towel. "You keep cooking, Carl. I'm ravenous."

They spent the rest of the day lounging around the apartment, catching up on what all was going on in their lives. They communicated regularly by phone, so there wasn't anything especially new or noteworthy, but there was nothing like having conversations face to face. Addison couldn't keep from smiling, overwhelmed by the joy of having her parents all to herself. She couldn't wait to introduce them to Noel, who was joining them for supper, but this first day they were in town was all hers.

Her father napped that afternoon while she and her mother sat out on the deck and talked about Addison's job. "I really like it, Mom. I know it's nothing special. I'm not out there saving lives or changing the world or getting rich, not by a long shot. But I don't need to get rich and I'm really quite content with making people's lives a little easier by taking care of the small things. I'm not just talking about the passengers, either. The flight crews can be just as out of sorts and confused as the passengers, and it makes a difference when I can sort things out for them." She gave her mother a wry look. "I honestly don't know how the world would function without us invisible people."

"You, my darling, are not an invisible person," Vivian declared, almost sharply. She reached out and put a hand on Addison's arm. "Why on earth would you say such a thing?"

Addison rolled her eyes, trying to brush off her mother's reprimand. "You know what I mean. Behind the scenes stagehands. The minions who handle the minutiae. The little gears inside the big machine." She linked her fingers together in demonstration. "No one sees those parts of the job, but we're the reason the whole place even functions."

Vivian said nothing for a few moments, the silence stretching out to the point of discomfort. Addison opened her mouth to say something, anything, but then, in a very quiet voice, her mother asked, "Is that how we made you feel, Addie? Like you were invisible?"

She sounded so distraught, that Addison felt an urgent need to assuage her. "Oh, no, Mom. Of course not. I mean, I—I didn't exactly fit in everywhere we went, but neither did you. In fact, you and dad kinda fall into the same category, don't you think? Always behind the camera, never in the shot."

It wasn't exactly true; her parents were recognizable figures in their field, and not just by the images they captured on film. They'd been in front of the camera so many times that a collection of theirs was often considered incomplete without a photo of them included in it.

It helped that they had the kind of faces that told stories of their own, features that camera lenses turned into works of art. Her mother's dark green eyes fringed with thick lashes, her long straight nose and high cheekbones, her strong jawline, framed by the waterfall of nearly black hair that she typically wore in a long braid, now threaded with strands of silver that only added nuance to her appearance.

And then there was her father. Carl had the long lean body of a runner, even though he professed to loathe the sport. He had the sandy blond hair of someone who spent a lot of time in the sunshine, a broad forehead with fine lines that deepened into grooves when he was engrossed in something, and ears that, according to him, were just a little too big. The laugh lines at the corners of his eyes spoke of his engaging character, and his ready smile hinted that there was always a terrible dad joke just waiting for an opportunity to be let out.

Addison could stare at their photos forever and never have her fill of them. They were two halves of a whole. Yin and yang. One began where the other one ended... leaving no space between them for anyone else.

Including Addison.

Oh, they were good at stopping to notice what was going on outside their two-person circle. They'd metaphorically uncoil from around each other and open their arms to draw their daughter in. They'd tell her they loved her, that she was the most brilliant creature in the world, that they couldn't imagine their lives without her in it. And she believed every word, without a doubt.

Then they'd go back to the business of being them, leaving Addison standing on the sidelines, uncertain of her place in their world.

Wondering about her place in the world in general.

Until now. Until Autumn Lake. Until her lovely little apartment above the Quill and Ink Stationery Shop.

Until her Garden Variety Lovers Club girlfriends.

Until Noel Stewart.

Vivian wasn't buying Addison's protestations. "Addie, darling." She straightened in her patio chair and pressed a hand to her chest. "I won't speak for your father, mainly because I have a feeling he'll have plenty to say about this himself, but I've never thought of you as being invisible. Not once. From the moment they laid you in my arms, I haven't been able to take my eyes off of you."

Addison's heart thudded behind her ribcage in response to her mother's words, the visceral reaction surprising even her. Her throat was tight with emotion, and her ears felt hot.

Vivian continued, an expression of what could only be motherly adoration on her face. "It's why we always insisted on bringing you with us, no matter where we went, no matter what country we visited, no matter how remote our assignments. I couldn't bear the thought of not seeing your angel face at the beginning and ending of each day."

The door of the apartment opened and Carl came out with a cup of coffee. His hair stuck out from his head on one side and his eyes were a little puffy from sleep, but he had one of his disarmingly sweet smiles on his face. "A vision of rare beauty," he declared, crossing the little deck to plant a kiss on top of Addison's head, then her mother's. "Can I get either of you something before I interject myself into this conversation? Coffee? Wine? Cookies?"

Addison held up her water bottle and her mother shook her head. "Sit, Carl. I'm glad you're here."

"Oh?" He sat the glider next to Addison and rested his arm across the back of it, tousling her hair briefly. "What are we discussing?"

Vivian sat forward, her eyes fixed on Addison, but she reached for her husband's hand. "I will speak for both of us now, Addie, since your father is here and can contribute as he'd like. We're so sorry—what an awful word that is. How inadequate and trite it is." She shook her head as if to rattle loose her frustration.

Addison glanced at her father whose brows were now drawn together in concern. He said nothing, waiting for cues from his wife.

"I'm sorry we haven't taken the time to put into words how important your very existence is to us, Addison. I love getting your texts and your phone calls, but it's our video chats that make my heart sing. Half the time I don't even pay attention to what you're saying, because all I want to do is stare at your perfect, lovely, pixie, angel face."

"Mom," Addison chided, but it was softened by her grin.

"I'm kidding," Vivian said. "I know I'm a terrible listener, but I'm working on it." Then she straightened and turned to her husband. "I owe you an apology, too, my love," she began, squeezing his fingers. "You've been wanting to take time off to spend here for years, and I've always come up with a reason to put it off."

Carl brought Vivian's hand to his mouth and kissed her fingers. "And your reason was because you believed that Addison wanted her space, that she needed a break from us."

"I should have trusted you, Carl. You know your daughter so well, and I should have listened to you." She leaned closer to him then reached up to smooth down his hair.

"No one loves your daughter as much as you do, Viv. We're here now, and you're the one who rearranged things so that we could make this trip. You don't need to apologize to me. Not ever." Carl cupped her cheek.

Vivian pressed her cheek into his hand. "Well, you're the one who—"

"Um, hello?" Addison interrupted, her grin widening at their saccharine interaction. "Would you two like me to step out of the room?"

In a way, this behavior was exactly why she sometimes felt like she was invisible, or at the very least, a spectator in their world. But in that moment, she realized that she loved them exactly the way they were. Carl and Vivian weren't perfect parents; no one was. There were times, yes, when it had felt like she had to wedge herself into their love bubble, but Addison had grown up with the unwavering knowledge that her parents loved each other, that they would fight tooth and nail to nurture and maintain their marriage no matter what the world brought their way.

That certainty, Addison realized in hindsight, was the foundation of who she was now. It was a big part of what had shaped her into the gentle, compassionate, and yes, even confidant young woman she'd become. The same young woman who had stepped out into the world with her head up and her game face on. Afraid, absolutely, but courageous, too. The same young woman who knew what she wanted, enjoyed both her work and her hobbies, who loved the people she surrounded herself with.

And now that she'd finally found her own place in this world, she could see clearly her place in her parents' world.

"Oh, Addison," her mother said, her cheeks pinking prettily, her eyes sparkling. "We're ridiculous, aren't we?"

"Not a bit. I want what you two have. I want it more than anything."

Her father pulled her up against his side and kissed her temple, reminding her in a surprisingly endearing way of Noel. "We want what we have for you, too. Because we love you."

"I know you love me, Daddy. Both of you. I've never not known."

"You're not invisible," her mother reiterated. "Let me hear you say it."

"I'm not invisible," Addison said, rolling her eyes. "But I'm never going to be the person in front of the camera, either. Just so you know. I'm a behind the scenes kind of girl, and I really like my life the way it is."

"We like the way your life is, too," her father echoed. "Except for this young man we have yet to meet. I'm not so sure about that whole thing."

Addison elbowed him. "You'll like him. I promise," she assured him.

That evening, the four of them filled Addison's little apartment with rambling conversations and easy laughter, surrounded by the exotic aromas of a home-cooked middle eastern meal made up of chicken tagine with seasoned cous-cous, air-fryer falafel balls and impossibly soft pita bread, and a robust and garlicky baba ghanoush dip.

As Addison had predicted, her parents had fallen head over heels in love with Noel. She'd caught her mother studying him on several occasions, her eyes slightly narrowed in concentration, but with a soft smile on her lips. Her father, too, had done his fair share of sizing him up, and from what Addison could tell, Noel measured up quite nicely.

The following morning, glorious Saturday sunlight shone down on their party as the group of friends gathered on Hazel Poleman's dock at the Garden Gate Guesthouse. Everyone brought something to contribute to what turned out to be an incredible lakeside picnic, and several of them took turns zipping around the lake on the jet skis. Even Noel had braved getting on one after Ward assured him it was just like driving a snow mobile, except on water, and he'd taken to it immediately.

At one point, Addison lost track of her parents, but Hazel pointed them out. They'd commandeered one of the john boats and were drifting lazily in the shallows of the bay. They sat with their heads bent together, deep in conversation, a scene right out of a romance movie.

Liz and Candy Needham came with a badminton set and a cornhole game, Juno brought large carafes of iced coffee and tea and an assortment of cookies and pastries she sold at the coffee shop.

After lunch, Hazel took Judy, Penny's mother, back to the guesthouse for an afternoon nap. Judy had early onset dementia, and although she'd seemed to enjoy the gathering of friends, it was evident to them all that the hustle and bustle of it all had taken its toll on her.

Addison watched as the two women made their way slowly and carefully across the lane to the beautiful old home that had been in Hazel's family for over a century. She loved the way they ambled along, arms linked, their matching floppy sunhats fluttering around their heads. It wasn't hard to imagine what it would be like to grow old in a place like Autumn Lake.

"Hey, you," Noel said as he came up behind her and slid an arm around her waist.

"Hey, yourself," she murmured, leaning back against him, not taking her eyes off the women who were now making their way up the curving walkway to the front steps of the guesthouse.

Noel waited to speak until Hazel and Judy had disappeared inside the house. "Ward got called away for about an hour so we won't be doing the lake tour until he gets back. How would you feel about taking one of the john boats out for a spin with me?"

Addison turned into him and draped her arms around his neck. "I can't think of anything I'd rather do right now."

When the sun started sinking toward the horizon, they built a small bonfire on the beach, eking as much pleasure out of the day as possible as they watched the peaches and golds reflected on the lake. The day had worn them all out in the best way possible, but no one wanted to be the first to call it a night. Finally, as the fire began to die down, Addison noticed both her parents yawn at the same time.

"All right, you two. Time to get you home to bed," she said with a chuckle, reluctantly easing out from under the blanket she and Noel had draped around their shoulders. Noel stood and offered her a hand up, then helped her gather their things. Vivian and Carl were a little slower to the ready, but they didn't put up any argument about calling it a night.

Noel had come in his own car, so they said their goodnights with fewer kisses than usual. "I miss you already," he whispered against her temple when he drew her close for a hug.

"I miss you already, too." She pressed a secret kiss against the tender spot just below his ear where she was sure she could feel his pulse under her lips. "See you tomorrow." She couldn't recall ever being so blissfully happy.

Twenty-four hours later, everything about her beautiful little world had turned upside down.

30
Noel

"I KNEW YOU LOOKED familiar to me," Vivian Wedgewood exclaimed suddenly, pointing at Noel. They were sitting around the table playing what could only be called a rousing game of Scrabble after supper that Sunday evening. Addison had apologized to him when they'd brought out the boardgame, explaining, "It's tradition. Sunday game night. Scrabble is one of our top three."

Noel had never played before, but he caught on quickly and found, to his surprise, that he was pretty good at it. Carl kept trying to make up words, which Addison inevitably called him on, and Vivian monitored everyone's spelling with an enormous old-school dictionary she'd pulled from one of Addison's many bookshelves.

Vivian stood and went back to the same spot where the dictionary had been and slid out a large coffee table book. She brought it back to the table and sat down again, moving her rack of Scrabble tiles over to make room for the book.

"Oh, Mom," Addison said, pushing to her feet suddenly. "No. Not now." She reached out with both hands, wiggling her fingers toward the book in a 'give it to me' gesture. "Come on. We're playing a game."

Vivian shook her head and opened the book up to somewhere in the middle, smoothing the pages out flat in front of her. "I can still play while I look through this," she told her daughter. Turning to Noel, she said, "I don't forget a face very easily, you know."

Noel looked from Addison to her mother and back again, but Addison suddenly seemed to be avoiding his gaze. "What book is that?" he asked, a little unsettled at Addison's agitation. He tipped his head so that he could better see the photos on the open pages.

"Addie hasn't shown this to you yet?" Vivian asked, picking the book up so that he could see the front cover. *This Land is Our Land*, it was called, and across the bottom, in large blocky letters, were the names of Carl and Vivian Wedgewood. "Why not?" Vivian asked, shooting a curious look at her daughter, who was still standing, both palms now pressed to the table. "Some of my favorite photos are in this book."

"Sit down, honey. You're going to see my tiles," Carl said cheerfully, covering them with one hand and tugging on Addison's shirt hem with the other. Vivian continued turning pages quickly, clearly searching for something specific.

But Addison didn't budge. "Mom," she said, shaking her head quickly, her eyes locked on her mother's face. It sounded like a warning to Noel.

Vivian seemed to realize that Addison wasn't just being modest, but she'd apparently found what she was looking for. "I knew it. It *is* you. It has to be." With a triumphant look in her eyes, she turned the heavy book around to show Noel, one finger exuberantly tapping the page.

The powerful, terrible image had been so burned into his mind all those years ago that he jerked backward as if he'd been struck. His hand knocked against his rack of tiles, sending the little pieces skittering across the table. A few fell on the floor at his feet.

The room went completely silent, and Noel could see a faint flickering of lights at the edges of his vision. He averted his gaze from the photo of the scruffy young boy offering up a bottle of water to a coal-blackened miner, the image made almost surreal by the eerie glow of floodlights in the background, the air thick with the anguish and uncertainty of a town waiting for news of the men trapped below the surface of the earth.

And suddenly, he was right back there in that tiny clearing, his heart pounding, his blood surging through his veins, his whole body tensing in preparation for the blow that would knock him sprawling, face-first, to the ground at his father's feet.

And then he'd see her. The scarecrow girl. The almost skeletal creature trying to hide behind her long dark hair that had fallen forward over her shoulder. The otherworldly creature with a camera pointed right at him, capturing forever his deepest wound, that moment of utter and complete humiliation and despair. And on her face, an expression of shock and horror... and soul-crushing pity.

Noel blinked, and the room and its startled occupants came back into existence. He was gripping the edge of the table as if he meant to tear the thing apart.

"Noel?" It was Carl who spoke first. He, too, started to push to his feet, but Vivian laid a hand on his arm to stay him. She'd closed the book and now held it against her chest.

Noel noted the collage of images on the back cover. Carl and Vivian at least a decade younger, standing together under the shade of an enormous tree.

A chestnut tree. The detached thought drifted slowly through his mind—he could actually see the ribbon of words floating around in there until it faded away. Another photo, this one of the scarecrow girl—no, of Addison, he could see now—perched on top of a gaudily painted chicken coop, a camera draped around her neck. She wore a giddy smile as she tossed a handful of feed to the flock of chickens on the ground below her. A breeze swept her long hair back from her face, and the light in her eyes seemed to spill out of her, making her look nothing like the wraith who'd borne witness to one of his darkest nights.

Addison was crouching beside him, near enough that he could smell her tantalizing perfume and see the tiny flecks of brown in her irises. *Like freckles,* he thought. *She has freckles in her eyes.*

"Noel? Are you—are you okay?" she murmured gently, reaching out like she was going to touch him, but her hand just hovered in the air an inch or two from his leg. Was she afraid of him?

She *was* afraid of him.

He met her father's gaze, and then darted a look at Vivian. They were all afraid of him.

"Noel?" Addison did touch him then, cupping his jaw, and he flinched at the warmth of her palm is if it had seared his skin.

"Excuse me," he managed to get out, then pushed back his chair and got to his feet. "Forgive me. I—I need to go."

He didn't miss the gleam of tears building in Addison's frightened eyes, or the shock and concern on her parents' faces. No one tried to stop him; or if they did, he wasn't aware of it. He somehow managed to grab his jacket off the coat tree—thank goodness he'd had the foresight to stick his wallet and car keys in one of the pockets—then he reached for the door, fumbling clumsily with the knob.

Suddenly Carl was there, reaching around to keep the door from openiing. "Son, are you okay to drive?" he asked.

"I'm fine, sir," Noel said in as steady a voice as he could muster. And he would be, once he got back to the safe confines of his rooms. If he could just hold it together long enough to drive around the lake and lock himself inside his suite at the resort, he'd be okay. Then he could let go and give in to the anxiety rippling just under the surface of his flesh. "Please open the door."

He had to get out of there, out of the little apartment that had once felt like such a sanctuary for him. Now, all he felt was exposed, shamed, and humiliated.

Carl hesitated a moment longer, glanced back over his shoulder at the women who were huddled together at the table, then turned the handle to let Noel out.

He took a deep, shuddering breath of the crisp night air, remembered his manners long enough to thank the man, then moved like an automaton toward the stairs that would take him down, down, down and away from this place and the people in it.

31
Addison

THE BOOK WAS A collection of images of the American manual labor workforce called *This Land is Our Land.* In it, her parents had captured stirring images of hardworking men and women engaged in jobs such as farming, construction, railroad, plumbing, mining, millwork, and more. Many of the images were paired with pictures of the same workers lounging on their front porches or gathered around a meal, sitting in church with their families, or walking a dog. It was visually stunning in a completely different way than was *Edge of the World,* the book about Iceland, and what made it extra special—and extra personal—to Addison was that her parents had included some of her own photos in it.

Before she'd stopped taking pictures.

The book always stirred up a maelstrom of mixed emotions in her. There was a wave of pride when she saw her name in the credits, always followed by that hollowed out feeling in the pit of her stomach when she showed anyone else the images. Her photos were taken from a girl's perspective and captured slices of life with a whole different flavor than the ones her parents took. While the majority of the subjects that Carl and Vivian shot were adults, Addison spent her time taking pictures of other children. Every once in a while, the scenes overlapped, and the lives of her subjects would intersect the lives of her parents' subjects. Those photos were often quite telling, especially when caught on camera by Addison.

Because when she would take pictures with her point-and-shoot digital camera, the characters being photographed rarely even noticed she was there. Addison kept to the sidelines while her parents worked front and center. She witnessed the behind-the-scenes tableaus, the background images, the stuff in the corners or brushed under the rug.

It was one of the photos in *This Land is Our Land* that had ended her fascination of taking pictures. It was an image that made her secretly proud, one that often garnered a visceral response from viewers in the same way it had in her at the moment she'd captured the shot.

But that's what it had been—a moment captured in time—and the moment had been a lie of the worst kind. When the lie had been exposed, Addison had stood frozen on the sidelines, too frightened to move, and intensely ashamed of her fear and self-preservation. When she'd finally found the courage to step forward, it had been too late.

She'd done it again. She could hardly believe it. She'd stood frozen on the sidelines while Noel—the man this time, not the boy he'd been back then—had pushed to his feet and fled the scene.

She hadn't even tried to stop him. And now, she knew it was too late. She knew he wouldn't answer her calls or respond to her texts. She knew he wouldn't show up on her doorstep with another plant. She knew he wouldn't spend another day on the lake with her family and friends... with people who'd quickly become his friends, too. She knew he wouldn't come to her ticket counter for his boarding pass. In fact, she knew he'd do everything possible to avoid ever having to engage with her again.

And she knew that it was all her fault.

What she *hadn't* known was that the man she'd been falling so hard for over the last few months was none other than the boy whose tragic past she'd immortalized forever on that fateful night so long ago. Somehow, she'd missed it. She'd been so caught up in the here and now that she hadn't connected the dots.

Noel had said he came from a mining family when they talked about Arnie's books. Although he'd been reticent to discuss any details, Noel had made it clear that he had a broken relationship with his father. He'd told her about going through anger management therapy to deal with some of those issues, and he'd taken full responsibility for his part in the situation at Carpe Diem with John Sheridan.

But it was his eyes that should have given him away. She should have recognized him instantly the first time she looked into those deep, dark eyes across her ticket counter. When Noel, the boy, had locked gazes with her, his face smeared with dirt and the blood he'd swiped across his cheek from his split lip, it had been more than her camera that had captured that image. His eyes had pierced right through to the core of who she was, and even after all these years, she still sometimes dreamed about those moments, her mind conjuring up scenarios of what might have been.

How had she missed it?

Of course, Vivian had recognized him. And Addison couldn't even be angry with her mother, even though she'd begged her not to bring out the book. All Vivian had intended was to bring to light the remarkable coincidence that photo represented, that they'd already met. And to show off her daughter's keen eye behind the camera, of course.

Addison had only been resistant to showing Noel the book because that time in her life—those images, in particular—had been such a monumental turning point for her. She hadn't been sure she was ready yet to share those most intimate parts of who she was, of who she'd been, with him. She'd thought it better to wait until he was ready to share his past with her, too.

Addison had no idea that she already knew far more about that part of his past than she could have imagined.

Ironically, the section of the book that included that photo had focused on extractive industries such as mining, quarrying, and the extraction of mineral fuels, and was appropriately titled *Beneath the Surface.* But Addison had never told her parents what lay beneath the surface of that picture.

She crouched down and began gathering up the Scrabble tiles that had been scattered in the melee.

Carl helped her, then returned to his seat, his face a mask of concern. "Please sit, sweetie." He offered her a hand, helping her to stand. "What just happened?" he asked, his usual affable nature markedly subdued. On the other side of the table, her mother still clutched the book against her body, her brow furrowed in thought.

Addison sighed and sank into the chair abandoned by Noel. She took a sip from the glass of ice water he'd left behind, her own thoughts still working at hyperspeed to put all the puzzle pieces together.

Then she told them. She told them about the monster hiding behind the disguise of a hero, about the brute who'd backhanded a child with such ferocity, and left him lying bleeding and motionless in the dirt. "That picture I took was a lie," she said, her voice breaking on the last syllable, and then she began to weep. Through her sobs, she went on, "I think—no, I *know*—that horrible, horrible beast of a man is Noel's father. I know it is. And I—I did nothing to stop him. I was shocked, stunned. Angry, too." She coughed to try to open up her airway as the words poured out of her. "I—I was horrified by what that man did right in front of me, but I was frozen in place by fear. I'd never seen an adult do anything like that to a child before. I—I just couldn't move."

Her parents were there on either side of her, their arms around her, folding her into a cocoon of tender solace, but it only made Addison feel claustrophobic. She squirmed out of their embrace. "I'm sorry," she said. "I know you're just trying to comfort me, but I'm not the one who needs comforting."

"Oh, Addie," her mother murmured as she pulled her chair around the table so that she could sit close, but not touching. "This whole situation is awful for everyone involved. Your poor, tender little heart. No wonder you put away your cameras. I should have known there was something you weren't telling us."

"But that's just it," Addison declared, her voice rising along with her self-loathing. "I never told—never told anyone," she stammered. "I stood there and watched it happen, then I let him—let Noel—get up and leave without helping him." She took the paper napkin her father handed her and blew her nose, not caring if it was clean or not. She was crying so hard that it was getting difficult to breathe and talk at the same time. "And then I was too ashamed of myself to tell anyone what I'd seen. I just walked away from the whole thing—from taking pictures. From him. From Noel." His name came out on a sob. "And I tried to forget it had happened."

Her father, she could tell, was at a complete loss. He didn't try to hug her again, and she was glad. She didn't feel worthy of their unconditional love at that moment, especially in light of what she now knew about the atrocity she'd been a witness to. But he rested his large hand on her shoulder, and the weight of it gave her a measure of comfort.

"Noel didn't get to forget it ever happened. He couldn't just walk away, could he?" She blew her nose again, but it didn't seem to be making much of a difference. "He's had to live with that—that monster his whole life, while I just put my cameras away, closed the stupid book, and put it all out of my mind."

"You were so young, Addie," her mother began.

"So was he," she shot back.

"You didn't understand what was happening," Vivian tried again.

"But I did. I saw that man hit that child. There was no misunderstanding on my part. I was just ashamed of myself. That's the only reason I didn't say anything. I just abandoned him, Mom. I could have done something, and I chose not to."

Her mother, with uncharacteristic tears streaking her cheeks, slid closer and took her daughter into her arms, refusing to let go even when she tried to resist. Finally, Addison gave in and sagged against her, sobbing into her shoulder. Then her father was there, too, kneeling on the floor beside them again, cradling them both to him.

It was a while before the three of them managed to gather themselves into a semblance of order. Together, they cleaned up the little kitchen, then her father made a pot of chamomile and lavender tea while the women made themselves comfortable on the loveseat. "Something to settle the spirit," he said, handing first Addison a cup, then his wife. He lowered himself to sit cross-legged on the floor at one end of the coffee table, close enough to rest a hand on his daughter's knee.

"What do I do now?" she asked her parents, hoping they'd give her the answers she didn't have. "Do you think I should go over there and try to talk to him?" As she'd suspected, he hadn't replied to the concerned text she'd sent, nor had he answered her call. "I'm so worried about him."

Carl patted her leg. "I think you need to give him a little time, honey. Your message gave him quite a lot to chew on," he added wryly.

"Oh, please don't remind me," she whimpered, closing her eyes in embarrassment. Her text had been simple: *Noel, please let me know you're okay, that you made it back to your suite safely. I'll try calling again in the morning, but you can call me any time before then, even if it's 3 in the morning.*

It was the message she'd left on his voicemail that had her squirming uncomfortably and hugging one of the throw cushions tightly to her stomach in an effort to quash the butterflies playing dodgeball in her gut. "Noel, it's Addison. I'm so sorry about the way things happened tonight. I'm sorry I just let you leave, that I didn't come after you. Both tonight and... and back then. And I'm sorry I didn't realize who you were. I didn't, Noel. I swear I didn't. I couldn't see that boy in the man I lo—I love today. How can I possibly make amends? How do I make this right? Please call me. Please. I do love you, Noel. So much." And then, before she could change her mind and erase it all, she'd ended the call.

Of course, two seconds later, she'd been in tears again, regretting every word she'd said, and wondering what on earth he must think of her.

"Your father is right, Addie. Give him time." Vivian reached over and tucked a curl behind her daughter's ear. "I saw the way he looked at you. He'll be back; I know he will. It might just take him some time to realize that he can't live without you."

"But what if I give him time, and he realizes that he *can* live without me?"

Carl shook his head. "I saw the way he looked at you, too, honey. And believe me, I wasn't exactly thrilled. Not many fathers are when they see a man look at his daughter that way." He gave her a careful grin. "He may not be ready to admit it yet, but he's a goner where you're concerned. I'd bet my Nikon Z9 *and* my 600 mm f/4 TC lens."

"Dad!" The camera was one of the most highly-valued professional models on the market, and the lens he'd included was more than twice as much. "You seem pretty sure of yourself."

"I'm pretty sure of your young man, daughter of mine."

Addison went to bed comforted by the indefatigable love of her parents, but she lay awake long hours into the night, praying for the whole awful situation they'd found themselves in. She added her regular request for a change of heart in John Sheridan and Paula Swinton, too. She desperately wanted Noel to keep his job, for his sake, but also for her sake. He couldn't very well avoid her if he was going to stay in a small town like Autumn Lake. Eventually, they'd run into each other, and now that he knew she loved him... "Well, there's no taking it back now, is there, God?" she whispered into the dark.

32
Noel

I'm leaving town for a bit, he tapped into his phone. *Not sure when I'll be back.*

Noel stared at the message, his thumb hovering over the send button. It sounded cold, even cruel, but he didn't know what else to say.

She claimed not to have known that he was the boy in that picture, not to have known that she'd photographed the horror of his life and then had it published in National Geographic magazine for the whole world to see.

A mockery. A lie. A fairytale of a story that painted the villain as the hero and the brutalized victim as the adoring subject.

Addison—his gentle, sweet, tender-hearted Addison—had wielded her camera like weapon that night and had cut his legs right out from under him. Not just once, but every time he saw that picture. Every time someone pointed it out to him.

And again, last night, when Vivian Wedgewood tapped the corner of the image and said, "I knew it was you."

Then again, Noel hadn't recognized Addison, either. Sure, now that he knew the identity of that stick-thin girl with her long black shroud of hair, he could see it, plain and clear. The way she still dipped her head and let her hair fall forward, the tilt of her head as she listened to him ramble, even the way she often hugged whatever she was holding to her chest, like she was trying to protect her heart. He could still picture her holding her camera just like that, right after she'd taken his picture. She could no longer be called waifish, that was for sure, and her hair was now a warm, dark mahogany and too short to hide behind. But her eyes were the same, wide with curiosity, warm with compassion... and then stark with pity.

She must have been going through that awkward stage between child and teenager, he decided. "Not much to look at back then," he said under his breath, then scrunched his eyes closed in shame at the unkind words, recognizing just how much he sounded like his father.

Disgusted with the whole situation, he sent the text and shoved his phone into his back pocket, then finished stuffing the last of his clothes from the closet into his suitcase. He wasn't planning on coming back to the resort, no matter how things played out. If he did somehow keep his job—if he even wanted the job anymore—he'd find a rental in one of the nearby cities, maybe even Evansville. Somewhere that wasn't Autumn Lake. There'd be no avoiding running into Addison if he stayed living in the small lake town. A twenty-five-minute commute was no problem, especially since he had such a great car to make it in.

He'd already called in to work that morning, explaining to human resources that he had a family emergency he needed to attend to and would either need to work remotely for the next few weeks, or he'd have to take a family leave of absence. It wasn't exactly the truth, but with his case still up in the air, he really couldn't afford to take time off without a good reason. Besides, he did plan to see his father while he was back in Bald Knob, whether Bruno wanted to see him or not.

"This time," he grumbled. "I'm not taking no for an answer. I'm not leaving the hollow until I get face time with you, Bruno Stewart." There were things he intended to say to the bitter old man, and nothing was going to stand in his way. Not even Aunt Gigi, although he wasn't a hundred percent sure she'd take issue with him confronting his father. The woman had been pushing for some kind of resolution, if not restoration, between them for years now, and she probably had an inkling that any hope of restoration would come with some kind of confrontation first.

"Confrontation, here we come," he said, snapping shut the clasp on his briefcase with a little more fervor than was necessary.

He let his attorney in on his plans, too, of course, and Joyce was less than happy about him leaving town. "You need to remain accessible to me at all times," she insisted. "I have a feeling this thing is picking up speed, and I need you to be prepared to get back here on a moment's notice. How's the reception out in Bald Knob?" She said it as though the words left a nasty taste in her mouth.

"Reception is fine," he assured her. "I'm taking my car, which will make a turnaround a lot easier. Flights on short notice can be tricky." Unless he planned things just right, usually flying took even longer than driving, but at least in the air, he could get work done.

His phone pinged in his pocket, but he ignored it as he did one last check of the apartment, making sure he'd left nothing of his behind. He'd emptied his fridge of the few perishable items in it, throwing away most of it, but opting to take the apples and the chunk of his favorite Jarlsberg cheese with him. Aunt Gigi would tease him about his fancy pants cheese, but he knew she loved the stuff as much as he did.

Housekeeping would empty his trash and clean the rooms, and they might even ask questions about the empty state of the place. Would it be Hannah, he wondered, or Sonya? If it was Sonya, she might not even notice, but Hannah would be concerned enough to say something, he was fairly certain. He thought about leaving a note, but then decided against it. He'd already told Fred St. Claire down at the Front Desk that he would be out of town for at least a week, maybe longer. That would have to suffice for now.

By the time he pulled into Aunt Gigi's driveway almost eight hours later, his backside was numb, his bladder was full, and he was ravenous. He'd stopped only for necessities; he'd been holding out for his aunt's Brunswick stew and skillet cornbread, a comfort food like no other in his book.

As he unfolded himself from his front seat, Aunt Gigi stepped out onto her front porch and hollered, "You made it!"

"I did, indeed," Noel said, mounting the steps with his things. He set down his suitcase to give her a quick hug. "Thanks for having me on such short notice."

She eyed his luggage and frowned. "You planning on staying awhile? Not that I mind, of course," she added. "You can move back to the holler for good and I'd die a happy woman."

"You're never going to die, Aunt Gigi," he teased, avoiding the question altogether. "Now let me in. I smell my favorite meal and I'm about to fall over from hunger." He also smelled the telltale garlicky, peppery aroma of ramps, the legendary wild leek that was a springtime staple on Appalachian tables. Noel silently prayed that she hadn't added any to the stew. Although he'd grown up with ramps as a big part of his diet, he had never acquired a taste for them. The flavor lingered in the mouth long after eating them, and the odor could cling to a person sometimes for days. It didn't help that everyone around him smelled the same. In his opinion, it only made it that much more unpalatable.

Bruno had never missed a chance to mock him for his aversion to them. "Ramps are part of your birthright, boy. Somethin' wrong with you? Think you're too good for the rest of us?"

Thankfully, Aunt Gigi hadn't forgotten, and over their bowls of ramp-free stew with cornbread crumbled into it, his aunt filled him in on all the local gossip. Apparently, Emma's family had raised enough money for her nose reconstruction surgery and she was scheduled to go under the knife this coming Thursday. Gigi was still taking meals to the Coopers, even though they didn't really need them. Shorty had finally managed to get his asthma under control with a new medication, and he'd started back to work at the gas station. "It's my excuse to go visit with CeeCee and their daughter, Rachel. Do you remember Rachel? She's several years younger than you, so I don't suppose you would. Anyway, she can't be left alone for more than a minute or two, poor thing, so it's hard for CeeCee to get out of the house much."

"You're a good woman, Aunt Gigi," he told her, and he meant it. He didn't know anyone else who was so ready and willing to look out for others the way his aunt did. "I hope the folks in this town appreciate you. Bald Knob wouldn't survive without you."

"Oh, pshaw. Knock it off. You'll make an old woman blush, and I can assure you, that's not a pleasant sight to see. Like one of those backwoods shriveled up dried apple dolls." She cackled at the thought.

While they did the dishes and cleaned up the kitchen, she told him that she'd been by the nursing home to visit Bruno that afternoon. "He's got a doctor's appointment tomorrow, and they always wipe him out. But he wants to see you, he assured me, and he promised me that he'll try his best to see you on Wednesday."

"Sounds good to me," he said. "I brought work with me, and I've got plenty to keep me busy." The resort had been quite amenable to him working remotely. Apparently, John Sheridan was continuing to cause a stir over Noel being allowed to return to the office at all.

Noel was glad to hear that his father had at least been warned of his impending visit. But some of his fervor to see the old man had ebbed over the long road trip, and now, with fatigue setting in and his mood mellowed by good food and the promise of a comfortable bed, he simply didn't want to think about it. He'd left Autumn Lake with a long list of things he'd been determined to say to the old man, things he'd wanted to get off his chest for years, especially now that Bruno couldn't fight back. Now, after hours of playing out scenario after scenario in his mind, he wasn't so sure confronting Bruno was such a good idea after all.

Aung Gigi, however, was clearly over the moon that he had made the trip to try again to see his father, and Noel didn't have the heart to tell her he was having second thoughts. In the morning, after a good night's rest and a strong cup of her coffee, surely, he'd have a better perspective on things.

"I'm beat," he said, leaning against the counter, his arms crossed. Aunt Gigi was sitting at the table sipping coffee that Noel was sure had been brewed that morning. "Are you okay if I shower now and call it a night?"

"You go right ahead," she told him, getting to her feet. "You know I watch Doc Martin on Monday nights so we can talk about it at Bunko on Tuesdays. That's why I'm chugging this caffeine so late. I have to be on my toes to understand what they're saying." She held up her mug and grinned, the missing tooth on one side of her mouth making him bite back a smile of his own the way it always did. She'd lost it a couple of years ago, and when she found out how much it would cost to get it replaced, she'd flat out refused to have the work done. "I'm old, I'm happy, and I certainly don't need all my teeth anymore," she'd told him, as if that made any sense at all. Noel was pretty sure she just didn't want him spending his money on her, but he'd learned over the years to pick his battles with her.

Not quite an hour later, he lay sprawled on the twin bed that had been designated as his since he was old enough to no longer need a crib. He'd replaced the mattress a few times since then, and it always surprised him at how comfortable it was, in spite of it being so narrow compared to what he was accustomed to. He'd spent the last fifteen minutes unpacking his things and setting up a work station on the small desk he'd spent hours at doing his homework as a boy. He'd have to give his aunt a few more details on the state of things at Carpe Diem, but that could wait a day or two, he decided.

His phone hadn't rung all day, but he'd gotten a few texts during the trip. One was from Paula, surprisingly enough, asking him if he could send her a copy of a file that he'd emailed to John last week. He wasn't sure why she couldn't just get it from John, but of course, he didn't ask. He let her know he'd get it to her first thing in the morning.

There was a check-in text from Joyce that he responded to, one from HR at the resort that he ignored—they were supposed to direct all communication to Joyce, after all—and one from a spammer claiming that the IRS needed him to contact them regarding his back taxes or they'd start garnishing his wages. He blocked the number, then plugged in his phone and set it on the nightstand beside his bed.

Nothing from Addison.

But then, after his icy text to her that morning, he hadn't really expected to hear anything from her. He'd hoped, yes... but he hadn't put much stock in that hope.

A few moments later, he picked up the phone and opened his voicemail. He stared at the few saved messages, most of which were from Addison, his body warming even at the sight of her name in his phone. *Why are you doing this to yourself?* his inner critic berated.

He hit play on the last message and pressed the phone to his ear, listening to Addison's shattered voice as she apologized repeatedly and begged him to call her. "I do love you, Noel. So much."

I do love you, Noel. I do love you, Noel. I do love you, Noel. So much. The words ricocheted around his heart like a pack of howling wolves, circling, closing in, tighter and tighter, making his chest ache.

It's not possible, he thought to himself. "It's not possible," he repeated out loud. He'd heard his father tell him over and over how worthless he was, how useless. "You're a waste of space," was one of Bruno's favorite taunts. Now that Addison knew who he really was, knew what he came from, he couldn't imagine she really meant what she'd said. "How can you possibly love someone like me?"

He put the phone down, turned off the lamp, and closed his eyes as darkness settled in around him. He listened to the various Cornish accents of Aunt Gigi's TV show from the living room at the front of the house. She kept the volume at ear-splitting, but it was something he adjusted to quickly when he visited. He'd left the curtains at his window open to let the ambient light of the starry sky in, but he turned his back to it, the vast velvet expanse making him feel hollow inside.

Noel lay awake long after Aunt Gigi turned off the television and went to bed, his mind circling again and again back to Sunday night with the Wedgewoods. Was it just last night?

How had he not made the connection before last night? It still rankled him that he'd been so blinded by his attraction to Addison that he'd missed it. She'd told him about her childhood, traipsing around after her photojournalist parents. Not a whole lot of details, but she'd explained that away when she'd said she didn't want people thinking she was a braggart. Besides, he—obviously—hadn't shared many details about his childhood, either, had he?

"What a mess," he groaned into his pillow, desperate for the sleep that wouldn't come.

NOEL AWOKE BEFORE HIS alarm clock feeling lethargic and unrested. He headed to the kitchen to brew a pot of coffee, but even after his first cup, he couldn't seem to clear the cobwebs. Since his aunt wasn't awake yet, he turned off the pot so the coffee wouldn't scorch, then headed back to his room to get some work done.

Elbow deep into a data collection spreadsheet that he was pushing himself to get filled in before noon, he declined breakfast when Aunt Gigi knocked on his door. At lunch, she offered him a sandwich, but he still wasn't where he wanted to be before he quit for the morning, so he insisted he'd fend for himself in another hour or so. When he finally left his room, the house was quiet, his aunt either napping or off visiting one of her friends or taking someone something they desperately needed.

He remembered, with secret relief, that she had her Bunko group that night, so he'd be on his own for supper, too. Maybe he'd head down to the Piggly Wiggly and pick up some groceries for the week while his aunt wouldn't be around to refuse them. There wouldn't be anything she could do about it if she came home and stuff was already in her fridge and pantry. He'd grab something from the deli for his supper while he was there.

Noel knew that Aunt Gigi knew that something was amiss. Every time she looked at him, he saw the glint of concern in her eyes. He knew he'd have to fess up sooner than later; it wasn't in her nature to let things go unaddressed. "Not in my house," she liked to say.

Sure enough, 'sooner' came the next morning, while he was checking his emails over coffee.

"So." Aunt Gigi shuffled into the kitchen in her zip-up house coat and flappy slippers, poured herself a cup of the dark brew, and topped his cup off, too. Then she dropped into the chair across the table from him. "I'd like to know what's going on with you before we head on over to see Bruno this afternoon. I'm old, Noel. I'm not good with surprises, and I need extra time to process bad news. Whatever it is you've got your long johns in a knot about, you'd better spit it out. Especially since your fancy suitcase tells me you're planning on staying for more than a minute."

Noel pressed his lips together, but not because he wasn't going to tell her anything. What good would there be in that? But where to start; that was the question. Finally, he set his phone face down on the table and said, "I found a job I really like, and now they're trying to get rid of me, and I found a woman I like even better, and now I'm trying to get rid of her."

Aunt Gigi studied him, her elbows on the table, her mug cradled between her hands. After an uncomfortable silence during which he refused to add anything else, she said, "I'm waiting to hear the part where you're going to fight for both."

"Ah, but see, that part doesn't exist." He shook his head ruefully. "Because I'm not sure the job is worth fighting for, and I know for a fact that the woman is too good for me, and therefore, not worth fighting for.

Me, I mean. I'm not worth fighting for. Not her. She... she deserves far more than I could ever be."

His aunt snorted. "Well, that sounds like a load of hooey. On both counts. You went after this job last year like it was the holy grail. Is it really the job that's the problem? Or you? Or someone else?"

Noel started to respond, but she held up a hand to stop him.

"And whoever this woman is, if she's got even a peanut of a brain—and she'd have to have at least that in order for you to fall for her—then she already knows that you're worth more than all the stars in the sky, and out here, kiddo, that's a whole lotta stars. Have you even lifted your head from that dang phone long enough to look at the sky the last two nights?"

Noel closed his eyes. He wasn't going to argue with her. Partly because she was right, at least about the job, but also because there was just too much going on in his head to make sense of it to himself, no less to put it into words that someone else might be able to understand.

"Why are you here, Noel?" she asked after a moment.

Noel opened his eyes and gave her a tired look. "I'm here to see Bruno. He wants to see me, right? Or so you keep telling me. So here I am."

Aunt Gigi grunted something into her mug as she took a sip of her coffee. It sounded suspiciously like a word that told him explicitly that she was calling his bluff.

Noel raised one eyebrow sardonically. "Very mature."

His aunt set her mug down a little harder than necessary and leaned forward over the table. She narrowed her eyes and pointed a knobby finger at him "Look who's calling the kettle black," she said. "You want to know why I think you're here?"

"I have a feeling you're going to tell me." Noel was beginning to wish he'd stayed holed up in his suite at Carpe Diem. He hadn't expected to be challenged by her. Aunt Gigi was supposed to take him in with open arms and tell him how amazing he was. Just like always. He never fully believed her, sure, but she was his biggest fan, and sometimes a guy needed a cheerleader. Like now, when the rest of the world seemed set against him.

"You're darn tootin' I'm going to tell you. I think you're here because you're running scared. Scared of life. Scared of love. Scared of committing to something bigger than yourself."

"Hardly," Noel shot back defensively. "What do you call my commitment to you and Bruno? I take care of my own. I make promises, and I keep them. It's what family does; isn't that what you always tell me?" He tried to keep the misery out of his voice, but he could feel his throat tightening up as he talked. "And what about this career that allows me to take care of you? I dragged myself, clawing and scratching, out of this cesspit of a town and made something of myself so that I *could* take care of my commitments. Yes, you helped, and I'll be eternally grateful for that leg up. It motivates me to keep moving onward and upward, to make your sacrifice worth it, because I know it truly was a sacrifice for you. If that's not commitment, Aunt Gigi, then I don't know what is."

She made an ugly scoffing noise. "That ain't commitment, honey. That's obligation. A commitment is a choice you make to engage with someone or something else for *their* betterment. An obligation is something you believe you *have* to do out of a sense of duty or pride, primarily because it makes *you* feel better. Now I'm not saying obligations are bad. When you make a commitment, obligations follow. That's the way it works. But don't you dare mix up the two, especially when you're telling stories to me."

Noel sat back in his chair. He'd never considered the difference before. But he wasn't done arguing. That wounded kid that still lived inside of him wanted to lash out, fight back, and his scrawny little fists were raised and ready. "I take care of Bruno so that you don't have to, Aunt Gigi. That's my commitment to you, and yes, it's something I choose to do. That hateful, vicious old man, though? Fine. You're right. He *is* an obligation to me, an obligation that is a byproduct of my commitment to you. I get nothing—*nothing*—out of paying his bills except the knowledge that you don't have to."

She kept quiet and just continued eyeing him over her cup.

He poked himself in the chest. "I am not afraid of commitment." Geez, he sounded like a stubborn kid.

"Which is why you'd rather be here visiting with that old hateful man you somehow can't bring yourself to give up on, rather than back in Autumn Lake fighting for a job you like and a woman you love."

"I don't—I'm not—" The denial died in his throat and Noel clamped his jaws closed, grinding his teeth together. He pushed to his feet and crossed to the sink where he dumped out the rest of his coffee. He was already on edge enough without the aide of more caffeine. He turned to face his aunt, propping his backside against the counter, and crossed his arms. Digging his fingers hard into his biceps, he opened his mouth to tell her that she didn't know what she was talking about, but all that came out was a sullen, "You just don't get it, do you?"

She sighed, her shoulders slumping, and her steely gaze softened. "Oh, kiddo. I *do* get it. I really do." She looked at him for several long moments, then in as gentle a voice as he'd heard her use in a very long time, asked, "When are you gonna stop running, child? Don't you ever want to come in for a landing?" Her mixed metaphors almost made him smile, but her words hit too close to home.

He'd been running, all right. As fast and as far away from all that pain as he could possibly get, only to find himself right back in the middle of it again and again and again.

Noel could feel her compassion wash over him in waves, and he held on to his anger as hard as he could. He wanted to open his mouth and roar, to shake his fists at God, to rail against the injustice of being despised by the one man in the world who should have wanted him, protected him, *loved* him above all others.

"Enough," he ground out, responding to his own wretched thoughts rather than to his aunt's questions. "Enough," he said again, this time louder, trying to wrap his head around what that meant to him.

"Enough running?" Aunt Gigi gently prodded, love and empathy and hope pouring out of her as she watched him wage his internal battle.

Try as he might, he couldn't look into her eyes and stay angry at her. Nor could he deny that everything she'd said just now was true. He took a deep breath, uncrossed his arms, and let the words spill out of him in a long exhale. "Enough running."

Aunt Gigi came over and wrapped her arms around him in a quick, fierce hug. "Good for you. Now, I'm going to make you a nice big breakfast, and we're going to talk about the part where you plant your feet and stand up for what you want." She reached up and grabbed his chin, giving his face a gentle shake. "Fight for what you deserve, Noel. Because you *are* worth fighting for. You *are* worth loving, and the people in your life are beyond lucky to have you." She gave him a sharp, narrow-eyed look. "Don't you ever let me hear you say otherwise again, got it?"

♥ · ♥ · ♥ · ♥ · ♥

THE VISIT WITH BRUNO that afternoon went nothing like Noel had expected, although he'd had very few preconceived notions of what would happen, once they got to his father's room. For starters, according to the young aide who checked them in, Bruno was up in his chair and waiting to see them.

"Would you like to go alone, or should I come along for moral support?" his aunt asked. She was serious, Noel realized, and he considered both options, but only briefly.

"Please come. He might be more comfortable if you're there." Noel was fairly certain no one would be very comfortable during the impending encounter, but the Bruno he knew would already be on the defensive, and now that Noel's head was in a better place after the morning spent in Aunt Gigi's counsel, he wanted to avoid making a scene, if at all possible.

Nurse Debbie was on duty, he was relieved to discover, and she greeted him with a warm smile and a firm handshake. "It's good to have you back, Noel. Your father has been asking about you. I'm sure he'll be glad to see you."

Noel wasn't so sure about that, but he didn't try to set her straight. He just nodded, then they followed the nurse as she led them through the building.

Debbie knocked sharply on Bruno's door and pushed into the room without waiting for an invitation. Aunt Gigi slipped in right behind her, but Noel hesitated, wondering if he should wait for the ladies to pave the way first. Then he thought better of it. Bruno already knew he was there, so holding back might only serve to make Noel seem afraid, and that was one thing he refused to be where his father was concerned.

Noel barely recognized the frail old man sitting in the recliner at the window that overlooked the back of the nursing home's property. The drapes were open and the blinds up so they could see outside to the beautiful spring day.

"I'll leave you three to it," Debbie said with an encouraging nod. She pointed at the call button on the remote strapped to the arm of Bruno's chair. "Just buzz if you need anything." Then she ducked out of the room, pulling the door closed behind her.

His father, partially backlit by the light streaming in the window behind him, was no longer the terrifying monster he'd once been. Shrunken, shoulders hunched forward over a chest that rose and fell laboriously, now little more than skin and bones, Bruno was nothing but an old man who'd given in to the ravages of both time and disease. Aunt Gigi had kept Noel informed of his father's medical condition and treatments, but he saw now that there was much more that she hadn't shared with him.

His father really was dying.

Bruno wore an oxygen canula in his nose, the tube connected to a large tank mounted on the wall near the head of his bed. He was clean-shaven and almost completely bald, making his sagging ears look enormous. His elbows were propped on the armrests of his chair, bony fingers loosely laced together over his abdomen. The backs of his hands were discolored and blotchy, crisscrossed with purple veins just beneath the skin.

"Hello, Bruno," Noel said, hating the catch in his voice. It wasn't nervousness that tightened around his throat, but a deep emotion he couldn't quite name, one that caught him off guard.

"Noel."

It was the first time he'd heard his name come out of his father's mouth in years, and it had been even longer than that since it had been spoken without rancor. The lump in his throat made it difficult to swallow, and afraid his voice wouldn't work, he said nothing.

"Been a long time," Bruno said, slowly and with much effort. He didn't unlace his fingers, and Noel wondered if holding his hands that way was to mask which one no longer worked. Bruno thrust his chin toward a couple of chairs nearby. "Sit."

Aunt Gigi nudged Noel further into the room, then she moved to Bruno's side and pressed a quick kiss to the top of his head. "Hello, little brother," she said, her tone motherly. "It'll just be a short visit, I promise. But I've brought your boy, just like you asked."

It turned out to be a shockingly short visit, indeed.

Aunt Gigi started the conversation with news of the goings-on at the mine. In spite of his father's current circumstances, the mines and the men and women who worked them had always been the most important pieces of Bruno's life.

His father managed to ask a few questions about men whose names Noel didn't recognize, before finally turning to look at Noel. He opened his mouth to say something but started coughing instead.

It was an awful, wet cough that wouldn't let up, and when it became clear that he couldn't catch his breath, Aunt Gigi pressed the nurse call button.

Noel stood and approached his father with great uncertainty. Should he do something? Pat him on the back? Go hunt Debbie down? Bruno was struggling to control the spasms of his body as the coughing continued. His eyes watered, his mouth opened and closed like he was trying to speak, and he dragged in harsh breaths of the life-preserving oxygen that hissed through the canula in his nose. At a loss for what else to do, Noel reached out and brushed his fingers over Bruno's tightly clasped hands. "I'm here, Dad."

The moment Noel touched him, Bruno unlaced his fingers, his stroke-affected limb flopping lifelessly off the side of the armrest, his good hand grasping Noel's. He squeezed Noel's fingers hard and didn't let go, locking gazes with him.

When Debbie bustled in, Bruno closed his eyes, released his grip on Noel's hand, and turned his face away.

Noel stood there, his fingers opening and closing in a fist at his side, unsure of what to do next. Should he stay in the room while the nurse did whatever she could to help Bruno? Or should he step out? Aunt Gigi's words from his last visit about the loss of one's dignity in a place like this echoed loudly in his mind.

His aunt took the decision from him when she slipped her hand into the crook of his elbow and guided him out into the hallway. "There's a family waiting room at the end of the hall," she told him, leading the way. "Debbie will know where to find us."

Half an hour later, Debbie informed them that Bruno was back in bed and was likely already asleep. "I think he's probably done in for the day," she said with a regretful expression. "I know you've come a long way to see him, Noel. I'm sorry."

In the car on the ride back to his aunt's house, Gigi explained, "He's been fighting that awful cough for several months now. It started out as bronchitis, Debbie told me, but it's turned into chronic pneumonia now. His heart is failing as a result of the stroke, and his poor old body just doesn't seem to have what it needs to stave off the inevitable. They can't get all that junk out of his lungs, poor thing, and once he starts coughing like that, it wears him out something awful."

"Should we try going back tomorrow?" The moment his father had said his name, something in Noel that he'd long thought dead and gone had sparked to life. There was still an ember of resentment, yes. The man had created a legacy of suffering that Noel would carry for the rest of his life.

But something else had reared its head, too. Something Noel wasn't sure he had the courage to acknowledge.

Hope.

Aunt Gigi shook her head slowly. "No," she finally said. "Unless he asks to see you again, I think the good Lord might have given you both just what you needed today. Let's leave things be for now."

He wondered, for the first time in his life, if he would actually *get* to see his father again, but he didn't say so out loud.

"Besides, you've got somewhere to be tomorrow, don't you?" she asked, nudging him across the console with her elbow.

His pulse quickened tellingly, and he glanced over at her, anticipation threading through him. "I do," he said.

An hour later, he was repacking his suitcase when his phone rang. He snatched it up off the desk, longing to see Addison's name on the screen, but it was Joyce.

"This is Noel," he said, doing his best to sound all business.

"How soon can you be back in town?" she asked without preamble. It was one of the things he liked about her, the way she got right to the point and didn't waste time.

"Actually, I'm packing up as we speak. I'd planned to head out first thing in the morning, which would get me there around two or three in the afternoon. Flying wouldn't get me there any earlier, in case you're wondering."

"Tomorrow afternoon is fine. We've got some negotiating to do, and I want you there in person, but this is good news, Noel. Great news."

"Wow. Okay. Do you want to share any of it with me?" He sat down on the edge of his bed, his heart racing.

"If you want me to bill you twice for it," she quipped. "I'll be going over everything with you in detail tomorrow."

Noel chuckled. "No, no. Tomorrow is fine." Like most attorneys, the woman billed in six-minute increments, but her rate per six-minute unit was borderline ludicrous. "I'll let you know when I get in."

"You do that," she said. "See you tomorrow." Then she hung up without waiting for his response.

33
Addison

Addison's parents and friends were doing their best to keep her too busy to fall apart, but there was nothing to hold back her misery at night, alone in her little guestroom, surrounded by the happily-ever-after couples in her collection of books that lined the walls. But every morning, she got up, applied a little extra foundation to hide the circles under her eyes, put on something colorful and cheerful, and went out to face the day.

She had no choice. After she got Noel's text, her parents had given her all of Monday to come undone. They'd even agreed to let her skip May's Monday Movie Night at the drive-in theater, even though Addison had been so looking forward to taking them to the community event. But that had been when Noel was going to be part of the party.

Tuesday morning, however, her mother had practically dragged Addison out of bed, her father had fed and caffeinated her, then they loaded her into the car and they'd gone thrift store shopping all day. They'd returned to the apartment on Larkspur Lane tired and grungy, but with a trunk full of treasures, and after showers all around, Carl whipped up an enormous batch of spaghetti—"Nothing better than leftover spaghetti!" he insisted when Addison asked him why so much—while Vivian and Addison perused what felt like hundreds of options before agreeing on a British detective series to binge watch.

They spent Wednesday morning sightseeing around Autumn Lake on foot, much the same way she and Noel had done that first Saturday they'd toured the town together, and it took all of her willpower not to think about how much she'd enjoyed herself that day. "I'm making new memories," she kept telling herself again and again. She wanted so much for her parents to love her little town; she wasn't going to mope around in misery and ruin things for them.

They sat at the counter at Juno's Coffee Bar for lunch, and Juno served them her signature roasted peppers and beef sandwiches, to which both Carl and Vivian gave their resounding stamp of approval. Then they headed over to The Cracked Spine for a surprise book signing and interview that Claire had somehow managed to orchestrate on such short notice. She'd let Addison in on her plans, but Carl and Vivian were surprised and delighted by the warm welcome they received upon entering the shop.

"I don't know how you pulled this off," Addison said to her friend as she watched her parents engaging with the small crowd that had come to see them. There were even folks from as far away as Indianapolis up north and Nashville to the south.

"I have my connections," Claire told her with a wink. Then she added, "But really, your parents pull in a crowd on their own. I just sent out a mass email with a flyer to every bookstore and library in a hundred-mile radius, but people are here because they want to meet Carl and Vivian."

That evening, they headed to Patsy's Pizza, and by the time they climbed the steps to Addison's deck, they all agreed that it had been a lovely day. Even Addison.

But alone in her room, she gazed out at the star-splashed night sky and wondered how everything had gone so wrong with Noel.

Thursday was another glorious spring day, so the Wedgewoods packed a picnic lunch and headed down the boardwalk toward the lake shore and joined several other families who were soaking up the sunshine and braving the chilly water. Addison made a hearty lentil soup that evening, and they finished the rest of the season of the detective show they'd started. Addison couldn't remember the last time her parents had seemed so relaxed. She really hoped they'd take time off like this on a regular basis; she loved seeing them this way.

On Friday, Addison and her parents headed out of Autumn Lake to spend the day wandering around Evansville. There were some wonderful sights to see, among them a haunted library, the only operational World War II-era naval landing ship in the United States, and the Angel Mounds, one of the best-preserved, pre-contact Native American sites in North America.

Carl and Vivian both brought cameras, but to Addison's surprise, her parents spent the day taking selfies of the three of them, rather than documenting the landmarks. "We're here to see you, honey," her father explained when she asked what else they wanted to see that day.

She knew how lucky she was to have parents like hers, and it broke her heart to think of Noel growing up with a father like the one she'd seen that night at the mines and then losing his mother so young. "I wish Noel could have had parents like you," she admitted to them as they meandered the brick-paved streets of historical downtown Evansville.

"Maybe he will one day," Vivian said, putting her arm around Addison and giving her a quick squeeze. "I don't think we'd mind one bit, would we, Carl?"

"You guys are too much," Addison said, although she secretly acknowledged that she wouldn't mind having him join their family, either. Not a single, tiny bit at all. But right now, such a thing just seemed like wishful thinking.

They stopped in at the eclectic River City Coffee for an afternoon pick-me-up, and after perusing the Evansville-inspired products the shop carried, they purchased matching Evansville t-shirts, which they wore proudly the rest of the day.

The day in the city ended at the Gerst Haus, an iconic German restaurant famous for its fresh wiener schnitzel and bratwurst, as well as their fishbowl goblets of German amber beer. By the time they got back to Autumn Lake, the sun was setting spectacularly over the lake, so they parked down by the boardwalk and sat on the shore to watch the show.

"Thank you for being here," Addison said in a hushed voice. The glorious sky demanded reverence, and she sat there between her parents, overwhelmed by gratitude.

As darkness fell, the night air grew chilly, and a breeze ruffled the water of the lake, nudging them into action. They drove the few blocks to Larkspur Lane, but as they pulled into the alley, Addison took her foot off the gas and let the car slow to a stop several yards away from her parking space.

Noel's car was parked in the only other spot behind the Quill and Ink.

"Oh, my," Vivian said from the passenger seat.

"Hm," Carl added from the back seat.

"What do I do?" Addison asked, turning frantically to look at her mother.

"Well, I'd start with pulling in and parking, darling."

"Then you can get out of the car," her father said, leaning forward between them and resting his elbows on the front seat console.

Vivian snickered. "So helpful, love."

"Thank you."

"You guys," Addison squawked. "You're not helping at all!"

"Park your car, Addie," Vivian said. "Start there."

Addison took her foot off the brake and angled her car into the open spot next to Noel's. She was half afraid to look over at it, so she made a big to-do about turning off the ignition and setting her emergency brake.

"He's not in his car," Carl said from the back seat.

"He must be upstairs already. Have you given him a key, darling?" Vivian asked.

"Mother! No, I have not given him a key to my apartment."

Vivian raised both hands in surrender. "It was just a question." When Addison just sat there, both hands gripping the steering wheel, her mother poked her in the ribs. "We're home. Get out."

"Oh. Right. Yes." She glanced over her shoulder at her father. "What do I say to him, Daddy?"

"Nothing," Carl replied almost flippantly. "Let him talk. I'm assuming that's what he's come to do."

"But—but then what?"

"Addison Wedgewood. Get your backside out of this car and go listen to whatever that man has to say. Now." Vivian held out a hand to her, palm up. "And give me your keys."

"Why?"

"Obey your mother."

"Why?"

"Because I'd like your father to take me for a moonlit ride without you in the car with us. It's a very romantic night out there, in case you hadn't noticed."

"Ew. Gross. Here." She started to take her housekey off the ring, but her mother snatched the whole set from her before she could.

"Nope. If this is a kiss and make up session, you two need to stay outside. I know all about what kiss and make up sessions lead to."

Addison rolled her eyes. "Oh, really?"

"How do you think you came about?" her father asked from the back seat.

"Oh, my gosh. You two are so disgusting." Addison pushed open her door and reached back inside to grab her purse. "Scarred for life, here," she quipped.

"You asked," her mother said, handing the bunch of keys to her husband, who slid out of the backseat and gave Addison a hug.

"Go get 'im, Tiger," her father said, patting her gently on the cheek.

"Thanks, Daddy."

"We're rooting for you both!" he added in a very loud voice, his head tilted up toward the deck above them. Then he climbed behind the wheel and backed out of the parking space, practically peeling out on the gravel in his hurry to be gone.

Addison just stood there, watching the taillights of her car disappear around the corner. Taking a deep breath, she finally looked up at her deck. Nothing. There was no sign of life up there. No handsome man leaning out over the rail to see her, no footsteps on the stairs as he came down to greet her. Great. And now her parents had driven off with her house key and she was going to be stuck waiting outside, all alone, while they were off doing something scandalous, no doubt, that Addison really didn't want to know about. She released a disappointed sigh, then turned toward the steps.

A movement above caught her eye, and she paused with one foot on the first step. A silhouetted form moved languidly against the bars of the deck railing, its tail flicking lazily with each step. The cat—no, it was a kitten, she realized—let out a scratchy little, "Mew."

"Kitty? What are you doing up there?" Addison called out, a bubble of delight bursting open inside her chest. Was she dreaming? She scrambled up the steps, almost tripping halfway up, and dropped to her knees to greet the furry little feline. It was all one color, a smokey gray, except for a white patch just between the ears and white socks on all four feet. "Oh, my goodness. Look at you," she cooed, her voice high, her heart racing, as the kitten traipsed over and started batting at Addison's fingers. "You look like you stepped in a puddle of starlight. Where did you come from, little one?"

Noel leaned forward on the wrought iron loveseat where he was sitting. "Addison."

"Oh!" Addison jerked in surprise, tipping backwards onto her backside, and surprising the kitten, who jumped into the air, then scampered away from her to hide behind Noel's legs. "I didn't see you there." Embarrassed, she scrambled to her feet, then stood facing him, not sure what to do with her hands. "How—how long have you been up here?"

Noel rose, but he didn't come any closer. The cat attacked his pant leg, snagging a tiny claw in the hem of it, then mewling loudly when it couldn't get loose. "Hey, buddy. Come here." Noel reached down and gingerly plucked the claw free, then brought the kitten up to hold against his chest. "We've been hanging out watching the sunset together," he said. "Addison, meet Cat. Cat, meet Addison." He leaned in close to the kitten's ear, but he kept his gaze locked on Addison. "She's that amazing woman I was telling you about."

For a moment, Addison wasn't sure her voice would work. What had her father said? *Let him talk.* Okay. That's what she'd do. "Nice to meet you, Cat." She didn't look away from Noel, either. "It's good to see you, Noel." Then she closed her mouth and leaned against the railing.

Noel cleared his throat, then reached into his back pocket and pulled out a crumpled pink bow. "She was wearing this when we first got here."

"Cat's a she, then," Addison acknowledged, trying not to let herself get too excited. Was the kitten a gift? For her?

"She's a she, and since I know you'd be a great cat mama, she's yours if you'll have her."

Addison felt the telltale prickling at the bridge of her nose that told her she'd be crying before long. "She's really mine?" she managed to say, her voice small and breathy.

Noel nodded, bringing the kitten up higher so that he and the little furball were almost cheek to cheek. "She's really yours."

Addison let her purse drop to the deck and she took a step toward him. "On one condition," Noel said.

"Oh yeah?" Addison stopped where she was and crossed her arms, barely able to contain the urge to pluck the kitten out of his hands. "And what is that condition, pray tell?"

"Addison," Noel said, his tone suddenly no longer playful. "I'm sorry for running the way I did. Twice now. I didn't even realize I was doing it, but apparently, that's been my go-to method of dealing with uncomfortable or tough situations." He chuckled ruefully. "By *not* dealing with them. By running from them."

Addison shifted her weight, wanting to go to him, but hearing her father's voice in her head. *Let him talk.* "I understand, Noel. I forgive you."

"And I'm sorry for doubting you the way I did. I should have known better," he said, shaking his head. The kitten reached up and batted at his nose, making Addison giggle. "Hey you," Noel gently chided, tucking the kitten into the crook of his arm and cradling her against his heart. "I should have believed you when you said that you were on my team. That you believed in me. It's not an easy thing for me to do, believing in people, I mean. I tend to forget that I'm not alone in this world, but that's no excuse, and I'm sorry. You've never given me any reason to doubt your friendship."

Addison's heart stuttered, and she took a tiny step back. Friendship? Was that what he wanted from her? She found that she was holding her breath.

"I'm in the rather painful process of learning some not-so-great things about myself," he continued. Even without the porch light on, she could easily make out the raw honesty and vulnerability in his expression. "I've been living in a haze of negative thinking for a long time now. I'm cynical about anything good and I've gotten really good at expecting the worst from people around me. It's unproductive and destructive, I know." He grimaced, but pressed on. "I really do see it for what it is, Addison, and I'm sorry. I've already taken some pretty big action steps toward changing how I think, which is a big part of the reason I'm here tonight. Me and Cat, both." The kitten, it seemed, had found the sound of his voice or the beat of his heart soothing, and her little round head nodded forward until her nose rested against Noel's palm. She blinked slowly, twice, then her eyelids drifted shut, bringing a soft smile to Noel's face. After a moment, he met

Addison's gaze and continued. "I'm really hoping that you meant what you said in the message you left me Sunday night."

She looked at her feet, glad for the dark, as her cheeks flamed with embarrassment. She wanted to ask which part he meant, but she couldn't bring herself to be so direct. The part about not recognizing him before that moment? In hindsight, her reaction toward her mother showing him *This Land is Our Land* sure made her claim look suspicious, even to her. Or did he mean the part about—.

"Did you mean it when you said you loved me, Addison?"

Well. That answered that.

Addison's breath released in a rush. "I—I did. I mean, I do," she mumbled, feeling flustered and foolish and completely exposed. "Yes," she added after a beat.

Then Noel was there, standing directly in front of her, the kitten still clutched to his chest. With his free hand, he gently cupped her cheek, and she lifted her gaze to meet his. "You don't know how relieved I am to hear it," he said, his voice hoarse with emotion. "I believe you, Addison, with everything in me. Even the scared boy—the one you crossed paths with all those years ago. That beat-up little kid who still lives inside of me believes you, too."

"I—I'm glad," she whispered as she uncrossed her arms and settled her hands at his waist. Her gaze drifted to his lips, and an urgency rose up in her to just lean forward and press her mouth to his, to kiss away all thoughts of doubt and shame and regret. *Let him talk*, her father insisted yet again.

"I love you, Addison Wedgewood. And I'm not running anymore. I want to be here for every moment of this... this amazing thing that's happening between us."

Addison nodded, afraid to speak lest she say something silly, mix up her words. But she wasn't nervous. Not anymore. She was so ecstatically happy that whatever words she could pin down in her head right now hardly even made sense to her. "Amazing. Yes," she managed to get out.

"I want you on my team, Addison, and I want you to know that I'm on your team, too." Noel rested his forehead against hers. "From here on out, I'm yours. If you'll have me. And that's my condition, by the way. You have to take me if you take Cat."

Addison thought her heart might just explode at that moment. "I couldn't imagine having one without the other," she said, happiness making her feel weightless. "And I'm not calling her Cat, just so you know."

The kitten stirred and stretched, yawning so widely that she let out a squeaky little yowl that startled her awake. She looked up to find them both smiling adoringly down at her and meowed softly.

Addison could no longer resist. "Come to mama, sweet girl. What shall we call you, hm?" She reached for the kitten, who came willingly, loose-limbed and languid and still half asleep. They stared at each other until the cat's eyelids started to drift closed. Addison kissed the white patch between her ears and said, "You have a star on your head, missy. I'm calling you Stella." Then she tucked the little creature up under her chin where it curled into a ball and began to purr. "Oh, Noel. Oh, my goodness. I'm in love," she said on a sigh, lifting shining eyes to his. "I can't believe she's mine."

"Wait a minute," Noel said, leaning back a bit. He was frowning, but she saw the humor in his eyes. "When you said you were in love, did you mean with her? Or me?"

"Both?" It came out a question, so she said it again, this time as a statement. "Both of you. I'm in love with both of you."

Noel rolled his eyes. "Great. My competition is a cat."

"In very different ways, though," Addison quickly clarified. Then she slipped her free hand around the back of his neck and drew him down so that their eyes were inches apart. "Want to kiss and make up?"

They were in the process of doing just that when someone cleared their throat on the stairs behind them, and Addison and Noel jerked apart in surprise. Her parents had come up without them even realizing it.

"Um, Carl. Vivian. Uh, hey," Noel stammered, and Addison ducked her head so that he wouldn't see her laughing at him. "We were—I was just—"

"Yes, yes," Carl nodded. "I know exactly what you were just doing to my daughter."

"Daddy!" Addison exclaimed, but it came out on a laugh. She turned so that her parents could see what she was holding. "Look who Noel brought with him. This is Stella. Isn't she the sweetest thing ever?"

Inside the apartment, Noel dished up the warm apple cobbler he'd brought with him from the Lux Solaris while Carl added generous scoops of ice cream to each plate. "I know it doesn't even compare to yours," he said to Addison over his shoulder. "But that's why I brought it. It's one more piece of evidence that my life is better with you in it."

"Oh, you're good," Carl hooted. "And he brought your favorite dulce de leche ice cream, Vivian."

"Dulce de leche is your favorite?" Noel asked in exaggerated surprise, grinning mischievously at Addison. He'd remembered, she thought with a smile. Of course, he remembered.

"You have just won me over completely, young man," Vivian called from the living room where she and Addison were playing with Stella. "If I had any doubts about you before, they have simply poofed out of existence."

Addison watched Noel as he bantered back and forth with her parents. It was like having her wishes come true all in one night. A girl couldn't possibly get any luckier, she thought to herself.

Suddenly, she recalled that all might be well in *her* little world, but Noel had the whole situation at Carpe Diem he was dealing with, and she hadn't even thought to ask him about it. She pushed to her feet and crossed the room to wrap her arms around him from behind. She rested her cheek against his back and said, "I'm a terrible girlfriend, Noel. I didn't even ask you about your job." She released him and stepped back. "How are things going over at the resort?"

Noel handed Addison two loaded plates. "Here you go," he said, kissing her on the nose. "And take this one to your mother."

Carl put the ice cream in the freezer, then the two men joined the women in the living room.

"Okay. Obviously, something's happened," Addison said, sending Noel the stink-eye. "You're acting way too nonchalant about everything. And I've already told my parents about poor John so you don't have to go back and explain things."

Vivian made a dismissive snort. "Poor John, my patootie. That man sounds like a bully."

Addison pointed her spoon at her mother. "He is a bully, Mom. But you always told me that hurt people hurt people." She and Noel were sitting on the floor on one side of the coffee table while her parents sat in the love seat. She nudged him with her elbow. "Someone somewhere in his life must have hurt John pretty bad for him to want to hurt someone as lovely as you are, Noel."

"Oh please," Noel countered. "I'm not that lovely. Remember how this whole thing started? I basically asked him if he wanted to fight me."

Vivian chortled gleefully. "Good for you."

"Mom," Addison admonished, but she applauded Noel for standing up for himself, even if it hadn't happened in an HR-compliant manner. To Noel, she said, "So, come on. Tell us what's going on. You still have a job, don't you?"

Noel took his sweet time chewing the enormous bite he'd just taken, then chased it with a swig of coffee before he finally told them what had happened since he'd returned to Autumn Lake.

His eyes shone brightly as he said, "You prayed for miracles, Addison, and that's what we got. In fact, I've been getting hit by miracles left and right all week, probably thanks to you. You didn't stop praying for me even though I took off, did you?"

She was shaking her head before he even finished. "Nope. In fact, I doubled my effort when you sent me that mean text on Monday."

"I'm sorry about that," Noel said, leaning toward her, his expression sincere. "Forgive me?"

"Yes," she whispered, then jumped when her mother clapped her hands in front of them.

"We're still here," Vivian said drolly.

"Right. Yes. Where was I?" Noel laughed and began again. "Thanks to your prayers, Miss Wedgewood, I came back to Autumn Lake to learn that Paula Swinton, John's numero uno sidekick, had changed her mind about supporting him. Remember, I told you what she said about needing the job?"

Addison nodded. The secretary had, in so many words, admitted to Noel that John was in the wrong, but that she would stand by the man to ensure that she kept her job.

"Well, she reached out to my attorney and asked if she could speak with us." He made air quotes and added, "Off the record."

"Off the record?" Vivian shot him a skeptical look.

"Right. So, Joyce and I met with her when I got back to town yesterday afternoon."

"And?" Addison prompted. "Why are you dragging this out? I'm dying here."

Noel chuckled. "Paula came prepared to negotiate for all three of our jobs. She explained to Joyce the same thing she'd told me about needing the job because of her son and having a history with John. She also said that she didn't want John to lose his job, but nor could she live with herself if she didn't do the right thing. So, Joyce asked her what she thought the right thing to do was, and Paula turned to me and said, 'I'll talk to John about dropping this charge, and I'd like you to forgive him for the way he's treated you. That way, we can all keep our jobs.'"

"Wow," Vivian murmured respectfully. "She sounds like quite a woman."

Noel chuckled and shook his head. "That was the surprising thing about all of this. She's always seemed uncomfortably subservient. Very old-school, the-boss-is-always-right kind of secretary. It was a little scary how cool as a cucumber she was."

"What did you all decide to do?" Addison asked, forgetting about her half-eaten dessert on the coffee table in front of her. She couldn't imagine either of the men would be too thrilled at Paula's suggestion.

Noel took her hand. "It wasn't much of a decision for me," he said, his voice softer now. "God—and my Aunt Gigi—had been working on me all week, and I'd already decided to forgive him, no matter how things ended."

"I can't wait to meet your aunt," Addison said, her heart swelling with gratitude for the woman who'd remained such a steady influence in Noel's life.

Noel grinned. "Oh, you will. She's already making plans for your first visit. And she'll love you almost as much as I do."

"How did John take it?" Carl asked, his brows furrowed in concern. Her kindhearted, compassionate father couldn't comprehend bully mentality; it just wasn't in his nature.

Noel shook his head. "He flat out refused to consider it."

Addison grimaced. "Yikes."

"Yeah, yikes. Well, to make a long story short, Paula took her written statement to HR, and HR asked Joyce what my intentions were. Joyce assured them that I wasn't interested in pressing harassment charges, and suggested that HR give John the chance to rescind his accusations against me and leave the company with a halfway decent severance package."

Vivian eyed Noel doubtfully. "Please tell me the man took it."

"Yes, he was smart enough to take it. And that's it. He's gone. Security ushered him out of the building this afternoon. Not because he was in trouble or causing a scene or anything," he explained. "It's just protocol when someone is laid off."

"Wow." Addison clapped in celebration. She could hardly believe it. "That really is a miracle, Noel. And just like that, it's over."

"Just like that," Noel echoed.

"What's going to happen to his position?" Vivian asked. "Is that something you plan to step into?"

"No." Noel shook his head. "I'm happy where I am. They're going to start interviewing for the position next week. In the meantime, I'll fill in where I'm needed, but Paula Swinton, I've quickly come to discover, is something else. I have a feeling she could run the whole department on her own if she wanted to. Which she doesn't. She's less than four years away from retiring with full benefits, and she's really looking forward to it."

"So, Noel. You're here to stay," Carl said, that ever-present twinkle in his eyes, but his tone was far more serious than usual. It wasn't really a question, Addison realized.

"I'm here to stay, sir," Noel replied without hesitating. "For as long as your daughter will have me."

Addison rested her cheek against Noel's shoulder. "I'll have you forever and ever," she declared happily, then reached over and scooped up Stella, who was sprawled, belly up, in a little blanket nest on the floor beside her. She cuddled the kitten to her chest and softly cooed, "I'm keeping both of you forever and ever."

34
Addison

~ ~ ~

SIX MONTHS LATER....

Addison sat on an insulated waterproof cushion on the beach just out of earshot of the group in camp chairs under the canopy down the way, their photography equipment at the ready. The sky was awash in iridescent waves of color swirling across the expanse overhead.

She hunched her shoulders around her ears, drawing the lower half of her face deeper into the fur-lined hood of her parka. She breathed slowly, trying not to steam things up too much, which would create tiny slivers of ice in the fur that would poke her in the face. She turned to the equally bundled up man at her side and asked, "Isn't it something?"

Only Noel's eyes and nose were visible as he met her gaze, but she could tell he was smiling. "I still can't believe we're doing this."

Addison giggled. "Right? Honeymooning with my parents. There's something wrong with us."

No one seemed to have noticed their withdrawal from the group who'd gathered on the beach to witness the show together, but Addison wasn't fooled. Her parents had gone out of their way to give her and Noel time alone together. The trip was a wedding gift from Carl and Vivian, but it was Addison who'd suggested they all go together right after the holidays, instead of right after their December 15th winter wedding.

"Come with us," Addison had insisted to her parents. "You know all the hot spots, you have all the connections, and you can show us around to make sure we see all the important things."

"We should probably get separate rooms," Carl had suggested.

"Um, yes, Dad." Addison had rolled her eyes at her father.

"Good. Because your mother and I can be very creative when it comes to staying warm—"

"Dad!" Addison had shrieked, at the same time her mother had covered her father's mouth to make him stop.

Noel had laughed good-naturedly, and had assured them all that he was completely on board with her parents joining them.

The timing of the trip had been providential. Addison had gone to Bald Knob with Noel a few times over the last several months. She and Aunt Gigi had become bosom buddies within minutes of meeting each other, and when Noel asked if she'd visit his father with him, she'd insisted on going. Bruno had greeted her politely, but he'd been so sick by then that Addison wasn't sure if he would remember who she was once she left the room. Aunt Gigi came to Autumn Lake for the week of the wedding, staying at The Garden Gate Bed and Breakfast where she had been warmly welcomed by the whole Garden Variety Lovers gang. She'd even promised to think about moving to Autumn Lake one day, although Noel had said he doubted she'd ever leave her beloved home in the hollow.

Bruno had died peacefully a few days after Aunt Gigi returned to Bald Knob to tell him all about his son's wedding. Noel had surprised himself by weeping like a baby when he heard the news, and Addison had cradled him in her arms and murmured wordless comforting sounds to him until he fell into an exhausted sleep against her chest. They'd made the sojourn back to the hollow for Bruno's funeral services, but they hadn't stayed long. Aunt Gigi had taken care of all the details, of course, and she'd insisted that it was time they lay the past to rest and get on with starting their new life together.

Their first Christmas together as a married couple had been precious and peaceful, a light snowfall blanketing the world outside their plant-filled window. Carl and Vivian had been on a photo shoot in Florida over the holidays, a gig that had been booked for over a year that they couldn't gracefully bow out of, but they'd video chatted that morning the way they always did when they couldn't be with Addison on Christmas.

She and Noel had joined several of the Garden Variety Lovers Club and their assorted families out at The Garden Gate for a mid-afternoon Christmas meal together, then the two of them had returned home shortly after dark, the quaint downtown streets aglow with twinkling Christmas lights. Stella, lounging in her cat hammock, had pretended not to be waiting for them, but the moment they changed into their cozy clothes and settled onto the loveseat together, the little minx climbed onto Addison's lap, curled into a ball, and began purring contentedly.

They'd been in Iceland for more than a week already and had experienced far more of the island than Addison ever had on her own. They sampled a variety of traditional Icelandic food on the Reykjavik Food Walk, then shared a delicious meal at the Friðheimar Tomato Restaurant where they served all things tomato themed, from tomato soup, to tomato beer, to tomato ice cream on green tomato pie. They had been to the renown Saga Museum with its wax figures depicting Icelandic history, as well as the iconic Perlan Museum with its rotating glass dome, overlooking the city from atop Oskjuhlid hill. They spent a day at a geothermal hot spring and had come back to their hotel that evening feeling beyond euphoric.

The drive from Reykjavik to Jokulsarlon was a good 235 miles, so they'd opted to book a four-day self-driving tour that included transportation, lodging, and a glacier boat tour once they reached Jokulsarlon. They'd made several stops along the way to take in the breathtaking scenery, including views of the waterfalls at Seljalandsfoss and Skogafoss, and a guided tour of the spectacular Vatnajokull Ice Cave. On the boat ride, they encountered a whole herd of grinning seals sunning on chunks of ice adrift in the near-black waters of the deep lagoon.

Now they were hunkered down on the black sands of Diamond Beach, the aurora borealis turning the polished chunks of ice washed up on the shore into glittering gemstones of rainbow colors. Pressed close to Noel's side, Addison barely felt the frigid cold of the January night.

Addison loved witnessing the splendors of this country through the unjaded perspective of her new husband. She cherished the moments his eyes widened in response to what he saw, what he tasted. She reveled in the way he talked about the things they were experiencing, and for the first time, she felt like she truly understood the remarkable gift her parents had given her by taking her to see the wonders of the world with them.

"It's so beautiful," Noel murmured for the fifth or sixth time in the last hour. "Thank you for sharing this with me."

"I wouldn't want to be here without you." Addison rested her head on his shoulder.

Several moments later, Noel spoke again. This time, his voice held a note of longing behind the wonder. "But it's not home."

She straightened slowly and turned to study him. His eyes met hers, and she saw the pinks and greens from the sky reflected in them. She reached up and pushed the fur of his parka hood back a little so she could see more of his face. "It's not home," she echoed, sliding her arm through his.

"This is all so amazing, Addison," Noel continued. He glanced up, only for a moment, then met her eyes again. "And I can hardly believe I'm saying this, sitting here under this kaleidoscope sky, but I miss Autumn Lake."

"I miss Stella," Addison said, laying her head back on his shoulder. The cat had been left in the care of "Auntie Claire," and although Addison had no doubt Stella was being spoiled rotten, she'd had to resist the urge to call daily to check in. Besides, the one time she'd convinced Claire to let her video chat with Stella, the cat was too busy playing with a feather boa to even bother with the phone. "Do you think she misses us?"

"I'm sure she does," Noel said with a low chuckle, then pressed a kiss to the top of her head. She sighed happily and they sat that way for several moments, watching the aerial show overhead.

"I have a gift for you." Noel spoke softly, almost offhandedly. But Addison thought she heard a smile in his voice, and her pulse hitched a little. Noel gave the best gifts, and Addison had stopped insisting that he was too generous toward her. She'd spent her whole life blending into the background, trying not to be a bother or a distraction, holding onto only the essentials so that she wouldn't be a burden to anyone. But Noel made her feel like she was the center of his world, and she was growing accustomed to the spotlight of his love being focused on her.

When he didn't continue, she pulled away a little so she could see his expression. He was, indeed, smiling. A little sheepishly, if she guessed right.

"You do?" she prompted, curiosity now dancing with anticipation behind her ribcage.

Noel gently withdrew his arm from her clutches and unzipped his parka enough to reach inside. He withdrew an envelope and held it out to her.

In the iridescent glow, she could easily read her name in Noel's precise handwriting. *Mrs. Addison Wedgewood-Stewart.* She still marveled at the sight of her name melded into his. "What is it?" she asked, although she knew Noel wouldn't give her any clues. She slipped off one glove so she could open the flap and pull out the document inside.

He surprised her by stopping her with one hand over hers. "This isn't me telling you what to do," he said, and Addison cocked her head, surprised at the sudden hesitance in his tone. "And I'm not setting a precedence of making decisions without your involvement."

"Okay," she said, wondering where this was coming from. For one thing, she trusted Noel to have her best interests at heart. He'd proven as much time and time again.

"I just—I wanted you to know—" He broke off, clearly at a loss for words, then squared his shoulders and started again. "My father made every decision in our household. Every single one and without explanation to my mother or me, even though so many of them directly affected us. Where we lived, what we ate, how we spent our time, who we spent that time with." He tapped the document in her hand. "This is a gift, Addison. Not an expectation or an assertion, and it comes with no strings attached. You are free to do with it what you want."

Addison nodded. "Okay," she said again. "Should I open it now?"

He dipped his chin. "Open it." He pulled out his phone and turned on the flashlight feature, directing it at the document she held.

The words 'Quit Claim Deed' were in bold at the top of the page. Addison turned to look at him, her brow furrowed. "A deed? To what?" she asked, then went back to reading. A moment later, she gasped, recognizing the address of their apartment. But it wasn't just the apartment number. It was the deed to the whole building, including The Quill and Ink Shop on the ground floor. "I—I don't understand...." Her voice trailed off as she flipped the page over, as though subconsciously hoping for further explanation on the backside. "My name is on this." It was in her married name, too.

Noel took a deep breath, squared his shoulders, and said, "I was in The Quill and Ink Shop last month. A week before Thanksgiving."

She remembered that day. He'd come upstairs to pick her up for a date, his cheeks pink, a satisfied grin lighting up his face. When she'd asked him what he was all smiles about, he'd told her that he was just happy to be spending their first Thanksgiving together. He'd handed her a small gift bag with the shop's logo on it; inside was a glazed ceramic pumpkin that fit in the palm of her hand. When she lifted the stem top, a green-eyed cat popped out, one that looked just like Stella. Addison had been enchanted. "I love my cat-in-a-pumpkin," she said. Her fingers were getting cold, so she slipped her glove back on.

"While I was there, I overheard Rita and Seth talking about moving away from Autumn Lake. I wasn't trying to eavesdrop, I swear."

Addison snorted. "Ha. I've heard that before."

Noel smiled wryly. "I really wasn't; not in the Quill and Ink or at The Cracked Spine. I always just seem to be in the wrong place at the right time," he added insistently.

Addison rolled her eyes but waited for him to go on.

"Anyway, I was in there killing time because I was so early picking you up, and I know how much you love it when I'm early," he teased. "And they weren't exactly speaking in hushed tones." He made a wry sound. Addison knew exactly what he meant. The couple was elderly, and although Rita could hear just fine, Seth wore hearing aides that he usually kept turned way down because he didn't actually *want* to hear everything going on around him. Over the years, Addison supposed, Rita had just gotten accustomed to speaking loudly when conversing with her husband.

"Rita was insisting that they needed to move closer to their daughter up in Indianapolis. She explained to me later that Jo—that's their daughter's name—has some health problems and they want to be there to help her out. Anyway, Seth clearly agreed, but was concerned about selling the building to someone who might not be interested in letting you—us, now—continue living in the apartment upstairs."

"Oh," Addison murmured, her heart skipping a beat at the thought of losing their home. "But they shouldn't be worried about me. I've never met Jo, but they talk about her all the time. If she needs them, they shouldn't be sticking around because of me."

"They care about you, Addison."

"And I think the world of them. They've been such great landlords," she said, trying to process everything she was hearing. Rita had said nothing about them leaving town the last time Addison had spoken with them.

"Well, now you're the landlord," Noel said. "And they no longer have to worry about you getting kicked out."

"I—I can't believe you did this. You bought my building." Addison noticed that her hands trembled a little, but she didn't know if it was from the cold or from being a little overwhelmed by Noel's gift. The rented apartment she called home was suddenly hers. Her own home. *Their* own home, she amended with a flutter of happiness. She pressed the deed to her chest, then, with some effort, hoisted herself up to her knees, her bulky winter clothing making her less than graceful.

"Where are you going?" Noel asked, grinning at her clumsiness, but giving her a hand up.

Without explanation, Addison hitched the bottom of her parka up high enough that she could straddle him, then she lowered herself to his lap and wrapped her arms around his neck. "Thank you," she said, pushing back his parka hood so she could kiss his forehead. "Thank you," she said again, kissing the tip of his nose this time. Once more, she said, "Thank you," and then pressed her mouth to his.

Noel's arms were around her, holding her close as he returned her kiss with rather ardent fervor. More than a few moments later, they came up for air, the blues and greens and pinks in the sky reflected in their eyes as they drank each other in.

"I love you," Noel whispered, their foreheads almost touching.

Addison sighed amorously. "Oh, Noel." She leaned back and stretched out her arms to the display overhead. "The Northern Lights dim in comparison to how much I love you."

Noel winced, and Addison gasped. "Sorry. Am I crushing you?"

"Hardly," he said with a chuckle. "But maybe don't lean back like that without warning. My knees don't bend that way." His legs were splayed straight out in front of him.

"I'm sorry," she said again, still giggling as she clambered out of his lap and settled back onto her own cushion beside him. She looped her arm through his and pressed in close to him. She let out a sigh of contentment, then after a few moments, said, "I don't even know what questions to ask about this." She held the deed out toward him. "I guess the first would be when are Seth and Rita moving?"

"Well, the sale is now final and the building is yours." Noel took the paper from her and tucked it into the envelope, then back inside his parka. "They can go whenever they want. But I think they're planning to be out of the building by the end of March."

Addison was still trying to wrap her head around the idea of owning the building she lived in. "So what's happening with The Quill and Ink? Did—did you buy that, too?" Surely not. She loved the little shop, but she couldn't imagine herself being a proprietress of a stationery shop, at least not long term. And she had no idea what to do with it if she wasn't going to take it over.

"I didn't," he said quickly, picking up on her tone. "They've sold the business, but the new owner has ties to Carpe Diem and is moving the shop into the resort," he explained. "They have agreed to be out of the building in ninety days."

"Wait. What does that mean? What's going to happen to that space, then?" Did that mean she'd have to be a landlord and try to find someone to rent it to? Did she even want to be a landlord?

Noel wrapped an arm around her shoulders, pulling her even closer. "That space, my beautiful wife, is yours to do with whatever you want."

"Whatever I want?" The possibilities flashing through her imagination were mind-boggling. "Really?"

Noel laughed softly. "You don't have to make any decisions right now, Addison. Take your time and think about it. You can rent it out if you want, or if you don't want to be a landlord, maybe you might want to set up a shop of your own." He gave her shoulders a quick squeeze. "Or maybe when we get around to working on those half-dozen grandchildren your parents have requested, you can convert it into a ground floor of your apartment. I know how much you love your place—"

"Our place," she interrupted him. "It's *our* place, Noel." Her cheeks warmed at the thought of having Noel's children, and she laid her head on his shoulder. "What's mine is yours, husband."

Noel pressed his cheek to the top of her head. "Our place. Yes. I know how much you love our place."

Addison leaned away from him and asked, "Do you? Love it, I mean?" Just because he'd agreed to live there with her didn't mean he didn't secretly long for something else. Something fancier. Bigger. Newer. It was awfully bijou compared to the poshness of the suite he'd moved out of.

Noel grinned and nodded. "I love our place. Our home." He pulled her back into his side. "I'm glad we came," he said softly. "But I'm really looking forward to going home with you, Mrs. Stewart."

Addison closed her eyes, picturing their cozy, colorful apartment and the gray fluffy cat waiting for them back on Larkspur Lane. "And I can't wait to go home with you, Mr. Stewart."

·♥·♥·♥·♥·♥·

Isn't it amazing how much forgiveness can change a person's life? I hope you found Noel and Addison's journeys towards the freedom forgiveness brings to be both inspiring and gratifying. I love it when I get to walk with characters through life-altering events and see them through to the other side where hope and love prevail.

There are more Autumn Lake Romances coming!
Visit me at **BeckyDoughty.com** and **subscribe to my mailing list** so you'll be the first to know when another one releases!

~ ~ ~

Have you met the Gustafson Girls?

Allow me to introduce you to Juliette, the eldest of four Gustafson sisters.

About Juliette & the Monday ManDates

JULIETTE IS PERFECTLY CONTENT with her quiet nights at home, especially when they include Chinese takeout and sappy romcoms.

But her sisters think she's teetering on the brink of spinsterhood. So they've come up with an intervention plan: weekly blind dates until their Jules finds her knight in shining armor... or until they run out of single guy friends.

They're calling it The Monday ManDates.

Survival skills kicking in, Juliette secretly names each new Monday man. There's TheraPaul, Frisky Frank, and TAZ the Rock Star, for starters. Then there's the Officer Manly Man, the policeman with a penchant for pulling Juliette over when she's at her very worst.

With a lineup like that, positively identifying her happily-ever-after seems like a long shot.

Then again, maybe, just maybe, she's looking for love in all the wrong places.

If you like family sagas, women's relationships, and series about sisters, you'll love The Gustafson Girls series. Clean and Wholesome, Christian Contemporary Romance with themes of Forgiveness, Restoration, and all things Family.

Keep reading for an excerpt from **Juliette & the Monday ManDates.**

From the Author

Dear Reader,

Did you enjoy reading along while Addison and Noel found their way home to each other in *The Apartment on Larkspur Lane*? I have a special place in my heart for sisters, for mothers and daughters, for women's relationships in general, and I'm having a lot of fun getting to know the women who make up the Garden Variety Lovers Club. I hope you are, too.

I write heartfelt and wholesome Contemporary Romance, Women's Fiction, and some Christian Fiction, too. You'll find romance, friendship, humor, a little mystery and suspense, and lots of family drama in my books. And usually a four-legged or feathered friend or two.

Visit me at **BeckyDoughty.com** and check out my other books and series. While you're there, **subscribe to my mailing list** and introduce yourself – I'd love to meet you.

Where hope lives and love prevails,
Becky Doughty

♥ ♥ ♥

Keep reading for an excerpt from…

JULIETTE

&

THE MONDAY MANDATES

The Gustafson Girls Book 1

If you like laugh-out-loud Contemporary Christian Romance,
come join the G-FOURce – the "Gustafson Four" sisters club
– in this heartwarming series about sisters, forgiveness,
and of course, happily ever after.

♥ ♥ ♥

Excerpt: Juliette & the Monday ManDates

Chapter 1

~ ~ ~

JULIETTE STARED WIDE-EYED INTO the rear-view mirror at the red and blue lights flashing behind her. Her palms began to sweat as her heart rate sky-rocketed, and it took her several minutes to pull her little PT Cruiser out of the dinner-hour traffic.

She waited, both hands gripping the steering wheel, as the officer approached her window. Finding it still closed, he tapped on it, and she jumped, letting out a tiny squeal. "Sorry!" she called through the glass, turning the car back on so she could operate the power windows. She worked the knobs, accidentally sending the backseat window up and down twice before she finally managed to get hers open. "Sorry," she repeated, peering up at the very tall officer whose eyes were hidden behind his sunglasses.

"Please turn off your engine, ma'am." His voice was firm, and Juliette scrambled to comply.

"Sorry," she muttered a third time, afraid now to look up at him. She toyed with the keys in her lap, sensing his eyes boring into the top of her head. She was sure she'd smell burning hair at any moment.

"May I see your license and registration, please?"

After wrestling with the latch on the glove compartment, she withdrew the paperwork for her car, then reached into the back seat to grab her purse from off the floor. Out of the corner of her eye, she saw him take a step back and put a hand on his holster.

The idea that she might be pulling out a weapon struck her as funny, and she had to bite her lip to keep from giggling. Her hands trembled, making it difficult to slide her license from its plastic casing in her wallet.

"Is everything all right, ma'am?"

"Yes, Officer." The late afternoon sun setting in the sky behind him made her squint. She couldn't tell if he was looking at her or not, but she caught a glimpse of her warped reflection in his sunglasses. "I'm just really nervous, I guess."

"Why are you so nervous?"

"I—I don't know," she stammered as she handed over her license. "I've never been pulled over before, and I'm trying not to freak out."

"I'm not going to hurt you."

"Oh. Good. Thanks." She grimaced. It sounded as though she'd been afraid of just that. "I mean, I know you're not going to hurt me. At least I think I do. I meant thanks for trying to reassure me. I can't help it, though; I get nervous easily." She should just close her mouth. She wasn't making things better by talking.

"Do you know how fast you were driving?"

"Um, I think so." She wrapped her damp fingers around the steering wheel again. "Actually, I'm not sure."

"Ten miles over the speed limit." His voice remained calm, patient, rattling her even more. "Do you know what the speed limit is here?"

"Um, I think so," she said again, a hot flush creeping up her chest and neck. "Actually, I—I'm not exactly sure about that either." Her voice cracked into a whisper.

The officer cleared his throat. "Ma'am, I'm a little concerned. You don't seem to know some pretty important pieces of information that someone who gets behind the wheel of a car should know." His patronizing tone irritated her. "The speed limit here is 35 miles per hour. You were driving 45." He paused, just long enough to make her squirm, before continuing. "Were you in a hurry to get somewhere?"

"No, not really." She shook her head and forgot about keeping her mouth shut. "I was just hungry, and I wasn't paying attention to how fast I was driving."

The officer chuckled, a low rumble that made Juliette's stomach flip-flop uncomfortably. "You were speeding because you were hungry? That's a first."

Her grip on the steering wheel tightened; he was mocking her.

Jerk, she thought to herself. "Well, it's the truth." She tried to glare at him, but the sun made it difficult, and she had to turn away again.

He leaned down to look around the inside of her car while she fumed in her seat. As if satisfied there was nothing suspicious about her, he straightened again, tore off a page from his ticket pad, and handed it to her along with her license.

"Look, Ms. Gustafson. Believe it or not, I appreciate your honesty. But being distracted is a dangerous way to drive, much more so than driving too fast because you *choose* to ignore the speed limit. Did you know that most accidents happen when a driver is distracted? Let this be a wake-up call for you. It's why we give tickets; not necessarily to punish drivers for bad behavior, but to encourage them to drive better." He pointed at the pink form she was holding. "Just follow the instructions on the ticket, okay?"

She couldn't believe it. He was actually *lecturing* her! First, he mocked her, then he lectured her. No longer nervous, she was offended. She nodded, her lips clamped shut, afraid of what she might say if she let any words slip out.

He patted the roof of her car. "Drive safely now, Ms. Gustafson."

"Thank you, Officer," she managed to squeeze out, her upbringing forcing her to be polite. "Not for the ticket, of course. Or the lecture." Why, oh why couldn't she just stop talking? "I mean, thank you for wishing me safe driving. Thank you for saying 'Drive safely now.'" Her voice trailed off. She stuck her keys in the ignition, turned on the car, and rolled up the window without looking at him again.

"Imbecile," she muttered, not sure if she was referring to him or herself.

·❤·❤·❤·❤·❤·

A TICKET. HER FIRST ever. She didn't know whether to cry or celebrate. And today, of all days. Today marked six months of life without Mike.

Juliette tucked her feet up underneath her as she nestled into the corner of her over-stuffed beige couch. This was *her* spot. It had always been her spot, and at this rate, it probably always would be. She maneuvered the TV tray over her knees until it was positioned just the way she liked it.

"Another wonderful meal with me, myself, and I. I can eat whatever I want, whenever I want, however I want, wherever I want. No one can tell me otherwise, and I *like* it this way." She raised her plastic fork in a defiant salute, then stabbed it into the middle of The Green Dragon food on her tray. She spun the utensil until it was loaded with noodles and shoved the whole bundle into her mouth. She couldn't close her lips around the bite, but she didn't care; she just chewed with her mouth open.

"Delicious!" she exclaimed when she could speak again. "It's you that I love, Mr. Chen Yu. Only you." She pointed the remote at the television and pressed play. A terribly acted romance-novel-come-to-life started up again where she'd left it to go pick up her takeout. The heroine was overly made up and vacuous. The male lead looked like he'd been shellacked from head to toe, not a hair or muscle out of place. Even his jeans were pressed. She actually *wanted* the woman to leave him. The story line was not making her cry, nor giving her anything else to relate to, and it was sucking all the joy out of her favorite food.

Just as she was debating whether she could stand another second of the sappy dialogue, her phone rang.

At first, she tried to ignore it. Then she thought it might be Mike and contemplated throwing the thing out the window. She let it ring instead, and the call eventually went to voicemail, beeping rudely at her. Sighing dramatically, she turned up the movie, preferring to see it through to the bitter end than to be stuck with her thoughts of Mike.

A few minutes later, the phone rang again. "Are you serious?" She pushed the TV tray away and scrambled for the purse she'd dropped on the floor at the end of the couch. It was Renata. "What do you want?" she muttered under her breath, while she considered whether she could handle talking to her sister right now.

Either she was calling to make sure Juliette wasn't drowning herself in the bathtub, or she was calling to try to coerce her into going on another family outing to Pizza Haven or the local dog park. "I don't even *have* a dog! Or a family, for that matter. Or a man." She sighed and brought the phone to her ear.

"Hi, Ren." She knew she sounded miserable, but she didn't care. Regardless of how she answered the phone, Renata believed Juliette was seriously depressed, and if she sounded otherwise, her sister reminded her she didn't have to fake it with her.

"How are you, sweetie?"

"Why do you call me sweetie?" Juliette voiced the first question that popped into her head, belligerence tattering the edges of her words. She softened her tone just a little. "In fact, you call all of us that."

"Do I?" Renata asked. "It must be because I think you're all so sweet. And actually, I don't call Phoebe that. She'd rip my head off and drop-kick it into outer space."

"Hm. Did you two have another run-in?" Juliette smirked at her own ridiculous question. Renata and Phoebe never had anything *but* run-ins.

As though reading her thoughts, Renata replied, "We don't have run-ins. We just think differently. But I didn't call you to talk about Phoebe. I called to find out how you're doing."

"I'm fine." Juliette opted for cryptic. She'd forgotten to turn down the movie and was having a hard time focusing on what Renata was saying.

"You're fine? Really? What is that noise? Do you have company?"

"I'm fine. Really. The noise is a movie. No, I don't have company. Any other questions?" Juliette rolled her eyes as the two main characters on screen started moving toward each other across a parking lot in slow motion.

"You're starting to sound like Phoebe." Juliette could hear the disdain in Renata's voice, and it made her bristle.

"That's not such a bad thing," Juliette said, defending their younger sister.

"Oh relax. I don't mean it's bad. I just mean you don't sound like you, because you're acting like her." Renata sighed. "Again, I didn't call to talk about Phoebe."

"What did you call about, Ren?" Juliette couldn't decide which was worse, this conversation or her movie.

"We had a G-FOURce yesterday."

All ears now, Juliette grabbed the remote and paused the lovers mid-lunge. "What? Why didn't anyone call me? I didn't know." She didn't remember scheduling a meeting with her sisters.

"Wait." A terrible thought occurred to her. "Renata, why didn't I know there was a G-FOURce yesterday?"

"Because we needed to meet without you. We're having a follow-up tomorrow, though, and you need to be there for that one."

"What's going on? I don't like the sound of this. In fact, I'm not sure I really want to be there." Juliette's mind was spinning. They'd met without her. That meant they'd met to talk about her. "This is another one of your interventions, isn't it?"

Renata didn't deny it. "We're worried about you, sweetie."

"Stop calling me that! I'm not your sweetie, Renata. I'm not your child, and I'm not some empty-headed twit who needs to be called placating names." Juliette pressed her forehead into the palm of her free hand and closed her eyes, immediately ashamed of her uncharacteristic outburst. "Look, I don't need an intervention, okay? Yes, I'm sad. Yes, I'm even slightly depressed. When I think about Mike, I get hot and sweaty, but not in a good way. I get sad, and then angry, and then wonder what's so wrong with me that he couldn't love me like I loved him."

"Wouldn't," Renata interjected. "Love is a decision, Juliette. That's why John and I are still married after all these years."

Ah yes. Mr. and Mrs. Perfect. "Regardless, my reactions are normal. I'm not on the verge of suicide, and I'm not going to go be a hermit on some isolated mountaintop. I just need a little time to lick my wounds and heal up a bit."

There was silence on the other end of the phone. "Ren? Are you still there?"

"Tomorrow. Five o'clock. Your place. That way, you can't ditch us. Come straight home from work, Juliette. Don't dawdle." The phone went dead in her hand.

"Yes, Mother," Juliette muttered. She glared down the sofa to her spot at the other end where her food waited patiently, trying not to congeal. Her plastic fork had been knocked to the floor in her scramble for the phone and was nowhere to be seen. She didn't really care; she wasn't so hungry anymore.

"I need a dog," she said. "One that will love me unconditionally. And eat my cold leftovers."

·♥·♥·♥·♥·♥·

Juliette & the Monday ManDates is available in print, ebook, and audiobook from **Becky's Bookshop** or any of your favorite online bookstores.